The Book of Us

ANDREA MICHAEL

OneMoreChapter

One More Chapter an imprint of
HarperCollins*Publishers*
The News Building
1 London Bridge Street
London SE1 9GF

www.harpercollins.co.uk

This paperback edition 2020

First published in Great Britain in ebook format by
HarperCollins*Publishers* 2020

A catalogue record for this book
is available from the British Library

ISBN: 9780008370213

This novel is entirely a work of fiction.
The names, characters and incidents portrayed in it are the work of the author's imagination. Any resemblance to actual persons, living or dead, events or localities is entirely coincidental.

Set in Birka by Palimpsest Book Production Ltd, Falkirk
Stirlingshire

Printed and bound in Great Britain by
CPI Group (UK) Ltd, Croydon CR0 4YY

For little girls with big dreams.
And for the old friends who keep them alive.

Some days
I am more wolf
than woman
and I am still learning
how to stop apologising
for my wild.

– 'Wolf and Woman', Nikita Gill

PART ONE

Chapter 1

Sorry to do this, Loll,

This has to be the three hundred billionth letter I've sent you (approximately) but you weren't answering and I haven't got time for bullshit anymore. So this is all nicely typed, properly addressed, no trace of my scraggy writing or those hearts over the 'I's you used to hate. It's proper, the way you like.

It's funny, I've been writing these letters for years, and now I finally have something important to say that isn't 'I'm sorry' or 'Please forgive me' or any of that other bullshit we know never works. You always said that if people cherished forgiveness, they would care enough not to make mistakes in the first place …

At this point, Lauren Richards honestly considered ripping up the letter. She'd been tricked into opening it, what with the sad Christmas songs still on the radio, and sitting alone in front of that huge tree with her glass of wine. Well, a few glasses of wine.

How the hell was she going to get that tree down? Darren

always did that part. Suppose she just left it up all year, until it started to rot through the expensive carpet? When people asked, their noses wrinkled in disdain, she could tell them it was Darren's fault, because he wasn't there to help. Not that many people visited the house these days anyway.

She averted her eyes from the beautiful tree, softly twinkling and totally perfect. Too perfect. She tipped the rest of the wine to the back of her throat and swallowed, blinking. Back to the sodding letter then.

… When we first met, you remember you said I was the best person you knew at living? Just pure chaos and destruction and fun. You loved it then, even when you pretended not to. Your mum thought I was a terrible influence, and your dad thought I was a hussy and you loved me anyway …

'And you proved him bloody right,' Lauren said to herself. Cass always got away with that, retelling the truth. Her parents *loved* Cass. They used to ask her to make Lauren over, take her out places, make her more ... just *more*. Cass was fun to be around, and Lauren had liked being near the edge of the spotlight. 'Why can't you be more like Cass?' her mother had sighed more than once, 'she's so confident, so vivacious.'

So I'm pulling out every trick in the book here, babe. I'm gonna need you to remember some time when we were happy. There were enough of them. The camping in the woods, and the puking off the side of the carousel at the fairground? That summer in Ibiza? I know, you'll be thinking 'she's listed vomiting as fun, and I hate camping and that summer in Spain I got burnt to fuck.'

Lauren almost laughed. Almost. She could hear Cass so clearly it was painful, and she couldn't stop reading. She could pause long enough to pour another glass of wine and snuggle down on the sofa, but she couldn't stop. Damn it, if she'd just ignored the letter in the first place she wouldn't be in this mess, enthralled by Cass all over again.

So you're holding on to that happy memory, right? Now I need you to remember the last thing you said to me. Need a little refresher? You told me you wished I was dead. Surprisingly strong words for sweet little Loll. I deserved it, obviously. But seeing as it's Christmas, I thought I'd get in touch to give you a very special gift – you'll be getting your wish!

I wonder how that feels. If you're at all sad at the idea of me not existing. Most likely, you're pissed off at me for telling you. But the thing is, babe, we both know that when I kick it, if you didn't know, you'd be even more pissed at me. So hold on to that, because there's more.

I'm thinking about the Big Book, and I'm pretty sure you have it. There's a chance you could have thrown it away, I guess – I know how stubborn you can be. It's been six years. But I'm really, really hoping that whatever tiny part of you that loved me, that loved us, kept hold of that book.

So whatcha say, Loll? Come punish me in person. Address is at the bottom. I won't say I know you'll come, because shit like that drives you nuts, and you'll end up doing the opposite.

But come, Loll. We've got some important things to talk about. It's time.

Love
Cass
Xxx

Lauren was trying to decide whether to scream or throw up. And yet, she knew she'd go. She was a pushover, and Cass needed her. She'd be angry as hell, and she'd grumble and cry and punish Cass for making her do it, but she'd go. Besides, it wasn't like she had anyone else to worry about, or ask permission from. It was just her now.

Her eyes slid to the address at the bottom – Blackpool! Gaudy illuminations and loud noises and fresh popcorn, a new party every night – she supposed that was a good enough reason for someone like Cassidy Jones.

When Cass had disappeared all those years ago – there one moment, all tears and destruction, and then suddenly gone – Lauren had been insane with rage. Even thinking about Cass had made her skin itch like she wanted to tear it off. She took a moment to assess if that was still how she felt. Did she still want to throttle her once best friend, want to cry at the very sight of her, or was it now a warm straight-jacket cuddle of a grudge, comfortably settled into? She had become accustomed to life without Cass. To monochrome routine and being invisible. People didn't really bother with you when you were shy – they seemed to think she was stuck-up, or aloof. Cass never had. Cass had understood.

At least before, she'd had Darren. That was why people got married, wasn't it? So they wouldn't be alone, especially at Christmas? Darren hadn't thought of that when he left her. She was still shaking at the injustice of it – leaving your wife on Christmas Eve. 'Lonely this Christmas' indeed.

She tried to take a breath, pushing away the image of Darren's shrugs as he explained it wasn't his *fault*, 'You don't *choose* who you fall in love with.' He'd looked so handsome, those painfully sharp cheekbones and his eyes bright against that blue jumper she'd bought him. He was leaving her, he wasn't sorry. Cupid's arrow had struck him and it wasn't down to him. It wasn't his fault, it was fate.

Lauren had sat there and looked at him in wonder. It wasn't his fault, *of course*, because he was *fated* to fall in love with a twenty-three-year-old beauty therapist who modelled part-time.

She'd almost choked on her hot chocolate. God, but he made good hot chocolate. He heated the milk in the pan, melted in marshmallows and added a sneaky shot of Baileys. Just like everything else in Darren's life, attention to detail mattered – perfection had to be achieved. Lauren wondered if she'd ever eat chocolate again, or if he'd ruined that for her too.

She'd spent Christmas Day caterwauling drunkenly in front of *Casablanca* and fallen asleep, waking up to the smell of burnt turkey and smoke billowing from the kitchen.

Cass would have found the whole thing hilarious. If they'd

still been friends, Cass would have come round with Chinese food and too many bottles of wine, and they would have sung at the top of their lungs until the early morning. She would have called Darren every name she could think of, but wouldn't have said, 'I told you so.' Cass would have listed her top thirty favourite things about Lauren, which she did every time Lauren had been disappointed or sad or let down, and she wouldn't pause once trying to find things to say. She would have held her hand, and stroked Lauren's hair whilst she cried.

There was something timely about this, losing Darren then Cass reappearing. Two opposite directions, opposing forces. It had always been like that. She could never have both of them at once.

Lauren conjured memories of Cass without effort, her blonde hair billowing, laughing over something ridiculous. Dancing at Inferno at those godawful uni nights, where they had downed Jägerbombs until one of them was sick, and then gone back and danced even more. She could see her at that final moment, tears in her eyes, skin patchy and flushed with guilt and anger as she apologised over and over again.

And then she couldn't see her at all.

Lauren tipped the last of the wine bottle into her glass, nodding her head as it emptied. An ending. Could Cass really be dying? She had a flair for the dramatic, just like her mother. Pulling fantastic stories out of an interaction on the bus, or a conversation in the queue for a coffee. Maybe this was one of those. A scheme, a final cry for attention. She wouldn't even be mad if it was.

She would go, Cass would say, 'Haha, tricked you! Knew you'd fall for that!' and she'd threaten to storm off. They'd fight and then everything would be fine. That would be it. It had to be.

She had lived the last six years of her life without Cassidy Jones, and they had not been okay at all. They had been greyscale, and quiet. But what if there weren't any more years left?

Lauren tottered upstairs, wine glass still in hand, trying to ignore the photographs on the wall, those smiling faces of two people who were always just making do. Doing what people did. Her fingertips traced the space on the wall that she had left bare, ready for softly-lit photographs of cherubim smiles and tiny handprints in ceramic. She missed those once future babies more than she missed her husband.

Darren had very carefully *not* said that Lauren's desire for a baby was obsessive. Crying every time she got her period was absolutely *not* irritating him. He'd just shrug and say it would happen when it happened, not to worry. 'We're still young, Loll, what's the rush? Let's live our lives!'

She supposed boredom was a bad reason to have a child. 'Living their lives' seemed to mean the same takeout from the same restaurant every Thursday, going to the cinema at the end of the month, a visit to the same hotel for their anniversary every year and an expensive holiday to somewhere warm that they would spend the next few months paying off. It meant having the same conversations about how Darren was overlooked for promotions when he was the best, how he deserved more money, how their friends had second homes abroad and he was embarrassed that they didn't. The future always carried the promise of reward. The present was something to be endured.

Lauren clung to the doorframe, surveying her room.

The bed was unmade. There had been no point – she only tossed and turned, scavenging for booze and biscuits before retreating back to it, burying her face in the covers and crying until she couldn't breathe. It wasn't necessarily that she missed Darren. It was the *unfairness* of it all that got to her.

She had to go back to work soon though. She had to get the grief and anger out now, before she messed up someone's paperwork and they lost their dream home. She placed the wine glass carefully on the side table and lay down across the bed on her stomach, reaching for the box underneath.

The box was slightly fluffy at the corners, beige cardboard showing beneath the purple. Dragging it out she snorted at the thick dust, pausing to run a finger through it. A relic of a different time.

She took a deep breath and threw the lid off, wondering if she'd feel different. Inside was an array of photographs, notebooks, odds and ends. A worn-bare keyring from when they'd gone to Disneyland. Those youthful photos, their cheeks pressed close as they pouted at the camera, their bright eyeshadow clashing with their lipstick. They were garish and loud and weirdly beautiful.

Lauren looked at herself, traced the cheekbones and the huge hair that Cass had teased out from curls into static. She always looked nervous in photos, but she didn't in this one. Her dark eyes were haughty, daring you to challenge her. Cass had that waifish look girls have when they know their own power – she was thin and coltish without being skinny, all odd sharp angles and huge blue eyes. She pulled you in. You only had to look at that picture to tell the girl was trouble.

And beneath it all, in the bottom of the box, was the Big Book. A chunky black Moleskin notebook that Cass had bought. It was a graduation gift for Lauren, a promise of their future adventures together. Lauren's clear black capitals had written, *Eat proper pizza in Italy*, followed by Cass's swirly scribble: *Try ayahuasca in South America*. After it, in her hand again, was *(If we feel safe)*.

Later, the pages were organised by country, then again by theme. They wanted to try wall climbing, canoeing, eat paella, drink absinthe. Cass wanted to find out which country's men were the best lovers, but Lauren was content to *Dance with a stranger*.

Even the warmth of the book in her hand tugged at her chest, this strange clawing ache that made her grit her teeth. It was different to Darren. Darren's leaving she had felt in the pit of her stomach, all rage and injustice and the sheer *cheek* of it.

The least he could have done was given her a *fucking* child. That was the first thing she'd thought when he said he was leaving – which wasn't a good sign, she supposed. But he was leaving her all alone. He would keep the friends that were always his, the family that adored him. If only she'd had someone to pour her love into, to survive for, she could have forgiven him.

Of course, she'd said nothing. He'd patted her on the shoulder before he left, commending her for being so understanding. She was always so good, so kind, so generous. Lauren had pressed her nails into her palms until she'd drawn blood. Her silence raged.

Lauren picked up that photograph again – *that* Cass was the one she'd met in the toilet stalls of the university bar. The one who was wild and fun and always up for adventure. The one who dragged her along because she needed to be forced to have fun. The one who listened when she finally did speak, however quiet she was. She had missed that girl. The Cass who came later – more mess and drama and betrayal – it was *her* Lauren was angry with. *This* Cass was perfect.

There was an entire folder in her phone full of text messages she had written, then saved, because she had no one to send them to. There was grief in that loss. A little shame, too.

Lauren used to talk to Cass in her head, back when her voice still represented comfort and stillness. In the midst of panic she could still imagine Cass talking slowly and gently, keeping her calm. At university, when her panic attacks had reached their peak, Cass would grasp her palm, pressing her thumb into the centre to distract her. She'd reminded her to breathe, talked her down until the waves crashed around them both and fizzled away. Then, she would always produce a chocolate bar from her bag and tell Lauren that everything was fine, that chocolate solved everything.

She hadn't conjured that voice for years – it just wasn't the same anymore.

But Cass not existing at all? No blonde-haired wild girl

wreaking havoc somewhere in the world – it just didn't seem right.

Lauren sipped on the last of her wine, snuggling down against her wrinkled pillows, frowning at that photograph. Her belly burned with a prickle of curiosity. The memory of slender fingers tapping her on the shoulder and warning her not to be stubborn. Telling her to take a risk.

Tomorrow was New Year's Eve. And Lauren would be driving to Blackpool. They had both known she could never say no to Cassidy Jones.

Chapter 2

Lauren shouldn't have been driving. Her dry mouth and fuzzy head told her this as she bumbled up the motorway. She seemed to feel hangovers deep in her bones these days, like she was filled with poison. She wound the window down and the sharp, cold air was a relief, blowing out the cobwebs.

As she crawled along, Lauren looked at the other people in the cars, all travelling somewhere for New Year's. Going towards people they loved, making promises for the year ahead. Lauren could almost hear the clink of the wine bottles in the back seats, the yowling sing-alongs from the twenty-somethings, convinced this would be *the best New Year's ever.* She and Cass had enough of those memories.

One was spent on the beach in Brighton, shivering but steadfastly remaining, gritted teeth and a vodka blanket to numb them. Lauren couldn't remember much beyond being mesmerised by the dark oiliness of the ocean at night, how the waves were deafening. She did recall curling up under a blanket, Cass's breath warm on her cheek as she whispered, 'This will be our year, Loll. *This* will be the one.'

The years had started to bleed together. She remembered the jealousy she felt at Cass's mum's parties, how Cass had always been sparkling at the centre of it all, showered with attention. The Christmas lights shone, and Cass had worn a pearlescent dress that caught the light like mermaid scales. People couldn't pass without reaching out a hand to touch her shoulder, as if entranced. Lauren wore black that year. Cass was the angel on the Christmas tree, and Lauren sparkled dully on the side. That always seemed to be the way.

There were the London lights one year, with the scramble of thousands of people and fingers numb with the cold. Darren had been annoyed about that one. He'd wanted her to himself back then.

After that came the New Year's festivities without her – the expensive meals in fancy hotels. An argument with Darren about something pointless. After a while, they stopped bothering. The promise of a new beginning starting with the chime of midnight didn't seem as exciting as before. They went out for dinner, like adults did. One year they had a party, but Lauren felt like a failure. Drinks were spilled, food was burnt. But she brought it on herself, of course. She was too highly strung, too anxious. She took everything too seriously, like the laughter of Darren's workmates as they chewed charred mini quiches and explained why their champagne was better than her prosecco. She'd started the new year hiding in the bathroom, and when she reappeared Darren asked her why she always had to worry and ruin everything for herself. Then came the years of sitting on the sofa, watching the fireworks through the window, a dine-in-for-two meal on the coffee table. They'd stopped sitting opposite each other a long time ago.

Why was no one else annoyed by the traffic? Lauren tugged at her hair in frustration. Her ring caught, tugging and splitting strands. That would teach her. She shouldn't have been wearing the damn thing anymore anyway. She pulled it off, letting it sit in her hair before she tugged it out and chucked it on the passenger seat. The traffic moved forward briefly, and Lauren held out for almost three minutes before reaching across and feeling for it, placing it back on her finger with a sigh of relief.

Her life seemed to split into two sections: with Cass, and after Cass. After was like watercolour, wishy-washy dullness like that overcast sky above the grey motorway. But there had been less pain. Cass had shone so brightly, all that colour and noise and excitement, that there had been no place for Lauren to be someone of her own. That's what she'd thought, after Cass was gone. Now it was *her* time to become someone.

But Cassidy Jones had been out of her life for six years now, and Lauren still hadn't made her own life colourful. Cass was oils on canvas, bold and messy. Lauren was the practice paper, the daubs of pastel that bled at the edges and merged. Not the good kind of mess. She wondered if Cass would look sick, whether she would finally fail to outshine everyone else in the room. It was awful to hope for that, though.

The car's speaker system rang shrilly, *Mum* flashing up on the dashboard. Lauren took a deep breath before answering, injecting a smile into her voice.

'Hi, Mum, how are you? Got any big plans for tonight?'

'Plans? We'll get fish and chips and watch the fireworks on the telly, same as every year. What are you talking about?'

Of course. No wonder I'm boring. It's in my genes.

'We were going to ask if you wanted to join us, sweetheart. How *are* you?' Her mother's voice dripped with sympathy, and it made Lauren's organs itch.

'I'm fine, Mum. Honestly. Feeling good ... new year, fresh slate and all that.' She pretended to believe it. That was the key to being a good lawyer, after all. Truth was relative. She hadn't liked that part of the job at all. Which explained why she'd ended up where she had.

'Lauren, your husband just left you for a younger woman. At Christmas.'

'I *said* I'm fine.' Her teeth were hurting. She must have been grinding them in her sleep again.

'No one would be fine after that. Why all this proud, brave stuff? We're family. Come home to us.'

Martha Martinez was not a woman people often said no to. She was capable of muffling their excuses with love, until they couldn't find a single reason to disappoint the lovely woman with the constant frown lines on her forehead.

It was the reason she'd so often escaped to her grandmother as a teenager. Her *abuela*'s home was warm, she was greeted with a bear hug and no one ever looked at her like she was a disappointment. Although maybe if her *abuela* was still around to see what a mess she'd made of her marriage, she'd feel differently. But at least she would have had back-up against her mum. No one else stood up to Martha.

Lauren often felt like her mother took up all the air in the room, and then siphoned it off to whoever she felt was deserving enough. Her brother usually won that one. Just one of the reasons she'd feigned sickness on Christmas Day. Hearing about her brother's impressive cases (he was a *real* lawyer, according to her parents) as a barrister, which news site had featured him, who he had helped. Then, dealing with her perfect sister-in-law, bouncing their gorgeous dark-haired son on her knee, feeling the velvet of his baby cheeks as he gripped her finger ... it would have killed her.

'I can't, Mum, I've got plans tonight.'

Her mother was rarely silent. It sat heavily between them, like a bowling ball, trundling down a lane towards its target. Lauren counted backwards from ten and waited for the impact.

'*Please* don't tell me you're going to beg him to come back to you. The idiot wants to go, let him go. It's embarrassing enough to be left, darling. Don't let him make you pathetic.'

That your entry speech for Mother of the Year Awards, Ma? Lauren said nothing, and wondered if one day she'd bite her tongue so hard her mouth would fill with blood.

'I don't want him back, Mum.' She was surprised to find she was telling the truth.

'Well, good,' Martha seemed marginally appeased. 'Don't you forget what he did to you. You called me drunk out of your mind at three in the morning on Boxing Day, howling about how you drove him away because you wanted a baby. I don't want to see you that broken again.'

Lauren twitched her mouth to release the tension and pretended to be fine. 'I remember. I don't want him. In fact, I wish him a lifetime of happiness with the teenager he's in love with. She can deal with washing his pants and making his dinner and listening to him whine about not getting promoted. See how long the magic lasts then.'

Martha laughed, and Lauren relaxed. Her mother always liked when she was sassy. She preferred her when she acted more like a conqueror, less like a victim. More like Cass.

'So where are you going? Taking yourself for a spa break? A good idea to get away and get refreshed. Though maybe you want to start thinking about money if you'll be getting divorced soon ...'

Lauren winced at the d-word, a sharp little pain in her chest. She wanted to blame it on the coffee that morning, but she couldn't. Divorced before thirty. Excellent. What a waste of an expensive party.

'Actually, I'm going to see Cassidy.'

Martha's gasp was a little dramatic for Lauren's taste. Her mother had *loved* Cass. She was always going on about how *beautiful* she was, how *elegant* and *stylish* and *bold.* Cass wouldn't have dreamed of being a human rights lawyer and ended up being a conveyancing solicitor. Cass wouldn't have been left for someone younger and more beautiful. And if someone had been stupid enough to leave Cass, she wouldn't have stayed in her house, screaming like a banshee, asking what she'd done to deserve it. She would have gone out and found someone new, evening out the playing field. Only fair.

Cass was big on fairness – crimes had to be paid, sins atoned for. Actions balanced the scale. Their friendship was a timeline peppered with Cass's offerings of apology, from a can of Diet Coke on the side in the morning to a box of doughnuts decorated with pink nipples (she'd borrowed, and lost, Lauren's best bra). Some were more labour intensive, like the hand-drawn cartoon of their friendship, from meeting in the nightclub all the way through to graduation.

Lauren's favourite apology remained the beautiful copy of *Alice in Wonderland*, a hardback with gold leaf edges on the pages. That one was because Lauren had an anxiety attack in her first law exam and Cass had said she was overreacting. She'd expected the quiet, comforting voice Cass always offered, the thumb in the middle of her palm. The soothing words that told her it would all be fine, that she could do anything. Instead, she was told to stop worrying, like it was something she could control. The same words everyone else had always used. The book had been placed outside her room, wrapped in a purple ribbon. On the inside cover was an inscription, the closest thing to a written apology. *Down the rabbit hole, we'll go together,* it read, in Cass's wayward scrawl.

They were always impressive, these tokens, dependable and preferable to the empty words and awkward silences. The insistence that everything was okay when it wasn't. They had found their balance. Cass would mess up, and then she would make it right. That was the way it always been.

Except for that last apology. There had only been words, and words weren't enough. Nothing would have been enough to undo that mistake. Except, Lauren hoped, maybe time.

Her mother's squawking brought her back to the present. 'Oh my goodness, all this time, and now Cassidy is back again? How is she?' Martha's excitement was untempered, and Lauren couldn't bear to burst her bubble.

'She's ... she's reaching out. And I thought it was time.'

'Yes, whatever it was you girls fell out about, it probably all seems very silly now, doesn't it?'

It most certainly did *not*. But it seemed less important. In the scheme of things.

'You never did say what happened between the two of you ...'

'And if I've held out this long, why break a habit?' Lauren clenched the steering wheel.

'Do you remember that time she told me off because I said you'd put on weight? She stood up and said, "Mrs Martinez, I know I'm a guest in your home, but your daughter is the most wonderful person I know, and she doesn't need to be criticised like that." Do you remember?' Martha laughed. Okay, so maybe one other person besides her grandmother stood up to Martha.

I remember you scowling and coming into my room later that evening to say how embarrassed you were and that I needed to exercise more so I didn't put you in that situation again. Lauren held her tongue, as always.

'She was a good friend. She always stuck up for me,' Lauren said dully.

'Well you always needed someone like Cassidy, didn't you? I'm so glad you found her at university or you would have stayed in your room and done nothing!'

'I might have got a first instead of a 2:1.'

'Yes, you would have spent three years with your head buried in books, crying because you had no friends. You don't always make it easy, you know, being so quiet. You don't let people get to know you. You're lucky Cassidy put in the time.'

It was a talent her mother had, managing to pinpoint her fears so terrifically, amplifying them until they were obvious. As if Lauren hadn't spent all these years hating herself for how grateful she'd been, for how much she'd depended on her one friend. How angry she was that one person in the world had seen her properly, without criticism, and then she was gone and Lauren had no one else. It was hardly what she wanted to be thinking about right now.

'Well, I've got to go, Mum. I'll give you a call when I'm home. Say happy New Year to Dad for me, okay? I love you.'

'You too, darling. Give my love to Cassidy, tell her I've missed her.'

Lauren rolled her eyes. 'I will.'

'And Lauren? Tell her you've missed her too.' Martha laughed and hung up, and Lauren couldn't help but snort at her mother. She would *not* tell her she'd missed her. Even if it was true.

Blackpool. Bloody *Blackpool.* They'd gone to university in Hertfordshire. Cass had grown up in North London. So how the hell had she ended up in Blackpool? Lauren conjured visions of Cass standing in the cold, shepherding kids on and off dodgems or a tired carousel. Would that be her life now? When she left all those years ago, Lauren had imagined her on a beach in Greece, dressed in jewels and designer swimsuits, endlessly adored by rich muscled men. Not in a grey, rainy town by the sea, lit up with tacky lights and strewn with L-plates and feather boas.

The Big Book sat on the passenger seat next to her, infinitely worn, with its thumbed pages and fraying black leather cover. It was a book of un-lived dreams, and she pushed it under her coat when she caught sight of it out of the corner of her eye. Who would want to do that to themselves, look back at all the things they failed to achieve? A lot of it had been travel, she remembered that much. They had been obsessed with all the places the world could offer.

She had been on holidays with Darren. But they tended to be four-star hotels at all-inclusive resorts, where you never saw the people who lived there, never had anything but buffets and booze and commenting on the scenery. They went to wonderful countries and stripped away the culture until there was just a pool and a sunset. It always made her feel a little uncomfortable, but Darren had a thing for luxury. '*They've made it the best of both worlds,*' he'd say, '*why wouldn't you want that?*' Why would she want to backpack across India and sleep in hostels when she could be here, in Mauritius, sipping Mai Tais? Why cycle through Vietnam when she could be on a beach in Mexico? Somewhere down the line, she had stopped craving adventure, focusing instead on home and family, preparing for the next part of their journey together.

If she'd known how it would all end, maybe she would have gone backpacking. Although the idea of being brave enough to do that without Cass was laughable. Her, by herself, out in the world? Impossible.

Lauren turned down a few streets, trundling along at a slower pace than she needed to. Under a grey sky, with winds rattling canopies and rain spitting on the floor, Blackpool looked post-apocalyptic. Lauren counted five people, sitting grumpily in a café, nursing cups of tea and shivering. Everything looked so incredibly *normal.*

She wondered what Cass's home would be like. It was easier than imagining her response when she opened the door. Her house would likely be a hippie den with oversized cushions and bright fabrics, the way her room had looked at uni. Cass was always getting into feng shui, or crystals, something pretty with a side of spiritual, before dropping it again. Her mum had been the same.

Barbara 'Babs' Jones had been an actress, model, backing singer, air hostess, aromatherapist, agony aunt and reiki healer. And those were the ones she'd stuck at for more than six months. In between those, Lauren was sure she remembered Cass talking about the failed doggy spa, selling health shakes and writing a couple of Mills and Boon-esque stories for magazines. Cass's mum had been fascinating, so different to her own straightforward mother. Barbara always looked effortless, it was something in the chin. It said '*no offence, but I don't care what you think of me*'. An inherent confidence lived in the Jones women's bones, made plain by hand movements and head tilts. Lauren had craved it so badly when she first met Cass that once she recognised it as a series of traits, she spent hours in the mirror trying to figure out the reasoning behind the magic. But, alas, it wasn't for the likes of her. It was just who they were, as natural as breathing.

Barbara loved an audience, she was always ready to hand you a glass of wine and tell you a hilarious story about a time she was in Bombay on a movie set, or Nicaragua, volunteering.

She had fit a lot of life into her life. She'd died young, too. And still, not as young as Cass would be. God, that was a horrible thought. Lauren physically shook it away as she gripped the steering wheel.

There it was. She pulled the car over and just looked. The street was leafy and pleasant, the little Victorian terrace was grey, with white window frames and a tiny paved entrance. There was nothing about it that told her Cass might live there, except the little evil eye that hung in the top corner of the doorframe. They'd got them in Turkey that first summer together, solid blue glass with a white eye painted on top. She touched it as she approached the door, fingertips chilled by the glass.

Lauren was quite sure she was going to vomit. The only way to put it off was to repeat, 'It's not a big deal, it's not a big deal,' over and over, until the words ceased to make sense. The rhythm was comforting, and she echoed it as she knocked on the door. Five seconds passed, and then five more. She knocked again, tapping her foot as she counted another five seconds. Okay, well ... she wasn't in. The relief of an anticlimax dripped from her fingertips. She would get back in her car, and go home. Maybe spend a night in a hotel by the service station. Surely those wouldn't be booked up on New Year's Eve? Enjoy some tiny room-service bottles and rubbish TV. She could even retrieve the Big Book from her car, leave it on Cass's doorstep as a gift. A sign that she came, that she tried—

'Well, well ... look what the cat dragged in.' Cass's voice was arch. It sounded mocking until Lauren turned around and saw her smile. It was ... shy. Grateful. Very unlike Cassidy Jones.

'Hi,' Lauren said.

'Hiya, babe,' Cass laughed, shaking her head, 'long time no see.'

She was the same, but different. Age, and life, but more than that, a slight greyness that hovered round the edges. Her thinness was no longer a sign of her diet of coffee and plain toast; it was now evidence of her sickness. She wore grey yoga pants and a jumper that hung from her. The blonde hair that had once flowed wildly down her back was cut into a tousled bob. She could have been anyone. Except for the way she leaned against the doorframe with her arms crossed, grinning.

'So a girl's gotta be dying to get your attention, huh?'

'Something like that.' Lauren twisted her ringless fingers, focusing on Cass's chin rather than her eyes. She was going to be cold, cool, sophisticated. She was the injured party here. Cass should be playing the role of the apologetic friend, eager to make amends. Somehow death had evened the scale, which didn't seem fair at all.

'Well, don't stand out here like a nutter, it's cold,' Cass turned and beckoned her in, watching to make sure she followed, 'still take two sugars in your coffee?'

Lauren trailed behind her, closing the door and taking in everything as she walked down the neat grey hallway. She followed Cass into the kitchen, where she was busying herself with the kettle. The kitchen was small and clean, with bright blue tiles and a spotless white floor. A plain wooden table with four chairs sat by the back door, looking out onto a frosty back garden with a sweet rainbow-striped birdhouse sat in the tree. The first sign of Cass. An abundance of colour that shouted amongst the neutrals.

Lauren sat down at the table, waiting for Cass to say something. But she didn't, she just let the kettle steam away, pottering with mugs and spoons and instant coffee.

'No sugar,' Lauren said suddenly, even though it was a lie.

'Okay,' Cass replied, not looking up, 'Geronimo.'

'What?'

Cass pointed to the black cat curling itself around Lauren's feet. 'Geronimo.'

'Why?'

Cass shrugged, 'I didn't name him.'

How did you even start to talk to someone who had once been a part of you? How did you ask, '*So how have the last six years been?*' without dredging up everything that went before? How did you stop being angry at someone simply because they were dying? There wasn't a switch she could flip, and yet, she drank the sight of Cass in because it was strange and wonderful. Like looking at one of those wacky mirrors at the circus. A reflection, but not a true one. Time was invisible until too much of it passed.

'Look,' Lauren stood up, talking to Cass's back, 'before all of this starts, I just ... I don't want to talk about the past, okay? Let's leave all that shit behind, I don't want to go over it all again. Let's just talk about the present and the future.'

Cass made a noise as she leaned over the sink, and Lauren couldn't tell if it was a laugh or a sob.

'So you don't want an apology? I've only been practising for six years. I finally got it perfect.'

Lauren clenched her teeth, trying to find the words, 'Cass—'

Just like that, the bristles were out. Cass straightened her back and placed the two mugs of coffee on the table, her pale hands with the flaked ruby nail varnish shaking slightly.

'Hey, babe, whatever you want. You're here. That has to be enough, I guess.'

'So it's my fault now?'

Cass blinked at her in shock, 'How could it be your fault, Loll? You came, after all these years. I'm grateful. Wish it hadn't taken me dying to get your attention. But hey, we take what we can get, right?'

She shrugged, picking up the cat and cradling him to her chest, tickling beneath his chin. He relaxed for a moment, then started to wriggle, demanding his freedom. Geronimo leapt from Cass's arms and escaped upstairs, leaving her hands with nothing to do but grasp her coffee cup.

'I don't know what I'm meant to say.' Lauren stared at Cass's bare feet.

'Well, I'm meant to say *I'm sorry*, and you're meant to say *I know*, and then we're meant to ponder silently for a moment before one of us makes a joke about something.' Cass looked at her hopefully, 'Know any good jokes?'

'Why are you acting like none of this matters?' Lauren asked.

'God, you really don't know me at all anymore, do you?' Cass put down her coffee cup and held out her hands to show her – they were visibly trembling. She quickly crossed her arms, trapping her hands in her armpits. 'It matters, Loll, it matters more than you know. I'm just trying to keep my shit together. You remember that much about me, at least?'

Lauren nodded. She did know. Something spiteful in her had needed proof. Some signal that she wasn't the only one struggling. She sipped her coffee, looking at the table, the scratch marks and sticky patches. Did Cass live here with a boyfriend, a partner? A husband? It was almost impossible to imagine, but so was this woman in front of her.

'How's Darren?' Cass sat down carefully, as Lauren's head whipped up. 'Might as well get the hard questions out of the way first.'

Loll snorted, nodding, 'Left me. Just before Christmas.'

'*This* Christmas?'

'Yup,' Lauren sipped, pretending it didn't hurt. 'Man, good coffee.'

'It's got caramel or something in it,' she said, and for a moment, it was so incredibly normal that Lauren felt her chest hurt.

'Guess you bet on the wrong horse there, babe.' Not quite an *I-told-you-so*, but just as sharp. Lauren couldn't feel too angry, she supposed. Cass was right, after all.

'Guess I did.'

'Are you terribly heartbroken?' Things were always like that in her world, Lauren remembered. They were always *terribly* or *awfully* ... as if she turned into Audrey Hepburn the minute she was trying to show empathy.

'No more than expected. What about you?'

'I'm not heartbroken at all,' Cass trilled, raising her cup. It was a poor impersonation of herself.

'That's not what I meant.'

'I know what you meant, Loll,' she twisted her cup around on the table, pushing the handle. 'I'm alone. There've been a few guys along the way. No one who stuck. When I knew I was sick again, well, it didn't seem fair. I felt like I was tricking them into a sad little life.'

She'd never heard Cass be selfless before. She had only wanted to be adored, to be seen. Now, she seemed to curl in on herself, her sleeves pulled down to her fingertips.

'How long do you have?'

Cass let out that half-laugh again, 'You know, that's all anyone wants to know. What does the crystal ball say, what's the deadline? It's like when old ladies ask how far along you are when you're pregnant. But in reverse, I guess.'

Lauren said nothing, and Cass sighed. 'I'm just ... can we finish our coffee first?'

'Whatever you want, Cass.' Lauren watched as the pale impersonation of Cassidy Jones put on that voice, the one that pretended to be brave.

'Best thing about dying – it's always whatever I want. Should have started dying *years* ago, everyone's been so awfully accommodating.' She gave a little smile and looked up, as if checking to see if Lauren still knew her, still knew how she spoke and what she really meant. Whatever she was searching for in Lauren's eyes, she seemed to find it.

'Do you want to go for a walk?'

*

The Blackpool Illuminations on New Year's Eve were a weird mix of drizzly grey skies, crashing waves, and the party spirit of young people pre-drinking in the afternoon. Loud youths walked back from the shops with six packs of beer, and bottles of wine under their arms. There was a sense of time passing, and simultaneously freezing. Nothing seemed to move or change, just the cold sea air pushing them back as they trudged.

'So, what do you do?' Cass asked. 'Are you a big-shot lawyer now?'

'I'm a solicitor, yeah.' Lauren pressed her lips together, holding back any further explanation. 'And you? Did you become a physio in the end or stay at the make-up counter?' *Did you stick with one thing, finally?*

'Nah,' Cass shook her head, 'didn't seem worth it after Mum. On to new things. I still do a pretty decent smoky eye, though. And I help a couple of the local oldies out with their exercises.'

Her thick mustard scarf was wrapped twice around her, and the colour clashed horribly, bringing out a yellow tone in her skin that spoke of illness.

'So what do you do?' It could have been any of a hundred things Cass had tried and quit. Nurse, model, waitress, dog walker.

'I work in an office. I'm an administrator for a homeless charity.' She shrugged, sneaking a peak at Lauren. 'Unexpected?'

'The word *administrator* and *I* in the same sentence from you? Sure.' Lauren smiled, 'How long have you done that?'

'About four and a half years.'

'Jesus.'

'I know,' Cass shook her head. 'Some things change.'

'Do you love it?'

Cass twitched her nose, shrugged one shoulder. 'It's fine. It's flexible. I like feeling like I'm doing something good. The money is enough and the people I work with are interesting.'

She raised a hand at an old couple walking on the other side of the street. They waved back, before returning to the task at hand – concentrating on staying upright. They gripped each other tightly, blue veins protruding from their clasped hands.

'I always wonder when I see old people if they're holding hands because they want to or they need to,' Lauren said suddenly, looking as the woman smiled at her husband with a kind of light in her eyes.

'Is there a difference?' Cass replied, checking her phone as it buzzed. 'All right if we take a detour?'

Lauren looked at her. 'Everything okay?'

'Sure, just got to pop round the corner.' She stopped suddenly, brushing her hair back from her face in frustration. She seemed to tremble again as she spoke. 'Look, you're here and everything, so I assume you're okay with meeting her? I know it won't be easy, but ...'

Cass's body was taut, her toe tapping as she watched Lauren. She crossed her arms, hip jutted in a way that was painfully familiar. Ready for a fight.

'Meeting who?'

Cass looked at her, confusion in the crease of her brow and her pursed lips. 'My daughter, obviously.'

Chapter 3

Lauren felt her stomach shift and clench. 'You have a *daughter*?'

'Yes.' Cass frowned in confusion.

'No, I'm sorry, that wasn't right. *You* have a *daughter*? *You*?'

They were walking briskly, Lauren marching ahead even as Cass struggled after her, her cheeks reddening with the cold air.

'You knew this, why are you being funny with me?' Cass stopped, taking a shuddering breath, 'It was why you stayed away, and I got it, but you're here now. I thought you'd come to terms with it ... what's with the anger?'

Lauren pressed her lips together, eyes resting anywhere but on Cass. It was an overreaction, sure, but it was unfair. All these years had passed, she was *dying*, and yet Cassidy Jones could still make her jealous. All she had wanted was a child, a little girl. She knew she shouldn't have wanted a girl over a boy, but she *did*. She'd wanted a girl she could teach to be strong, and fierce. A girl who wasn't raised in a pink bedroom wearing pink tutus and ballet slippers, who was taught to be seen and not heard. This daughter she had imagined she would have one day, she'd be allowed to play in the mud, and be loud and silly and messy. The way she hadn't been.

Lauren could taste the loss, metallic and sour. Of course, Cass had a girl. Cass, who had been irresponsible and flighty and had done what she'd done – *she* got to have a child. Lauren suddenly heard Cass's words clearly.

'I didn't know. How would I know? I don't know anything!' She knew she sounded hysterical, her voice struggling to project. *Little mouse*, her family always called her, *angry little mouse*.

Cass's face lost all colour, eyes widening in panic. 'Oh God. Oh God, he said he'd told you. That's why you never returned any of my letters.' Her eyes flicked to the house behind Lauren, her hand raising slightly, then falling. The fact that she was looking past Lauren enraged her even more. 'I wouldn't have ... I would have *said* something—'

'Who? Who told me what? And what *letters*? This was the first letter I've ever had from you. Six years, nothing, then *boom,* here's Cassidy Jones with her drama!' Lauren could feel the bitterness spilling out and she couldn't hold it back.

'Drama!' Cass hissed, eyes wide. 'Dying isn't *drama,* Loll.'

'It is when you do it.'

Cass seemed to deflate, leaning back against a tree. Its roots had collapsed the surrounding pavement, leaving the stones uneven and broken. Her fingertips traced the bark and Lauren was drawn to the sight, her soft, pale fingers moving back and forth. She had done that on the inside of Lauren's arm when they were younger, just below the elbow. It was in second year she'd first started, when Lauren couldn't sleep at all, worrying and fretting about life and exams and failure. Cass had let her rest her head on her lap and stroked spirals on the inside of her arm, telling her everything would be okay. A lifetime ago. She had believed her then. She watched as Cassidy shook her head, seeming to build up the energy for that bitter little voice.

'That fucking bastard.'

'Who?' Lauren sighed.

'Darren, obviously.'

'Darren, my Darren?'

Cass rolled her eyes. 'Loll, doesn't it seem strange to you that I've sent you hundreds of letters in the last six years, and you only received one? After he left?'

'You think Darren was smart enough to hide my letters all this time? He barely remembers to pay the gas bill.' Lauren snorted. Besides, the man was incapable of not expressing every thought he had, whenever he had one. Which was why when he left, at least it had been upfront. Painful, and irritating as hell, but he'd come to her and said he was leaving. It was the one decent thing about him. There'd been no running around, no lying. He'd cheated, he loved this woman, he was leaving. That was it. Done.

The idea that he could have been stealing her post ... and since when did Cassidy Jones write letters, rather than leave a drunk voicemail at three in the morning? She could still remember them, the crying and snivelling, the apologies, the excuses. It was too late by then, what they'd had was broken. She'd stopped being Cass the minute she betrayed her.

'And how often were you working, Loll? How late did you

get home, how early did you leave? You don't think there's any chance he could have just scooped up the post without you noticing?' Cass's grey-blue eyes were round with pity, and Lauren hated that even more.

'Oh, so it's my fault? I destroyed my marriage because I'm a workaholic?' She could hear herself, that stupid teenage answer-back tone. *Petulant, stupid woman. Stop talking. You're in the street. It isn't proper.* Her mother's worried voice echoing around her skull.

Cass sighed, closing her eyes briefly. Her voice was calm and even, 'I didn't say that. I just know you. Or, I knew you. This isn't about you. This is about Darren lying.'

'So you're saying he hid your letters to me? Why?'

'Because he didn't want us to be friends. He never did, you know that,' Cass said lightly, her eyes flickering again to the window, a slow nod and a quirk of her lips. She held up a single finger, mouthing, 'One minute.'

Lauren looked behind her, but saw only the flicker of a white net curtain.

'He told me you knew about my kid, that it hurt too much, that you didn't want to see me,' Cass stared at the ground. 'And I understood, you know, of course, but it didn't seem ... I don't know, it just didn't seem like you. I always thought if I just kept sending the letters, you'd come around ... but now I get it. You didn't know, you never knew. All this time I thought you hated me—'

'I *did* hate you! I *hated* you!' Lauren said, feeling herself trembling.

'And you're going to hate me again. Now you know. He

said you'd never been able to get over it, and I hadn't thought he was just protecting himself.' Cass hovered on the edge of tears, pressing her lips together as she looked at Lauren in silent apology, shaking her head.

Lauren tried to make sense of it, her emotions twisting tendrils around her vocal cords. She knew the answer, it was obvious. It was suddenly as if she'd always known. They said nothing.

Cass used all of the tree to support her weight, as if she couldn't find the energy to stand. Her eyes flicked behind her, and she straightened, whispering to Lauren, 'Just breathe, okay? Just keep breathing and everything will be fine. We'll sort this all out back at the house.' The same words she'd always used, the same promises. *How could they ever sort this out?*

Suddenly, the front door opened behind her, and Lauren whirled around to see a little girl coming running out, sprinting across to Cass. Her brown hair was in two high pigtails, and her trainers lit up as she moved. Her jeans were a little too big, a heart-shaped patch on the side, and her T-shirt said, *Girl Power*.

'Hey there, munchkin, cool your jets. No need to run anywhere.' Cass tried for a smile, but it was drawn and tight, her eyes flittering up to Lauren to assess the situation.

Cass turned the little girl around to face her, and it was clear. So clear.

'Vee, this is Loll, my very best friend in the whole world,' she looked towards Lauren cautiously, like she was a wild thing, not to be trusted. 'Loll, this is my daughter, Veronica.'

Lauren almost laughed then, at the second meaningless betrayal. Cass knew that was her grandmother's name, a name she'd planned to save for her own child.

Abuela Veronica had been the only person to ever really see her as strong. As something beyond the scared little girl that everyone else seemed to want her to be. She had these dark eyes that demanded more of you, and permanently pursed lips like she wanted to laugh but was holding it in.

Veronica had been the one to tell her to do law, if she wanted to do law. That she was only as weak as she allowed herself to be. That it didn't matter what they thought.

She was unlike anyone else's grandmother. Sure, she did the motherly stuff, and she squeezed baby cheeks and made amazing paella. She cared about her family. But she absolutely didn't care about what anyone else thought. She poured herself a large glass of port most nights, she giggled when she ate chocolates, holding them daintily between her solid fingers. She started a swing dance class in her seventies, and though everyone knew she'd loved her husband, she never felt the need for another companion. She had her life, and she was satisfied.

Lauren's favourite thing about her grandmother, beyond that funny, wild spirit, was that she had chosen her own name. When she came to England with her kids, and her husband died, she decided she could either be afraid, or she could be in control. So she gave herself a new name, for a new life. And she lived it, well.

Cass knew that. She knew how much that name meant.

'Veronica,' she exhaled, shaking her head. 'Really? *Veronica*?'

'Yes,' the little girl said, a little pout appearing on her lips, 'but I like Vee best.' She held out her hand, so that Lauren couldn't resist bending down to accommodate her.

'Very nice to meet you, Vee,' she heard the break in her voice and stood back up again, staring up to the sky until the tears dried. Her heart beat in her throat, vicious and rapid. The little girl appraised her.

'Are you sick like Cassy is? Is that why you're sad?'

'No,' she pressed her lips together, shaking her head and trying desperately for a smile. 'I'm just so glad to meet you, and to see your mum again. We have a lot to catch up on.'

Veronica nodded in approval, turning back to Cass to smile at her, taking her hand. God, she looked like him. Not a lot, but just enough to matter. An echo of her father about the tips of her ears and the tilt of her chin. It was always arrogant on Darren, but with Vee's delicate features it was pleasantly obstinate. Lauren couldn't help but trace Vee's features for more of him, like there were clues in her skin. She tried to remember if she'd seen any of Darren's baby pictures, but his family weren't like that. His mother was never a soft woman. She'd had a pinched look at their wedding, standing there sipping her champagne like she'd never been so put out. And she was an unsuspecting grandmother. How insane.

Unless she knew. Was this all some big game, where everyone knew everything except her? She had to be kept in the dark because she was so fragile, so incapable? '*Let me worry about it, it's too much for you*,' Darren had always said. '*I didn't want you to get upset*,' her mother said whenever there was big news. She didn't know about her brother's baby until a month before the birth. '*You just get so worked up*,' the voices seemed to repeat, over and over. '*I'll never lie to you, Loll*,' was Cassidy's refrain, fighting against the others, '*even if it hurts*.' She'd kept that promise at least.

Lauren was unspooling, she could feel it, jumping off into a dark pool of water, unwilling to come back. *Step back from the paranoia, take a deep breath and a step back.*

'Hello?' A chubby little hand shook hers, and she refocused. 'Auntie Loll? I said are you going to have dinner with us? We get to have a special New Year's dinner. Cassy said you might come – it's macaroni cheese. My favourite.'

Auntie Loll. Lauren let herself be led along by Veronica, the small child holding a hand of each woman like she knew she had to keep them moving. She chatted away and even though she tried, Lauren couldn't catch the words. They looked like a family. She couldn't get the idea out of her head.

'Did the cat get mean again, baby?' Cass asked her daughter, scanning her face. 'He didn't scratch you?'

'No ... it was my fault. I shouldn't have cuddled him when he didn't want to be cuddled.'

'That's true.' Cass shook her hand and grinned at the floor.

'Jasper isn't as nice as Geronimo. Do you like cats, Auntie Loll?' Veronica turned her huge eyes to Lauren now, and the fact that they were the same colour as Cass's, but her hair was brown like Darren's ... it just threw her.

'Huh?' she blinked.

'Baby, Auntie Loll isn't feeling very well – maybe wait to chat at dinner, okay?'

'Okay,' the girl's voice quivered with disappointment. 'Sorry.'

'Oh no, you don't have to be sorry!' Lauren squeezed her hand, 'I'm not feeling well right now, but when we get back home I would love to talk about cats. I had a cat growing up called Tigger and he was a big fluffy monster. I'll tell you all about him.'

Vee grinned, nodding. 'Good.'

The walk seemed to last forever. Lauren was sure she was walking through fog, or wet tissue paper. Something was pushing back, making it hard to see. She just had to keep breathing and moving, that was all she had to do. *Steady breaths, don't look at either of them. It will all be fine.*

Oh, but Veronica was gorgeous. There was mud under her fingernails and scuffs on her trainers and she spoke eloquently and clearly. She was confident. Maybe if Lauren had had a daughter, she would have been meek and mild. She hadn't thought so, but everyone else seemed to. She might never have been strong enough. Clearly, Darren wasn't the problem after all. It was her. She was the reason they hadn't had children.

As soon as the key was in the lock, Lauren felt it.

'Bathroom?' she gasped.

'Top of the stairs.'

She galloped up, losing a trainer in the process, and collapsed into the bathroom with enough time to slam the door and reach the toilet. There wasn't much to throw up – she hadn't been eating. That didn't stop her body from retching, over and over, until her throat hurt and her stomach cramped. She wasn't sure if the bile was red from last night's wine or she'd scratched the lining of her throat.

Lauren clung to the toilet seat, resting her head on her arm.

She could die here. She could outdo Cass, for once. She would die of shock on her bathroom floor, and that would show her who was dramatic.

Except that was stupid. But what *wasn't* stupid was finally getting angry instead of sad. She should be finding an appropriate outlet for her rage. Someone who wasn't a dying mother or a five-year-old.

Lauren scrambled for the phone in her coat pocket and pressed the button. She felt strangely drunk, elated even, at having the chance to scream at him. It somehow hadn't been his fault when he left. He'd fallen in love, it just *happened*, he couldn't help it. It wasn't like he'd *chosen* to hurt her. And before that, all those years ago ... he was shocked, disgusted by the accusation. He could never even have *dreamed* of hurting her like that. It was *offensive that she even considered it*, those were his words ... God, how he must have been laughing at her naivety, her stupidity. These lies were longer than their marriage.

Her heart pounded as the phone rang.

'Lauren? Why are you calling?' Darren sounded genuinely puzzled, and she couldn't blame him. He could have counted on her pride. She wouldn't have called him again for the rest of her life if not for this.

'*You bastard. You lying bastard.*' Her voice was low and croaky, and yes, that was blood she tasted. She quite liked how her words sounded when they bled.

'Who told you?' Darren replied too quickly, and before she'd even answered he'd blathered on, his voice high and wavering. 'Look, obviously we'll wait until after the divorce comes through to tell anyone, it's not a *big deal* or anything. We just put it on social media so Sasha could show off the ring, that was all. There's no rush—'

Lauren pressed her palm into her forehead, as though she was trying to stop her brain falling out.

'You're getting married.'

'Well, yeah, but it was spontaneous, sweetheart, it wasn't—'

'We're still *married*, dickhead.' Lauren suddenly felt like her nineteen-year-old self again, holding hands with Cass, drunk and obnoxious as they told boys to fuck off and find someone else to gawk at, because they wanted to dance. She felt powerful.

'Well yeah, but it's over, so ...'

'Whatever, I wasn't calling about that, although wow, continually lowering my expectations after all these years. Impressive.' Her throat was too dry to laugh, so she coughed.

'Look, what do you want, Lauren? I don't think it's healthy for us to talk at this time.'

'Oh, okay, well I'll be quick. I just kind of wanted to know about that whole thing where you *knocked up my best friend and then hid it for six years!*' Screaming hurt, but it was a good hurt. It gave her burning lungs something to do.

He laughed. He actually laughed. 'Bloody hell, all those years and Cassidy finally got her claws back into you? Didn't see that one coming. Thought you didn't forgive, Lauren, that's what you said, wasn't it? Once people lose your trust it's gone for good?'

'Still married you, didn't I?' she hissed. 'Aren't you sorry?'

'Sorry? I hid it for you! You, crazy-desperate for a family, to know that Cass had what you wanted? You think you wouldn't have gone mental over that? I was protecting you.'

'You're a liar. Everything you said, you denied it, you made it seem impossible. And it happened, it all happened ...' Lauren felt herself unravelling.

'It was better this way. You know what Cass was like back then. You were better off without her, we both were. Without the drama, the drunken hysterics.' Darren's voice softened, 'I didn't want to lose you.'

'So I had to lose her?' Lauren wanted to burst into tears like a child at the unfairness of it all. 'Have you even met her, your kid?'

She didn't know why she asked, it barely mattered. Everything had changed the moment he lied. Everything could have been different.

'No! My God, no, Lauren, never! I told her I wasn't interested. I send her some money every month, because it seemed like the right thing to do, but—'

Lauren snorted, 'How noble.'

'Look, I didn't want to be a dad. You know that. I went along with it for you, because it was what you wanted, but I never wanted that. Not yet anyway. And certainly not with *her*, for fuck's sake.'

'You ... you stole my letters? Every opportunity you had to make things right, every time a letter came to the door. Stacking up the lies over and over,' she was rambling, she could hear the madness in her voice. 'I honestly didn't think you were even that smart.'

He laughed at that. 'I was smart enough to protect myself. To protect my marriage.'

'Only to throw it away when something better came along.'

'You'd rather I stayed with you even when I wanted to be with someone else?'

'I'd rather you died a painful death in some sort of ridiculous clown-related accident,' she threw out, channelling a teenage Cass. But oh, to wish him dead when Cass was dying ... that wasn't right. Her anger had bubbled up and it was like a burst tap, spitting hot hatred everywhere. 'I didn't mean that.'

'Yes, you did. Maybe until the divorce we shouldn't speak, so we can interact like civil adults when it comes to separating the assets, right?'

Lauren wasn't even sure where to start. So she didn't. She hung up the phone and rested her head on her arm again. She might have fallen asleep, she wasn't sure, but there was a gentle tap on the door, and then she saw Cass's pale arm sneaking around the frame, handing her a mug.

'Ginger tea. Settles the stomach.'

Lauren half-laughed, blowing on it, 'Prefer vodka.'

'Later.' Cass pushed back the door, leaning her head on the frame. 'What did he say?'

'That he lied to protect me.'

'You know that isn't true, Loll.'

Lauren closed her eyes. 'I don't want to talk about him.'

'Good. Let's talk about you.'

Lauren shook her head, drowsy as a child. 'No. No talking about me. And no talking about death.'

Lauren pushed herself up from the floor and Cass offered her hand. 'I think it's time for bed. Come on now, up you get.'

She coaxed and cajoled, her voice so soothing that Lauren couldn't even get grouchy at being treated like a child. She led her into the dark room, and tucked her up in a single bed, plastic stars faintly glowing on the ceiling. In the corner of the room, a space-themed mobile swung in the breeze through the window, sun and moon orbiting each other around an unsteady Earth.

'Is this Vee's room?' she said in surprise, failing to focus on the stars.

'She won't mind.' Cass rested a cool palm on her forehead, 'Sleep, Loll. The rest will sort itself.'

She stayed a few moments longer, her thumb resting in the middle of Lauren's palm, applying light pressure, just as she always had whenever Lauren had drowned in anxiety, struggling to breathe.

Now, she was beyond all that – she was simply numb and exhausted. She pulled her hand away, and Cass nodded as she left.

Sleep came like death, engulfing her in darkness.

When she awoke, she padded down the stairs to see the remains of dinner on the table, and Vee asleep, curled into Cass on the sofa, her little dark head nuzzled under the blanket, Cass's arms tight around her. Cass's eyes were on the fireworks on the screen, but she seemed to be looking past them. She looked up as Lauren peered around the corner.

'I saved you some dinner,' she whispered, 'nothing much, but it's in the microwave if you want?'

Lauren smiled, the force pulling at the skin at the corner of her mouth. She walked through to the kitchen, set the microwave and waited. She suddenly saw, as she hadn't before, the plastic princess cup on the draining board, the photos on the fridge. If she had taken one more second to look around earlier, she wouldn't have been blindsided.

Cass looked like a mum, the way she stroked Veronica's cheek, and smiled at her enthusiasm. The way she had gripped her hand, and checked both ways as they crossed the road. She was really a mother. Maybe even a good one. It was cruel of her to be shocked by that.

The microwave beeped loudly, and she burnt her fingertips as she pulled out a bowl of macaroni cheese with a slice of garlic bread stuck in the top. Absolutely no nutritional value, but she ate desperately, burning her tongue in eagerness. It was the first time she'd been hungry in days.

She watched Cass settled on the sofa, absentmindedly stroking her daughter's hair. Her smile was tired, and she shuffled slightly when Lauren came in. Lauren chose the seat across from her, curling into the padded armchair and resting her bowl on her knee.

Cass kept her eyes on the television. 'No shouting or arguing unless it's a whisper, okay? Dealing with a grouchy, sleepy kid is not my favourite.'

'Agreed,' Lauren said, her eyes hovering on the sleeping child. 'I can imagine that's not fun.'

Cass shook her head. 'A couple of years ago she had croup, it was a nightmare. Seeing her in pain, not being able to help, killed me. It's worse to be the bystander sometimes, you know?'

The fireworks on the screen were over the top, bursting into flashes of pink and blue against the colours of the London Eye.

'You remember when we went?' Cass's eye tilted from the screen back to Lauren.

'Worst New Year's ever,' she laughed, still watching that repetitive motion of Cass's hand stroking Veronica's hair. 'We were freezing and drunk, and we had to pee outside because of the queues ...'

'We got neck ache looking up and that guy vomited all over your shoes!'

'My back! On my leather jacket!' Lauren smiled, placing her bowl on the side table.

'Wearing a leather jacket out on the coldest night of the year – a classic Loll move.'

Lauren tilted her head. 'Was it?'

Cass snorted, 'You kidding? Every *single time* we went out, you would never put a proper coat on because your outfit didn't look right, or you didn't want to look bulky, or you didn't want to carry it, and you'd spend the whole night cold and miserable.' She shook her head. 'Or worse, you'd decide to drink more to keep you warm and that would get you in trouble.'

'I'd forgotten that. Seems so unlike me.'

Cass smiled. 'Bet you've got a spare coat in the car now, haven't you?'

'Something like that.' She had a second pair of gloves, two hats and an extra jumper in there, just in case. Always prepared for every eventuality. Somehow, the idea of discomfort had become more harrowing as she grew up. Being cold, being tired, being pissed off, it just never seemed worth it. It was better to prepare, to keep herself happy enough. She'd thought that would be a good trait as a future parent, always being the one with the baby wipes and the spare bottle of water.

The house was small, but homely. Everything was neat and in its proper place. The walls were a cheery pale yellow, and the bookcases were full, haphazardly stacked. Each book seemed to have broken spines and folded down corners. They had been loved, thumbed through, re-read over and over. Lauren remembered those books and the cases from Cass's bedroom at her mum's house. It had driven her mad, those books, how *used* they looked. '*Don't you have any respect for them?*' she'd asked, aghast at the teacup rims on covers, the folded pieces of paper as bookmarks sticking out from different ones. '*Of course, I love them,*' Cass had replied and Lauren remembered simply not understanding how you could love something so much you'd destroy it.

'What are you gonna do, Cass?' Lauren was surprised by the desperation in her voice. 'Is there treatment, something you can do? What's actually wrong?'

Cass assessed her sleeping daughter, looking for the rise and fall of her chest, little ears that weren't overhearing.

'The big "C" of course, just like Mum,' Cass said lightly. 'Always figured it would get me sooner or later, so, here it is.'

'What does that mean? It's inherited?'

'A certain gene makes you more susceptible.' She shrugged gently. 'Win some, lose some.'

Lauren simply stared.

'Hey, you said less drama, I'm doing less drama.'

'I shouldn't have said that. I was just ... overwhelmed.'

'I know,' Cass said. 'But it's no more than I deserve, is it?'

Lauren didn't know what to say. Cass had that same knack as her mother – a discomfiting sort of mind reading. Her mother got her insecurities, and Cass got those thoughts she was ashamed of having. *You betrayed me, you deserve this.* Lauren shook her head.

Cass looked back at the screen, now showing the steady hum of people trying to leave the Embankment, an unholy mess of coats and scarves bumbling along in a plodding stream. Lauren looked at the clock on the wall: almost 1 a.m., and they hadn't really talked at all.

'Isn't there something you could do?' she asked, and once again Cass's mask appeared, that blasé raised eyebrow that seemed to ask who the hell she thought she was, turning up and asking questions.

'You mean like two rounds of chemo? Or a double mastectomy, maybe? Been there, done that. T-shirt doesn't fit the same.' She tilted her head, the small tug of a smile about her lips, 'Come on, you have to laugh. If you don't laugh, you cry and I haven't got time for that. Not yet anyway.'

'Cass. Tell me.'

Cassidy took a deep breath, eyes still on her daughter. 'I knew I had the gene before Vee was born. I'd had tests just before Mum died. She didn't want me to, wanted me to be like her, living without fear. But I needed to know. You saw her at the end. For once in my life, I wanted to be prepared.' She shuffled a little, looking down at her daughter. 'There'd been a bit of panic when I was pregnant. Vee was okay, but there were a few concerns. Had the chemo, and it worked. All good. Came back clear, on we went with our lives. They said a good way to limit future issues was the mastectomy, so I did it. This has been going on a long while, Loll, you're just here for the final act.'

She paused, reaching up to brush hair away from her face, 'Mum was bitter and angry in the end. She hated me for being there, for witnessing her disappearance. Then she hated me when I left. She was in a fog most days and it was like she became small, collapsed in on herself. There was no joy. Before, she'd been the life and soul of the party. First one on the dodgems, first on the dance floor ...'

'Loudest laugh in North London,' Lauren supplied gently.

Cass snorted, 'Exactly! And cancer took that from her. She wasn't herself at the end, not really. It was like *Invasion of the Body Snatchers*. I didn't want to lose my mum but when it was over, I was *relieved*. The pain and loss had turned her into someone hateful. It's awful, but I was pleased it was over. And that fucked me up.'

She trailed off. They both knew where it went from there. It had been bad enough in the run-up to Barbara's death with the drinking and the lost jobs and the distance. Cancelling plans and turning up frantic, talking gibberish. A night, a confrontation, and a disappearance.

'Loll, come sit here,' she whispered, patting the seat next to her on the sofa.

Lauren went, moving delicately, settling herself in so as not to nudge Vee. She couldn't stop looking at the little girl, how beautiful she was, the very best parts of Cass. Asleep she looked vulnerable and in need of protection. And yet, this sort of hysterical rage seemed to bubble when she looked at her – it was too painful, like looking directly into the sun. This beautiful little girl was a symbol of betrayal and lies. She couldn't stop scanning her for parts of Darren, as if she'd suddenly sit up and say something he used to say, or run a thumb over her eyebrow like he did. She couldn't hate an innocent child, could she? Surely she wasn't capable of that.

'She calls you *Cassy*,' she said. 'Why?'

Cass offered a one-shouldered shrug in reply. 'Who knows why kids do what they do? It makes her happy.'

'Is she ... has Veronica got the gene, the thing your mum had?'

Cass bit her lip. 'She'll be higher risk, having a mother and grandmother who both croaked early. It's fifty-fifty, they say. She can't be tested until she's older. I like to believe she'll be fine, living a long and hopefully happy life.'

It was just a flicker of her lip, but Lauren saw the fear flash across her face, the understanding of loss and what she'd be leaving behind. A reluctance to go.

'So you wanna know why you're here, Loll?' Cass smiled suddenly, emotion hidden behind her charm. 'I know you do.'

'To bring you the book. And find out about Vee.'

'I don't just want the book, I want *you* with the book.' Cass looked very pleased with herself, and Lauren knew that look almost as well as that bitten lip and anxious face that looked back from the mirror each morning. Cass was bargaining. She'd told her once in a market in Greece that you should *always look as if you'll be getting exactly what you deserve, one way or the other. The only factor that changes is how long it takes. Time is the only variable.* She was always coming out with bullshit like that, and often Loll, whilst delighted at how smart it all sounded, just chalked it up to Cass being Cass. Wanting to be alluring and make a story out of everything.

Cass reached over and took her hand. 'I want us to do the things in the Big Book. The way we always meant to, before jobs and careers and husbands and dying mothers and fucked-up grieving and mistakes got in the way.'

'You want me to quit my job and go backpacking with you?' Lauren wondered if she was still drunk.

'I want to live. And I want you there to live with me. You don't have to quit your job if you don't want to. Take a sabbatical, or a break, or something. I bet … have you got any holiday left?' Oh dear, a question. Already there was a chink in her bargaining. *Never question, always tell.*

Lauren thought about how she'd afford the mortgage on that big family home they'd bought, and whether she could buy Darren out. It was unlikely. She'd have to sell up and move into somewhere smaller. She needed her job. She needed just one thing in her life to stay the same. The world had tilted, there were too many changes, so many mistakes and lies … it was hard to breathe just thinking about it. She felt untethered. Why hadn't Cass shouted yet, why hadn't they argued? They would, eventually, they would yell and scream and dredge it all up, just for Cass to die anyway. The shame of Darren's lies, and those memories, stuck in her throat like gravel.

'I ... I can't,' she stuttered, looking at Cass. 'I'm so sorry, but I can't.'

'Is this about ...' She lowered her chin to Veronica, still sleeping soundly, and Lauren shook her head.

'I have a job, I have a life. I'm sorry about everything, I really am, but ...'

The silence settled like dust, and Cass honestly looked like she didn't know what to say. She wasn't expecting a rejection. She never had, Lauren remembered. People always wanted to do things for her.

'I should have known not to spring this on you. You always need time to process. You didn't come because you were ready to forgive me, you just came because you felt sorry for me.' Cass blinked away tears, shaking her head, trying to smile. 'I understand, I do. I got my hopes up. It was too much to ask.'

Lauren said nothing, looking at the floor.

'I guess money is a reason too?' Cass asked, quietly hopeful.

'Partly,' she sighed, 'divorces are expensive, I hear. Especially when he's rushing it through to get remarried.' She choked out a laugh at that, raising her eyes to the ceiling. 'God, what a mess.'

'That man was a colossal waste,' Cass said bitterly, jaw clenched.

Lauren rested her eyes on the beautiful little girl beside her, reaching out gingerly to stroke her cheek, but stopping herself. 'Maybe not completely.'

'He sent us money. I've never touched it, Loll, not one penny. I didn't ask him for it. Cheques arrive at the house each month, and a bit more at Christmas, and I've put it all away. I thought we could use it for all of us to go on this adventure. Kind of poetic, I guess. Paying for a reunion tour. But we don't have to, you can have it, if you want.'

Lauren shook her head, eyes still on Veronica. 'No, keep it for her ... What is she going to do without you, Cass? How is she ever going to be okay?'

Cass smiled, but her lips quivered a little, her eyes glassier than before. 'I've got it all planned out. She's going to have so many wonderful memories with her mother. She's going to have this big adventure, and *that's* what she'll remember, this gift I'll give her.'

'You're going to take her on this trip?'

Cass nodded, awaiting judgement.

'How long?'

'As long as it takes.'

They sat in silence for what felt like hours, watching the little girl as she slept.

'You know ... you know how sorry I am, right, Loll? I know there's nothing that could ever undo it, and I know you never forgive,' Cass stared at the television, stroking her daughter's hair, soothing herself rather than the child. 'But I want you to know I'm taking my punishment. It's actually the kind of torture that would almost make me believe in God. A delicious sort of irony, to have the worst thing you ever did, the thing that destroyed your life actually bring you something wonderful.'

'Cass ...'

She pasted a smile on her face. 'I know what you're thinking. I'm sick so you've been robbed of your chance to be angry.

But we can have it out, tomorrow. I'll drop Vee in with a neighbour and you can properly yell at me.'

'You're making me sound like a horrible person,' Lauren sighed, wriggling in her seat.

'I'm just trying to make it fair, make it even.'

It was impossible to even imagine how to make something like that right, and Lauren could feel Cass realising it too.

'You could always come on this trip with us, make my final few months a misery? Put my hand in warm water when I'm asleep, and cut my hair with nail scissors? Come and punish me, it'll be fun.' She smiled so desperately, wide-mouthed and strained, that Lauren could only chortle politely and announce she was going to bed.

There was too much to say, too many half-finished sentences and words that would return days later to haunt them. *Why didn't I just say that? Why didn't I ask this?* Cass took Veronica upstairs to her room, with Lauren returning to the child's bedroom, following behind them. The window ledge halfway up had a selection of photographs in frames. Vee at playgroup, her sweet little monogrammed jumper. Cass, holding her baby close, looking exhausted and oh-so young. Lauren wondered who had taken the picture, who else she had in her life to soften the blow when everyone else was gone.

As she lay there in that lovely little room with the plug-in night light and the collection of fluffy toys, Lauren tried to imagine a world where Cassidy Jones was gone before she even got to know who she had become. It was only then, fist stuffed in her mouth, cover pulled over her head, that she allowed herself to cry.

Chapter 4

'Get up! Get up! Auntie Loll, you have to get up!' There were little stubby legs jumping on the bed, and a lumpy body landed on her. 'Oof! Get up! It's New Year! We're having pancakes! Hellooo?'

Lauren lay very still, one eye open as she waited for the impatient hands to lift the cover. When Veronica's face peered round, she grabbed her quickly, tickling as the girl shrieked and laughed.

'Stop, stop!' Vee kicked her legs, and Lauren stopped.

'Not a nice way to be woken up, little miss!'

Veronica acknowledged this with a tilt of her head. The movement was so Cass that it made her chest hurt. She searched for Darren in that little face, looking for the arrogance behind the eyebrows, but there was nothing. She was pure Cass.

Vee jumped down onto the floor and went onto her tiptoes, kissing her on the cheek. 'Good morning, Auntie Loll, happy New Year.'

'Much nicer, thank you. Happy New Year!' She let herself be dragged down the stairs by the insistent child, to see Cass at the stove, her blonde hair tied back in a blue-spotted scarf.

'Morning, bacon with your pancakes?'

'Yes, please!' Cass's pancakes had been legendary throughout the university dorms. The girl couldn't make beans on toast without setting off the fire alarms, but fluffy American pancakes, perfectly round and golden, drowned in maple syrup and nearly-but-not-quite burnt bacon? Excellent every time.

'We're going to the rides!' Vee clapped her hands as the pancakes came to the table. 'You'll come too.'

Lauren looked across to Cass, raising an eyebrow in question.

'The pier, we're going to the pier. Baby, you gotta *ask* Loll if she's coming, not just tell her she is.'

'But it's easier to tell people,' the little girl frowned.

Lauren fought a smile, her expression mirroring Cass's. It felt nice, to share something simple like that with her.

'I guess that's true.' Lauren shrugged. 'I'll come. I'm not going on any rides though.'

'What's the point, then?' Veronica asked, truly perplexed.

'Vee, kinda rude.' Cass nudged her with her elbow, placing the plate of bacon and bottle of syrup in the middle of the table, and sitting down herself. 'The point is your auntie will spend time with us. That'll be nice, won't it?'

'*Very* nice,' Veronica nodded, wide smile on her face, 'but it would be better if you went on the roller-coaster.'

Lauren shook her head. 'Nuh-uh. I'm a big scaredy-cat. If you're *very* lucky though, I might go on the teacups with you.'

The little girl considered this, a forkful of pancake halfway to her face. 'Hmm, I'll think about it.'

'Well, that's very kind of you,' Lauren laughed, her eyes

flitting to Cass again, who was wearing a look of something like relief.

'Your Auntie Loll doesn't like big scary rides,' Cass said to her daughter, sparing a glance for Lauren, who smiled at the tabletop. She knew Cass was thinking of the day they skived off uni to go to a theme park, and just before the ride started, Lauren panicked. She'd been strapped in and started crying and struggled to breathe. They let her out, and Cass went with her, never once telling her she was silly. She just bought her an ice-cream cone and suggested they walk around the maze instead.

Lauren remembered being so shocked that someone wouldn't mock her for her weakness. Her parents were always telling her how embarrassingly fearful she was. Cass was the only person who ever let her be who she was. And now she was letting her be awkward and angry and confused, without question. Just gratitude.

'But they're the most fun!' Vee looked shocked that anyone could deny the joy of a roller-coaster.

Lauren was almost convinced, but later that morning, as she looked up at the rickety old wooden framework, she felt her stomach drop.

'*That?*' She pointed. 'You want to go on *that*?'

Vee grinned up at her, pulling on her hand. 'Of course, it's the best one!'

'Leave poor Auntie Loll alone, pudding, come on. I'll come with you.' Cass steered her daughter over to the roller-coaster, where there was no queue. No one was there, and Lauren stood in the cold, hands in her pockets, shoulders braced against the chill. She was wearing a grey coat, brown boots and black tights. Against the grey background of the pier, the sky blending into the water, Lauren was sure she was almost invisible.

Cass and Veronica didn't have that problem, it was easy to see them across the pier, Veronica's bright little yellow rain mac and black-and-white tights standing out almost as much as Cass's deep-green coat and red scarf. They were little chunks of brightness in the dismal landscape.

Lauren wondered whether she should have stopped Cass, asked if it was safe for her. They hadn't talked about the state of her illness, what she was dealing with. She looked frail, but she had always had a pallor that erred on the side of sleepless nights. Once, a painter at a party said her skin looked like that of a porcelain doll. Cass had been delighted, tracing her own cheek in surprise. She loved a compliment. Lauren was sure he'd tried to sell them drugs later on that evening. Now she still looked like porcelain, but she was fragile. Easily broken. Lauren pressed her nails into her palm. There would be no talking Cass out of having fun.

The response would be the same as it always was, whenever Cass did anything dangerous or foolish or strange: *Well, gotta die someday.* Whether it was trying the week-old Chinese food for a dare, or getting pierced in a back-alley studio, or walking over to that scowling boy with the neck tattoo to demand a date, Cass never turned down the chance to take a risk.

She watched that little cart creep to the top of the roller-coaster, Vee's yellow coat blinking in the distance, so high up in the sky. She held her breath, trying not to panic. So many things could go wrong. They could be hurt. Or killed. Wasn't there a story in the newspaper about a girl getting killed on a roller-coaster? Nothing was certain, everything could turn upside down in a second. Your best friend could betray you, your husband could leave you, you could realise you'd wasted the last six years of your life being angry about the wrong thing. You could meet a child who made you jealous of your dying friend, but also made your stomach cramp with loss. You could realise your life was not the way it was meant to be. You could blame your idiot husband and your critical mother and your beautiful, selfish friend, and realise you created your own undoing all along, with every choice you made.

God, she needed them to be okay.

They seemed to hover at the top, and then they were falling, slipping through the air and tracing the loops. Lauren's heart thumped desperately, and she held her breath. The little figures in the distance held their arms up as they fell. She imagined she could hear their screams. Her eyes followed their movements in a panic, time seemingly endless as they moved this way and that, until finally they were deposited back to the ground and she could breathe again.

She watched as Veronica jumped up and down in delight, clapping her hands, and hugging her mother. Cass looked breathless, but there was colour in her cheeks, and her red scarf flapped in the wind.

Veronica's grin was huge as she ran over. 'Did you see us? Did you see us? We were so high and then we just went *zoom*!' Her hand indicated the descent. Her eyes were so bright and vibrant, wide with excitement. 'We were like birds, *hoot hoot*!' She lifted her arms to swoop around the two adults, holding her coat up like a cape. She then launched herself at Cass, who was forced to bend and catch her, cradling her close.

Lauren watched her face, the strain in her movements, the downward tilt of her mouth as she gritted her teeth. There it was, illness hovering behind her eyes and in the joints of her fingers. It made Lauren wince a little just to watch.

'Gently, sweetheart, gently.' Cass kissed her daughter's rosy cheek and swung her back and forth, rotating from the hips. 'Besides, you know we're not birds! What are we?'

'We're wolves!' Veronica yelped, throwing both her arms up, '*Arroooo!*'

Cass threw her head back too, joining her. '*Arroooooo!*'

Lauren's cheeks coloured in embarrassment, and she had to physically stop herself from stepping back from them. Her eyes sought out Cass's and she wondered if she remembered, or if she'd just plucked a random phrase from the air to entertain her daughter.

Cass met her gaze defiantly, not leaving her eyes as she spoke to Veronica. 'Vee, tell Auntie Loll why we're wolves.'

'Because we're a pack,' Vee ticked them off on her fingers, 'and we protect each other, and we keep each other warm, and we're pretty ...'

Cass pressed her lips together, and almost rolled her eyes as she squeezed Veronica and put her down.

'Yes, wolves are very pretty. But we're a pack, right?'

'Right,' the little girl nodded definitively. 'And Auntie Loll too, right? She's part of our pack?'

'I don't know, baby.' Cass tilted her head at Lauren. 'What do you think?'

It was a strange thing, to watch them both watching her, their heads at that same angle, each quirking that same eyebrow.

'Can you howl, Auntie Loll? You need to have a good howl to be a wolf,' the little girl said with authority, hands on hips. 'Let's hear your howl.'

Lauren snorted, shaking her head. 'I'm sorry, lovely one, I'm not a wolf. I'm a deer ... no, something less elegant ... I'm a pheasant. Or a dormouse, I'm a dormouse.'

'What's a pheasant?' she frowned.

'A very silly bird.' She shook her head, then, as the awkwardness made her skin itch, she checked her watch. 'Look, I better get back. Back to work tomorrow, long drive and everything ...'

Disappointment flashed across Cass's face, but she nodded. 'Of course, thanks for coming. Look, we'll walk you back to the car.'

'No, no, enjoy the pier. I'm sure there's another terrifying ride to go on – enjoy your New Year's Day!' She flapped her arms, as if to keep them at bay. 'I left the book for you, Cass, it's on your kitchen table ... Good luck with it.'

Cass bit her lip, nodding slowly, before turning to Veronica. 'Baby, say goodbye to Auntie Loll.'

'Bye.' The little girl reached out her arms and Lauren crouched down, letting herself be nestled into, Vee's hair tickling her nose. This child who would have been her step-daughter, the living symbol of the ultimate betrayal. Yet she whispered in Lauren's ear, 'Well, *I* think you're a wolf,' and she struggled to hold in the tears.

Lauren squeezed her briefly, feeling her chest contract. She had to get out of there. This was too much. This wasn't her life. She wasn't part of this, she wasn't one of them. And tomorrow she had to go back to work and pretend her husband hadn't left her, Cass wasn't sick, Veronica didn't exist and that everything was normal.

'Um, Loll, do you, I mean ... do you want my number, or ... anything?' Cass looked so small suddenly, like a strong breeze from the waves could carry her away. Lauren wanted her to be sassy, and courageous, to yell, 'Hey bitch, take my number, we'll talk,' just as brash as she used to be. But instead she just stood there, with this aching desperation on her face, like a lifeline was walking away from her.

'I'll write to you,' Lauren stuttered as she took a few steps, 'that's what we do now, isn't it? We're all cool and old school and we write letters.'

She had to force herself to slow down, because she knew it looked like she was running away, her feet catching paving stones as she stared resolutely ahead. When she had crossed the road and made it down a side path, she looked back. They were still there, standing on the pier, holding hands, the tall thin woman in the green coat, and the little girl in her yellow mac, the only visible thing against the grey.

It was okay to leave them, it was okay not to get involved. She wasn't one of the pack, she wasn't part of any of this. She was just the woman who had married Veronica's biological father. She was just someone who knew Cass when they were younger. That was it. No one would expect anything else. She had more than enough of her own shit to deal with.

When she reached the car, her heart was pounding and her ears hurt from the cold. She shivered as she waited for the heating to get going, and stared across at the little house, the Christmas tree visible in the front window. She couldn't give up her life again for Cassidy Jones. She had to focus on herself. It seemed that was how all of this had started, that determination not to be in Cass's shadow anymore, to finally be her own person instead of the plain little friend always along for the ride.

Cass was asking again. *Come along, Loll, it's my party but you're invited.* She wondered if the howling was a mistake or not. Veronica throwing her head back like a young cub, it had torn right through her. Cass had to have known, had to have remembered.

*

It had been the second year of uni, because they lived with Emily and Rachel, who insisted on having ridiculous parties every weekend. Ones that descended into screaming matches about other people's boyfriends and acceptable boundaries. It became boring, so they used to camp out in the pub across the road, the Resurgence. Lauren had a soft spot for the bartender, Luke, who always smiled and gave them free packs of salt-and-vinegar crisps. Mainly because he had a soft spot for Cass. Lauren was used to that turn of events by then. There'd been something particular about that night though, and Lauren strove to remember.

Something to do with Babs. A serious diagnosis, or a bad week of chemo. The years of her sickness blended together, she had always been waiting for treatment or undergoing it. Cass had always been either pretending she wasn't worried, or escaping into drugs and booze. The years were hard to keep straight.

This night though, Lauren recalled the specifics. She remembered the purple jumper that Cass wore, how she pulled the sleeves over her fingertips. How her eyes looked even more blue against her pale skin. She kept coughing from the damp in the house.

'I should be with her,' Cass had said, wallowing in self-pity, 'she's going through this alone.'

'And you're sick and you could make her worse. Focus on getting better. Or focus on passing your course.'

Cass had raised an eyebrow. 'Something you want to say there, Loll?'

'Don't change course again, even if it bores you?'

'Well, what's the point of all this really, if I'm not passionate about the thing I'm studying? If it's not *meant to be*?'

'If it's not easy, you mean.' Lauren had sipped her pint of cider, her eyes flitting to Luke behind the bar and the way he rolled his shirt sleeves up.

'Excuse me, I'm having an existential crisis here,' Cass had nudged her, 'plus don't you have a boyfriend?'

'I have a ... Darren. We don't have a label.'

Cass rolled her eyes, then rested her head on Lauren's shoulder, nuzzling in. 'I don't know what I'm doing, Loll. I don't know what I'd do without you.'

Lauren snorted, 'That is absolutely not true, and you know it.'

Cass lifted her head and smirked. 'Okay, well I wouldn't know how to be myself.'

'You mean maybe you'd be a completely normal, well-balanced person without me?' Lauren faux-gasped, 'The horror!'

Cass sat back, her fingertips tapping the sticky darkwood table insistently. 'You joke, but I'm being serious. You're like ... my tribe.'

'We can't be a tribe by ourselves.'

'We can,' Cass nodded, eyes wide, 'and maybe we'll add more people if they prove themselves worthy.' Her gaze strayed towards the bar briefly, where Luke was polishing glasses and looked across the bar at her. She turned back to Lauren, 'But we're definitely a tribe.'

'And how will these people prove they're worthy? Slay a dragon? Rescue a princess? Run through a burning building?'

Cass's eyes were sometimes shocking in how blue they were. She blinked, then laughed. 'No, they just have to be there when we need them.'

Lauren couldn't think of a joke to make, and she knew Cass's thoughts were returning to her mother and the chemo. She could imagine Barbara, sitting in her chair, making all the other people around her laugh, asking the nurses if they could switch out the solution in her drip for wine. A nice sauvignon blanc, if you please.

It was impossible to imagine her not looking glamorous, her golden blonde hair curled elegantly, wearing her best navy wraparound dress and her heels. Barbara always wore heels, no matter if she was in a hospital ward or on a camping ground. When she'd first met Lauren, she pulled her in for a bear hug against her ample bosom, asked her how she felt about marriage, and offered her a glass of wine. Lauren had blinked, looked at Cass, who had shrugged, and said she thought it was probably very nice for people who were into that sort of thing, but currently she was quite happy dating.

Barbara had a laugh like a foghorn, and she bundled Lauren through to the kitchen. 'Thank God! Finally a normal friend, hey, baby?'

'Normal?' Lauren's heart had sunk. Here she was in Cassidy Jones's house, seeing the things that mattered to her in her childhood bedroom (a stuffed whale called Winston, and her eternally broken-spined book collection) and meeting her mother. And she had been dismissed as *normal* immediately. What an awful word, *normal.* They knew how they sparkled, and they recognised her dullness.

'Not a fuck-up!' Barbara elaborated, handing her a generously poured glass of wine. 'Someone simpatico! Friends should be on the same page. Every other "friend" Cass has had seems to be from a different book entirely!'

It was horrible to admit, but when Cass loved you, she shone a light on you, and Lauren loved that warmth. When Cass was with her, she felt her prettiest, smartest and loveliest self. Until she was in the shadows again. Cass had slipped an arm around her friend, staring at her mother defiantly, as if trying to prove her wrong. *Look, I found someone who gets me. I am lovable. I have a friend, I have everything I need.* Lauren could tell what that look meant, from the jut of her lip, the tilt of her chin, their heads next to each other, as if posing for a picture. Barbara suddenly laughed and clapped her hands together, wine sloshing out of her near-empty glass and onto the cream carpet.

In the pub, Lauren had looked at Cass, resolutely drinking her cider and staring into space, the empty bar suddenly so silent. It was her job, as her friend, to get her through this. To listen as she offloaded, and be there when she cried. Cass had done it enough times for her, over things much less important than a dying parent. But she needed to know she was strong enough.

'You remember what your mum used to call us?' Lauren said, remembering a comment that Babs had once made, when they came downstairs in their matching Halloween outfits and garish make-up. 'She called us a pack.'

'A pack's the same as a tribe.'

'No, it's not. Because a tribe can be people. But we're not people. We're wolves.'

'Wolves?'

'Sharp teeth and pretty fur and fucking deadly.' Lauren tried her best to sound like Cass, energetic and passionate. 'Wolves can deal with anything, no matter how cold it gets, right?'

'I get it, Loll, and I appreciate it, but ...'

'Nope, we're wolves. And what do wolves do?' Lauren asked, grinning.

'I don't—'

'*Arooooo!*' Lauren howled, enjoying the look of shock on

Cass's face. 'Join in or I'll keep going! *Arooooo!*'

'I'm not going to—'

'*Arrrrooooo*!' Lauren howled louder, seeing Luke jump across the bar and narrowly avoid smashing a pint glass. 'Are you a strong wolf, or are you a puny human?'

Cass fought the smile, but it seemed to spread across her face despite her attempts. 'I'm most definitely a wolf.'

'Prove it,' said Lauren, crossing her arms.

'*Arrooooo!*' howled Cass, using all the air in her lungs until she couldn't howl any longer for laughing. In that moment, Lauren knew she'd done her job.

It was painful to think about now, the moment she'd been strong enough to care for Cass. Everyone always thought she was weak, but she wasn't. She was just quiet. Cass knew. Cass had always known what she was capable of.

Now there was a wolf pack of two again. She had been replaced by Veronica. They thought they needed her, but they didn't, not really. They'd have their adventure as mother and daughter. She didn't need to be a third wheel. But the whole way home she couldn't stop thinking of that little girl in the yellow coat, staring out at the sea, and wondering whose hand she'd have to hold when her mother was gone.

Chapter 5

The drive home had been awful. Long, and stuck in traffic. Lauren didn't feel buoyant with the hope of a new year. She felt foggy. She had to stop four times for coffee and bought a bag of doughnuts to eat in the car. All that 'New Year, New You' rubbish, and the truth was she was a twenty-nine-year-old soon-to-be-divorcee with nothing much going for her. May as well eat the doughnuts. Leaving powdered-sugar finger marks on the steering wheel felt symbolic. She was making a mess. She was allowed to make a mess.

Lauren kept thinking about Veronica, how her eyes had lit up at the roller-coaster, how Cass's gaze had softened as she stroked her hair. How Darren was already engaged. He must have been cheating for a good long stretch. It was hardly the biggest lie, in the grand scheme of things. Why hadn't she looked more carefully at the list in the Big Book, before handing it over? Perhaps there were things she still wanted to do. She should have apologised. Cass had, and yet, was that ever going to be enough? How did words suddenly wipe away all the damage? Everything hurt. There was too much to think about, and in the end, the concentration she needed for driving took over. When she eventually made it home, she collapsed into her bed and slept, relieved that she was too exhausted to think anymore.

*

Lauren hated her work clothes. She always felt like she was pretending to be a grown-up. She'd tried to copy her colleagues, but it never looked right. She was still young, and yet she dressed more maturely in the hopes that people would take her seriously. She felt a hundred years old. The only way to get into work most days was to trick herself into it, repeating something comforting in distraction. Before Christmas it was, *Holiday soon, holiday soon*. Before that, it was simple pleasures like *Thai food for lunch* or *Shopping after work*. Now, there wasn't really anything to say.

It's okay, it's all okay, she settled for repeating before brushing her teeth, looking at those red-rimmed eyes in the bathroom mirror. She repeated it as she walked to her car, as she drove to work and as she buzzed herself into the office. As she sat down at her desk, she silently congratulated herself on tricking her body into work. She would only have to do that every weekday morning for the rest of her life.

She had dreamt of Cass, unsurprisingly. She had dreamt that Cass and Veronica went on their adventures, and kept sending her postcards. At first they had read, *Wish you were here,* but soon they turned cruel. *We didn't want you anyway and we're having more fun without you,* was scribbled on the backs of rolling hills and seaside scenes. They had kept coming, the postcards, shooting through the letterbox with vicious intent, until she was drowning in a sea of pictures, bleeding from thousands of tiny cuts that never should have hurt at all.

'Morning,' she said to passing colleagues, and they nodded back as they sat at their desks. She went through her paperwork, opened her email inbox and started to sift through the responses.

'Lauren,' her boss, Glen, walked over. 'Happy New Year.'

'Happy New Year. Good Christmas?' she replied softly. Glen looked rather like an overbaked ham – rotund and a deep pink. Lauren often worried about his blood pressure, but then he'd say something awful and she'd hope he'd keel over. It was a complicated relationship.

'Yes, yes. Very good and all that. Look, I've had Mrs Keener on the phone already this morning, and she left eight messages over the holiday.' He leaned on the edge of her desk and looked down at her, an expression of disappointment on his face. 'She says the process has taken too long, and we're risking her losing the house she wants. I've had these conversations about time management with you before.'

Lauren felt her neck grow warm, and noticed an orange stain on the collar of Glen's grey jacket. 'There's been absolutely nothing else I could do, you know what it's like this time of year. I'm waiting on data from the registry, I've had to email her buyers three times with the forms – and it was Christmas. We're still on track for within ten weeks.'

Glen didn't look convinced. 'Look, Lauren, I know you work hard, but you need to be a bit better at keeping your clients happy. We don't have this with Nadia or Mairead, and they are both in their early twenties. They've picked up that their clients will be happier if they're kept in the loop. The more unhappy a client is, the more likely we're going to get negative reviews, even when the purchase goes through without a hitch. Chat to Mrs Keener, let her know what the hold-up is and that she'll get the house she wants.'

Lauren bit her lip. She'd already called Mrs Keener three times before Christmas, assuring her that everything was running smoothly, letting her know what stage the process was at and what they were aiming for next. She'd let her know it was her number-one priority, that she would highlight any issues along the way and that she wanted her to have a good Christmas. And still the woman called.

'Glen, you know there are certain clients who are more anxious and more pushy – there always are,' she said. *And it's funny how they always seem to be passed on to me.* She looked across the room at Nadia and Mairead, their stylish black dresses with tailored jackets and statement necklaces. They looked at her, then looked away again.

'Yes, and I know that when our clients leave bad reviews, it's bad for my business.' Glen stood up. 'I'd like you to take responsibility for your workload, Lauren. These are people's *homes*. If you're not going to take it seriously, we'll have to reassess your place here.'

Lauren blinked as he walked off, leaving her papers in disarray on her desk as he stood up from it. What was *with* the universe right now?

It wasn't that she hated conveyancing, necessarily. It was just that she had been training, all those years, because she wanted to be a human rights lawyer. She loved looking for the details in a story, the titbits in the paperwork that could build a case for innocence, or a suspicion of conviction. She didn't necessarily want to stand up in court and speak for anyone, but she'd wanted to be part of change. She'd wanted to protect people. She took in information like a sponge and all those years working towards this big goal that no one thought she could achieve, it was meant to be for something.

But she had been stressed and anxious, and everyone told her it was too much for her. Her mum, Darren, her course tutors. No one seemed to like her having feelings about anything, it seemed. It was better to sit at this desk in this awful place where everyone seemed to think she was an inconvenience, because she wasn't twenty-four and wearing a tight skirt and telling clients lies to keep them sweet.

It had been okay, when she had Darren. They were planning a family. That was what people did – they had families and bought homes, and had dinner parties and called their parents. They spent money on new curtains and had a box hidden under the bed with baby onesies and tiny, adorable shoes. Because they made plans for the future, and their plans sustained them.

But there were no plans. Her life spread out before her like a carpet being unrolled. Anything could happen, and that knowledge didn't bring the same joy it had years ago. It was terrifying. The future was vast and unyielding.

She could go on this trip. She could. She could call Cass, arrange the time off. She might even laugh the way she used to. Her entire life she had been the stable one, the sensible one. She had given up their travel plans because she had to study, and then she had a job, and then there was no Cass to hold her hand along the way.

What if she went?

It was impossible to comprehend, for more than a five-minute daydream. She had to stay and tidy up her life. She could already hear her mother's judgemental tone as she accused her of running away. It was best to stay and stick it out. Better than being the unnecessary third wheel on a mother-daughter bonding trip. Seeing Cass's love for her daughter was a fresh knife wound every time Vee smiled. Searching the little girl's face for echoes of her father, conjuring images of the night they made her. The trip would kill her.

No, better to be safe. To stay still. Lauren's hand paused over the telephone, fingertips hovering over the keys. Mrs Keener or Cass? It was hard to tell who she was meant to call. One call for one direction, and one for another.

Coffee first, that would help. She launched herself across the room, nodding back to *Hellos* and *Happy New Years* until she was sure her face would crack with the effort of smiling politely. When she got to the coffee machine, thankfully there was only Nigel.

'All right, cracker, happy New Year and all that.' He grinned at her, then paused. 'God, you look like absolute shite, y'all right, love?'

Nigel was in IT. He had no time for anyone's politics, and his main concern was insuring that no fraudulent activity was happening through the company. Luckily, most of the older bosses didn't really understand what he did, so he'd throw some tech jargon at them and they'd go away. Lauren wished she could do that.

'Um, yeah, cheers, Nige,' she tried to laugh, getting herself a mug out of the cupboard. 'Although, I suppose, if you were gonna recommend your divorce lawyer, I wouldn't say no.'

His eyes softened, and he nodded. 'Sorry, mate, that's crap. I'll send you her number, she's a world-class beast, razor-sharp jaws. Goes in for the kill, if that's what you're looking for?'

'I don't know what I'm looking for.' She shrugged, pressing the button on the coffee machine. 'A way out, I guess.'

He scratched his head, his red hair becoming even more fluffy with the movement. 'You were always too good for that estate-agent prick anyway. Thought he was God's gift, didn't he?'

'Apparently his girlfriend – sorry, fiancée – agrees,' Lauren snorted, keeping her eyes on the entrance to the kitchen. Nadia would have a field day with this information.

'Shut the front door! Motherfucker!' Nigel hooted, then made a face. 'Sorry. Want to get a drink later? Drown your sorrows? I think I was drunk for a month when Angela left.'

She smiled at him. 'Thanks, but I've spent enough time drunk. Time for me to dry out.'

'Okay, well I'll send the number over. Take the bastard for all he's got. And keep your chin up.'

Nigel nudged her as she left, and she felt deeply grateful. He was probably her only friend at work. Everyone else was so focused on seeming like the best, on making their money and winning awards – it didn't seem right. To listen to people moaning about a hundred-pound fee on the million-pound mansion they were selling, when every morning Lauren passed a homeless girl on her way from the car park to the office.

Maybe she should take Darren for everything. Keep the house, take his car. If the fact that he was cheating and already engaged wasn't enough, the secret love child with her best friend was surely great grounds for divorce. She laughed out loud at the thought of it, clapping her hand over her mouth. Oh God, she was losing it.

The phone rang, and she answered. 'Lauren, it's Mrs Keener on the line for you. She sounds quite upset.'

Oh great.

'Thanks, Kemmy, put her through.'

She waited for the click, and took a breath, making her voice bright and bold.

'Good morning, Mrs Keener, happy New Year.'

'Is it? Is it a happy new year when I still don't know when I'll be into my house, and might end up being *homeless*? Is that a good start to the new year?'

'Now, Mrs Keener, I know the process can be frustrating, but—'

'Frustrating! Do you know how many times I've had to call your office to find out what's going on? Do you? Tell me how many times!' The woman's voice was starting to get squeaky, and Lauren felt her chest start to hurt.

'From our records, it seems you've called eight times. I was just about to—'

'Oh don't tell me,' she cut her off, 'you were just about to call me.'

'Well, we've all been off for the Christmas period, as I mentioned when I called on the twentieth—'

'So you're allowed to go and enjoy your Christmas when I don't know if I should even unpack my tree?' Mrs Keener was clearly enjoying herself, and Lauren felt her breathing become uneven. She hated this. People loved to call up and shout at her. This was why she could never have made it as a big-shot lawyer. Always too soft, too sensitive.

She took a few breaths. 'Mrs Keener, nothing has changed since I called you. The office has been closed. The process is continuing, and we're still within the ten-week goal for completion. Your buyers have yet to send back a few of the forms I sent, but that happens at this time of year. If you have their details, maybe you should prompt them.' *Instead of bugging me.*

'Oh so it's *their* fault? Typical. I could have you fired, you know.'

It was one of those moments where she knew *exactly* what Cass would say in response.

'You know what, lady, you'd be doing me a favour.' The words were out of Lauren's mouth before she'd even realised what she'd said.

'Excuse me?'

Was there a way to spin this, beyond stuttering and apologising? Probably not. But she was damned if she was going to carry on bowing her head to that vile little woman. Cass wouldn't.

'Mrs Keener, I *assure you*, I have done everything I possibly can to speed this up. I didn't want you to have to call eight times, I didn't have a great Christmas whilst you were stressed, and to be perfectly honest, if you wanted to get me fired, I would probably thank you for it. I am trying so hard to make sure you get this house sold at the correct price, but it's not just down to me, it's down to your buyers, their solicitors, the registry, so many other factors. But I can assure you, I'm doing everything I can.' She breathed out slowly, hoping the woman had taken enough of that in to back off.

'Well, if that's how you feel about your job, why on earth should I trust you with my house? You probably just leave the office at half four and go about your life with no thought at all for poor people like me, stuck in limbo, whilst you're off gallivanting.'

She snapped. She knew it was coming. *Damn.* It was like Cass had got inside her head, the memory of a sassy nineteen-year-old controlling what came out of her mouth.

'Actually, Mrs Keener, I was here until about seven every night in the run-up to Christmas, doing my best for my clients, which is probably why I didn't notice my husband's affair with the woman he's now decided to marry. So perhaps if I cared less about *poor people like you* making a £650,000 profit on your sale, my marriage would still be intact. I'll forward you on to Nadia who can have the *immense* pleasure of dealing with your sale, and I'm sure you can expect it to be completed by spring. Goodbye!'

She slammed down the phone and squeaked. *Oh God.* Could she legitimately blame Cass for this? Burrowing her way into her head and reminding her of what a pushover she was? Or maybe she was still in shock from Darren and the cheating and Veronica's existence. Well, if you were going to do it, it was best to go the whole hog.

She downed her coffee, washed up her mug and went into Glen's office. Twenty minutes later she was walking out with the few personal items from her desk packed in her handbag, and fifteen packs of Post-it notes that Nigel had handed her as she walked to her car, telling her she should at least get something from the bastards. He gave her a hug and said she was certainly starting the new year with a bang.

'It was my choice,' she said incredulously, grinning at him. 'I chose to leave.'

'Well, good on you, lovely. Smart choice. Bold.'

She nodded in agreement, sitting in her car in a daze. Lauren had made a choice, and the world hadn't fallen apart. She had changed something. And she was going to do it again. How miraculous.

When Lauren returned home, it was like she was looking at it all with new eyes. The house itself was beautiful, there was no doubt about it. Visitors always commented on how much light there was, how the cream carpets were still fluffy and clean, how the roll-top bath was a delight. They fawned over this symbol of their success.

But still, there was no one here to see when she was sat alone eating a microwave meal and wondering why Darren was home late again. Wondering if this was really all there was. She didn't love this house. She didn't love her job, or her life. This house was a symbol of absolutely everything she didn't want anymore. Cass would have told her that happiness came first, above all – what else was there beyond being happy?

The thought of being free of it brought a smile to her face, and she grabbed her phone and texted Darren.

I've taken half the savings from our joint account. You can have the house, sell it, buy me out, whatever. Sort out the divorce, seeing as you're the one in such a hurry. Have a nice life. :)

With that, she threw the phone onto the sofa, knowing that soon enough it would start ringing. The less she was bothered, the more it would offend Darren. She knew that much by now. He had to be the centre of it all.

Lauren remembered that the first goal in the Big Book was written in her own neat, thin writing: *Design a life we're proud of.* For all she cared, this life could burn to the ground. It was time for another. She went upstairs to pack.

Chapter 6

The drive to Blackpool was different this time – it was still grey and dull, and traffic was still traffic, but something had changed. She blasted rock-and-roll hits from the speakers and yelled along, out of tune and joyous. There was something beautiful about destruction, about the chance to start again.

She was excited, she realised. It was such a strange sensation. In the back of the car she had her suitcase with all the clothes she actually liked wearing (none of those impersonal attempts at business wear) and that huge backpack. The one she'd bought and never got around to using. Darren begged her to throw it out – *When are you ever going to go backpacking, Lauren, we're not teenagers anymore* – but she'd steadfastly refused. One of the few things she stood her ground on.

She stopped halfway to get petrol, and as she wandered around the attached shopping centre in search of snacks, Lauren spotted something – a little stuffed-rabbit toy with a soft brown body and a white fluffy bob of a tail. She bought it immediately. Finally, a child to spoil. It felt a little like an apology for the way she had stared at Vee, scanning her for signs of the betrayal that created her. She couldn't resent a child. Not if she bought gifts.

Lauren picked up some food for dinner, revelling at the presumption, and threw in a few fancy chocolate bars and some pick 'n' mix. Something for Cass. She loved jelly beans, but only the orange and yellow ones. Lauren carefully only scooped those colours into the pot, smiling to herself at the thought of it. She had quit her job! She would have an adventure.

It was almost unthinkable after years of sleepwalking. The promise of anxiety sat in the back of her throat, questions of how she'd survive and what people would think ready to hound her. But she hummed a tune to herself to keep them out.

When she returned to her car, Lauren felt her pocket vibrate. Darren. She probably shouldn't answer, but maybe it would speed things up.

'Hello?'

'I've been trying to call you – why haven't you answered?' Ooh, he sounded annoyed. *Excellent.* She decided, just as she had with her job, to emulate Cass. That seemed to get the best responses in these situations. She couldn't be trusted to be herself. Act like Cass.

'Didn't feel like it,' she shrugged, munching on a jelly bean from the bag. 'What's up?

'*What's up?* You've left the house. Where are you? Where are you going?'

The irritation in his voice was a balm. Lauren thought back to that night he told he was leaving, all heartfelt apologies, his clear explanation that *fate* had a role to play in all of this. He begged her not to blame him, she couldn't blame him. He was just trying to do the right thing.

'That's really none of your business. Is there something specific I can help you with?' She chewed louder.

'Come on, Lauren, don't be unreasonable,' his voice was soothing, rational. 'This isn't like you at all.'

Yes, I'm showing some sort of backbone, I imagine that's surprising, she thought to herself. 'You're right, it's not like me. But it could be.'

'You're not making any sense. Look, come back so we can sort this out like adults. We need to get divorced.'

'Correction: *you* need to get divorced. So you can get married again. And to be fair, if I register the papers it'll have to be on grounds of an affair, unless you'd like me to put "*struck by the hand of fate*" under reasons for separating?'

'How can you put "affair", I was upfront and told you—'

'You left me before Christmas and now you're engaged, but there was no affair? Do you think a divorce lawyer is going to buy that?'

'Doesn't matter, can't prove it.'

She knew that tone of voice. He did it when he was at work, on the phone, crowing to some seller about how he'd done such a great job, what a solid deal it was. It was the cocky tone of voice that made her snort.

'Okay, so even if I couldn't find emails and texts and photos and social media check-ins at expensive restaurants, how about finding out you had a secret love child with my former best friend? And that you'd been sending her money over the years? Think they'd rule in your favour on that one?' She laughed to herself. 'Look, here's the thing you have to accept: you're the arsehole here. So start acting like it. Apply for the paperwork, and when you've got something for me to sign, I'll tell you where to send it.'

He was silent for a moment, and she could tell he was desperate to roar at her, or slam the phone down.

'This is all Cass. Back in your life for five minutes and you're already back to being a teenager again. It's demented. You're being incredibly childish, you know,' Darren grumbled, and she knew she'd won.

'I know. Wonderful, isn't it?'

She hung up with satisfaction, singing to herself as she got back into the car. She couldn't wait to see Cass's face. It had been the longest time since she'd done something fun and unexpected. Her usual idea of spontaneity was ordering something that wasn't a sandwich for lunch at the office.

When Lauren arrived outside Cass's house, she sat, vibrating with anticipation. There was so much they hadn't discussed. Where they would go, what they would do. How long she had left to have this adventure. And they still hadn't talked about the one thing that tore them apart. At some point she would have to have that conversation. She would have to acknowledge the gaping wound, the loss she'd felt all those years ago, and how angry she still was, even when Cass was dying. She wasn't allowed to be angry, and she couldn't figure out how she could hate her and love her and be fearful of losing her again all at the same time.

As long as Lauren kept all of that at the back of her mind,

she could continue moving forward. Denial, as always, was the answer to success. She would have to keep herself in check, bite her tongue as she had done for all these years. As she seemed to have no trouble doing with everyone but Cassidy. Besides, Vee didn't need to see them fighting.

She jumped out of the car, clutching her shopping bags and the little bunny toy, and walked across the road. If she paused, she would stop completely, so she pressed on the bell, once, twice, then again. Too insistent. Too desperate.

The door opened and Cass stood there, blinking. Then she smiled, and the sun came out.

'Well ...'

Lauren couldn't fight her own grin as she gestured with the shopping bags. 'You going to let me in? We've got places to go and adventures to plan.'

Cass laughed in delight. 'You're right. Come in. Vee will be beside herself.'

She tucked her hair behind her ear, Cass's signature gesture of nervousness, and Lauren felt okay again. Things were going to be okay. She followed through to the living room, placing the bags on the floor.

'Hey, Veronica, you've got a visitor!' Cass yelled over her shoulder. There was a thunderous racket as small feet stamped down the stairs, and suddenly she was enveloped in a hug.

'Auntie Loll!' Vee cried, her arms grasping around her waist. Lauren felt her heart contract. 'You came back!'

'Well, we didn't have enough time, did we?'

The little girl shook her head, looking up at her. 'Are you staying for dinner?'

'I'm making dinner,' she replied, then looked over at Cass, 'if that's okay?'

Cass laughed. 'Me not having to cook? That is more than okay!' She paused, looking at Lauren, blinking a little too much. Then she frowned and looked at the ceiling, before adjusting her smile. 'Thank you.'

She mouthed it more than said it, but Lauren felt it anyway.

'Will you stay here, or ...?'

'I thought I'd get a room nearby, don't want to take Vee's bed from her again.'

'I don't mind!' Vee insisted, taking her hand and shaking it back and forth. 'Really.'

'No, it's okay, I'll go and settle in, and then I'll come back and we'll have dinner. You can help me cook, right?'

Vee nodded intently, and Cass stroked her hair. 'This one, queen of cheese on toast, aren't you, babe?'

'And noodles, I can make noodles. And crud-ites.'

Cass snorted, 'Crudit*és,* babe. And yes, you are the winner at cucumber sticks. It's all in how you arrange it on the plate.'

Vee looked up at Lauren with a smile, the dimples in her cheeks so similar to Darren's that it hurt. They conjured moments from happier times – saying their vows, curled around each other on their honeymoon. That child's smile was a rock in her stomach, a reminder that her marriage was a lie. Had always been a lie.

She had to keep smiling. She had to be kind beyond the pain.

'Are you here to come on Cassy's big adventure with us?'

'I think I am.' She took a breath, her face hurting with the effort of smiling. 'Where will we go?'

'Everywhere!'

That evening, after dinner, Cass placed the Big Book on the table. Vee climbed up on her lap, and Lauren sat next to them. The book's leather coating was worn and battered, and Cass traced it gently with her fingertips.

'Um, do we think this is appropriate for little eyes?' Lauren tilted her head at Vee, and Cass widened her eyes.

'Ah, yeah, maybe we should cross out the ones we already did, too.'

Veronica pursed her lips in irritation, 'Come on, come on. I want to see.'

Lauren opened the book and took a deep breath. '*1. Design a life we're proud of.*'

She looked at Cass, who looked at her daughter and smiled, bouncing her up and down on her lap a little. Her lips then pursed as she stared resolutely upwards, holding back tears. Lauren looked away, ashamed. Cass had designed her life completely, making her own choices. She had a daughter, and a home and a job she liked. Lauren had stumbled into her life without even realising she was making decisions. It was like she woke up one day and realised she'd been sleepwalking. That sort of living stopped here. She had already made a bunch of choices today, ones that would set her on a different path. She could be proud of that, at least.

'Swim around the Great Barrier Reef,' Lauren said, nodding. 'Did you do that?'

'Nope, you?'

'Nope.'

'What's the great reef?' Vee asked, twisting to look at her mother.

'It's this beautiful underwater world of brightly coloured coral, with turtles and fish and beautifulness,' Cass smiled, squeezing her daughter close, '*and* you have a great uncle in Australia who I'm sure would love to meet you.'

'Jack!' Lauren recalled with a smile. 'He was always a good time.'

Jack was so clearly Barbara's brother it was almost impossible to tell them apart. He was just as much the life of the party, handing them drinks and telling stories about fighting alligators or meeting celebrities. You could never tell which was fact or fiction. Most of the time you didn't care, either. Just like Barbara. A little bit of magic in the Jones's family tree.

'He asked if I'd like to live with him, after Mum died, but ... well, it didn't seem fair,' Cass gestured at the bundle of five-year old in her arms. 'I would really like to see him again. He was always good to me.'

'Okay, so Australia! Bet we can tick off a few more on the list there too.' Lauren flicked through the pages, 'Going surfing! That's an easy fit. Skydive? I'm not so into that one anymore ...'

Cass shook her head. 'Me neither. I think I just put it on there because it's the kind of thing you put on a bucket list. We need to be able to ignore the ones we don't care about.'

Lauren exhaled. 'Thank God. I thought you were going to call me a wuss.'

Cass shook her head. 'Life is scary and risky enough – we only take the risks that are worth it.'

'Agreed,' Lauren smiled, and lifted her beer, clinking the bottle against Cass's. It was starting to feel like this was possible.

Her phone rang, and she saw Darren's name flash up, but ignored it, turning it off entirely.

'Ahem,' a quiet, polite voice said, and both adults looked down at Veronica, who looked particularly serious. 'Am *I* allowed to choose things I want to do?'

Lauren looked at Cass, who nodded. 'Of course, sweets, but we'll try and tie it in with the book.'

'Can I add it to the book?'

Lauren nodded and handed the little girl a pencil. Veronica grabbed the book and pulled it towards her, writing methodically, her tongue stuck out at an angle in concentration. She seemed to take an age to write one word, and then focused on doing a drawing alongside it, in case it wasn't clear. When Cass peered over her shoulder, she couldn't hold the smile in, grinning across at Lauren.

'You know, I think that is going to fit in perfectly with some plans your auntie and I made years ago. Shall we see if Loll can guess?'

Vee looked intrigued.

'See the Northern Lights. Sleep in an igloo. Sled with huskies,' Cass said, raising an eyebrow. 'Loll, do you think we could make time for a *very good* little girl to meet an important bearded man with some excellent reindeer?'

Lauren pretended to think about it. 'You know, I think it would be really silly to go all the way to Lapland and not meet up with Santa, don't you?'

Veronica clapped her hands in delight, before restraining herself. 'Um ... you don't think he'll be on holiday? Because he worked so hard over Christmas?'

Lauren patted the little girl's hand. 'Even when he's relaxing at home, I'm sure Santa would be really pleased to see you. Maybe we should do that first, because it's closer than Oz?'

Cass shrugged her agreement, then turned her head at the doorbell ringing. 'That'll be Barry.'

'Barry!' Vee jumped up, 'I'll get it.'

'Look through the letterbox first!' Cass warned, then stood up, wincing a little. She waved away Lauren's look of concern and walked over to the sidebar to grab a shopping bag.

'It's him!' Vee's yell echoed through the corridor, and they could hear her opening the door. The male voice that greeted her was wispy and croaked a little in that way old voices did. Voices that had lived long lives and softened with experience.

"Ello, love, your mam in?'

'Through here, Barry,' Cass called out, then rolled her eyes at Lauren, with a smile. 'He always asks, and I'm always here.'

The elderly man who walked through the door was clearly a gentleman, taking off his flat cap as he entered the room, nodding his head and smiling toothily. His hair was white and sparse, with perhaps more coming out of his ears than the top of his head. He stood straight, like he was wearing a suit instead of his stained jeans and checked shirt.

'How you feeling, petal? You and the little miss all right?'

Cass squeezed his hand. 'You know us, Barry, we're always all right. This is my friend Loll.'

Barry nodded at her. 'Ah, the best friend. Yes, Sandy said you'd be here.'

'Sandy knows?!' Vee clapped her hands and gave Lauren a significant look, 'Sandy is psychic.'

'Oh,' Lauren replied, 'that's ... nice.'

'I don't think it is, really,' Vee shrugged, sitting back down at the table, before turning to Barry. 'Find any treasures today?'

Barry grinned and produced a shell in the same way a magician produced a coin – with a flourish. 'For you, petal.'

'Ooh, it's a good one! Thank you!'

Barry beamed and Cass offered him a cup of tea, but he waved the offer away.

'No thanks, love, I'm meeting the fellas at the pub, and you've got your lovely guest.'

Cass nodded and handed him the bag, 'Well, your shirts are done, not very well, mind, but ... and we had a bit of spare beef that was going to waste, so I made you a couple of sandwiches.'

'You're too good to me.' His gratefulness was a little too raw, his eyes slightly watery as he grasped the bag.

'No one could be too good to you, Barry,' Cass rubbed his arm.

Lauren watched the interaction with curiosity, trying to figure out what the connection was. Cassidy Jones mending shirts, sewing, cooking? Her nature was to find underdogs and defend them, but caring wasn't necessarily her thing.

Barry raised a hand and waved, so Lauren waved back.

'Thanks for my treasure, Barry!' Vee said, flipping the shell between her fingers.

Cass showed the older man out and Lauren took the chance to find out more.

'What does Barry do, Vee?'

'Finds treasure on the beach,' the little girl smiled, holding up her shell. 'Look!'

Lauren accepted the shell and turned it over between her fingertips, tracing the lines and searching for the shine.

'Is he looking for gold?'

Veronica shook her head, like the idea was preposterous. 'No!'

'So he collects shells?' Apparently, she wasn't very good at getting the truth out of kids, even when they weren't being obtuse. Maybe it was good she'd never become a 'proper' lawyer.

Cass walked back in. 'He's the dustbin man on the pier. Lovely bloke. Lost his wife a couple of years ago. I try and help out when I can.' She settled back into her seat a little awkwardly, she looked like she ached.

'That's nice, Cass.'

She turned her head, only slightly, a wry smile that looked more like a wince. 'Oh, I guess you would be surprised by that. Nice wasn't really my thing.'

Lauren blushed, looking down at the table. 'Not true. You had your moments.'

'Cassy is *very* kind,' Veronica said sternly, looking at Lauren with a frown. 'She makes Barry sandwiches, and takes Sandy cake on Sunday, and gives Freddie too much money on the rides at the pier because he's only young and times are far!'

'Hard,' Cass laughed, squeezing her daughter, 'times are hard, kid.'

Lauren held up her hands. 'That is very kind, you're right. It sounds like you and your mum help a lot of people.'

Veronica nodded, those wide eyes unblinking. 'Even small stuff can make people happy.'

It sounded like something she'd learnt by rote.

Cass laughed. 'Hey, good-cop-bad-cop, ease up on your auntie. She knows a different version of your mum. One who was a lot wilder.'

'Wild like a wolf?'

Cass considered it. 'Wild like a hurricane.'

Veronica made a face. 'Jeez!'

'Indeed.'

Lauren laughed, watching the back and forth between the two of them, a slight ache in her stomach that she tried to ignore. It wasn't jealousy, that wouldn't be right, even though Lauren was alone, and Cass had her beautiful daughter, who would defend her no matter what. The one thing she had wanted from Darren, and Cass got it instead of her. But she would be here for Cass when it was all ending, even after everything. That made her nice too, right? The truth, that this was a convenient escape from a life she disliked, seemed to hover around her earlobes, whispering guilt.

'What about you, Auntie Loll? What do you want to do?' Vee's little face looked across at her intently, bringing her back into the conversation.

'What do I want to do when?'

'Cassy has the coral, and I have Santa, what about you?'

Lauren shrugged. 'I like both those places.'

'No,' Veronica shook her head, suddenly stubborn. 'You have to have your own place.'

Cassy nudged her, shaking out her legs. 'Oi, stop being bossy.'

Lauren laughed. 'Don't tell her that, we need more bossy women – they're the ones who'll be running the world.'

Cass pushed the book back across the table, and Lauren scanned it, taking in the scribbles with a pang. All those things they'd meant to do, some complete nonsense, relics of another time, and others so obviously theirs that she'd never dared do them with someone else. She never wanted to stop and think, *Cass should be here,* so instead she didn't do them at all.

'You're going to think it's boring.'

'So what?' Cass shrugged. Even that was telling. Years ago she would have said, *'I'm sure it will be, darling, but I'll listen anyway.'*

'Andalucía – I want to eat tapas and drink sangria, watch flamenco. No bull fights though, because they make me sad.'

'The whole world to choose from and you want to go to Spain?' Cass asked. 'Really?'

Lauren pushed the book back and pointed at the writing. *I want to show Cass the real Spain, my Spain.*

That had always been the plan, to take her to where her *abuela* was from. To dance, and drink and speak Spanish. To let that part of her shine through, the version that had only really been around when her grandmother was alive. The wild part of her. Somehow, Cass brought it out again, and she'd wanted to ... thank her, she supposed. She wanted to share her history and culture with the one person who knew her.

The one other person who didn't see her as quiet and mousy. In Spain, she had been so sure, things would be different. She would be the tour guide, the one in charge. She would channel her *abuela*, and take pride in all the snippets of her heritage. She hadn't been back to Spain since her grandmother had died, and it was Cassidy she had wanted by her side when she did.

The pain in Lauren's chest told her that much was still true.

Cass coughed a little, her smile wavering before she reaffixed it, shiny and new. 'Okay, Spain it is. You'll be able to show off your language skills, Vee.'

The little girl grinned. '*Muy bien,* Mama!'

Lauren blinked. 'They teach kids languages at this age?'

'She picks stuff up,' Cass waved it away like it was nothing. 'You know, I think some sangria and tapas sounds like exactly what we'll need to warm us up after the North Pole, don't you?'

They chattered away about packing and clothes, and Cass said she'd email Uncle Jack to see if he was up for a visit, but something about the whole exchange didn't seem right. A five-year-old learning Spanish? Was that really normal in schools these days? Lauren had the sense that Cass was hiding something from her, but that was nothing new.

That night, Lauren lay in her hotel room and thought about where it all started, the moment Cassidy Jones came into her life. It was almost hard to pinpoint, through the drunken haze of university and exams and boys and double vodka Red Bulls. It seemed like Cass had been there from the beginning, there for every moment of her university life. But she hadn't.

It had been the start of the second term, and Lauren had been miserable. Her flatmates had dragged her out, insisting she was no fun because she'd rather sit in her room and study instead of joining them. They were right, she was no fun. She was going to study law and prove her parents wrong, and that meant concentrating and avoiding distractions.

Yet there she was, at the uni bar on a Tuesday night, wondering how soon she could escape. She'd been queuing for the toilets when she heard her.

'Hey, you, little help?'

Cass had pink slashes in her blonde hair back then, and it was tied in little bunches so that her curls flowed over her shoulders like streamers.

'Me?'

She had nodded, beckoning her to the cubicle. When people asked how they met, Lauren always liked to say, 'Well, she dragged me into a toilet cubicle and I thought she was going to offer me drugs.'

What had actually happened was a very drunk Cassidy asking her to hold the door from the inside, so she could pee without the door closing. She was babbling on about how her mother always said one embarrassing scenario under your control was better than a bunch you have no say in. Lauren had no idea what she was talking about, but focused solely on the wide variety of graffiti on the door.

In a swell of bravery, she asked Cass to hold the door for her after, instead of returning to the queue again. When they'd come back out into the bathroom, standing side by side at the sinks, Lauren hadn't been able to stop looking at Cass. Her smeared pink lipstick, hot-pink fishnet tights and black Doc Martens all seemed to bely the way she washed her hands like a doctor before surgery.

'Buy you a drink?' Cass had offered, her eyes meeting Lauren's in the mirror. Lauren looked at their reflections, side by side, her own flushed cheeks and huge dark curls contrasting with Cass's paleness. She'd nodded, as if it was no big deal.

Cass had reached for her hand as they'd woven through the crowds in the club, and she let her drag her along to the bar, grinning when they arrived.

'I'm Cassidy,' she'd yelled, still grasping her hand, attempting to shake it. She was sandwiched between too many people to fully move her arm, so settled for squeezing her fingers.

'Lauren,' she had shouted back.

'Are you sure?' Cass peered at her like she was lying.

'Your name is *Cassidy* but am *I* sure? Yeah, I'm sure!' Lauren had laughed, trying to figure out what the girl's deal was. Was she drunk, purposefully fanciful, mentally ill? Was she going to be a best friend for the evening, or would she buy her a drink and head back to her multiple admirers?

Cass shrugged, before turning to immediately catch the bartender's attention.

'Hey Robbie, sweetheart, I'll have a vodka Red Bull, and a ...' she turned, gesturing at Lauren.

'Vodka orange.'

'Vodka orange for my friend Loll, here.' She spoke like she'd learnt how to from old movies. It seemed weirdly disconnected, that voice coming from those shocking pink lips. She took the drinks, grinned at the barman but didn't pay. He just smiled and shrugged as Cassidy handed her the drink and led her towards the beer garden.

Loll. Lauren had never really had a nickname before, she'd always just figured she wasn't that sort of person. Her dad, when he was feeling particularly nostalgic, would call her *Ardillita* because of that time she'd wandered off at the park as a kid and stuffed her pockets full of conkers. Somehow, throughout the years, that had become *little mouse*, the mocking name her family used when she got upset and squeaky. A name that silenced her.

But *Loll*, well, that was something else. Something short and strong and a little strange. Something this girl had given her. They shared a cigarette even though Lauren didn't smoke, and talked about all the usual things. What halls they were in, what courses they were doing. What they wanted to be when they grew up. Cass was thinking of changing from psychology ('I'm not good at staying out of people's lives') but was intrigued by Lauren's decision to study law.

'You're going to change the world then?'

'Maybe,' she'd replied. Something about this girl made her want to believe her own words. Stand up for the things she believed. Be more than the little mouse.

'And what if you can't?'

'Excuse me?'

'What if you can't change the world?' Cass had asked, a smirk playing around her lips.

Lauren's pause had been weighted, distinct. She needed to say the right thing, to watch this girl's eyes widen in surprise, her lips flicker to a smile.

'Who are you to tell me what kind of change has value? Or what the hell I can or can't do?' She had immediately regretted it, the words sounding wrong coming from her, like she was playing a bad character in a shitty movie.

Cass paused, then laughed. 'You're an interesting sort of person, new friend Loll,' Cass had said, trying to blow smoke rings as she stubbed out the cigarette. She gripped Lauren's hand and grinned. 'I think we're going to remember this night as something really important.'

They had danced, and drunk more, and when Lauren finally got back to her dorms that night, her flatmates had been back for hours and were shocked that she'd finally shown herself to be so normal.

She figured it was enough to lie there in bed, not taking her make-up off and letting the room spin. She'd had fun, she'd met someone who thought she was interesting. It didn't have to be anything more than that. Except at midday, a blonde girl in an oversized grey jumper arrived with bacon sandwiches and a bunch of movies and told her to put the kettle on. A friendship grew from nothing, a few moments of interest on a dark dance floor, and whispered secrets shared over mugs of tea under a duvet. Somehow, Cassidy Jones simply became part of the furniture, someone she told secrets to and asked questions of. Someone who reminded her she could do things, who calmed her mind and pushed her out of her comfort zone. Somehow, she was having adventures all the time. And there had been the promise of so many more to come.

Lauren wondered if that was still the case, staring at the cracked ceiling of the hotel room and imagining it caving in, a wrinkled man in a bathtub staring at her in shock. The image blinked away. That first meeting, that was when Loll was born. Cass was the only one who called her that.

She had to admit, she'd missed it.

Chapter 7

The week that passed created a sort of routine. One where Lauren had inexplicably become part of their lives, but she and Cass still didn't talk about anything real. They revealed parts of themselves in snippets. Cass talked about Vee, but not in the way most parents did, with this obsessive pride that expected interest in their children. There was a wonder in the way she spoke about her daughter's likes and dislikes, flecked with guilt, as though talking about her at all was like rubbing salt in a wound. Sometimes, it was.

Lauren learnt that Veronica only drank her hot chocolate if it was stirred three times clockwise and three times anti-clockwise. That she loved puffins but hated woodpeckers. That she liked to mix ketchup and mayonnaise into a horrid pink concoction before she dipped her chips into it. That she hated stories where the prince turns up and does all the rescuing and that she'd broken her ankle last year playing on a skateboard. The last two were not a surprise.

Vee was exactly the kind of daughter she expected Cass to have – wild and inquisitive, wanting attention and yet enjoying how others interacted. She seemed to like watching

Lauren and Cass together. She'd wait quietly, head tilted to the side, trying to understand what they were talking about. Sometimes she'd come in and make herself comfortable, taking a hand or squishing down next to someone on the sofa. Other times she'd just wait, as if she was expecting something magical to happen.

Lauren already loved her. Apart from those shocking moments that seemed to come out of nowhere, where she'd look at her and wonder if her life would have been different if Vee had never existed. Where she almost wished it was so. They passed like waves crashing, frothing up guilt. Those moments always sent her running to buy something for Veronica, to offer her something, to show everyone around her that she was okay with everything, really, she was. And still, it annoyed her that Darren hadn't wanted to be part of this little girl's life, hadn't fought for her. There was a living, breathing part of himself out in the world, and he didn't care.

There were too many feelings – she was angry at everyone, and yet this little girl existed and that wasn't going to change. Better to love her, and push her own pain down somewhere dark and hidden. Children couldn't be blamed for their parents, that was the rule. Even when they seemed to look out from behind their eyes.

They were young, Lauren realised. They were incredibly young in the world, and Darren would go on to have other children down the line, the same way he'd have another wife, another home. Lives could change instantly, everything you set up falling away. She could have hundreds of other adventures before this was all over. She could meet someone else, fall in love, and have this all be a bad dream. A misstart, taking off from the finish line too soon. She'd get a do-over, if she did this right.

But Cass wouldn't. Cass got this and no more. She had fit a lot more life into the last six years. Hell, she'd fit a lot more life into all her years. She didn't do drudgery or sameness. She felt fear and loved it, like sitting in that cart, teetering at the edge of the roller-coaster track, waiting for the fun to start. You could always tell what kind of person they were from that; the ones who gripped the safety bar, white-knuckled, wondering if they were going to vomit or fall out, or the ones who threw up their hand and interrupted their screams with laughter, a grin on their face. Then there were the ones like Lauren, who were too scared to go on at all.

'Can we go to the park, please?' Vee had sidled in quietly, holding a book open and munching on an apple. Her hair was tied in two long plaits and she seemed to be buzzing with boredom. School started on Monday, and there was a question to be answered there.

Cass looked up from the computer, where she was scrunching up her face and trying to work out connecting flights. 'Sure, go wrap up warm though. No point getting sick before our big adventure!'

Lauren felt the look the child wanted to share with her, the sense of irony and sadness. Cass would be sick before their big adventure, and during it. Her sickness was the only reason for their trip at all. She shot Vee a smile. 'Bet I can swing higher on the swings than you.'

'No way!' She thundered up the stairs to get her coat, the book and half-eaten apple left on the side.

Cass rolled her eyes and went to pick up the book, folding the corner of the page over, and taking a bite out of the apple. 'Waste not. And stop wincing. It's not a library book, it's hers.'

'I can't help it – it's sacrilege!' Lauren felt comfortable, for the moment, until awkwardness crept in. Laughing about the things they'd always teased each other about felt like a bad impersonation. They hadn't earnt it, not yet.

When she was with Cass, they were organising, making careful, meticulous plans the way they never had when they were younger. Because things were different now. Not only was there a change in comfort levels, the fact that now they wanted soft beds and safe surroundings, places they could actually sleep, places they could safely take a five-year-old, but it had to be special, it had to be right. Each place had to make memories. Especially for Veronica. She had to be able to look back at this as a time that was sacred, magical. There would be pain enough later.

Lauren was concerned about whether Cass would be well enough to travel. But every time she tried to bring it up, Cass brushed it off. She had a warning look in her eyes that Lauren remembered well. So they added that to the list of things they didn't talk about.

The sky was the same grey it had been since she'd arrived, but at least the cold wasn't biting and the wind had abated. They strolled, not quite arm in arm, but companionably, as Vee broke out into a run when they entered the park. She was so like a puppy, needing to burn off her energy.

'Don't worry about her, she does that. It's like she saves up all her madness and needs to run it off,' Cass said, as if reading her mind. 'I wonder if she'll always be that way. Maybe she'll become a runner or something.'

'More like a daredevil speed demon,' Lauren replied, trying to keep away thoughts of Veronica growing up, and Cass not being there.

'You don't have to do that, you know. Protect me. I'm okay with everything. Honestly.'

Lauren huffed a little as they wandered along the path, the greenery only a faint whisper amongst the sludgy mud.

'How can you possibly be *okay*? You don't get points for being the martyr, Cass.'

'Yeah, but your remaining time is a little less awful,' Cass sighed, looking past Lauren to an approaching figure. The man was in his mid-thirties, his dark hair just curling out from beneath a ridiculous bobble hat. He had the collar of his coat turned up against the wind, a multicoloured knit scarf around his neck, and his hands tucked into his pockets, shivering a little.

'Paul!' Cass called out, waving him over. 'Hi!'

Oh, here we go again, Lauren thought. It was uncharitable, but Cass was still the same person after all. And yes, there were his eyes, lighting up as he approached, focused on Cass. The same way they always did with men like him. Another willing victim. He wanted to rescue her, just like they all did.

Vee got there first, speeding along like a little jet, almost launching herself at him. 'Mr T! Happy New Year!' She stopped short of hugging him, but bounced on her heels. 'We're just here with my mum, and my auntie is visiting, and we're going to have adventures. Did you have a nice Christmas?'

The man blinked at the onslaught. 'Happy New Year, Veronica. I had a lovely Christmas, thank you. Are you ready for school to start?'

'No,' she said with a grin. 'I have to go play on the slide now.'

He nodded at her seriously, giving a salute. 'Go forth, play well.'

She rolled her eyes and ran off. By that time, Cass and Lauren had arrived.

'Ah, there's trouble, Happy New Year.'

Cass's smile was wide, unusually real, no coquetry or foolishness. 'Hello, darling, happy New Year. Paul, this is my friend Loll.'

'Lauren,' she interjected, reaching out a hand in a formal way that made her feel embarrassed, even as he took her hand.

'Paul Thompson, I'm Vee's teacher.'

'Vee's *teacher*?' Well, that was a new low, even for Cass.

'I wish she'd stop calling me Mr T,' Paul laughed awkwardly, 'that was *clearly* your doing.'

Cass looked away, shrugging as the smile tinged her lips. 'I admit nothing.'

'I wouldn't mind,' Paul turned to Lauren earnestly, 'but it's caught on with the other kids. It'll be in the teachers' lounge soon enough.'

Lauren couldn't help but smile back at the man, so awkward yet so clearly unbothered by his trials.

'It's nice to meet you,' he said, focusing his gaze on her, 'I've heard so much about you.'

'You too. I mean, that it's nice—'

'Oh, I'm sure no one's mentioned me, don't worry.'

He smiled, but Lauren knew that tone. One of Cass's admirers, waiting for his chance. They veered from harmless to obsessed, and she *knew* that. She knew, even after all these years, the way she could make men want to do things for her. It didn't hurt that she looked more fragile now, like spun glass, all delicate tendrils of hair and huge eyes. Oh God, she was jealous of Cass for being ill? That was a new level of despicable.

'Paul is part of the resistance, Loll, he's going to help us.'

Of course he would, Lauren thought with sympathy, *how could he stop himself?*

'And how am I going to do that?' Paul asked, a crease appearing above his right eyebrow.

Lauren wondered whether she should be noticing that crease, or the dimples that appeared when he smiled. She was meant to be in mourning for her relationship. And yet, she actually felt relieved to be alone. To be ... untethered.

'It's time,' Cass said simply, looking over to the play area, where Vee was hanging upside down from the climbing frame, clapping hands with another girl. Lauren winced in fear, visualising her falling and crushing her neck, but Cass put up a hand to hold her back. It was her decision, her child. And she wasn't worried. It wasn't Lauren's job to worry. That hurt, just a bit.

'Time,' Paul repeated.

'*Time,*' Cass intoned meaningfully, wiggling her eyebrows at him.

'Do we need to be so cloak and dagger, really?' Lauren huffed, and then realised how harsh she must have sounded to the man. *Yes, you're dying, get over it. Stop being melodramatic.*

Oh God, she was awful. Shut up, Lauren, shut up.

'We're planning that trip we talked about, Paul,' Cass said gently, nudging Lauren in the ribs with her sharp elbows, 'and I'm going to need written permission to take her out of school, right? Whatever that compassionate leave she'd get after I'm gone, why shouldn't she have it while I'm here? Put it to good use. You agreed.'

'I do agree ... *in principle,*' he admitted, 'but ...'

'No,' Cass held up a hand, 'this is what I want. For my ending, my journey, this is what I want for her and for me, and for Loll.'

Lauren blinked at this, turning her head towards Cass, who gave nothing away.

'So take it to the headteacher, or whoever it is. The people who follow pointless rules who can tell me it's okay for me to take my kid abroad for a couple of months. How much can she really be missing?'

It was quite obvious Paul wasn't as easy-going as he seemed. Two red spots appeared on his cheeks. 'Well, that's a lovely way to sum up the difference I'm making to young lives, thanks.'

'Is it allowed?' Lauren asked.

Paul shook his head, meeting her eyes. 'I honestly don't know, we haven't really had this situation before. I know we'll have to set up a homework schedule so she doesn't miss out, we might have to Skype or something, and you'll have to prove you're up to a home-learning schedule. The head will definitely have to be involved, and the governors.'

Cass looked unconcerned, but Lauren supposed she had the advantage. She was dying, she just wanted to do whatever she felt like – there would be no consequences for her. But everyone else would be left to pick up the pieces.

'How long will you be gone?'

The real question Paul wanted to ask, the one everyone asks, sat beneath his words.

'How long do you think we can push for?' Cass asked, avoiding Paul's eyes, looking over at her daughter, who was now hanging like a monkey from the bars.

'The less time she's gone, the less worried they'll be about her catching up. She'll probably be under extra supervision ... after.' Paul looked awkward, balling his fists into his coat pocket, shifting his weight side to side as he tried to find the words. 'Cass, in all honesty, have you thought about what this is going to be like for Veronica?'

Lauren watched as Cass's eyes flashed briefly, and she turned to the teacher, 'Paul, you think I think of anything else but how my baby is going to deal with everything when I'm gone? You know everything I'm doing is for her.'

'No, actually, I don't know that.' Paul stood his ground, and in that moment Lauren changed her mind about him. He wasn't another man to have his will bent to Cass's whims. Maybe he had potential after all. Maybe he could make sure that Vee had the best care anyone could have under the circumstances. 'I think you're only thinking short-term – you want to take her on holiday, give her these wonderful memories. What's she going to do after, Cass? What's she going to do when her friends all forge new friendships? When she feels lonely hanging out with two adults? Kids need structure, they need support ...'

Paul spoke with passion and Lauren could clearly see in that moment why he did what he did. It was easy to look at a man with a bobble hat and a silly scarf and judge him. He wasn't weak.

He wasn't wrong, either. Veronica would need her friends, would need normality. It wasn't fair to wrench her out of everything on some selfish quest. And yet ... they couldn't go without her. She needed to be there, she needed that time. They all did.

'A month,' Lauren heard herself say. 'We'll be gone a month. We'll register for home schooling, we'll do everything they ask. We'll send homework remotely. And if we time it right, we'll have a week of half term, right? So it'll only be three weeks. I imagine we'll need to present something to the governors, and the local authority, perhaps? I'll look into the paperwork ...'

'Woah,' Paul looked at her, 'someone's a planner.'

'Lawyer.' Cass tilted her head towards Lauren, 'Someone has to be the adult in this situation.'

Even that admission of her talents had deflated Lauren. She was the boring adult who dealt with the paperwork.

Paul smiled at her, a real smile. 'Well I'm glad someone's thinking this through. Three weeks is something we can work with. I'll give you my email address, Lauren. Send me what you've got as a proposal, and I'll see what I can do.'

He held out his hand with such expectation that Lauren blinked.

'Give him your phone, Loll,' Cass sighed, suddenly irritable. She watched Veronica, who was running around with her friends, her braids swinging behind her as she pulled up short to wave.

Even as Lauren handed over her phone, she watched the rigid line of Cass's shoulders, the pressing together of her lips as she tried to remain composed. Lauren would have recognised that micro-moment anywhere. She had seen it a hundred times before, as Cass wrestled her emotions. When pretending to be happy at her mother's latest beau, or when a boy turned cruel at her rejections. When Barbara got sick, when she met Darren for the first time ... Cass's attempts at stoicism were the same. Woefully inadequate.

'She'll be happy, Paul. She'll be so happy, for those four weeks. That's the point,' Cass's voice trembled, but she didn't look back.

Paul's brow creased in pity, but he seemed to know her well enough not to step closer. 'But four happy weeks won't make up for a life without her mother.'

'It might,' Cass said, turning to him, looking at Lauren. 'We can make it special. I've ... I've got it sorted, just ... I'll take care of my daughter. I just need you two to sort out the practicalities, you know that's never been my strength.'

Lauren snorted at her tone, imperious as ever. It seemed that Paul shared her opinion, bowing dramatically.

'Glad to be of service, my lady.'

Cass's lip lifted, just a little, and she turned her sunshine on them both, reaching out a hand to each of them. 'Oh ignore me, being grouchy. I do appreciate you, both, and all you're doing to make this happen. I just ... I want to give her this. I haven't been able to give her everything I wanted, and I need to do this.'

'I know,' Lauren said, squeezing back, 'and we will. We just have to do things properly. Crossing i's and dotting t's.'

'I second that,' Paul nodded, 'Look. We'll work together and do what we can.'

He paused, his eyes searching Cass, scanning her. 'And you're looking after yourself, right?'

Cass smiled wryly, crossing her arms. 'Oh how I miss the days when people asked me how my Christmas was. See you on Wednesday for the pub quiz?'

Paul shook his head. 'First week back, I'm going to be exhausted. Tell Barry I said not to try to answer any of those music questions. Man's tone deaf.'

Cass nodded, threading her arm through Lauren's. 'Well, I'll have Loll to replace you. She's a know-it-all, I'm sure we'll be on a winning streak.'

Lauren gritted her teeth. Another one of those *compliments*.

'I'm sure you will.' Paul smiled at her, and she couldn't help but smile back, noticing those dimples again. 'I'll be in touch, Lauren, and we'll work out a plan to sort this one out.'

'Right,' she nodded, wondering what that feeling was, like she was being seen properly. It felt strangely gratifying.

Cass seemed to be bored now she'd gotten what she wanted,

shivering slightly in the cold, so she waved and dragged Lauren off, calling out to Veronica as they approached the playground. The child waved, paused to see if she was being told she had to leave, and seeing they were just walking along, realised she could carry on playing.

'Keep it in your pants, Loll, you've only been single a few weeks,' Cass laughed, her grip on Lauren's arm vice-like.

'Ooh, someone doesn't like sharing,' Lauren found her voice, trying to sound playful, sound like her old self. But this time there was clearly a bite underneath. The years apart had stopped her hiding how she felt.

'I think we better stay off that topic, don't you?'

'That's up to me, isn't it?'

'It's all up to you, Loll. You're the good one here. Whatever you want, babe.'

'I ...' Lauren shook her head, trailing off. She never knew what she wanted. Cass knew that.

'Or we could just carry on pretending everything's okay, until we can't pretend anymore? And if we're *very, very lucky,* I'll be dead before then,' Cass replied, and they walked on in silence, until Veronica zoomed over, waving goodbye to her friends, talking ten to the dozen about all the adventures they'd have.

That night Lauren lay in her bed at the hotel, listening to the sounds on the pier, hen and stag parties roaming in search of booze and adventures, and not even three glasses of gin could quiet her sudden fear that this trip was a terrible, terrible idea.

Chapter 8

Getting to pick up Veronica from school was like a gift Cass was giving her. She got to stand at the school gates and make idle chit-chat with the mums and dads, and for ten minutes pretend that this was her life, the one she'd dreamed for herself.

Cass kept acting like it was a huge favour she was doing, but she must have known how eager Lauren was. Or maybe she sensed that edge of fright Lauren felt sometimes, looking at her daughter. She wondered if Cass looked for signs of Darren too.

Vee was always thrilled to see her, which surprised her every time. That huge sparkling grin that engulfed her face as she ran full pelt at Lauren. She didn't know how her heart could expand any more than when that kid ran towards her, pushing out the poison.

'Auntie Loll!'

She caught Vee and swung her round. 'Hey there, Fluffy!'

Vee frowned, 'That's a rubbish nickname.'

'Not for a wolf,' Lauren laughed, taking her hand. 'It's an excellent name for a wolf.'

'Nooo,' Vee seemed to be holding back from rolling her eyes, and the look was so Cass that Lauren took a sharp breath. 'A *good* wolf name is fierce. Like Fang or Jumper or Growly.'

'You wanna be called Growly?'

Vee laughed and shook her head. 'No, not really.'

'I guess we'll have to work on our wolf-names, huh?' Lauren said as Veronica swung their joined hands back and forth with enthusiasm. 'So do you want to go to the park on the way home?'

Vee wrinkled her nose, shook her head. 'Can we go see Sandy, please?'

'Um ... what if she's busy working?'

The young girl looked at her in amusement. 'Auntie Loll, she knows we're coming. *That's her job.*'

'Ahh right, psychic.'

They started walking towards the pier. Something about going to see the old woman made her feel uncomfortable. And it wasn't that she thought there was anything to her 'gifts'. The only thing Sandy needed to seem *more* like a fraud was to put a tea towel on her head and talk about communing with the ghost of Princess Di.

'Why do you like going to see Sandy? You want to know the future? Want to hear that you'll be rich and famous?' Lauren asked, hoping the old con was busy.

'No, that's boring. I just like Sandy. She's funny and grouchy. And she pretends she doesn't like seeing us when she does.' Veronica raised an eyebrow like she was a super detective.

'How do you know?'

'Because she's lonely and a cranky-pants, and she always has my favourite biscuits in her cupboard. She doesn't even eat biscuits!'

Holy crap, this kid saw everything.

Lauren didn't say anything, but Vee grinned at her. 'I'm very smart. That's what Mr T says.'

'So you like Mr Thompson?'

Vee nodded. 'He's nice and he's never mean if you forget things and last week he showed us how to make these space boxes for our spellings so we shoot for the stars.'

Lauren tried not to cringe at how cheesy that was. She could imagine Cass responding to that, calling Paul a nerd and poking fun at how earnest he was. Lauren had been enjoying her back-and-forth emails with Paul, though she was always on edge about how far a man would go to make sure Cass was happy. It stuck in her side like a little thorn, irritating and uncomfortable. He seemed to care about Veronica's happiness above everything else though, which was what mattered most, as far as Lauren was concerned.

They arrived at the beach and the little hut on the pier that acted as Sandy's 'office'. The old woman was outside, her madly dyed orange hair standing out against the grey of the sky. Sandy seemed to think that wearing at least five shawls better indicated that she had a connection with the divine. Her large jewelled rings and shell necklace set the tone better than those huge round glasses she wore, attached to a string around her neck but almost always placed atop her head.

Lauren didn't trust her. Her movements were birdlike and jumpy, and she always had this little frown on her face, her lips puckered in distaste when Lauren arrived. The pucker made her upper-lip hair more visible. She was standing outside smoking a fag dramatically, hand on hip, staring out at the sea as though engaged in a battle of wills. Sandy did everything dramatically.

The faded paint on the side of the hut declared *Psychic* in gold letters, and the face of the woman with bright eyes and a shining crystal ball didn't look like Sandy at all. Lauren hoped they could make this quick.

'Little miss!' Sandy grinned at Vee, choking back a cough. 'I *knew* you'd be to see me today.'

'See?' Vee shook Lauren's hand, before running over to the older lady and giving her a hug. 'Anything exciting today?'

'Oh, the alignment of the stars, my luvvy, it's always mystical and exciting. A man who will find his true love, a family torn apart by an ancient secret ...' Sandy's stony gaze turned to Lauren. 'And three girls on an adventure that will change them all.'

Lauren resisted rolling her eyes and adopted a neutral expression. 'Interesting. We don't want to interrupt you from your work ...'

Please, please let her say she's busy ...

Sandy waved the concern away with a weathered hand. 'Come in, I'll put the kettle on.'

Vee bounced into the little hut and sat on the cushion on the floor. The front of the hut was all draped materials and Moroccan lamps, casting interesting shadows on the wall. The smell of incense was heady and made Lauren feel a little sick. It was hard to think in this tiny space where the old woman's strange hair and owl features were even more prominent. Perhaps that was the point. Confuse the customer, put them on edge so they believed whatever garbled rubbish you told them.

'Milk or sugar?'

She called back from behind the curtain, and Lauren looked at Vee, unsure if she was included in this invitation.

'Milk, please,' she replied, hesitant.

Sandy returned with a tray, two chipped mugs of Earl Grey and a wine glass full of milk for Vee, with a pack of chocolate bourbons. Vee gave her a look, as if to say, 'Told you.'

'So, how are the travel plans going?' Sandy asked, settling herself carefully into her chair.

I thought you'd know, Lauren longed to say, but she held her tongue.

'Good, we're almost ready, aren't we?' Lauren tried to include Vee in the conversation, 'Just waiting on a response from the school about taking Vee out for a few weeks.'

Vee wrinkled her nose. 'There's going to be lessons. And homework.'

Sandy considered this. 'Yes, but you'll have loads of fun around it, won't you?'

Vee nodded, playing with a small buddha statue on the side. Sandy's eyes narrowed as she looked at Lauren.

'Veronica, pet, I think I feel a vision coming on. It's telling me I need a shell from the beach. One that's uncracked.' She held her palm against her forehead in a way that Lauren personally thought was a bit over the top.

Vee jumped up, eager to respond to the hands of the unknown.

'Can I?' she asked Lauren, who nodded helplessly.

'Don't go too far down to the sea. And stay in sight.'

Sandy nodded. 'We'll move our tea outside so we can see you.'

'As the spirits command,' Lauren bit out, picking up her teacup and shuffling outside into the cold. The wind was bitter and powerful. The sea raged grey and frothing, pounding against the shore.

They waited until Vee was bent over stones, inspecting them with care, placing them back down delicately instead of throwing them. She wasn't like other kids.

'I think it's a bad idea, this trip,' Sandy said, her eyes not leaving Veronica.

Lauren turned to her. 'Have the spirits told you that?'

The older woman glowered at her. 'My gut tells me that. Cassidy isn't going to survive a trip like that. Is that what you want for the little one? Her mother dying on her holiday?'

Lauren sighed. 'I don't know why you think I have any say in this. It's Cass. She gets what she wants.'

'She needs someone to stand up to her.'

'That's never really been my strong suit.' Lauren couldn't help but feel she was getting the raw deal. Sandy was upset with Cass, but was taking it out on her. As if she was the parent in all this.

'I love those girls like they were my own, and I'm telling you, this is a bad idea.' At least she spoke normally when she was insistent. Nothing to be blamed on the divine.

'You shouldn't be telling me, tell Cass.'

'I have.'

'And I imagine that went well.'

The old woman coughed, lighting up another cigarette. The scent made Lauren wrinkle her nose.

The tea, at least, was warm and offered a distraction from the weather and the company.

'Why don't you like me?' Lauren asked suddenly, feeling bold.

'I don't trust people who don't forgive,' Sandy said. 'You have all this angry, bitter energy coming off you in waves. It's not good for Cassidy, and it's certainly not good for Veronica at a time like this.'

Oh well, I'm sorry my energy isn't compatible. Lauren bit her tongue, quite literally, clamping her teeth down and setting her jaw. As the old woman stared her down, she felt incredibly vulnerable, naked. 'You don't know what we've been through.' *You don't know what she did. You want me to be the bad guy.*

'A best friend who hasn't been around for six years, and a five-year-old daughter? I don't have to be psychic to see what's happened there.'

'And yet I'm the bad guy?' Lauren felt like a huffy teenager.

Sandy narrowed her eyes. 'We're all the bad guys. It's people like you though, the ones who ball up their anger and don't let go of it because they're too nice to face up to it – you're the dangerous ones.'

'Dangerous?' Lauren tried not to gasp. 'I could never be dangerous.'

Sandy raised an eyebrow and nodded. 'Oh yes, you're all sweet and quiet, trampled all over by everyone, by Cassidy. You don't think that energy goes somewhere?'

'How is that my fault?'

'You need to be responsible for your life and choices. This frustration that's rolling off you, it's poison' – Sandy leaned in, her pinched features catching the light – 'and I'll tell you this for nothing, sunshine, people love those Jones girls. They're part of this community and they've had a hard few years. If you're not going to help, you're better off leaving.'

Lauren felt like she was drowning. 'Sandy, I'm here because she called, because she wanted me here.'

The old woman smiled, shaking her head. 'That's not why you're here. You're here because you're unhappy.'

'Both things can be true.'

She shook her head again. 'You've got to sort yourself out, sort out all that anger and jealousy and ... disappointment. They don't need that from you.'

Jealousy. To have an outsider minimise her relationship with Cass down to the basest, most shameful emotion, it was excruciating. And even then, she bit her tongue. Stayed quiet, stayed meek.

As always, Cass was the one who had people jumping across themselves to save and defend her. She was so beautiful, so fragile. So in need. And now, instead of being the ugly stepsister, or plump mousy sidekick, Lauren was cast as the villain. What would Cass say in this moment?

'Well, maybe I could pay you fifty quid, Sandy, and you could clear my chakras, or my auras or something? Would that be best for Cass and Veronica?'

Sandy exhaled, something that sounded like a chuckle. 'There's that anger. You know, I've been here from the beginning.

I've seen that girl pregnant and scared and lonely. I've seen her as a new mother, pretending she was fine, begrudgingly accepting help. And I've seen her turn away people who loved her, who could have made her life easier, because she didn't think she deserved to be happy.'

Maybe she doesn't, was the first thought that crept in Lauren's consciousness and Sandy looked at her in triumph, as if she could read her mind. Lauren shook the horrible thought away, determined to be a good person. To be the loving, kind, hopeful person she was before.

'When she was in hospital with that baby, it was me who took her letters to the postbox. Letters to you, begging forgiveness, wanting you by her side. Those first few months, every time I stopped by, there was another letter on the table. She must have written hundreds over the years.'

'I never got them! She knows that!'

Sandy looked unimpressed, as if she was telling her the dog ate her homework.

'No, really! My husband ... he ... he lied. Over and over again. I wouldn't have even thought he was paying enough attention to lie like that. If I'd have had just one letter I would have been here.' She knew it was true as she said it. No matter what had happened, if Cassidy Jones called, you came running. However much you might want to resist.

No wonder Darren had lied. He'd known how easily she would have been won back. How much she'd missed Cass.

Rat bastard.

Sandy wasn't bothered by Lauren's story though, and carried

on as if she hadn't spoken. There was no making amends, no proving her worth. She'd been cast as the bad one. Not just disappointing or boring, or less pretty. Not just *less* to Cassidy's *more*, but another person actually thought she was a bad human being.

'She had a young fella for a while,' Sandy continued, stony-faced. 'He would have married her, I think. Loved Veronica as much as anyone could. But that girl, she pushes away anyone who could love her.'

'She always has.'

Sandy shook her head. 'No, it's about forgiveness. She betrayed you. And she's spent the rest of her life atoning, sabotaging any chance she had at happiness. You could set her free, but you're too busy feeling sorry for yourself.'

They looked up as Vee came back through the door, halting the not-quite-argument. The child could sense something was off.

'Did you have your vision?' she asked. 'What did it tell you?'

'Nothing splits three ways, luvvy,' Sandy whispered dramatically, hand at her heart. 'There's a reason the animals march in two by two, that we live in couples. Just because someone tries to make a three, that bond between two can never be broken.'

Sandy gave Lauren a dirty look, as if to warn her off trying anything.

Veronica looked between them, frowning. 'Here's your shell, Sandy. I think we should go now, Auntie Loll.'

She hugged the older lady carefully, as if she might break,

and snuck one of the biscuits from the plate into her pocket seamlessly.

Lauren got up, and put on a friendly face, like a well-behaved child. 'Thank you for the tea. Will we see you later at the pub quiz?'

Sandy's craggy face was like a cliff edge. 'Only the spirits can tell us.'

Lauren was agitated as they walked back, and along with struggling against the wind, Veronica struggled to keep up with her. It wasn't until they got away from the seafront that they could catch their breath.

'Why don't you like Sandy?'

'Why would you say that?'

Vee rolled her eyes and gave a disbelieving look that was so like her mother's that Lauren had to blink.

'Okay, well ... because she doesn't like me.'

The child's face creased in confusion. 'Why doesn't she like you?'

'She thinks I might hurt you or your mum, I suppose.' You were meant to be honest with kids, right? And this one was certainly smart enough to tell if she was lying.

Vee tugged at her hand. 'You would *never* do that. You love Cassy.'

Lauren hesitated, but didn't deny it. 'Sandy's just confused. Sometimes adults don't have all the answers.'

Vee shook her head, her little mouth set in a pout. 'That is extra bad for a psychic though. She might not make enough money and have to close her shop.'

'I'm sure that won't—'

'And THEN I won't have any biscuits!'

Lauren laughed. 'Glad you're focusing on the important things there, kid.'

The afternoon was taken up with dinner and homework, where Cass came in and ruffled her daughter's hair, pulling her into her arms with such an intense relief that Lauren had to look away.

They had found an evening routine – Cass would come back and take over homework duty whilst Lauren cooked dinner. They would sit together and eat, talking about their days. Mainly, they listened to Vee talk about whatever was going on at school, or what Mr T did, or some pictures she'd drawn of the North Pole. Then they watched a few episodes of something on TV, read a story and bed. Sometimes Lauren left before the story, went to her hotel room, but sometimes she was requested to be present for those interactive tales of angels and fairies and demons with big fangs but kind hearts. Cass told a story without hiding the fact that she made it up as she went along, that nothing quite made sense until suddenly it did. But that was part of the fun. As always, Cass's stories were chaotic and rambling, but so incredibly alive.

They were waiting to be given permission on their adventure, and Lauren could tell Cass was getting frustrated. She had made a decision, she wanted to go. Lauren, on the other hand, was grateful for the normality of it all, the quiet domesticity.

That night was pub-quiz night, so Nadia from next door, a gothy teenager who was all scowls and badly dyed hair (until she saw Veronica, whom she loved), was babysitting.

'You know the old me would give Nadia a fiver less and threaten to expose the fact that they have now watched the same Disney movie sixteen times, and she knows all the words to the songs.'

'The old you would have charmed her into working for free,' Lauren snorted as they ambled over to the pub.

'She offered. I didn't feel like using the dying card was particularly fair. Hey, maybe I am growing up!' The unease that settled around Lauren's shoulders whenever Cass used the d-word was starting to become less heavy. But that didn't stop her desperate desire to change the subject as soon as possible.

'I had a telling-off from Sandy today,' she said, keeping her pace slow and her voice light. 'Apparently I'm putting you in danger with my negative vibes.'

Cass shrugged and flicked her hands as if shooing the problem away. 'Don't mind her. She's lovely, just protective.'

'Yes, because in her mind I'm the bad guy and you're the angel.'

Cass's eyes narrowed, but her smile was stuck on, resolute. 'You expected me to tell these people about my business, our business? I was meant to turn up to a new town, pregnant and alone, and when they were kind to me I should have told them things that would make them think I was awful?'

'She seemed to know everything.'

Cass raised an eyebrow. 'Yeah, well ... that's Sandy.'

'What, it's her psychic powers?'

'She's just ... painfully aware. Like she has antennae or something. She was a nurse, back in the day. She was in the ward, advising or visiting or something, just after I gave birth,' Cass took a deep breath, screwing her eyes shut briefly. 'She noticed I was scared to look at Vee. I would hold her but I wouldn't look at her. In case … in case …'

'In case you saw him.'

'I got over it eventually,' Cass shrugged, waving it away. 'The fear of seeing the most beautiful thing you've ever made as a reminder of the worst thing you've ever done – it was pretty fucking scary. Plus, I was high as a kite. Things are easier when you stop thinking so much.'

Why did it always feel to Lauren like she needed to apologise? Even now, when she was so sure she had the moral high ground, that she hadn't done anything wrong, she wanted to apologise. And that made her angry all over again. Mousy little Lauren, falling back into old habits like putting on old clothes.

It was always easy back then to just keep quiet and get along, keeping Cass by her side rather than standing her ground and risk losing her over something stupid. That was the same thing she applied to everyone in her life, even though Cass was probably the only one who would have withstood her anger, welcomed it even.

But she'd still lost her.

'You know I'm sorry, you must know that? I spent so long trying … but there's no apology big enough, nothing I could give that would—' Cass spoke quickly, knowing she would cut her off. Neither of them knew how to apologise in any way but the one they had – gifts and silence.

'Let's forget it,' Lauren said sharply, walking more quickly.

Cass exhaled, but nodded, saying nothing. 'But if the old bag appears at the pub quiz *maybe* you could tell her you've had a chat with the spirits and they think I'm cool?'

Cass's face erupted into a childlike delight, and Lauren couldn't help but feel proud. 'Babe, I don't think ghosts hang around to judge who's cool, but I'll try my best to get her on side. And if not, when I'm done with this mortal coil and all that, I'll come back and judge you from the other side.'

'You'd whisper in my ear when you hated my outfits?' Lauren fought through the awkwardness, desperate to keep joking, keep smiling.

'I would throw them out the window' – Cass paused, looking down at Lauren's ensemble – 'especially that coat, Loll. Jesus. Do you own anything that has an actual *colour?*'

Drab and dull as always, the sidekick to the beautiful burning ball of energy. Cass was the supernova and Lauren was the satellite – practical but ultimately without any secrets or mystery.

'Maybe we should add it to the book – a new wardrobe for a new me?'

Cass suddenly looked pained, her voice tinged with regret. 'Don't be a new you, Loll, the old one was perfect. Just perfect.'

No, she wasn't, Lauren thought, noticing the softness of Cass's palm as she reached out and squeezed her hand. *She was just weak, and a pushover, which is exactly what you liked about her.* It was hard to mind though, when she thought about how good they'd been together, how well they had balanced each other out. Wild and timid, soft and loud, loving and vicious. They got to be two people, and by loving the other they just about made a whole. It was this thought that remained tender, and they held hands all the way up to the pub door.

Chapter 9

The pub was loud and rowdy, and the tables had a sticky sheen of weeks' old beer. Lauren felt immediately like she was part of a pleasant routine, as perfectly fitting as a well-worn chair. It was comforting.

She desperately hoped Sandy wouldn't turn up tonight after their earlier conversation. It was hard enough to be in Blackpool, to look at Veronica and see Darren in her movements. To think of that night every time Vee tilted her head, or looked at her frankly, unguarded. It was even harder to look at Cass struggling and wonder if she was allowed to still be mad at her. Sandy didn't seem to think so.

Did years of apologies count if you never got them? Would it have changed anything if she had? They settled themselves down in the corner at a large dark wooden table with a nasty green cushioned bench against the wall. Barry waved at them from across the bar, lifting his hands in imitation of a drink. Cass and Lauren looked at each other and nodded, Cass giving the thumbs up.

Lauren already adored Barry. He was such a gentle soul, nodding good morning to strangers as they walked down the pier, always ready with an interesting fact about the town, or the beach, or the history of the paving stones. In many ways, he seemed to barely exist, whistling away to himself as he did his job – people didn't notice him.

Even after a day of pushing his cart along, he went out again for an evening walk and always ended up saving the day in some adventure, whether it was a lost dog on the beach or an inconsolable bride-to-be crying into her bag of chips. Lauren liked Barry so much that she'd started drinking bitter, just because she didn't want to offend him by asking for a glass of wine.

'So, we're onto a winner tonight, right, my sweethearts?' he said as he set the pints down on the table and rubbed his hands together.

Pub quiz night was taken very seriously, and at least once a month, Lauren was informed, the team had won the coveted £50 bar tab. A few years ago, they'd won every week, and had been threatened with disbarment, but old Dave the quiz master started getting his nephew to help out with 'younger' questions, and the balance had been restored.

'Where's Sandy? Communing with Casper?' Barry chortled, looking at Justine, Nadia's mum from next door.

She shook her head, grinning as she sipped her gin and tonic. 'I guess you don't have voicemail for ghosts.'

'Sandy wasn't sure if she'd make it,' Lauren chimed in, hoping the relief wasn't too evident.

'Lauren's devastated,' Cass added, arching an eyebrow. She placed two packets of crisps in the middle of the table, ripping the foil bags to make them into plates.

'Who else are we expecting, then?' Barry asked, getting crumbs in his whiskers, then blinked. 'Well look at you two, scrabbling around like mice.'

Cass and Lauren looked at each other and paused, their fingers each grasping crisps of roughly the same size.

'You have to eat them in order,' Lauren said.

'Otherwise, what's the point?' Cass finished, biting her lip, then grinning. The two women didn't look at each other, but somehow, stupidly, it was that shared, automatic reaction that made them feel close. Maybe it would be all right, after all.

Dave, with his forever-red face trundled over and handed out the sheets and pens, giving a warning that they'd start soon.

'I guess we're a small group tonight then,' Barry said, smiling. 'Me on my own with all these lovely ladies. I'll take care of the football questions.'

Justine snorted, 'Barry, I've been going to Bloomfield Road since I was knee-high to a grasshopper – give over with all that.'

Cass wiggled her eyebrows and said nothing, sipping her pint. The door opened suddenly, letting in a cold breeze, and in blustered Paul, hands full of paperwork, that ridiculous scarf getting caught in his coat as he walked through the pub.

'Hello! I have news!' he plonked the paperwork down in a pile on the table and Barry withheld a grumble at covering the quiz sheets. 'Everything's gone through, you're good to go.'

Lauren looked at Cass, expecting her to light up, grin, cheer ... something. Instead she pressed her lips together and nodded, not saying anything. The corners of her lips twitched up in acknowledgement. It was really happening.

Paul didn't seem to notice her lack of enthusiasm, turning to Lauren, '—and it's all down to this woman here. That letter? Brilliance! Utter brilliance! They couldn't question anything because you'd covered it all. And all those examples from other boroughs, and the page of references from grief and child psychologists on the benefits of closure and positive experience ...'

Lauren could feel herself blushing as Paul babbled on about her accomplishments, but worse than that, she could feel Cass's eyes on her, and knew she was seeing something she didn't like.

'Cass, your friend is an absolute genius,' Paul said, all earnest puppy-dog enthusiasm, and Lauren suddenly wished he'd shut up.

Cass just looked up lazily. 'I know, she's a good find, isn't she? Wasted in property, weren't you, Loll?'

Lauren felt her chest tighten, as if it was a trick question. 'It was just a bit of paperwork, there wasn't anything brilliant about it ...' She felt like she should hang her head, just keep the conversation moving forward.

'Now, don't do that, Loll, putting yourself down. You're a grown-up now, aren't you? Thought lawyers were all cut-throat bastards making money from the plight of the innocent? Or is it the guilty?'

'Well, I was making money from the plight of people waiting three weeks for a basic environmental search, so I really couldn't tell you,' Lauren bit back, feeling her words press like a bruise. Why did this always happen? It was always men. Men were the problem. Everything else was fine unless there was a bloke in the room looking between the two of them and wondering which one was an easier option. The introverted shy one or the party girl who craved attention? Except those roles didn't really fit anymore. Or, at least, they shouldn't have.

No one really knew what to say, so Paul simply handed Lauren the confirmation letter and pushed his paperwork into his bag, getting himself a drink.

'What's going on there?' Cass asked, her eyes following him to the bar.

'Nothing. Jesus,' Lauren huffed, 'we worked together on the application. For *you*, I might add. What, did you have a thing?'

Cass shook her head. 'No, never. He's Vee's teacher.'

'Wouldn't have stopped you before.'

'Being a mum isn't always about getting what you want, Lauren. Maybe you'll learn that one day.'

It stung more than it should have, and Lauren recoiled a little, standing up suddenly.

'Where you going, love? The quiz is starting soon!' Barry frowned at her.

'Toilet – be right back,' she made a quick escape, darting across the room, weaving in between people to make it through to the ladies' room. She splashed some water on her neck, then simply stood, looking at herself in the mirror. She saw a strained woman with dark hair, who was pretty enough. She wore her anxiousness around her eyes, and in the hollows of her collarbone. She was a long way away from the round-faced girl that Cass met and took along with her. The less pretty friend. And yet, immediately she was back to feeling like that person.

When Cass bestowed her love, it was like light. You became the most beautiful, special person in the universe. But when she turned her back on you, it was like you didn't even exist. She was starting to look older than she was, Lauren thought, noticing the prominent blue veins along with the bloodshot eyes and that tension around her mouth. Her lips were always pressed together to stop herself from saying anything.

Cass walked in, stood next to her, so that their reflections were side by side. She said nothing. Lauren noticed the lightness of her, the fluttery bird movements made by the clear beating pulse in her neck. The sinews and bones starting to show beneath skin, like when sand is washed away on the shore. Her short hair was beautifully cropped and stylish, but she was tired. Her eyes were red too.

'I'm sorry, Loll,' she said, looking at her reflection, meeting her eyes in the mirror as if it was easier. 'I'm so, so sorry. I don't know how to talk to you anymore. I don't know how to joke with you, or be that person I used to be. I used to be the adventurous one, dragging you off to do things that scared you, because you needed it. And now I'm just tired all the time and everything seems hard.'

Lauren sighed, nudging her. 'You don't have to keep doing that. Making me do scary things.'

'Don't I?' She raised an eyebrow in the mirror.

'Okay, well you probably do, but you used to be *kinder* about it. Instead of tearing me down if someone's nice to me.'

'You're right. You're so right. I'm just ... I'm angry. I'm angry and jealous at everyone who gets to live and be here. Even if here is just to hear Barry swear about how the music question is always about this modern garbage and what happened to the bloody Rolling Stones anyway.'

She half-laughed a little at that, almost like a hiccup – involuntary. Her eyes watered, and she gripped Lauren's hand, still looking at their reflections side by side. 'I didn't mean what I said about being a mum. You'll be an amazing one. I just don't like seeing that look of surprise when you notice I'm all right at it.'

'What?'

'You do this thing where you widen your eyes and get this little smile, and I *know* you're thinking, *the old Cass wouldn't be making lasagne and practising spellings, she would have been doing tequila shots and hanging upside down from the monkey bars in the park*, and I hate it. I don't know why, but I hate it.'

'You hate nostalgia?'

'I hate thinking that you believe I'm doing a bad job and *you* could do it better. That if he'd just knocked *you* up instead, everything would have been fine.'

Those words were a little too close to Lauren's thoughts for comfort. If Darren had managed to get her pregnant, she would have been fine. He could have left and she would have had a kid. She certainly wouldn't have fallen foul of a few letters and some emotional whim to see her old best friend.

Cass seemed to see the truth in her eyes, and squeezed her hand. 'I'm *really* glad you're here, Loll. We're gonna fix everything, I promise. *I'm* going to fix it.'

There was that determination, the Cass who had promised her she was going to give her adventures and make her brave. The Cass who had bought her the Big Book on her graduation and said she was going to do amazing things with her life. Who had told her she was proud when her mother was busy faffing with her high heels and comparing the ceremony to her brother's, and no one else had thought to say it. She was still here, that girl who reminded her she could do something wonderful.

Cass tilted her head to the side, resting it awkwardly on Lauren's shoulder, their reflections strangely separate from them.

'I don't want to leave,' Cass said, sighing.

They stayed like that for a few moments, looking at themselves and wondering where to go next.

'At least we're going on an adventure. There are things to do and see and eat. Things for Vee to look at in wonder.'

Cass smiled, nodding as she lifted her head. 'Why do you think we have all our important moments in toilets?'

'Well, that's an easy one,' Lauren said, directing her towards the door. 'We're both full of shit.'

PART TWO

Finland

Chapter 10

Lauren had been so overwhelmed with how wonderful Vee was that she'd almost forgotten she was still a kid. And kids tended to get grouchy, bored, tired and hungry on a three-and-a-half-hour flight. Even with the promise of Santa at the other end. When they arrived in Finland, Lauren started to realise it wasn't so much that Vee was a regular child – it was that she was just like her mother.

Cass looked so tired she was swaying on her feet as they waited for the luggage to swing around the carousel, shivering just a little. Lauren steadied herself, determined to grab the luggage as it arrived, their huge bags ready to cover their adventure all the way from hunting the Northern Lights to swimming the Great Barrier Reef. Lauren was exhausted already. It was becoming clear that her role on this holiday was not only as organiser, but carer.

Luckily, organising came naturally to her – which was why they had a shuttle waiting for them outside the airport to speed them straight to their resort. If she had to deal with two grouchy sleep-deprived Jones girls, she was going to do it in comfort.

Vee was even too tired to *ooh* and *ah* at the scenery as she leaned her head on the window and looked out, glassy-eyed. Cass put an arm around her, her head resting back against the chair.

Lauren, however, didn't want to miss her chance. She opened the window a crack so that she could breathe in that cold, sharp air and see the last vestige of daylight falling across the horizon. The trees were sprinkled with snow and even though her travel companions were not capable of being excited yet, Lauren couldn't help but smile.

A month ago she had been sitting alone at home wondering where her life had gone, and now, her life was here. There was a childish glee that surfaced at the snow and the road signs and the jangling music on the radio of the taxi. As long as she didn't look at Cass's pale face and think about how vulnerable she looked when she was sleeping, everything was fine.

The resort was a snowy paradise, wintry lodges and little huts selling hot chocolate, sweet treats and warm clothing, perfectly designed like little square boxes in the setting of a snowglobe. They were greeted by a cheery young woman at the front desk who immediately took their bags and led them through to their home for the week.

Lauren shook Vee's hand a little. 'Hey, are you excited to see where we're going to sleep?'

'Sleep,' Vee nodded, leaning against her arm, trudging in her snow boots as they followed their guide. Cass snorted in agreement.

'Well, are you excited about the reindeer, or the huskies, or Santa? Tomorrow we can go and play in the snow and I'll teach you to ski if you want?'

Veronica looked up at her, eyes almost rolling back. 'Auntie Loll, I'm very tired now but I will be excited tomorrow.'

'I'm assuming that wasn't sarcasm.' Lauren looked across at Cass, who shook her head.

'Unfortunately, it's just plain honesty.'

Lauren huffed, 'Well, *I'm* excited.'

It was an understatement. She was giddy, bouncing on her heels as they approached their door.

'What's this? I thought we were staying in a lodge and visiting an igloo?'

'And *I* thought staying in a glass igloo would be a bit more special,' Lauren grinned. 'Surprise!'

The Jones girls looked at each other, and suddenly Lauren was on the outside again, trying to impress everyone, trying to be beautiful and interesting enough to compete with them. They walked into the room and looked around.

'This is so cool!' Vee said, showing some of the enthusiasm Lauren craved. 'I can see the sky!'

Their guide wished them a pleasant evening and closed the door behind them.

'This is a bit insane, Loll. How much did it cost?' Cass looked around them in concern, ignoring the beautiful haze of stars visible through the curved glass ceiling at the front of the lodge. Instead, she focused on the lodge behind, the second double bed in the centre of the room, the bunk beds that Vee was already climbing up. She walked through the kitchen area to the bathroom, and called out, 'Jesus, Loll, there's a sauna in here!'

'It's Finland,' Lauren shrugged, 'but don't you think it's

amazing? I thought that's what Darren's money was for, to make this unforgettable?'

'I love it!' Vee said from the top bunk, reaching out to touch the wooden ceiling with her fingertips.

'But that money is also going to be for Vee ... *after*,' Cass said, gesturing around them. 'Did we really need all this? We could fit six people in here!'

'Well, maybe you should have set some boundaries when I asked you about budgets weeks ago!' Lauren argued. 'Remember, when I said, "What about the money?" and you said, "Whatever, babe, you know best." I guess I should have known that was just you wanting to get out of a boring conversation.'

Before Cass could retort, Vee yelled, 'Stop fighting! I don't want you to fight. Santa will be mad and I have important wishes for him so don't make him angry!'

The little girl's head was hovering over the entrance to the top bunk, her cheeks red and her scowl clearly visible.

'All right, munchkin, I'm sorry, we're both sorry, aren't we, Loll?' Cass nodded towards her daughter, and Lauren held up her hands.

'I'm very sorry. We're all tired, aren't we? Shall we go to bed and tomorrow I'll see if they can move us to a smaller lodge?'

Cass shook her head, pushing those blonde wisps behind her ears. 'Don't do that. I'm sorry, I just had a moment. There's a reason we've lived on a shoestring these last few years. This trip is meant to be about brilliant experiences. I shouldn't have gotten my knickers in a twist.'

Vee giggled at the mention of underwear, crawling down

the bunk-bed ladder. Lauren rushed over to hover behind her as she moved, feet grasping for the next step down. When Vee reached the bottom, she jumped down to the ground with a flourish. 'Ta da!'

'And that is why we never had a bunk bed,' Cass smirked, before pointing to the bathroom and handing over a washbag from her case. 'Here. Teeth, face, pjs. Spit spot.'

Vee followed instructions, skipping off to the bathroom.

Even that small smirk felt like a dig. *You'd know if you had children, Loll. You'd know what to pick and how to think. You wouldn't waste money if you'd had to live like we've lived.*

That night she lay in the bed in the igloo section, Cass insisting she'd sleep better in the darkness of the lodge, Vee safe on the lower bunk bed to her left. Lauren stared at that perfect green sky, pulsating with streams of colour and light, and wondered why even when she tried her hardest, it was never quite enough. *A great start.*

'Wake up, sleepyhead!'

A sing-song voice, along with a gentle bouncing on the bed welcomed Lauren back to the land of the living.

'Breakfast!' Cass grinned, flopping onto the bed and throwing a squashed cereal bar at her head. 'Or at least, the closest we'll get until we leave to scavenge for supplies.'

'Is today husky day? When do we see Santa? Can we play in the snow? What about the rolly-bolly-lally?'

'Aurora borealis,' Cass corrected gently, placing a hand on her head. 'Chill with the questions, let your aunt have a coffee first.'

'Coffee? Where?' Lauren croaked, pulling herself up into a

seated position. She felt suddenly on display, the light filtering through the glass igloo's ceiling, Cass and Vee sat on the end of the double bed. Cass reached behind her for a mug and passed it over.

'After a shower and a good sleep, I am officially eighty-five per cent less B-I-T-C-H today.'

Vee's eyes narrowed as she thought about the spelling, and Lauren stepped in to distract her, 'Today is about the huskies! *Aroooo!*'

'*Arooooo!*' Vee joined in, throwing her head so far back as she knelt up on the bed that she fell backwards giggling.

'That was a very enthusiastic howl,' Lauren grinned. 'Good job. So we need to get wrapped up very, very warm.'

'And we need to go find ourselves a decent breakfast.'

Something in Lauren's chest ached a little as she saw Vee all wrapped up in her snow gear. She imagined what she'd been like as a little baby, a toddler swaddled in puffy snowsuits and knitted hats. Her little red cheeks and bright eyes, how adorable she would have been. That shard in her chest was either jealousy or resentment, and Lauren didn't like the feeling of either. She wondered if Cass had ever given Darren photos, but that seemed too much like an invitation. Cass would never have invited him into their lives. She was happy as a single parent. They had their own language of looks, gestures and sounds.

Even now as she watched them, Cass bending down to zip up her daughter's jacket, their heads seemed to tilt the same way, their voices matching each other in lilt and laughter. Vee's mannerisms weren't quite Cass, she was too open for all that, but there was that edge of overconfidence that was almost necessary in a kid, a way to make friends and survive. Most adults lost it, but Cass, somehow, retained it – a smile that suggested she knew best and she wouldn't hear otherwise. It had always annoyed her, but now that feeling was merged with nostalgia.

But it was impossible to stay irritated surrounded by so much snow. Even when she'd been skiing with Darren, surrounded by his impossible workmates who masqueraded as their friends, it hadn't dampened her enthusiasm. Snow was pure and bright, and immediately made her feel like a child again. And unlike back home, this snow wasn't likely to end up a muddy grey mess by the end of the day, ruined by humans tracking through it.

They bundled up and walked through to the main dining hall, Vee chattering away about wolves and huskies and dogs, giving every possible fact that she could possibly fit into one breath. By the time they reached the dining hall, she seemed to have run out of things to say.

'I'm not hungry, I want to do stuff!' She clapped her hands, waddling across to the window and staring out with glee at the reindeer tied up at the side. 'Look!'

Cass nudged Lauren with her sharp elbow. 'Good call on this place. It's made her so happy.'

'And what about you?'

Cass smirked a little. 'When have I ever been *truly* happy, babe? Not sure I'm cut out for that sort of thing. But I'm well enough.'

She strode off to the buffet bar, returning with plates of waffles, pancakes and fruit salad, assisted by a man who wasn't wearing a name tag or uniform.

'This lovely young man saw I was struggling and offered to help me carry the trays!' Cass exclaimed as she sat, turning on the full force of her charm, meeting his eyes. 'Thank you *so* much, it's really appreciated.'

He sort of guffawed, shifting his weight from one leg to the other, as if waiting to be dismissed.

'Thank you for your help,' Cass repeated, the smile not wavering for a second, 'maybe we'll see you around the resort.'

With that, she turned her focus back to Vee, chatting with her about how you had to eat even when you were excited, and how she might faint from hunger on the husky ride if she didn't have a few bites.

The young man hovered for a few moments more, Lauren meeting his eyes with a pitying smile. He left, turning on his heel and saying nothing. Even though her hair was shorter and her mini-me was at her side, there were some things about Cass that hadn't changed. The ability to get what she needed from people and then drop them, for starters.

Hell, hadn't that been how she convinced Lauren in the first place? This was what she wanted. A babysitter and carer on her final journey. And then, with perfect timing, she looked across the table with that shy smile, reaching out a hand to grab Lauren's.

'I'm so grateful you're here, Loll. Vee, baby, aren't you glad Auntie Loll came with us and organised all this stuff?'

Vee's glowing look matched her mother's. And of course, Lauren fell for it, the same way she always had.

Chapter 11

Lauren took her role as photographer very seriously on this trip. It was her job to ensure that Vee had excellent memories of her mother, and the photographs to go with it. Sure, it ached a little to be on the outside, but she never stayed there for long. Vee would take her hand and lead her over to look at the huskies, or to stroke the reindeer. It was only when Vee suggested she take a photo of her and Cass that she recoiled a little, unwilling to so clearly put everything in the past. Her photos with Cass had never been lies – she'd always been truly happy in those prints, her wide grin authentic and undeniable. She refused to pretend now. It was too soon. She waved off the offer and said she looked a mess. Cass looked uncomfortable but didn't argue.

Seeing Vee's face light up during the husky ride was worth all of Lauren's worries. Her little hand reaching out to plunge her fingers into the soft fur, the wild animal nuzzling gently. Cass seemed to vibrate with a motherly terror, as if the sled dog might turn on her, but she held herself back, letting her daughter explore. Strength came in many guises.

She watched as Cass and Vee snuggled up under a blanket

on the sledge, really only made for one person, and Lauren settled onto the sledge next to them, hiding behind her phone as she took photo after photo. They were so gorgeous together, each image was almost flawless, their red cheeks and eyes bright in fur-hood halos.

It was not okay to feel jealous or left out at a time like this. That was not what grown-ups did. It certainly wasn't what good people did – feel jealous of a dying woman. The sledge drivers made a noise, and off the huskies went, dragging them behind so swiftly Lauren almost lost her phone, clasping it tight and snuggling down further. Oh, how lovely it was not to be responsible for anything in this moment, just listening to her own heartbeat as they sped across the snow.

The sled dogs were invigorated by the speed, kicking up snow beneath their paws, and even as she was scared, she felt the desire to throw her hands up and shout, just like she'd seen Cass and Vee do on the roller-coaster. Instead, she hunkered down further, slipping her hands into her armpits for warmth.

She could hear Cass whooping, intermingling with Vee's cheers as they yelled against the cold air through their face warmers. Lauren tried to focus on herself – she was here, she was doing things, she'd made this happen.

They stopped not long after for warm drinks – a fruity hot tea or hot chocolate. She chose the healthy option, whilst her companions both chose chocolate. Cass convinced her daughter that the drink had been made to her exact specifications – stirring it three times clockwise, then anticlockwise.

Lauren and Cass stood together as Vee seemed to have very

intense conversations with each of the dogs, asking them how they were, if they were tired, whether going fast was as fun for them as it was for the humans they pulled along.

Cass nudged her, a little smile on her face. 'Cheer up, grumpy-face. Look how happy she is.'

'I'm not grumpy, I'm just...'

'Thinking about *what-ifs* and *might-have-beens*?'

Lauren said nothing, inclining her head half an inch.

'I think about that a lot too. But honestly, it's better to stop thinking altogether – you do more living that way.'

And what was there to say after that? The darkness, which had never really left, seemed to settle around them like a midnight cloak, and the stars popped as if someone suddenly turned on the lights. It was time to head back. Even Lauren, so full of jealousy and aching with loss, couldn't help but smile as she tilted her head back at the sky.

'Hey, Loll, you're gonna be our driver!' Cass grabbed her hand and pulled her over to their sled.

'Excuse me?'

'Listen,' Vee said, holding a finger up to her lips. 'Shhh!'

Lauren did as she was told, listening to the guide as he explained they'd have a chance to steer, but that you had to be strong and authoritative.

'Hardly me,' Lauren snorted. 'You do it.'

'I don't have the energy.' Cass shrugged as if it was no big deal, when really, Lauren could see her itching to take hold and jump on the back, controlling their direction. Maybe she wasn't the only one missing things.

'Come on, Loll, you need to be a little scared sometimes.'

I'm scared all the time, she wanted to yell. Only her fear of sounding pathetic stopped her. It was true – she was scared of being alone and being invisible, and time passing her by, the way it had, unnoticeably, these last six years. She was afraid she would wake up one day and lose her voice because she never said anything worth listening to.

'Okay, let's do it. But if I kill you—' Lauren joked, then stopped with a wince.

Cass shrugged as if the words meant nothing, her face a blank. Then she grinned. 'You'll only have yourself to blame. Especially after arranging this whole holiday. What a waste!'

That was always one of the comforting things about Cass – if it could be made into a joke, it would be. It was better to laugh than to cry. Better to be silly than serious. Lauren had forgotten how much she used to laugh over things that weren't funny.

Vee settled down in the cart with her mother, Lauren standing unsteadily on the back, listening to the directions, mumbling them to herself over and over, lips moving but no sound escaping.

What if something went wrong? What if she fell off and was left freezing in the snow? What if the dogs got angry at her and turned on them?

As if she seemed to know, Cass lifted her hand up and grasped Lauren's tightly. Mittens made it difficult, but she felt the pressure as Cass tried to press into her palm, the way she always had. Anxiety release in moments of terror. She squeezed back once, then gently pulled her hand back. It was enough that someone noticed, and cared, that she was afraid.

She took a breath and left that worry behind, letting it drain away. Every day at work had been full of those voices, building up into a wall of *what-ifs* and *almosts*. Not the good kind, not the maybe-one-day kind of daydreams. It was more the feeling that everything she did was probably wrong, and everyone knew it.

God, she wanted to tell her brain it was such a waste of time to turn on her like that. They could have been so productive, done great things together. Lauren was pretty sure that studying broke her. The pressure of learning and working and getting married and losing Cass – she had simply broken, and her brain wasn't really her friend anymore. She was just a weaker, delicate sort of person. That was what they all said. Her mother, Darren, her tutors. She was just *so sensitive.* She couldn't expect to change now.

Except ... Cass had never seen her that way. Cass had never doubted she was a wolf.

'Go!' she said suddenly, fingers clenched in anticipation. The dogs did as they were told, picking up speed and depending on Lauren to shift her weight this way and that to guide them. She furrowed her brow, feeling her head start to hurt with the tension of concentration. *Keep steady, keep still, don't let them down, don't let them get hurt, don't fuck this up.*

When the dogs finally slowed, and she remembered to breathe, her heart was racing, her fingertips shaking from the numb coldness and exhilaration.

'That was amazing!' Vee jumped up. 'Auntie Loll, you led the pack! *Aroooo!*'

She threw her head back as she howled, and suddenly all the dogs turned their heads towards her. Cass put a gloved hand over her daughter's mouth quickly. They waited, and the huskies seemed to get bored, distracted by food from their trainers and the promise of bed.

'Maybe don't howl in front of them. We don't know what we're saying in wolf – it might be rude and we don't want to offend the pack,' Lauren said, her voice hoarse from the cold air.

It had been fun, though, hadn't it? She'd felt empowered in the pockets between the terror. At least Vee knew her Auntie Loll wasn't a stick-in-the-mud. She could be just as fun as Cass. At the very least she could do as she'd done all those years ago, and pretend. Pretend she was fine with staying out and meeting strangers. Pretend that she didn't need to have a few drinks for courage before getting all dressed up for a night out. She'd been Cass's shadow once, and it was easy enough to stand behind her again.

'Why is it so dark already?' Vee whined, taking the hand of each woman and walking in between them. 'Does this mean I have to go to bed?'

'No, silly,' Cass rolled her eyes, 'we haven't even built a snowman yet. Let's do that, and maybe get some schnapps for Mama.'

Lauren raised an eyebrow.

'Is that not right? Oh, something local and painfully alcoholic, you know what I mean.'

'And perhaps find something on the dinner menu for a certain person that isn't Prancer or Blitzen,' Lauren added.

'Good point.'

The afternoon passed easily enough, sharing a bottle of wine in the curve of the glass igloo as they watched Vee build a snow castle. They didn't talk, Cass pretending to read a book, but really only propping it up in her lap whilst she stared at her daughter. She was clearly trying to take a mental picture, remembering the way strands of hair fell out from her turquoise bobble hat, and the redness of her nose as she chewed her neck warmer in concentration.

Lauren got out her sketch pad, something she hadn't done in years, but felt was appropriate for this trip down memory lane. She'd almost forgotten she used to draw. Everything from wiggly doodles, to cartoons, to portraits. She had loved to capture something perfectly, whether it was an idea or a perfect copy of reality.

There had stopped being time for drawing. The studying, the work, Darren – time seemed to move so slowly, hour by hour, but then she had looked up and years had passed without her doing anything much at all.

She sketched Vee, her little form made rotund from the snow clothes, the briefest outline of pencil on white paper. But it became a little too painful, to be watching her with the same intensity as Cass. Wondering about *what-ifs* and Darren and that night. She closed her eyes and pushed the images away.

Instead she started drawing the huskies from earlier, looking at photos on her phone to help her focus on the shapes. The points of their ears and the roundness of their paws, the fan of their tails. She drew wolves around the page, in different styles – pouncing cartoons that looked like cave drawings, all simple swirling lines and rough shading. Then wolves made of triangles, all angular and bloodthirsty, staring at you like they saw dinner.

It was therapeutic, simply letting the pencil trace the page. She thought of Vee's howl and how they froze in fear, and started drawing a young wolf cub, her head thrown back in a joyful exclamation. Lauren wondered how she'd ever howled in that pub all those years ago, unafraid to be silly, make noise or draw attention. Now, half the time she went to speak it felt like her voice was out of practice.

Vee trundled in, tracking snow on the tiles. She wiped the back of her forehead with her mittened hand, a dramatic gesture.

'Phew,' she said, attempting to pull off her boots whilst still standing. 'Can I have a warm drink, please?'

Cass helped her out of her boots, placing a hand gently on her head before whipping the hat off. 'Well, as you asked so nicely.'

She headed to the kitchen area whilst Vee climbed up on the bed next to Lauren, unzipping her jacket as she nuzzled in to her side, peering at the sketch pad.

'Wow, those are pretty wolves. I like that one with the spiky teeth.' She did her own impersonation of bared jaws, holding her hands up as splayed claws.

'You like the fierce ones?'

They were made of geometric shapes, and something about them made Lauren feel on edge, like they were prowling around outside somewhere and had only paused when she trapped them on the page.

Vee shrugged. 'They're cool. They're pretty, but scary too.'

'I guess no one would care if they were just your average home pooch, huh?'

'Doggies are cute, but they wouldn't be wild. We went so fast! And you were the pack leader! You told them what to do!'

'Huh, I guess I did.' Lauren grinned, squeezing the girl briefly around the shoulders, then releasing her as Cass approached with her hot apple juice.

'So what's the plan tomorrow, pack-leader?' Cass asked, lowering herself gently into a chair, then leaning over to top up Lauren's wine. Lauren raised her glass in thanks.

'Tomorrow, we get some snow time in the morning, so I'm going to ski for the first time in years, and then the afternoon we get to see a certain magical old man.'

'Are you skiing, Cassy?' Vee asked, pulling at the threads on her jumper.

'I used to surf, so I might try snowboarding on the nursery slope. Something new! You wanna try it with me, muffin? Or we could go down the hill on a sled or in a rubber ring, that might be fun!'

The little girl narrowed her eyes in thought. 'I want to learn to ski like Aunt Loll. Can you teach me?'

Lauren didn't have time to say yes before seeing the look on Cass's face, that dark cloud again. She could switch in an instant. Rejection always did that to her. It made her cruel without a moment's notice. And picking Lauren over Cassidy Jones? Oh, it seemed like there could be nothing worse.

'Of course, going to grow up a posh girl, are we, baby?'

Cass's voice was sharp, 'Be out in the French Alps in your teen years?'

'Cass,' Lauren frowned. 'Don't.'

'No, it's fine, I just didn't think ... I'm surprised you ski actually, Loll. Bit too much risk, isn't it? Thought you'd be scared.'

The vitriol in Cass's voice wasn't surprising – Lauren had been here before. When she chose a weekend away in Paris over a trip to Birmingham for a rave with Cass. When she decided to move in with Darren. When she said she wanted a baby. Cass had a metal exterior, but her insides were shards of glass. If you shook her, she'd jangle.

'It's a controlled risk, I know what I'm doing on the slopes. Do you not want me to teach her? Are you worried about Vee's safety?'

That was the only way, back her into a corner of logic and truth because it was clear why she didn't want her to go – she wanted her baby to look at her with joy and adoration. She didn't want to share with Lauren. Cass was silent, and Lauren floundered for a way to make it all go away.

'Hey, I know, why don't we all try snowboarding together? We can all learn something new?'

Cass huffed, 'You know, Loll, just once it might be worth trying to have a backbone. Stop snapping yourself in half to be loved by everyone.'

Lauren stood up, pausing to smile at Vee, before she walked past her old friend. 'And maybe you should think that just because you're D-Y-I-N-G, it doesn't give you the right to be a B-I-T-C-H.'

She walked past her, through to the back of the lodge, unsure of where to hide away.

Cass raised her voice, 'Well—'

'*Stop*!' Vee yelled, hands on hips as she stood on the bed. 'Stop being mean! I'll go with you, Cassy, just stop being mean.'

Cass looked across the room at Lauren, suddenly so incredibly vulnerable, her lips trembling with the force of not crying. She nodded at her friend before turning back to her daughter, reaching for her hands.

'I'm sorry, munchkin, of course you should go skiing. Mama's just tired, and grouchy.'

'Well, sleep then,' the little girl retorted, not sure how to continue being angry when her mother looked so sad.

'That's a very good idea,' Cass nodded, looking past Vee to the snow outside. 'Why don't you and Auntie Loll go on an expedition to find some food? I'll have a nap and I'll be much nicer when I wake up.'

'Well, okay,' Vee pursed her lips as if she was pretending to be angry, but jumped down from the bed and gave Cass's hand a pat. 'Sleep lots and we'll bring you ice cream!'

'Ice cream?! All this snow and you want ice cream?' Loll exclaimed as she put on her jacket, fingertips trembling just a little.

'Snow is just non-tasty ice cream, really,' Vee replied, letting Cass help her pull on her shoes.

'Kid's kind of got a point.'

Cass's words were directed to Lauren, but she didn't meet her eyes. She knew she should be gentle and understanding of Cass's outbursts; she'd dealt with them for years, of course, the little sparks of criticism and harsh words that suggested Lauren was simply too dull to be believed. But she was doing this for *her*. She was the one who'd been betrayed, lied to, dumped and then manipulated – was it too much to ask that people be nice to her?

Except ... she felt guilty. She'd shouted at Cass, and even though she knew Cass would want her to be normal with her, to call her out no matter how sick she was ... it didn't feel right.

She bundled Vee up and out of the lodge, stomping through the snow, holding the little girl's hand as she chattered away. How much did Vee see of her mother, how much was different and how much was the same? After about ten steps, Lauren paused and looked back. Cass was still sitting in that chair, staring up at the white, cloudless sky.

When they returned, Cass was asleep, but outside in the snow, *I'm sorry,* had been spelled out in capital letters, with a heart at the end, and her snowy boots sat by the front door.

Chapter 12

'Hello? Can you see me? I can't see you.'

Paul's voice was tinny over the laptop speaker, but eventually the black square came to life, and there he was with his beaming smile. 'Well hello! Glad to see we have full attendance for today's class.'

'They told me I wasn't allowed to play in the snow if they had to stay in and learn.' Cass faux-pouted, then grinned, leaning her chin on her hand as she looked at the camera. 'How are you?'

'Good,' Paul smiled, 'not as good as you guys, off having an adventure. Are you having a good time, Veronica?'

'Yes, Mr T,' she sighed, looking out behind her at the snow, 'but I was building a snow castle yesterday and then it snowed again so I have to start from scratch.'

'Well now you have the opportunity to make a better one!'

Vee's pout looked exactly like her mother's, but hers was genuine. '*Yes*, but it was very tiring and I'm only little.'

Paul hid his smile behind a hand, picking up some files and putting them down for no reason. Lauren felt like he was grinning at her, even though there was no way that could be true. The screen was fuzzy as anything.

'And how is Madam Secretary this morning?' This, she assumed, was addressed to her. Paul had joked about her paperwork skills, her need to be precise, in control and have absolutely everything in triplicate. Which, when you were organising home schooling for a kid and had to get travel insurance for a dying woman ... well, she was pretty sure it was a compliment.

'Good, eager to get on the slopes,' she always spoke too loudly on video calls. Why was she so awkward?

'Ah, a snow bunny. Of course.'

What did that mean, exactly? Did she seem like the kind of person who skied in the winter? She'd always felt frightfully like she didn't fit in with any of them when they'd gone on Darren's trips. He'd make such a big deal of buying expensive drinks to be part of the *après-ski*, or choosing designer ski-wear that was mainly impractical. He desperately wanted to be part of that world, she realised now. He was searching as much as she was, pretending just as she had been.

As if she'd conjured him, her phone started ringing. Looking at the screen, she tilted her head up and shared a look with Cass. She apologised to Paul for the interruption and said she'd be right back. He probably wanted to talk to Cass anyway.

'Hello?'

'Finally, I've called a hundred times!'

She rolled her eyes, reaching out a fingertip to the glass window. 'You called thirty-six times, don't be dramatic. What do you need?'

'You quit your job?' Darren asked. 'I just spoke with your boss and he said—'

'Yes, I quit. It made me miserable so I quit.'

'Well that's not very grown-up, is it, Lauren?'

She barely held in the laugh. 'That's what you did with our marriage, didn't you? It didn't make you as happy as something else, so you quit. Why can't I quit things?'

'I got you that job. How do you think it looks—'

'It looks like I don't owe my soon-to-be ex-husband anything. And those people thought you were a moron. They called you Slime Ball and said you wore too much hair gel.' She paused, thinking about it. 'You do, by the way. Wear too much hair gel.'

Darren sighed, 'Look, Lauren, I really think you should come home so we can do this properly, like adults.'

'Ummm ... no. Been an adult long enough. I didn't get to have my post-studies gap year, and I'm having it now. Sold the house yet?'

'The market's not—'

'Ooh,' she hissed like a child, 'lost your edge? I thought you could sell anything? Unless you'd rather move your mistress into our marital home? Because that's fine, you just need to buy me out.'

'I thought you didn't care—'

'I didn't, but this phone call is boring and you're pissing me off. Plus I happen to know how much money you sent to Cass over the years. I'm sure that wouldn't go down well in court, would it? Siphoning off money to pay for your love child?'

'Lauren, look, you're above all that stuff with money, it doesn't matter to you. But I—'

'Need it to feel like a semi-decent human being?' Lauren laughed, 'Or are you worried your fiancée won't stick around if you don't have a tidy sum to spend on a spectacle of a wedding?'

Darren went silent, and she had to stop herself from asking if anyone was still there, as there was only vague breathing at the end of the line. When he did speak, his voice was quiet and dull. 'Look, you never really loved me anyway. You never wanted to stay with me. You put up with me. So yeah, I've been a dick and I fell in love with someone else, in a way that I never loved you. But let's not pretend I didn't do us both a favour. You were just too much of a coward to leave.'

Rage bubbled up, hit the top of the pot ... but disintegrated. He was right. He was a dickhead and a cheater and was so full of shit all the time, but he was right. Yet, on the other hand ... 'So I should be punished for showing loyalty?'

'We should be set free, sweetheart, both of us. And I'm sure Cass is poisoning you against me every day you're with her—'

'We've had more important things to talk about,' she cut him off, and noted he didn't ask questions.

'Look, just come home and we'll talk. We'll get it all sorted, and who knows, maybe we'll even be friends. We were always good friends, weren't we?'

Lauren wondered how she had ever been married to this man. He was either stupid or insane. Or she was, for never seeing it before. Never listening to Cass when she said he was more dangerous than dull. 'You destroyed my relationship with my best friend. You lied, you made me believe ... and now I've lost all this time for a man who didn't love me anyway.'

'Cass was bad for you. You were nervous and excitable, always running around after her, up and down. She put pressure on you to look after her, deal with her madness.' He sounded so kind, suddenly, so much like the caring husband who always wanted to limit her pain, limit her fear. Keep things simple and greyscale and structured. 'Just come home, and we'll sort it out together.'

'It's not my home anymore,' she said, and put the phone down. Let him call thirty-six more times if he needed to. Every time she spoke to him, she felt her backbone strengthening along with her resolve.

As much as Cass could be cruel and changeable, acting like her during these conversations was keeping Lauren strong. She was pretending not to be a pushover anymore. Cass had always brought that out in her, the belief that she was stronger than everyone else thought. Probably why Darren hated her so much. She made *Lauren* into *Loll*, and oh, how she'd missed being Loll.

When she walked back into the lodge area, Vee was writing in her workbook, her forehead incredibly close to the table as she leaned into the page, tongue poking out from the side of her mouth. The adult voices stopped abruptly.

Perhaps Cass was moaning about what a nightmare this was already, that it was a let-down. Maybe she was poisoning the well with Paul. She'd done that before, annoyed when someone paid Lauren a little too much attention, was a little too friendly. There were people who were *hers*, who were there to adore *her.* Getting distracted by her mousy friend was not the plan.

'What are we talking about?' she asked as she walked over.

'How you're getting divorced,' Vee said without looking up from her writing. 'That means when people aren't married anymore because they're not happy.'

'That's right, well done. What are you writing?' Lauren slipped into the chair, shooting Cass a look. She made sure she stayed off camera, and felt a little relief. She could see him but he couldn't see her.

'Spellings. Mr T says when you spell well people know you're smart.'

'And then you can make a hundred copies of paperwork like your Aunt Loll.' Cass shot her a smile, an apology. So they had been talking about her.

'Well if you guys are studying, I'll sit over here and do some work too,' she said, taking herself over to the sofa. 'Call if you need anything.'

It seemed strange, then, as if the room was suspended in time. Voices were quiet and Cass didn't really say much after that, just sitting present as her daughter did her work. Lauren sat on her phone, typing in endless pointless web searches:

What to do with a law degree?

What to do with property knowledge?

Interesting jobs for lawyers.

Children and grief counselling.

The last one sat in the search box, the cursor blinking until she clicked *Enter*. She shouldn't have been worrying about that yet, but Cass didn't seem to be, and someone had to. If Cass had gone to therapy when her mother got sick, things might have been different. Maybe they would have still been friends.

She liked hearing Paul's voice in the background, she realised. It was a comforting presence, knowing that Vee was well taken care of, that she would go back to school and not be behind, and everything would be well. Except, what happened when they went home? Would she hang around whilst Cass got worse? Was Vee meant to stay with Sandy or one of Cass's lovely, but decidedly kooky, friends?

Cass had always lived in the moment, but dying wasn't really the time for that. Lauren would have to decide whether she stayed there till the end, living in Blackpool, watching Cass disappear. She might become hateful, just as her mother had, wasting away and demanding no one see her.

But it would be worth it. To try to get back what they had, just for a little bit. To look at the woman who had shared her secrets and held her hand and told her she was wonderful. The only real friend she'd ever had. Even if sometimes she hated her. She would stay until this was all over. She would be brave for Cass, because she would do the same for her. The thought was terrifying.

Eventually, the lesson ended. Vee was given her homework, which she pulled a face at, but bore, writing it all down. She walked over to wave at the screen with the other two.

'Thank you for agreeing to do this,' Lauren said, knowing just how much he'd fought to protect Vee and her future, and how ardently he would have argued their case. It meant more work for him too, preparing all the work, taking time to do these extra lessons. But of course, men had done stupider things for Cassidy Jones.

'Yes, I really appreciate it, darling.' Cass shot her a look, as if she'd stolen her line. *Oh, it was going to be another one of those days.*

'My absolute pleasure. Have a hot chocolate for me. I'll miss you guys at the pub quiz.'

His face froze on the screen as they disconnected, that perpetual hopeful expression seasoned with the slightest shadow of worry. Today he was wearing a dark blue jumper, and Lauren tried to ignore how it made his eyes alarmingly bright.

'Okay, snow time.' Lauren clapped her hands together.

'You know, you guys go,' Cass said suddenly, eyes wide and innocent. 'I'm not feeling that great.'

'You keep saying that!' Vee said seriously, tugging on her hand.

'What, I can't *keep* feeling unwell?' Cass snorted, 'I wish that were the case, munchkin.'

Lauren didn't know what to do – step in and defend Cass, take her daughter skiing and avoid any complications? Except Cass had done this before. Sat out of the race because she felt hard done by. It was never selfless, it was always to put a damp towel on the party so no one else could enjoy it too. She should grow a backbone though, just like Cass said.

'Okay then, Vee, shall we go ski?'

The little girl froze, still holding onto Cass's hand. 'I ... no, I think I want to snowboard with Cassy.'

'Vee ...' Cass shook her head, but Lauren wondered if her eyes shone with success instead of tiredness.

'Okay, I'm going to go then. I'll see you guys later.' Lauren walked off too slowly, pathetic in how much she wanted them to stop her going.

'Loll,' Cass stood, walking over, the hollows of her eyes suddenly more prominent as she whispered, 'this wasn't a play, babe. I don't feel safe going out on the slopes, my legs are jelly from yesterday and all I want to do is sleep without worrying that I'm ruining her holiday. Take her for me, please.'

'You're sure? You're not going to turn around the minute I say yes and accuse me of trying to steal your daughter?'

Cass laughed, a solid laugh that took up space and reverberated, rather than fizzling into thin air.

'God, it's good to be around someone who really knows me.'

That sounded like a blessing, so they headed out, Cass waving at them with a smile plastered on her face.

They stood on the nursery slope, Vee bundled up safe from both weather and falls, and Lauren tried to share what she knew. She secretly wished there was someone to take a photo of them together in this moment, as she held Vee's hand and guided her down the hill. There weren't too many people on the slope yet, and gradually becoming accustomed to the swishing, curving movement of the skis, Veronica looked up at her and grinned, arms out in celebration.

'I did it!'

'You're amazing!' Lauren exclaimed as she caught her.

How lovely, to be able to tell kids the truth. To have someone you could be honest with, at least in your feelings. *You're wonderful, you're amazing, I'm so glad you're here, you're so much fun, I'm so impressed by you.* Those compliments were reserved for lovers, good friends, and children. Children seemed to thrive on them, growing towards kind words like the sun.

Lauren started to trust herself, that she wouldn't see Darren's judgement peering out of Veronica's eyes, because how could she be like him? She was so completely herself.

After an hour or so, they retreated to the café by the gondola entrance for sustenance, sweaty and aching with the effort of holding themselves up.

'That was so much fun!' Vee said, watching carefully as Lauren stirred the hot chocolate three times clockwise, followed by three times anticlockwise. She nodded as it was presented to her, a queen giving her approval.

'It really was!' Lauren sipped at her hot chocolate, closing her eyes. God, it was good to enjoy things. To savour simple pleasures that weren't designed to make you forget or disappear, or even survive. Things that existed just to be enjoyed. 'So, are you excited about seeing Santa this afternoon?'

Vee shrugged, a little smile on her face. She swirled the straw around in her hot chocolate, licking the cream. 'I don't know. What if he can't give me what I wish for?'

'Well, he's not a genie, sweetheart, but if there's something you want for next Christmas, I'm sure he'll try really hard to make it happen.'

Vee frowned. 'Who do you think Santa asks when he wants things?'

'Himself, I suppose.'

'That must be good.'

They sat slurping their drinks, but something didn't feel right to Lauren. She wasn't sure if it was meant to be her job to probe a little further, or whether Cass would want her to wait.

'You know if there's something you want from Santa, you can ask me too? I'll see what I can do.'

Vee laughed, a flash of pity in her eyes, as if this silly adult really didn't understand. 'Thanks, Auntie Loll, but you're not magic.'

That much Lauren had to agree with.

The afternoon was not as tense as the morning, with a bundled-up Cass coming out to meet them for lunch, cheering on Vee from the base of the mountain as she showed off her new skills.

'I'm glad you took her,' she said quietly to Lauren, standing by her side. 'I know I don't make it easy.'

'Where would be the fun in that?' Lauren replied.

Cass reached for her hand, taking her back to their early twenties, huddled together under covers, watching movies, talking about how their lives would be. 'Really, Loll. It means so much. Not just for you to help with Vee, but for you to be here. It's exhausting trying to be who everyone else thinks I am. You're the only person who ever knew the truth.'

'That you can be a grouchy bitch?' It was the kind of thing she would have said back then, and it fell from her lips before she could think.

Cass beamed at her. 'Exactly. Exactly!'

They sat down to a simple lunch, watching in horror as surrounding tables got the Rudolph Special, a reindeer burger with a bright glacé cherry speared through the top of the golden bun. They tried to distract Vee, sensing their animal lover would be distraught.

Lauren took photos and they laughed into their sandwiches and told snowman jokes. It was what she'd hoped their holiday would be. Cass and Lauren each ordered a beer, and they arrived in huge glass tankards that Cass struggled to lift. Even that made them laugh.

They talked about their last night in Finland, and how tomorrow they would play in the snow before leaving for their flight. Cass was determined that she'd go down the mountain in a rubber ring. Nothing was going to stop her.

Lauren watched as Vee started to twitch with agitation, desperate in her need to see Santa Claus. She had been so incredibly patient, but now the adults were taking too long to finish their huge drinks, and she really wanted to go.

She led the way, Lauren and Cass bumbling behind, strangely euphoric from the beer. They staggered along in the snow behind her, clinging to each other in support. There had been more laughter that afternoon than there had been in the whole time since they had reappeared into each other's lives. Lauren holding onto Cass as they tried not to fall was so reminiscent of uni days, rambling back home after the club, that it physically hurt. The nostalgia was a living, breathing shard sitting in her chest. It was too easily disturbed by laughter and lightness.

They heard Vee's squeak of delight and grinned at each

other, the darkness falling around them as she called out, 'Hurry up, look!'

When the adults turned the corner, they could see why she was beside herself. Santa's lodge was a twinkly wonderland, lit up across a little bridge over a frozen river. It looked like every kid's dream – the warmth of the room inside was clear through the windows, all red fabric and a huge Christmas tree with presents piled up underneath.

A young woman dressed as an elf stepped outside to greet them, bending down to Vee's level.

'You must be Veronica! Are you ready to see Santa?'

Vee nodded seriously, her eyes suddenly huge.

Lauren and Cass followed her in, phones at the ready to capture each moment of glee on the little girl's face.

They sat across the room at a table, and sipped at hot apple cider whilst Vee approached a very convincing Father Christmas, rotund and red faced as he shuffled in his chair. His smile was kind, and he leaned in as Vee spoke to him quietly. Cass and Lauren shared a moment of comfortable silence, watching this person they adored look so happy.

'And what would you like for Christmas, Veronica?' the man intoned in his soft accent.

They watched Vee blink as one of the elves took a photograph.

'Christmas is a long time away, so can I have my present early? I'll be very, very, very good!'

Santa nodded thoughtfully, stroking his beard. 'Well, tell me what it is, and I'll see what I can do.'

She looked over at Cass and Lauren, then leaned in,

whispering into the old man's ear. His eyes widened, and his beard twitched slightly. Lauren noticed how the corners of his eyes turned down, as if he was struggling for composure. He stared at Cass, then at her, then back to Vee.

'Oh, Veronica, I don't know if I can control that,' he said softly, patting her arm. 'Is there anything else you would like?'

Vee looked lost, searching for something beyond the room, an idea she could grab at.

'Well ... maybe you could send me my daddy? Can you find him?'

Her nonchalant tone made the women blink, and the old man looked even more surprised.

'I'm sure I must have a daddy somewhere, Santa, so maybe you could find him. I don't mind waiting until Christmas for that though.' She nodded resolutely, back straight.

The old man seemed to collapse in on himself. 'Are you sure you wouldn't like something else? A lovely new bike, or some other toy?'

'Oh no, Santa, I'm having adventures with my mum and auntie. We can't pack much.'

Lauren felt her heart clasp and creak as if someone was trying to open it with a crowbar. Poor little Vee.

'Really, Veronica, I think you should have this present,' Santa insisted, trying to hand it over to her. 'If you don't want to take it, you can give it to someone else you think might like it.'

Vee nodded. 'Okay, thank you.'

She took the present, and smiled. Just as she started to walk towards her grown-ups, the elf suddenly thrust another present into her hands. 'Take this one too, please. Elves like to give gifts as well.'

The young woman looked heartbroken as she smiled at Vee, handing her another box wrapped in green paper with a huge red bow.

Vee smiled and shrugged, thanking her politely as she struggled to carry the parcels over to the adults. Cass said nothing about what they'd overheard, and Lauren felt obligated to fill the silence, the strange stiffness that suddenly existed between them.

'Shall we go and feed the reindeer?' She injected a cheery tone into her voice.

'Yes, please,' Vee said, smiling as if nothing was amiss. 'Can you hold my present?'

Cass took one of the presents from her and took her daughter's hand, following after Lauren as she led them out into the snow.

'Thank you!' the elf cried out from behind them, her squawk echoing through the chilled air.

The reindeer were around the back of the lodge, and Vee's previous questions seemed to be forgotten as she beamed at the creatures, asking their handler about them and feeding them carrots and apples. Cass took photographs on autopilot, smiling blandly and saying nothing.

She had asked about her father.

Lauren wondered how those conversations had gone before, if Cass had been her typical self and simply refused to talk about it. If she'd lied and been kind, or told some twisted version of the truth.

It was more likely she'd played a careful game of misdirection and distraction, until her daughter was too exhausted to ask again, and she could pretend all was well.

They ate a simple dinner in the resort restaurant, subconsciously plying Veronica with anything she might want. Yes, of course you can have that huge burger you'll never finish. Yes, you can order dessert. Of course, you can have a fizzy drink, even though it'll make you crazy caffeinated and you won't sleep.

They shared a bottle of wine, and Cass drank more quickly than usual. She held up her side of the conversation, but luckily, Veronica was distracted enough by her presents. As much as she wasn't a child invested in having *things*, there was so much joy in the fact that not only did this come from Santa, but the elf thought she was *such* a good girl she should have another present. Lauren kept up a constant stream of babble as Vee opened the presents and exclaimed in delight.

The first was a toy husky, its white fur fluffy and its bright blue eyes like marbles. Vee immediately clasped it to her chest and yipped in delight. 'Look! A wolf!'

'What will you call it?'

She pouted as she considered, 'Storm.'

'Good name,' Cass offered, the barest twitch of a smile though her mind was clearly elsewhere.

'What's the other one?'

The strangely shaped box was opened to reveal a small turquoise ukulele. Lauren turned to Cass with a grin. 'Do you remember?'

Cass's smile, finally, shone through, suddenly authentic. She nodded.

'Do you still have it?'

She shook her head. 'I don't think so. It got lost somewhere along the way.'

'What is this?' Vee plucked a string. 'A tiny guitar?'

'It's called a ukulele, your mum used to play,' Lauren said with a smile. 'Maybe she'll teach you.'

Vee's eyes lit up with a hopefulness that even Cass couldn't say no to.

'We'll have a go when we get back to the lodge, see if I can remember anything.'

'I'll see if I can find any videos of your mum playing,' Lauren said with a grin. 'I'm sure I at least have a picture somewhere.'

She wondered what happened to all those photos and videos. An entire lifetime of her face pressed close to Cass's, too much make-up to hide the splotchy skin, flushed with booze and excitement. She hoped they were still somewhere. Not just in that box under the bed, but in the ether, in the cloud. It had been hard to look at them when she went online, which was why she'd shut down her social media account back then. She didn't really have time for it anyway. She didn't have friends from uni she needed to impress with her wedding pics. She didn't have an ultrasound to put as her profile picture, a constant update with what kind of fruit her baby was now. She'd justified that it was all fake anyway, that real friends phoned and visited, but the truth was that there had only been Cass, like a shining sun, and without her it was clear she had neglected the chance to make other friends. Social media was excellent at making you look busy but feel lonely.

That night in the lodge, the tension had lifted slightly. Cass sat on the bed in the centre of the room, leg tucked under her as she played the ukulele. A strand of blonde hair fell across her face, and she kept blowing it out of the way. Her fingers looked bony but strong.

Vee sat curled into her side, resting her fingertips on her mother's thigh as she watched the strings, paying avid attention to the way her fingers moved across the frets. Cass half hummed, half sang, a tune that came and went. Her voice wasn't the best; it had a jangling quality to it, as if someone was shaking a bird mid-warble. But it was pleasant and sweet, the sharp bursts of song in between silence.

Lauren went to take a picture but stopped, instead videoing the moment. Capturing the sounds and the movement as Vee looked up at her mother, with Cass smiling to herself and fiddling with strings ... it felt necessary. She was the safeguard. The memory keeper.

God, some things would only exist between her and Cass soon enough. Their truths would become her truths when Cass was gone. How lonely, to carry all your memories alone. Leaving them open to time to change how you remember.

Vee wriggled off the bed and climbed into Lauren's lap, her legs digging into Lauren's thighs as she added her own weight to the chair. She took over the role of camerawoman and took the phone, directing it at Cass and zooming so far in only her face was visible, that hair falling forward, a halo of soft golden light from the side light behind her.

Lauren dared not move, feeling an immense sense of loss as Veronica sat on her lap as if she'd been doing it since was a child. Maybe she had, but with someone else.

Cass looked up from strumming and smiled at the camera, before pulling a funny face.

'Cassy, you ruined it!' Vee laughed, ending the video, and handed the phone back to Lauren.

Silence settled like a breath in. Waiting.

'Pumpkin, why did you ask Santa about finding your daddy?' Cass asked gently, eyes on her fingertips as they danced around the frets, rather than on her daughter.

'Because Santa didn't think he could give me my other wish,' Vee wriggled uncomfortably on Lauren's lap, fiddling with the fraying edge of her jumper.

'And what was that?' Lauren gave the little girl a brief squeeze.

'I wanted Santa to make sure Cassy is with me next Christmas, but he said he couldn't promise,' her bottom lip started wobbling. 'If Cassy isn't here ... who's going to look after me?'

Cass's tears were sudden, loud and noisy, her cry like an explosion that she desperately tried to muffle, her hands over her face to hide it. She immediately tried to compose herself, struggling to breathe as she snuffled and snorted into her hands.

Lauren looked down at Vee, who stared up at her in shock. 'I made her cry.'

'It's okay,' she cuddled her, trying to make her voice soothing, when really, she quite wanted to cry as well, 'adults get upset too sometimes.'

Vee jumped off her lap and ran over to Cass, struggling to hug her as she curled in on herself, shuddering as she tried to breathe.

'I'm sorry, Cassy ... Mummy, I'm sorry.' Vee stroked her mother's hair like she was a distressed pet, and looked at Lauren in anguish before reaching for her new husky toy. 'You can have Storm? Storm will look after you and keep you safe. Cassy, don't cry.'

Cass's breathing slowed and she opened an arm to let her daughter into her embrace. Vee still held the fluffy toy and held it up in offering. Cass rested her head on her daughter's, eyes still closed as she tried to breathe.

'I'm sorry, sweetheart, I didn't mean to scare you. Everything's fine.' She took a few more breaths, rocking side to side a little as she rubbed her cheek against Vee's. She wiped her cheeks as she pulled back, extricating herself so she could kneel down in front of her daughter.

'I'm sorry I can't stay. You know if I could, I would stay here with you all the days of your life. I don't want to miss any of your adventures. I want to see every part of your wonderful life,' she stroked Vee's cheek with her thumb. 'But you have to know you will be well looked after by people who love you. I would never let you be alone, you know? I would never let you be lonely or scared.'

Vee's little face was brave as she looked down at her husky toy, stroking the soft fur.

'You believe me, don't you, Vee? You know I'd never lie to you?'

Her daughter nodded, and Cass rewarded her with a kiss on the cheek.

'So, if you don't have to worry about being looked after, do you still care about having a dad?'

Vee shrugged with one shoulder. 'I don't know. Samira says her dad sits on the sofa and yells at the TV, and Jess says her dad farts all the time.'

Cass shared a look of amusement with Lauren. 'Well then, you see? You have so many people who love you, you don't need a big fart monster, do you?'

Vee paused. '... No.'

'And Lee has his two mummies, doesn't he? And Nathan has his daddy and his nana, and Elise is raised by her grandparents, isn't she?' Cass continued, desperation suddenly ringing in her voice. 'And I never had a daddy, and I turned out okay.'

Vee nodded, but there was some niggling doubt hanging around behind her eyes, as if she wanted to be told a happy ending to a story that probably didn't have one.

'But ... I have a daddy?'

Cass closed her eyes in defeat. 'I don't know how to talk to you about this, baby girl. He ... he wasn't a very nice man. He wasn't an evil, bad man, but he wasn't someone who would be a good daddy.'

Lauren shifted in her chair, feeling suddenly overwhelmed. *Darren*. Darren knew she'd existed and never cared enough to do anything about it. Darren, who made up part of her, who had helped create her.

'But he gave me you, which was very nice of him, really, wasn't it?' Cass smiled, nudging her daughter.

'But ...'

Cass sighed and held up a hand. 'Okay, look, I'm gonna make a deal with you. Or rather, your Auntie Loll is going to make a deal. When you get to eighteen, if you still really want to meet your dad, Loll will make it happen, okay?' She looked at Lauren with a peculiar kind of apology in her eyes. 'Right?'

Lauren nodded, 'Sure, okay.'

God, what had she promised now? That her life would be forever tied to Darren's, just like it was to Cass's? She'd always be between them, even when Cass was gone. Her and Veronica, stuck in the middle. At least she wasn't alone anymore.

Vee looked satisfied at last and smiled, sighing deeply so that all the tension seemed to run out of her little arms. Her eyes flitted beyond the adults to the front of the lodge, and she pointed. 'Woah. Rory-Bory-Alice.'

They shuffled to the bed at the front of the lodge, lying back and looking up. Veronica was squidged in the middle, wriggling to accommodate Storm, who had become a regular member of the family, it seemed.

'Woah,' Lauren said, watching as the colours in the sky seemed to fizz with life and vibrancy.

'Woah,' Vee repeated, her eyes huge and desperate to take it all in.

'Yeah,' Cass whispered, looking at her daughter. 'Woah.'

*

Lauren woke suddenly, a sharp pain in her neck making her gasp. The Northern Lights still hovered in the sky and she looked to her left to find Vee and Cass still in her bed. Cass looked up from her sleeping daughter, splayed at odd angles between them, and smiled.

'Hi,' she whispered, stroking Vee's hair.

'Hi.'

Lauren shuffled, suddenly uncomfortable. All those years of sharing a bed, sharing mascara and cans of cider and everything else seemed very far away.

'I'm sorry I sucked you in to the promise about you-know-who,' Cass whispered.

'Did you mean it? After everything, you'd let him near her?'

'If she still wants that then, let her. Eighteen is old enough to be disappointed. I wish I'd known my father, even if he was a bastard. I would have liked the opportunity to decide that for myself.'

Lauren thought of her own father, his softly spoken words and warm hugs. His love language was food, a generational hangover from her *abuela*. When Lauren had been lost, or sad, or overwhelmed, her dad had been there, offering her *tortilla*, or Padrón peppers, or chunks of watermelon.

'It'll will all be okay in the end, *Ardillita,* if it's not, then it's not over yet,' he used to say, ruffling her hair.

It was hard to imagine Darren being like that with a child. As much as she'd wished for it during their marriage, tried to convince herself it was possible, there was a blank space in her mind.

'Maybe he'll be different by then anyway.' Lauren shuffled closer, turning on her side.

Cass snorted gently. 'You don't change, do you, Loll? Always believing the best in people. That's good, though. I hope Vee's like that too. You get hurt more, but it makes you a better person.'

'By the time she reaches eighteen, she won't be bothered anymore. She'll have learnt how people can be,' Lauren offered.

'Maybe. But it should be her choice. I can't protect her.'

They sat in silence for a while, looking at the sleeping girl between them, how she stuck out her bottom lip in exhaustion, the stuffed toy grasped in a tightly clenched fist.

'How did he react when you told him?' Lauren asked. Yes, it was so long ago it barely mattered, but somehow it still mattered to her.

'I didn't, really,' Cass sighed, eyes on Vee as if worried she might wake. 'I sent you a letter, telling you. Apologising to *you*.' She tried to sidestep it as quickly as she could. 'Nothing came, not for a while. I just thought you were mad and didn't want to know.

'A few weeks later he calls me and says you two have talked it over and you want me to ... get rid of it.'

Lauren blinked. 'I never got a letter.'

'Well yeah, I know that now,' Cass snorted. 'So anyway, I packed my bags, sold Mum's house, decided I had always wanted to live near the seaside, and off I went.'

Lauren tried to find a way to ask the question, almost feeling guilty as she looked at the beautiful child lying there.

'And you didn't think ... you didn't ... I mean you weren't very maternal. You didn't want kids, so why ...?'

'Why did I go through with it when anyone could have told you I was incredibly selfish and would make a terrible mother?' Cass smiled to herself. 'I know, I thought the same thing. And the truth is, my reasons were selfish.'

'You wanted someone? You were on your own after your mum?' Lauren tried to imagine what it was like to be Cass back then, broken and grieving for her mother, without any friends, realising she was pregnant. She'd been a mess during that time, a drunken screaming banshee half the time, a malevolent spirit the rest. Her life was garbage, everyone else had everything worked out, nothing was good enough, no one cared. The few people she'd strung along over the years, suddenly seeing her without the charm, dropped her. People stopped returning her texts or calls. Even the bartenders in her favourite pubs wouldn't serve her anymore, knowing how much abuse they'd be subjected to if she turned on them again.

Lauren had spent so many nights picking Cass up from bars, trying to look after her, finding her passed out in club toilets. But she was doing her post-grad, and exams had started and everything got that bit harder. Trying to love Cass whilst she hissed insults and drunken comments became too difficult. The voice in her head that always told her she was worthless had started to sound like Cass.

She was a genius at a well-timed barb – she knew how to hit you at your weakest point. It was instinct. She spat poison back then and hit the mark every time.

'It's a shame,' Cass said suddenly, looking at her daughter with so much love that Lauren felt an ache in her chest. 'You were just starting to like me again, and now I have to tell you something that'll make you judge me.'

Then why tell me? Lauren thought desperately, wanting to hold on to this moment of quiet underneath a memorable sky. This journey was about healing, not about breaking things further.

'The BRCA gene, I knew I had it when Mum died. Towards the end when she was cruel and angry and out of her mind on painkillers, she said I'd know how she felt, that it was a curse she'd passed on to me.' Cass tried to shrug it off. 'I was so terrified of dying back then, Loll, you have no idea. I was sad about Mum and I felt lonely, but more than anything I was scared of dying the way she did – early, and angry and bitter that she had to leave.'

'You don't feel like that now?'

'I haven't reached that point yet, but I'm hoping this will help' – she gestured around her – 'this trip, getting this time with Vee, with you. Getting to feel like I'm doing and seeing things I always wanted to. Seeing my Uncle Jack again too. I want to feel like I'm going out on a high, rather than wasting away and becoming invisible.'

Lauren nodded, impressed by her attitude.

'I know I've been unkind and cranky, I'm trying not to be,' Cass said.

'You get a few passes. Besides, I haven't been great either. We're learning how to be with each other again,' Lauren replied, then paused. 'Why would any of that make me judge you?'

'You know two of the things that can limit the risk of cancer when you have that gene?' Cass stroked Vee's hair gently, eyes roving her face for confirmation she was asleep. 'Pregnancy and breast-feeding.'

There was silence whilst Lauren tried to figure out what she was saying. And then suddenly, she understood.

Cassidy Jones never changed. She always did what was best for her.

'You had a child because you thought it would stop you dying?' Lauren hissed.

'See, I knew you'd be judgemental. Why do you think people *have* children, Loll? To stop themselves dying. To make sure their legacy lives on. To see themselves, but better, stronger, younger, full of possibility. To have someone to look after them in old age. I'm not subjecting Veronica to that, at least,' she snorted.

'That's not why people have children!' Lauren huffed.

'Because society tells them to, because of pressure from their mothers, because they hate their jobs? Because they love that other person so much they want to see their features shared?' Cass laughed gently, shaking her head. 'To trap someone in a relationship or a marriage? To get benefits or move up the housing ladder. There are more reasons than you'd think, Loll, and most of them are crap.'

'Well, okay then, if you're such an expert on the human condition, what are the good reasons?'

'There's only one,' Cass said, shaking her head. 'Because you want them so much it hurts not to have them.'

Lauren felt that recognition like a punch in the gut, and

almost physically recoiled. She rolled onto her back and stared up at the green and purple hues of the sky, not sure of what to say.

'I love her, Loll. You must see that,' Cass sighed. 'She's the most perfect thing I've ever done. The way things begin doesn't mean that's the way they end up.'

'Just like you and me,' Lauren said, unable to move, and yet unable to leave.

PART THREE

Spain

Chapter 13

Lauren hadn't spoken to Cass in approximately eighteen hours, if you included the ones where she was sleeping. It was easy enough to disguise her inner mess of emotions. She took pictures, pasted on a smile and focused all her energy on making that child feel so incredibly cherished.

She knew that perhaps she was being unfair. It wasn't clear whether she was angry, upset, sad for Vee or just plain jealous. Lauren thought that by the time the plane landed in Seville, she might have had a handle on her feelings, might have worked out how she felt, why she felt it, and would have a plan to move forward. Instead, she was stuck in stone. Cass had betrayed her friend, got knocked up by someone she hated, and it was worth it, if it kept her alive for a few more years. Like pregnancy was an anti-cancer pill.

Except, the other half of her heart argued, if that was the case, she could have given Vee away when she was a baby, and she hadn't. It was painful to think back to that time, where Cass was such a ball of destruction and Lauren was trying to bury her fear of that wave of anxiety that seemed to crash over her. They were both alone. Cass got a daughter,

Lauren had Darren, and that was how it worked out. Cass got the better deal.

Even whilst she was in a strop, Lauren managed everything to do with their travel. She found their luggage, directed them to the taxi rank, gave the name of the hotel. Even in her anger, she was efficient.

Her Spanish was rusty, but she tentatively chatted to the taxi driver, who seemed cheerfully impressed by her attempts. He offered gentle corrections to pronunciation, and asked why they were there. 'We always wanted to come,' she replied in Spanish, looking behind her to the two people in the back seat. Vee sat squashed in to her mother's side, pointing out of the window at all the things they saw. Cass was distracted, stroking her hair and barely replying. She was in pain today. The set of her jaw was different when she braced herself against pain. It almost changed her face completely.

The taxi driver, Manuel, dropped them off as close to their accommodation as possible, pointing down the narrow path with vibrant-blue patterned tiles against a yellow wall.

She tipped generously, and Manuel gave her his card. 'You need to get around, you call me, I'll look after you. Practise your Spanish! *Adiós.*' He wiggled his bushy eyebrows and jumped back into his cab.

'Getting chatted up?' Cass asked, trying for humour but sounding flat and tired.

'He looks like one of my uncles.' Lauren rolled her eyes, then waved the card. 'But we have a cab driver for the rest of our trip.'

She hoisted a bag over her shoulder then took hold of two

handles to wheel the cases behind her. Cass and Vee followed her, holding hands like trusting children trailing behind their mother.

The front of the hotel was subtle, a worn wooden sign swinging above the door that read *Casa de los Sueños*. Vee clapped, pointing.

'Dream house!' she laughed.

'God, your Spanish is probably better than mine,' Lauren smiled, before struggling to get through the door with all the bags. Inside, a huge reception area decorated in the traditional style, all vibrant colours and small tiles, made it look like the drawing room of a grand old villa. Huge plants stood in terracotta pots and through the back there was a large central garden with a water feature.

'Woah,' Vee said, looking up to the painting on the ceiling.

'*¡Buenas tardes, señoritas!*' an older lady, her greying hair tied back in a headscarf grinned at them, flinging her arms up, 'Welcome to *Casa de los Sueños*. I am Nuria Lopez, and this is my home.'

Lauren smiled, too embarrassed to try her Spanish again.

'*Buenas tardes, Nuria. ¡Soy Veronica!*' Vee grinned up at the lady, hands on her hips in a Wonder Woman pose. She awaited a pat on the head and congratulations on being such a smart girl. She was not disappointed.

'*¡Muy bien!*' Nuria clapped, smiling and hooting. 'Very impressive! You should meet my granddaughter, Isabel, she does not have much English. Be *amigas*, yes? Anyway, check in!'

Nuria clapped her hands, her strong, sturdy arms wobbling

a little with the movement. 'You have the apartment. Breakfast is on the rooftop bar, you are welcome to go up for drinks and tapas in the evenings. I give you a map?'

Lauren nodded, tentatively asking about a few of the local tourist spots in Spanish.

'*¿Ay, y tu? ¡Español!*' Nuria's voice had a range of tones that Lauren wasn't used to, high and squeaky, yet loud. It echoed sharply.

Lauren tried to explain her heritage, her father's Spanish roots, her English mother learning the language for him. Her *abuela*, the woman she adored and the world she'd left behind to come to England. It had been years since she had spoken Spanish beyond singing along to the odd song. Her language skills were a jumbled mess, long pauses and stutters, and she always felt like people were looking at her when she tried. But still, she had to try, because her *abuela* would have wanted her to.

Nuria smiled, looking behind to Cass with curiosity. Whether she was wondering about their relationship, or how suddenly grey and worn Cass looked, Lauren wasn't sure.

'Juan will take your bags for you,' Nuria nodded, before filling her lungs and yelling, 'Juan! *¡Ven aqui!*'

Lauren blinked in shock.

'My son,' Nuria rolled her eyes. 'Lazy, slow boy. But guests like him.'

As Juan rounded the corner, Lauren could see why. He looked like something from the front of a romance novel, chiselled arms and a strong jaw with designer stubble. His eyes hovered on Cass, who resolutely ignored him, her eyes returning to scan him when he wasn't looking. He nodded at Lauren and picked up their bags, loading them all up before setting off, tilting his head so that they would follow him.

She shared a look with Cass, so brief and yet completely understood. Half a smirk, the barest tilt of an eyebrow. A look they had shared a hundred times before when a cute boy had walked into the student union. For a moment, everything was fixed.

The apartment had a beautiful view over the skyline of Seville, and in the distance they could make out the cathedral, casting a shadow and demanding attention.

'What now?' Vee clapped her hands. 'I'm going to order food in the restaurant, Sandy told me what to say.'

'*Sandy* speaks Spanish? That's who's been teaching you?' Lauren wandered back in from dumping her bag in her bedroom. After sharing the lodge, she suddenly felt so far away from the two of them. Separate, and on the outside once more.

'Sandy lived in Spain for about fifteen years. Her husband was a Spaniard. Madrid, I think.' Cass shuffled back on the bed, the life seeming to drain out of her the more horizontal she got. 'She only came back when he died. Didn't want to look at the places she loved and miss him.'

Lauren suddenly felt bad, like she should have been gentler with the older woman. Even if she was a charlatan on the beachfront with her crystal ball and incense sticks.

'Give her a chance, you'll like her. She's ballsy,' Cass said, as if reading her mind.

'Cassy, are you going to sleep?' Vee asked, brow furrowed

in concern as she climbed up onto the bed and rested a hand on her mother's forehead. 'You warm?'

Cass caught her hand and placed a gentle kiss on it. 'I'm just tired, pumpkin, it's been a long couple of days. Lots of adventure. Why don't you and Loll go explore a bit?'

The little girl looked put out, and Lauren couldn't help but feel rejected as Vee shook her head. 'No, I want all of us to go. Together.' She reached for the ukulele and shuffled back into the space next to Cass, who placed her hand on her daughter's ankle before closing her eyes.

Lauren, so suddenly dismissed, walked back into her bedroom and lay on the bed, eyes open, staring at the ceiling and wondering what to do. She checked her phone, to find there had been no calls from Darren.

That sparked a peculiar disappointment. It had to be that she missed having the opportunity to reject and annoy him, rather than being lonely. But really, what had changed? She had traded one person for another. At least with Cass, came Vee. Vee who would rather sit in a hotel room than explore Spain alone with her.

It seemed she would always be in the shadow of Cassidy Jones, no matter what stage of her life she was in. Except she was Vee's mother, and she was dying. She could almost hear Cass's voice. *It's not always about you, Loll, sometimes people have their own shit going on.*

Nodding in response to the imaginary voice, Lauren jumped up, splashed some water on her face, adjusted her ponytail and left the apartment, closing the door gently behind her. If she was going to spend some time thinking, she may as well do it with a drink in her hand and an excellent view.

The rooftop bar was everything she'd hoped for – comfy seats, a great vantage point over the city to sigh over, and no one else around. Nuria was cleaning glasses over by the bar, holding them up to the light with the ferociousness of someone who didn't settle for less than perfection.

'Oh!' her face changed to a wide smile. 'A drink? Sangria, yes?'

Lauren shrugged, then nodded, thanking her.

Sangria brought back memories of the original Veronica, her grandmother. She'd been a wild woman, liable to kiss you as well as smack you. She had a big laugh, Lauren remembered, and her solemn face would bloom when she saw someone she knew. At the weekends in the summer, there were family barbecues, huge parties with cousins and second cousins. Her dad always tried his best, but was too formal, too quiet. Lauren, back then at least, had been chatty, seamlessly fitting in with these other dark-haired kids who munched on cake and ran around causing trouble. There had always been sangria, a non-alcoholic version on the kids' table to match the adults'. When she reached sixteen, her grandmother took her aside, a leathery hand on hers, to tell her the recipe. 'Great sangria is not just measurements,' she'd said, 'it's art.'

Her *abuela*'s sangria was deadly – two cups and you'd be out of it the next morning, wondering what the hell happened.

Nuria brought over a jug and two glasses, setting them

down on the table. Lauren was about to mention that Cass wasn't joining her, but the older woman sat down. Oh. Apparently she had company. Well, that was what she'd wanted, wasn't it?

'Your friend, she is sick?' Nuria poured the drinks, then held her glass up. '*Salud.*'

Lauren sipped, the flavours creating a wave of nostalgia that crashed down over her, with just the slightest disappointment – not quite the same as *Abuela*'s, and she couldn't remember the recipe.

It was gone, just like all the other things you really wished you'd paid attention to at the time.

'Yes, she's sick.'

'She doesn't have long?'

Lauren simply shook her head, 'I don't think so, no. We're ... we're making memories. For her daughter.' *For us too.*

Nuria nodded. 'I know this. Me and my husband, we raise my granddaughter. My daughter, her husband, both die in a car crash.'

'I'm so sorry.'

Lauren traced the woman's face for signs of despair or brokenness, but there were none. Only sadness and acceptance.

'It must be hard work.'

It wasn't what she meant, not really. She meant it must be awful to look at their granddaughter every day and see their lost child. It must be a sharp knife to the heart every birthday or Christmas or school play. Every time little Isabel would look up and think that she should have been seeing her parents.

Oh God, would Vee have that for the rest of her life? The feeling like every special event was only half a moment?

'No, the hotel is hard work. Bossing around my lazy son, that is hard work. Raising a child ... is an honour.'

They sat quietly for a moment. 'You will look after the girl, when your friend is gone?' Nuria continued.

Lauren had been wondering that herself. To ask would make her seem eager, like it was something she wanted. She felt guilty even thinking about it. Cass would see the desperation in her eyes. That ache to be a mother. It was too much to hope that she might be the best thing for Vee. How could she be, when she was really just an anxious young woman in the middle of a messy divorce with Veronica's biological father? She was weak, emotional, incapable. Maybe Sandy was the better choice. But oh, how she loved her already, in that same way that she'd loved Cass – she wanted to take care of her and make her safe and stop all the destruction.

'I don't know. She hasn't said.'

'If you do, you get used to being second to a ghost. Every time you yell, her mama would have been kind. You cry, her mama would have been strong. You do everything right, and she loves you? She still wants her.'

'I've been used to that all my life, actually,' Lauren laughed, gulping down the sangria a little too quickly.

'Some people sparkle,' Nuria shrugged, 'the rest of us are cleaning up when they finish shaking glitter on the floor.'

Lauren snorted again, lifting up her glass to toast the truth of it.

'You want to make your time here special, yes? Let me help. I tell you how to make memories.'

They sat there for another half an hour, trading stories. Lauren talked about her grandmother, her kindness and strength, how inspirational she'd been. Of the business she'd started in her home town, organising the young women to form a sort of union, exporting their embroidery to the Mediterranean. When she left for England, she had left them clear instructions: always be kind but don't be a fool. Lauren had loved to hear that as a child – that her *abuela*, at nineteen, had organised a business, helping women support themselves, and had negotiated with buyers and tourists and anyone else she had to in order to get them paid.

Lauren was so sure she would do amazing things too. Her father said her grandmother was called 'the terrier' in her town. Once she got her teeth into something, she never let go. She was the same right into her eighties. Organising days out for her group of friends, getting a sneaky discount on the side. She'd died after a night of dancing, a glass of port by her chair and a smile on her face.

Classy even in death.

Lauren told Nuria all of this, wrapping the stories around her like a patchwork quilt, snuggling down in their familiarity. She hadn't had anyone to tell in a long time.

'She was called Veronica?' Nuria asked. 'Like the little one?'

Lauren nodded. 'Coincidence.'

Nuria didn't look so sure. 'Your friend, she is a strange one.'

'She is. But she's also a bit magic.' Lauren felt better for her loyalty. The sunshine washed the streets in an orange-gold hue and she didn't want to close her eyes for fear it would be dark again, and the day would have gone.

It was nice to know she could talk to people, she could look after herself and be interesting enough alone. She didn't need to be anyone's sidekick.

Years ago this would have felt impossible, sitting chatting to a stranger, not wondering what they thought of her or how she might screw it up. She attributed it to being around Cass – growing sassy and strong again, the way she'd been before, when she had her by her side. Remembering that you could say what you felt, when you felt it, and the world wouldn't end.

'Tonight, you go to the flamenco. Find the magic. I make it happen for you.' Nuria patted her hand as she stood up, 'You need to live too.'

It was a strange thing to say, Lauren thought as she sipped the dregs of her sangria. They had finished the jug between them, gradually, barely noticeable, but time had passed and she had been allowed to air the memories of her grandmother, her mother and her uncles, their loud brashness and silly stories. She needed to live too. What a strange thought.

So many years had passed just plodding by, it was almost impossible to think. They had celebrated birthdays, and New Years, and Christmases and anniversaries. They had noted time moving on just like everyone else. But heartbeats keep better time than clocks ever could.

And the last time Lauren felt alive was at nineteen years old, holding Cass's hand as they danced wildly into the early hours. When Cass squeezed her hand and grinned and screamed that she was beautiful.

Everything else was just pretty packaging and good intentions. She hadn't been alive for a very long time.

*

Lauren took time getting ready that night. She wasn't *competing* exactly, but it felt important to start making an effort again. Sure, all her clothes were still muted colours, but speaking a language she hadn't used in years had awakened something. Given her access to a different part of her.

Her father always joked that people had different personalities in different languages. He said when Lauren's mother had spoken Spanish properly for the first time all those years ago, her temperament was different to her inherent Britishness. The way certain languages made your lips move, it was impossible to fight it.

Lauren felt it in herself, a kind of sassiness in the way she rolled her tongue, or moved her hands. It was like remembering a dance, you had to be confident even when you were fudging the steps. She wore a black wrap dress and took the time to curl her hair, outlining her eyes in black liner to draw attention to how dark they were. She looked 'the part' as far as she was concerned, and when she looked in the mirror, she dared to smile at her reflection – she looked pretty. She would never turn heads or stop traffic, but she didn't always have to be in the shadows.

Cass made an effort too, reinvigorated by her afternoon

siesta. There was more colour in her cheeks, and when Lauren had returned, throwing a cereal bar onto the bed, she'd eaten it with enthusiasm and a smile on her face.

Cass wore colours like they couldn't clash. Her pale pink top was starting to hang off her, but she ignored it, pinning it along with the waistband of her royal blue trousers. Her ballet pumps were green with gold spots. Somehow, though, Lauren didn't feel drab in comparison; she felt like a counterbalance. An equal opposite. They needed to be on either side of the spectrum to keep everything working.

Vee wore her rainbow dress, the vertical stripes rippling as the skirt swirled out around her. She was her mother's daughter – this child would never be forgotten, ignored or overlooked. She wouldn't stand for it.

They were just heading out when the computer buzzed with an incoming video call.

'Hello!' The screen blinked into life, a frozen bunch of fuzzy figures with a cream background. 'Hello, can you see us?'

'Who is that? Paul?'

'Yes, we're here, hold on!' a different voice called out from the speakers as the three of them peered into the screen in interest.

The image suddenly flashed to life and there was a group staring back at them: Paul, Sandy and Barry, along with Justine and Nadia.

'Are you in the pub?' Cass asked, squinting at the background.

'They changed the bloody day, can you believe it?' Barry huffed. 'Trying to stop us winning, that's what it is! Getting rid of the competition!'

'Luckily we found out just in time,' Sandy said, getting closer to the screen, her sharp features assessing them. 'How are you? Is everything okay? No bust-ups yet?'

'Everyone still has all their limbs,' Cass snorted. 'It's so good to see you all!'

'You guys are all dressed up, looking lovely,' Paul said with a wide smile, but was greeted with a glare from Veronica.

'I don't want to do homework now – we're going for dinner and *I'm* going to have tapas,' Vee announced with a sense of importance, looking at Paul as if she expected him to complain. He held up his hands.

'I would not let spellings get in the way of tapas. Have some *patatas bravas* for me.'

Vee nodded without knowing what he was talking about, in the hopes that it would speed things up.

'Send us a postcard, girls, we miss you.' Barry clutched his cap in his hands, looking mournfully into the camera. 'Now bugger off because we'll get disqualified for using technological whoosamiwhotsits.'

'Charming!' Cass laughed. 'You called us!'

'Short and sweet, darlin',' he grinned. 'See you soon.'

As quickly as they appeared, they were gone.

'You've got some good people,' Lauren said as they headed down the stairs. She kept an eye on Cass, who had been a little unsteady with stairs of late, her legs a little weaker than they used to be. She managed fine, half an eyebrow raised in annoyance at her own slower pace, and Lauren's eyes tracing her every move.

'Even if they're a little overprotective at times.'

Lauren stepped back, taking the hint.

Nuria greeted them at the desk, smiling widely, arms outspread. 'Look at you! Beautiful! So beautiful!' She came out to walk them to the door, Vee twirling to make her skirt swirl around her.

She gave them directions to the flamenco bar, promising them a night that would show them the truth of love and passion. 'But not you,' she said to Vee, who grinned, 'for you it is just pretty dancing.'

As they left, Lauren felt the eyes of Nuria's son, Juan, watching them. But not her, of course. Cass. He watched her with the smirking interest of a twenty-something who didn't have to worry about being rejected. But Cass didn't look back. The only way Lauren knew she was aware was the flick of her head as she shook out her hair. The straightness of her back as she took Vee's hand and walked out of the door, hips swinging.

The streets were narrow and cobbled, each building seeming to lean on the next as they followed Nuria's instructions to the flamenco bar. They slipped in, Lauren explaining in Spanish that Nuria had sent them. The staff treated them like honoured guests, leading them further in to the cavernous building, the columns and tile work offering as much beauty as the stage. A band was set up at the back of the stage, and they were taken to a small, round table in the crowd.

In whispers, the staff said they'd bring a little of everything to try, as Nuria had recommended. Lauren, for once, enjoyed not being in control, letting someone else who knew better take care of them. Wine was brought over, juice for Vee, and the tasting began.

The music played in the background, the skiddle of fingers upon strings, plucked and strummed in a heavy rhythm. Warm and steady like a heartbeat, with the trills of nerves and excitement overlaying it.

The dancers took centre stage and there was a voracity, a heavy desire that thrummed in the movements of their legs, the stamping of their feet. The woman was beautiful, and not only in the colours and spots and frills of her dress. It was her strength. The way she held her arms, the sharpness of her castanets and the clack of her heels. Her gaze, too, was intense, a look of determination that bordered on hatred. Lauren wondered if this was what love was. Passion and craziness, a lack of control.

Cass, most likely, would say yes. She was staring at the stage, her look of wonder matching her daughter's. Her concept of love had always been about power, who was in control, the follower and the leader, like the dance. Of course, Cass would love this. For Lauren, although it was beautiful, a connection to a culture she had almost forgotten, it felt ... wrong. Love should be comfortable and kind, easy. Yet, really, what would she know? She had done anything for an easy life, and here she was. Maybe flamenco had a lesson to teach her.

The man joined the dance, offering a counterbalance to the woman. His strength rivalled hers, but didn't dominate. When one pushed, the other pulled. They took turns in the spotlight, each circling the other, letting them lead the way.

It made Lauren think of Darren on the day of her graduation.

He had bought her an expensive bracelet, but he was sure to tell everyone around them how much it cost, and how he could afford that because he *didn't* go to university. It was her day, and somehow he had managed to belittle her, to make it about him. Her mother had been *thrilled.* Lauren had shaken it off, so sure she was being overly sensitive, that it was selfish to resent a gift given on a special day. Only Cass gave her a look like she wasn't impressed.

She'd been the only person who thought Lauren could do better. Why hadn't she heard it at the time?

Now, the signs were obvious. A handsome, charming man had somehow chosen someone quiet and meek, who would do everything she could to avoid an argument. *Keep your head down, just get on with it, don't expect too much.*

Those were her mother's words, and as much as she'd railed against them, spitting venom when they were said, apparently she had fallen in to living by them. Somewhere along the line, she'd stopped fighting. The moment she lost Cass, or just before. *Expect less, be happy.*

The applause rang out as they stamped their feet in time, getting faster and more intense as their arms echoed their movements. The woman's red dress swung around her, the red flower vibrant against her black hair. *I want to look like that. Like I'm powerful*. The thought was gone as soon as it appeared, a whisper amongst the rhythm of the guitar.

'I'll be back,' she mouthed to Cass, escaping amongst the cheers and whoops of the crowd, out into the street. She pulled out her phone and scrolled down to that number.

He answered immediately, surprise evident in his voice.

'Lauren?'

'Why did you choose me?' she asked, surprised by how her voice stayed steady. 'All those years ago, why did you choose me? I was so grateful, I didn't think to question it.'

'I thought you'd make a good wife,' Darren said after a pause. 'I knew you'd support my career, and look after me, and put me first. We may not have been crazy all-over-each-other but it was the smart choice, for my future. For both our futures.'

Oh God, he chose me like part of his investment portfolio. All those words, they just confirmed what she'd always known – she was boring, bland and straightforward. She was the smart choice. She was never desired, never wanted that way. He'd never loved her so much that he thought he'd die if she wasn't there. It was a business arrangement without the money.

'And you were, Lauren, you were an excellent wife. You did a great job. But I just ... I see now that isn't how you're meant to pick a person.'

She wasn't sure if this pain in her stomach was worse than the affair, or the new engagement. It didn't really rival the pain she felt over Cass and all those years she'd wasted. She wanted to say it was because of him, but it wasn't. It was because of herself. Darren hadn't wanted Cass, he'd wanted her. So that made him the best person in the world. Even if he wasn't.

'Did you ... did you ever really love me?' God, she hated herself for being weak. For twisting the knife.

He paused. 'Oh, Lauren, come on. Don't do this.'

She closed her eyes. 'No, I need to hear it. Do it, tell the truth.'

'Now I know, now I've met someone and know what it feels like, what it should feel like ... no, I never loved you.'

'So you stood there on our wedding day and just thought, *fuck it, she'll do*?' Lauren laughed, suddenly hoarse.

'No, I cared about you ... look, I can't go through all this again, okay? I'm getting married and I'm going to do it right this time. Let's not pretend you were head over heels. I was just the one man who didn't want to shag your best mate over you. It's not my fault she made you feel like shit.'

Lauren felt her stomach clench in anger. 'And yet ... here we are. You made me believe ...'

'You made that choice, Lauren. You chose your boyfriend over your friend.'

God, when he decided to tell the truth, he really went for it. It was so exhausting to hate him, to nurture that shock and distrust. She blamed him more than Cass, and she knew that wasn't fair. The betrayals weren't equal – losing Cass, losing the concept of Cass, the one person who knew who she really was. That was worse. And yet, he had lied when she had told the truth. That had to count for something.

'So how are those divorce papers coming along?' She tried for a friendly, upbeat tone, but her voice rang like a death knell. She could hear it, that sense of helplessness.

'Wasn't sure where to send them.'

'I'll email you the address.' She snorted to herself – he could enjoy the postage costs to Australia.

'Where are you now?' Darren asked, and she was honestly surprised he was interested.

'Spain.'

'Seeing family?'

She shook her head, even though he couldn't see, 'Making family.'

Chapter 14

'That was 'mazing, wasn't it 'mazing?' Vee said, so sleepy she wobbled against them, each adult holding a hand.

'Yes, yes it was. I think we need to get Aunt Loll wearing some of those polka dots and bright colours, get her out of her funk.' Cass was back to being herself, it seemed, perked up by sleep and a good show. Her cheeks were flushed and there was something behind her eyes that looked like a scheme. Lauren recognised that look.

'What are you up to?'

'Updating your fashion sense, darling,' Cass winked. 'Nothing wrong with that, is there?'

Lauren shrugged, relieved that Vee was too tired to jump on the bandwagon.

When they reached the hotel, Nuria was gone, her son sitting behind the reception desk in her place, a bored look on his face as he scrolled through his phone.

'*Buenas noches*,' he called out to them as they walked up the stairs. Cass didn't turn around, leaving Lauren to nod awkwardly back at him.

Vee conked out in her bed, they sat having a drink on the

sofa, some of the wine Nuria had left in the room for them.

'You still angry at me? For having her?' Cass asked, carefully stretching out her legs and sighing.

'I'm not angry about that, that's not what ...' Lauren shook her head. 'I'm just angry, okay? I'm angry about everything. You and me, and her, and him and everything.'

'Do you think maybe you're angry about the wrong things?'

Lauren rolled her eyes. 'I think I'm making up for years of not being able to be angry because you weren't there. You're the only person who lets me be angry.'

'Yeah, sorry I wasn't there, kinda busy raising a child, trying to stay alive.' Cass stuck out her tongue.

'Some days there's no point us talking.'

Cass laughed. 'Well, your *some* days are going to be *all* days soon enough. May as well talk to me whilst I'm still around.'

'Oh, don't use the dying card, you're better than that.'

'Exploiting what I have to get what I want, no matter how emotionally manipulative? It's like you don't even know me,' Cass laughed, sticking her tongue out like a child.

Before she could stop herself, Lauren laughed. It escaped like a bubble, popping when it hit the air.

'You know, one of the hundred things I'm angry about is that I treated life like it didn't matter if I threw it away. I settled and plodded and didn't wait for the big stuff. I pretended and made it look like a life.'

'Everyone does,' Cass said, downing the last of her wine.

'You don't. You didn't.'

'No, I did the opposite. I destroyed it.'

'No, you didn't, Cass. You took something selfish and you made it selfless.' Lauren downed the last of her wine and stood up, more than ready to sleep. Cass evidently wasn't ready for that. 'I'm sorry I keep being awful. I just ... I want to yell at everyone, and you're unlucky enough to be here.'

'Hey, I deserve it. And if we've worked through your years of unexpressed rage by the end of this trip, I will crown myself a miracle worker.' Cass smiled with such affection that Loll's chest hurt a little.

'Do you remember when we went on that roller-coaster when we bunked off lectures? That day when you panicked and wanted to be let off?'

'And you came with me, even though you really wanted to go on it?' Lauren replied, struggling to follow the conversation.

'Yeah.'

Cass's eyes were focused on the wall. 'I've been dreaming about that lately. Over and over. Sometimes I make you stay on, and once it starts, we zoom through the air holding hands and you laugh, so happy that you took a risk. Maybe I should have pushed you. That's what I always used to do.'

'I'm glad you didn't. I felt like I was going to die,' Lauren said, then winced. *Bad choice of words.*

'The last few days it's changed, the dream. We're still on the roller-coaster, but you get out and I carry on alone.' Cass took a shuddering breath, shaking her head. 'There's no laughter in that one, just darkness as the track goes into a tunnel.'

'And then what happens?'

'Nothing. Nothing happens. And it's terrifying.'

Lauren sat down again, trying to find something comforting to say. Trying to find a way to tell her that everything would be all right, the same way she had done for her for all those years. But she'd be lying. And Cass had never lied.

'I'm here, Cass. You're not alone. I'm not getting off the ride.' She put her hand on Cass's, feeling the tendons and bone. Still as pale as ever, her dark nail varnish chipped. She pressed her thumb into the centre of Cass's palm.

'It's not the same. I know it's my fault. I broke it and it won't ever be the same.' She sounded like Veronica, a sad child with a broken toy, her words slurring ever so slightly.

Lauren was taken back to those times that she cried in Cass's lap whilst she stroked her hair. A bad grade that wasn't so bad, a boy who snubbed her, a cutting remark from her mother. All those things that felt like the end of the world, but didn't matter at all. Cass had been there. All of that wasn't undone because of what came later. One moment didn't destroy a history. But it changed it.

'Maybe it doesn't have to be the same,' Lauren said gently. 'Maybe it can be something new.'

Cass nodded, head lowered, but said nothing. It was too late for all that.

Lauren felt gravity pressing down on her, until it was hard to stand straight. The wine had flooded her fingertips and made her fuzzy.

There had been too much thinking and talking and breathing. Something about the primal looks on the faces of the flamenco dancers had disturbed her. It had made her feel uneasy. Add to that Cass's regret and Darren's lack thereof, well, she was exhausted. She was stuck between these two people who had claimed to love her. She was left hoping that at least one of them was telling the truth.

'What about Darren?'

'What about him?' Lauren shrugged, wanting to push the idea of him away, cauterise the wound so it couldn't keep bleeding. 'He's an arsehole. He's a liar.'

'Terribly good timing, babe,' Cass said, and she turned back to look at her. Cass's eyes were unyielding, as if she refused to look away, refused to lose whatever challenge she'd set herself.

'What is?'

'Making me into a martyr before I die.'

*

The next morning, she awoke to the sound of singing. Vee's to be precise. Her sweet little voice was tremulous but determined as she plucked at her ukulele. She was singing 'You Are My Sunshine' and Lauren's heart expanded even before she entered the room.

'Knock knock,' she said, tapping the door with her knuckles. 'Do you need another audience member?'

She peered around and saw Cass still lying in bed, lounging with a small smile.

'You okay?'

She nodded but her smile was strained.

'Need painkillers?'

'Taken them,' she said, 'but I could kill for some breakfast.'

'Ooh, I want some breakfast, I want some breakfast ...' Vee sang along to the same tune, 'it makes me happy, in my belly. You'll never know, dear, how I love breakfast, so don't take my breakfast away.'

The adults clapped and whooped, and as Lauren was about to return to her room to get dressed, her phone buzzed.

'Oh, we've got a lesson with Paul in ten minutes! I forgot! Some organiser I am. I mean, he trusted me to be responsible for this and I—'

Cass rolled her eyes. 'Chill, would you? You can't panic about *everything*. Paul won't mind, no one cares, people forget stuff. Relax.'

Her voice was sharp and irritated, like there was no place for this version of Lauren. She needed her to be better than that. Needed her not to be a boring worrier who overthought everything.

'Look, I'll sort out the munchkin and get everything set up. You go get us some breakfast from the buffet and bring it back,' Cass raised an eyebrow like she was expecting an argument. 'No stress, no worry, just everyone working together to make sure this little noggin is educated.'

She pretended to knock on Vee's head. 'Don't want this staying empty, do we? Need to fill it with all sorts of equations and learny stuff.'

As she walked down the corridor to the lift, Lauren wondered if she would have made a bad mum if everything had worked out as she'd planned. Being scared and worried all the time was exhausting enough when it was just about you. Having the fear of damaging someone else, being responsible for their pain and unhappiness? It was almost unfathomable how much that might have destroyed her. How she'd spiral under the pressure. She'd barely been able to manage her studies without destroying herself.

By the time she returned to the room, struggling to carry a tray piled high with fruit, yoghurt, croissants, cheese, ham and toast, the lesson was in session.

'Here she is!' Paul's voice rang out warmly through the speaker, and she put down the food so she could wave at the screen.

'Went on a run for sustenance,' she said, watching as Cass ripped a croissant in half and stuffed it into her mouth, sighing with relief.

'I hear you forgot about me this morning – I'm hurt!' Paul's voice was cheerful, but Lauren looked to Cass in betrayal.

'Oh, don't worry, darling, no matter how hurt you are, it won't compare to Loll's pain. She'll hold onto this moment for *years*, telling herself how awful she is. Until she can be distracted by something else to worry about.'

No one knew what to say after that, so Lauren excused herself to have her breakfast out on the balcony, pretending not to be upset. She wished she'd brought a book. Instead she was stuck sitting with her feelings, when she couldn't trust her brain to not drag the darkest thoughts in her arsenal out into the light. It wasn't fun.

When the lesson was over, and she ventured back in, Paul tried to catch her attention, asking her about the trip, what her favourite bits had been, what they were planning that day. Like trying to get answers from a child, he offered her too much gentleness – he pitied her, she could tell. Another man blinded by the sun from Cass's smile, putting up with her along the way.

She cut him short, explaining they had to get on, and he probably had classes of his own to get back to. Paul recoiled, just a little, those light eyes showing surprise before he covered it.

'Okay, well, I'll talk to you guys in a little while, and I'll send over some more homework. It's a good thing Veronica is so brainy or we'd have to do more sessions.'

'Who knows where she gets that from,' Lauren said, thinking of Darren. Paul frowned at her, and she shrugged. *Right. Don't insult the dying woman.*

He signed off, and Vee looked up at her. 'We can go have adventures now, right?'

Lauren nodded. 'Let's go see if your mum's ready.'

When they walked into the bedroom, Cass was back in bed. She stretched and rolled, looking at them.

'I'm not feeling so great anymore,' she said. 'Why don't you go on without me today? I'll get my rest and be ready for this evening.'

'But ...' Vee blinked at her, 'you'll miss stuff.'

'You go find the best places and then you can show me them tomorrow. Sometimes I'm going to need to rest on this trip, baby, I'm sorry. It's just how it is.'

The look of abject disappointment on the little girl's face almost broke Lauren's heart.

'And you,' Cass looked at her. 'No panicking. You can look after her, she's fine. Nothing's going to happen.'

'You'll call us if you feel worse and we need to go to hospital? I've got the name of the recommended doctor and it won't take long if you want to get checked—'

'How is that not panicking?'

'It's planning, it's different.'

Cass sighed like a teenager. 'Fine, okay, I'll call if I need you. Go take lots of pictures and have fun!'

Whilst Vee was getting her sparkly ladybird backpack together, Lauren leaned over until her lips almost touched Cass's earlobes. 'If you think this is it, don't send her away now without getting the chance to say goodbye.'

She pulled back, and waited. Cass looked straight up at the ceiling, unmoving, until she suddenly beckoned with two crooked fingers. Lauren moved forward again and Cass clutched her arm.

'Loll, if this is to be my final moment, I need to tell you ...' She made her hands into a cone and yelled, '*Stop being so fucking dramatic!*'

'You'll call us if you feel worse and we need to go to hospital? I've got the name of the recommended doctor and he won't take long if you want to get checked—'

'How is that for panicking?'

'It's planning, it's different.'

Cass sighed like a teenager. 'Fine. Okay, I'll call if I need you. Go take lots of pictures and have fun!'

Whilst Viv was getting her jacket, Jack tried to keep it together. Lauren leaned over and hugged him, then squeezed Cass's hand. 'If you think this is it, don't send her away now without getting the chance to say goodbye.'

She pulled back, and waited. Cass looked straight up at the ceiling, unresponsive until she suddenly beckoned with two crooked fingers. Lauren moved forward again and Cass clutched her arm.

'Look, if this is to be my final moment, I need to tell you ...' She made her hands into a cone and yelled, 'Stop being such a drama queen!'

Chapter 15

'Do you think Cassy is okay?' Vee asked for the third time that morning.

They had wandered around the city, looking at the buildings, walking the streets. Lauren felt an incredible pressure to be impressive, to be fun. She knew she was more reserved, more quiet than Cass. She hoped Vee wasn't bored with her. She kept stopping to offer ice cream. The first two times, Vee was thrilled. But now she was sick of ice cream and it didn't distract her from the fact that Cass wasn't there.

'I'm sure she's fine, she just needs to rest more. Travelling can make you tired,' she swung her hand back and forth. 'Don't worry.'

'Cassy said you're going to take me to meet my daddy.' That little face was intent, her eyes not leaving Lauren's. She was exactly the same as her mother – winning was all about the eye contact.

Oh God. Not this, please not this. The idea of Darren getting to see Vee, judging her as too much like Cass, assessing her that way he used to Lauren, where his eyes scanned up and down looking for imperfections ... it killed her. Or worse, he'd see himself in her, want to be part of her life. It was awful enough that her brain conjured images of them together, Cass and Darren, when she looked at Vee. The idea that he would get to know her was even more painful.

'She said when you're older you get to decide. Why do you call her *Cassy* and not *Mum*?' She hoped the question would distract her. That much, she had learnt. There was no stopping questions, just pausing them and distracting with other ones.

'That's what I call her,' Vee frowned, like it was obvious. 'She's my Cassy.'

'You've never called her *Mummy*?'

Vee shrugged.

'Shall we go see the gardens?'

Vee took Lauren's hand and meandered along like she was tasked with keeping the adult happy.

'What's that?'

She followed the little girl's pointing finger but couldn't see anything beneath the bridge. 'The water?'

'No,' Vee huffed, dragging her over to the side of the bridge and pointing at a small padlock. 'This.'

'Oh, people put locks on bridges,' Lauren said.

'Because they might get stolen?'

Lauren laughed, unsure if Vee was offering the same snarky response her mother would have, or asking a genuine question.

'No, people lock their love in. They think of their loved one and put the lock there to show they'll always love them. Then they throw the key in the water. If they ever wanted to be separated from their love, they'd have to swim and find the exact key to unlock it' – she gestured at the number of locks on the railings – 'which would be hard.'

Vee nodded. 'Can I get one?'

Lauren grinned, 'Have you got a crush on someone?'

'No. Gross. I want one for Cassy,' Vee said, 'to lock her to me.'

Lauren opened her mouth to say *something*. Anything. That it didn't work that way, or that she'd always have Cass with her *inside her heart*, or whatever. Everything sounded cheesy and awful.

'Okay, we'll find a lock before we go. I promise.'

'Don't tell her,' Vee frowned, suddenly serious. 'She won't want me to lock her to a bridge.'

'Um, it's not—'

'No telling.'

'Why not?'

'Because she'll share one with you and not with me!' Vee stamped her foot, her lips pursed and eyes wide. Daring her to argue.

For the first time, Lauren wondered what it felt like for Veronica, to meet someone who knew her mum longer than she had. Someone who had a history with her, before Blackpool. She thought back to Sandy's warning about animals grouping into two, and three not being able to break that bond. They weren't a three, they were two pairs – her and Cass, and Cass and Vee. The two halves of Cass's life. Perhaps she wasn't the only one afraid of being left on the outside.

'Sweetheart, you know everything's going to be okay, right?'

Vee looked up at her with the expression of a child who had heard the same line enough times to know better. She nodded like she knew she was supposed to, offering a smile that didn't reach her eyes.

'Can we go back and see if Cassy's better?'

It was fear, Lauren realised. The jut of the bottom lip and the way she dragged her hand across her face. It was the same fear Lauren had whenever she left Cass alone – that when she went back she'd be gone, and never have a chance to say the things she needed to.

They'd never had a proper talk about what Veronica knew about her mother's sickness. Did she understand what was happening? Was it all angel's wings and sitting on clouds that she had in mind for her mother? Or was it incomprehensible, that much pain, when you were five?

'Yeah okay,' Lauren held out a hand, and she took it willingly, 'she's had a couple of hours to sleep, she might feel strong enough to see the gardens. We could book a cab to go there so she doesn't have to walk much.'

Vee seemed to wave off details the same way her mother did – she didn't mind how it happened, just that someone else was taking care of it.

By the time they reached the hotel, Vee was almost running, dragging Lauren behind her as she rushed to get to the room. Lauren reached to find the key card, then stopped. There was a terrible noise. A deep groaning sound that reverberated through the walls.

'She's hurt!' Vee's eyes widened as she looked at Lauren, expecting her to do something. 'Cassy!' Her little fists banged on the door, and Lauren tried to calm her, but she was insistent. She needed her mum.

The problem was, Lauren knew what those sounds meant. Or at least, she thought she did.

Vee snatched the key card from her and rushed in, only to stop dead as she stared at the tanned back facing them, unaware of the interruption.

Lauren grabbed Vee, spinning her away so she faced the front door.

Cass's head peered around the strong silhouette and blinked, 'Oh s ... sugar plum fairies! You're back early!' She was drunk, if not something else, trying to sound cheerful even as the blood rushed to her face. She looked at the ceiling. 'We'll be done in just a minute, okay?'

The man seemed to take this as a sign to pick up his pace, so Lauren rushed Vee out the door, pulling it sharply behind them. 'Let's get some ice cream on the roof. You didn't get to see the rooftop for breakfast!'

She kept up a steady stream of chatter, trying to keep Vee distracted whilst simultaneously stopping her from answering any questions. Thankfully Nuria was at the bar, serving lunch and drinks to a few groups dotted around at different tables.

'*Buenas tardes*. Sorry, I'll be with you soon. So busy! No idea where my stupid, lazy son is!'

I do, Lauren thought to herself, looking down at Veronica. Why did Cass always do this? It was such predictable behaviour. Losing herself in the nearest pretty boy with a neck tattoo or a dangerous smile. As they sat quietly, Lauren desperately trying to think of something to say to let that little girl unsee what she'd just seen, another child came over. She was all huge eyes and dark curly hair that she tugged at nervously.

'*Hola, soy Isabel*,' she said to Veronica, smiling as she explained that her grandmother had said she spoke Spanish, and would she like to come play with her puppy?

Veronica looked back at Lauren, not so much asking permission, but looking for direction. Should she go? Would that be easier? Lauren nodded gently.

'I'll come get you in a little bit.'

Nuria walked past, 'My husband will watch them, don't worry.'

Don't worry. The easiest thing in the world to say. When most people worry, they overthink. Maybe they get a little nervous, or unable to eat. Butterflies and nausea. Worry was in your head, and yet it wasn't. It was so clearly in your body.

When Lauren worried, her heart beat in her throat and her body flushed, on edge as if she didn't know whether to run or fight. She stayed in that moment for what felt like hours, before getting up and stomping downstairs. She threw the door open, relieved to see Nuria's son was getting dressed.

'Get out!' she yelled in Spanish, suddenly finding a whole vocabulary she didn't even realise she had at her fingertips. 'Fucking a woman in front of her child, you animal bastard! I'll tell your mother!'

He snorted with amusement as he slid past her, blowing Cass a kiss.

'I'll put a great review on TripAdvisor!' Cass called out as he closed the door behind him.

She burst out laughing, but even that appeared to be in

slow motion. An easy, lazy sound as she stretched her arms above her head, the sheet slipping. It was uncomfortable to see her so thin, the sharp protrusion of her collarbone was like a cliff edge. She'd always been relaxed with her body, unbothered by what other people thought. It was a relief, in a way, to see that hadn't changed, even as her appearance had. Which Lauren may have cared about if she wasn't almost blacking out with rage.

'Is Vee okay?' Cass asked, eyes wide like it was absolutely no big deal.

'Oh, you care, now, do you? What *the fuck* was that?'

'Juan. Julio? Something with an "'h",' Cass laughed. 'Did you see that arse? Delicious. Glad I ticked that one off the list. And of course I care about my daughter, Loll, don't be ridiculous.'

'That's what this was about? Fucking some nobody because we thought it would be a good idea at twenty-one?'

'I thought it was a good idea today,' Cass snorted.

'And what, you're high?'

Cass grinned like a Cheshire cat. 'Some good shit.'

'And what about Vee?'

Cass rolled her eyes. 'Well if you'd stayed out and followed your bloody five-point plan, your hundreds of hours of castles and gardens and architecture, this wouldn't have happened!'

'So it's *my* fault you pretended to feel ill so you could stay behind, get high and fuck some stranger?'

'Ugh, Lauren, stop being so fucking *boring*. People have sex, okay? They smoke and drink and have flaws. They live.' She stood up, pulling her dress over herself, before walking to the kitchen and pouring herself a glass of water, glugging the whole thing down.

'She wanted to come home because she was worried something would happen to you,' Lauren said. 'She missed you. I kept trying to distract her. Maybe I would have tried harder if I'd known what she was coming back to.'

Cass ran a hand through her blonde bob, tugging at it.

'I *needed this*, Loll. Surely you can see that?'

'You needed me to look after your kid so you could act like a teenager again?'

'*Yes!* Yes, I did. You wouldn't understand. You don't have kids.'

And there it was again, that little knife in her gut every time it was thrown in her face.

'This has nothing to do with kids.' Lauren felt her lip curl in disgust. 'This is just you being you. Cassidy Jones, can't figure out how to deal with her life, so it's better to fuck whatever guy will have you, even if you have to be out of your head to do it. How many times has Vee had to see that? How many random men have been in and out of your house? I don't know why I'd thought you had your shit together, you're clearly the same as you always were.'

She could feel the rage growing, the need to say all the things she hadn't said. But this wasn't the time. It was too much.

'And what's that, Loll? Seeing as you know me so much? I'm a bitch? I'm a troublemaker? I'm a bad mother?'

'You're a slut.'

Cass blinked.

She looked honestly shocked, letting out a strange laugh at sounded as if it would fall down the stairs into a sob.

'Well good for you for finally saying it, Loll. Knew you lways thought it. Well done for having the balls to be honest, guess.'

Lauren took a breath, exhaling sharply. 'Look, I didn't—'

'Yeah. You did.'

The silence became a tableau: Lauren standing over a resplendent Cass, tapping her fingertips on the table. Cass seemed to be formulating a response, but struggled to find the words.

Eventually, she spoke. 'Ask me when the last time I had sex was, Lauren.'

'I'm not doing this.'

'Because you don't want the answer.' Cass pulled out a chair at the table, gesturing for Lauren to sit opposite her. 'I had sex two years ago. Barry introduced me to his nephew who was visiting. We went on a couple of dates. It was nice, we said goodbye as friends.'

Lauren didn't say anything.

'I didn't want to bring anyone into her life when I knew mine was short. I wanted to give her everything I had of myself.' Cass tried to catch Lauren's eye, but Lauren refused. 'But we're near the end, Loll. And you know how much I just wanted to be held? Just wanted to be in that space with someone I fancied. You forget how, you know. You forget how to be attracted, forget how to see the world that way.'

Lauren didn't say anything, but she joined her at the table.

'I am a *good* mother. I did everything right. I did it the way

I thought you'd do it, if you were her mum. You've been my fucking head every day from the moment she was bo whispering in my ear. *Don't be a fuck-up, Cass, don't be selfis You destroyed everything for this, better make it worth it.*'

'Oh, Cass, look—'

Cass shook her head. 'No, you wanted to talk about it, let's talk about it. You wanted a baby, and I had one. I have lived every day knowing you probably would have done a better job. There were nights when she was sick and I was on my own, and I was tempted to drive over and leave her with you, so you could have what you wanted.'

'Why didn't you?'

'Because the idea of being away from her feels like my guts are being ripped out.' The light had changed, the potential of the day fading to the laziness of siesta time. Lauren wondered how Vee was, if she was having fun, if she was going to be scarred by all of this. 'If I'd given her to you, none of this would have happened. I'd be alone, living a party lifestyle, and you'd have what you wanted. And we'd be even. Maybe I wouldn't be sick.'

'What on earth does that mean?'

Cass sighed. 'Everything has a price, Loll. Every action has a consequence. I betrayed you, and I never repaid the debt.'

'And that's why you got cancer? Not genes, or chance or bad luck?' Lauren resisted rolling her eyes.

'Karma,' Cass looked at her, unblinking, daring her to say otherwise.

'You can't honestly believe that? That you're being punished?'

Cass's shoulders drooped, as if all of the energy had escaped from her body. She was like a puppet, with no master. She looked to Lauren, tears in her eyes as she tried to smile, shoulder lifted in a half-shrug. 'Who knows? But we can't say I don't deserve it, can we?'

'No one *deserves* this, Cass. For goodness' sake! Bad things don't happen to bad people, and there isn't some rule of the universe punishing you. If you were being punished, you wouldn't have Veronica, would you? She's wonderful. She's a gift.'

'That's the worst punishment of all,' Cass snorted, wiping her eyes. She jutted her chin, trying to compose herself. Within seconds, her face was a blank again.

Silence surrounded them, Lauren sitting opposite her, unsure of what to do next. Frozen.

'What will you tell Vee about what she saw?' she asked.

Cass winced, then seemed to brace herself, throwing her shoulders back. 'I'll tell her that when people are not well, sometimes they do silly things. And that even mums are human and make mistakes.'

Lauren twitched her lips.

'That's not enough? I know. But here's what you need to learn – kids will accept mistakes if you're honest with them. They're understanding. They don't hold a grudge. Not if you love them as much as you can.'

'Shall I go get her then? Nuria will know where they are.' Lauren wasn't really sure what to do now the rage had left her.

Cass was in the wrong, she was sure of it. Acting like a teenager, with no worries as to what her daughter had seen or how it would affect her in the long run. She was so sure that she'd be forgiven, because she always had been. Cassidy Jones was infinitely lovable, and people forgave her without a second thought. Except Lauren. Lauren was the only one who never let it go.

'I'll go see if she wants to do something. Maybe we could pick up with your sightseeing plans?'

Lauren gave a shrug. She refrained from mentioning the hundred-point plan that Cass had hated merely moments ago. Apparently it was all squared away now. Nice and neat, the way Cass liked it. She got what she wanted, and you weren't allowed to be angry with her.

Cass paused at the entrance to the bedroom, and even without lifting her head, Lauren could feel her eyes on her.

'I *am* different now, you know. You remember me the way I was at the end, but if you could try to remember why we were friends in the first place, that might make this all a bit easier.'

Lauren forced herself to meet Cass's eyes, but said nothing.

'Sometimes, it's really easy to believe that you hate me.'

Cass said it with an easy air, as if she knew it couldn't possibly be true. Lauren sat at the table, wondering what that said about her if it was.

Chapter 16

The afternoon was tense, the sun beating down like an unyielding reminder: just because something looks perfect, doesn't mean it feels like it. Either way, Vee seemed okay, which was the only thing that mattered. She had, apparently, listened and understood, accepted the apology with a nod. But when they came back to their rooms, she went straight to the sofa to pick up Storm the husky toy, and took him over to Cass.

'Say sorry to Storm too. You were lying on him.'

Lauren fought a smile and failed, as Cass turned a laugh into a cough.

'You're right, I'm very sorry, Storm. I did not mean to upset you, it was very rude of me. *Aroo aroo, woof woof*.'

She nodded at Vee. 'Is that okay?'

'I don't know, I don't speak dog.' The little girl turned to the stuffed toy, 'Is that okay?'

She lifted the dog's nose to her ear and listened, nodding. 'Storm says okay but he would like some chocolate.'

'Hmm,' Lauren said, 'well, chocolate makes dogs sick, but

maybe you could have his chocolate for him. Do you think he'll mind?'

On this, apparently, Vee did not need to consult the toy dog. 'He won't mind.'

'How fortunate,' Cass replied. 'Okay, let's go on an adventure to eat some chocolate.'

The three of them wandered the city together this time, pointing out things, doing exactly what Vee wanted without question, and pretending that the awkward encounter of that afternoon had never happened. It seemed almost easy, but Lauren couldn't help but notice that Vee stuck closer to her, reaching for her hand instead of Cass's, directing her comments to her. If Cass noticed, she didn't say anything.

The gardens were luscious and vibrant, each area leading to another palatial building. Lauren imagined kings and queens walking amongst the greenery, making plans or avoiding their daily lives for the shortest time. She listened to hints of phrases from the Spanish guides, and translated them back, before teaching Vee a song in Spanish, one of the few she remembered from her childhood.

'My *abuela*, my grandmother, taught me that song,' she told Vee as they wandered. 'She was called Veronica too. It's my favourite name.'

The little girl's eyes lit up, before getting distracted by a little alcove in the corner and insisting they follow her.

'Why did you name her that? Coincidence, spite?' she asked Cass. 'You knew what that name meant to me.'

Cass shook her head, adjusting her hat. 'I'll tell you, soon enough.'

'Cryptic bullshit, wonderful.' She checked to make sure Vee couldn't hear her, 'Saving all the bad stuff for your death bed? How very like you.'

'Wahey, I'm glad we can joke about dying now, good stuff.' Cass nudged her as they walked, trying to make it normal again. 'I'll tell you in time, I'm still trying to figure out how this all goes. How long before I can stop putting it off.'

'Oh God, there's not more secrets?' Lauren said dramatically, hand against her forehead. 'You've sold Vee into the circus where she'll have to juggle husky pups? I'll have to chase the circus down, bring her back and save the day? Because that sounds exhausting.'

'But maybe still better than a day job?' Cass said.

Lauren snorted, 'Pickings are not so much slim as boring and unpleasant. I want to fight the power, not help rich people get richer.'

'Don't charities and places need lawyers to look over their files and check strategies? Some place that's not a law office, but where your skills would be useful?'

'I have excellent skills – my fingertips are impermeable against paper cuts. That's got to count for something, right?'

Cass rolled her eyes. 'I just mean ... stop thinking about what you can't do. But also, stop thinking that your job has to be this big thing that defines your life. It's a way to make money so you can do things and survive. Your life's passion can be something else. It can be volunteering, or creating something, or helping people.'

'You weren't passionate about your job?'

'I enjoyed it, mainly for the people and the fact that I could count the good I'd done. By the end of each week I could tally up the people I'd helped, even if it was just making a cup of tea or listening to a scared mum or helping an old man fill out paperwork. I was trying to be good. To make up for some of the bad.'

'I thought you didn't believe in good and bad. Everything's grey, everyone's complicated.'

Cass pressed her lips together, trying to find the words. 'When you're faced with a deadline, you try to find some meaning in it all. Which is difficult because there is no fucking reason we're here, except to live. So I tried to just focus on doing more good than damage.'

'Suddenly worrying about the upstairs and downstairs scenario then?'

Cass shook her head. 'If there's some omnipresent, omnipotent deity, she's smart enough to know that life is strange and people are stranger. I just ... I've had things to make up for. So that's what I'm trying to do.'

Lauren's stomach clenched a little, though if it was at the idea of Cass feeling guilty, or Cass not being around, she wasn't sure. The image of her in the hotel room, declaring her cancer was a punishment, her red eyes defiant, stayed in her mind. She always felt more than she showed. Lauren knew that. She'd always known that.

'Well, next stop is the cathedral, so if you're wondering about the big life things, I guess that's the place.'

The Seville Cathedral was unlike anything else she'd ever seen. The balance of Gothic towers and strong structures, the brickwork in the sunshine, the pure hugeness of it all. Vee tilted her head up until she almost fell backwards.

'That's big.'

Lauren felt her voice echo. She meandered around in that way people did as tourists, not really sure where to commit her attention. There was so much to be in awe of.

She kept an eye on Vee, who made an effort not to wander too far, whilst staring up at the ceiling and spinning around. When Lauren looked for Cass, she found her at the back, lighting a candle, briefly closing her eyes.

She wondered if it was a wish for her health, for Vee, or for something else. Maybe there was still hope, somewhere.

Lauren sidled up next to Cass when she opened her eyes. 'Making a wish?' she whispered, facing forward.

'Lighting a candle for Mum. She's been on my mind a lot recently.'

It wasn't hard to see why. She was making the same journey as Barbara, but was so desperate to walk a different path. She was going to keep her sense of humour, that much she'd promised. Lauren wasn't sure she should expect that much. She knew how cruel Cass could be when she was in pain.

'That makes sense.' Lauren distracted herself by reaching into her pockets for euros, sticking them in the donation box and lighting a candle from Cass's flame.

Barbara Jones had been an amazing woman. She was wild and free and endlessly fun. She wasn't judgemental, and just accepted that everyone had their path in life, their role to play. She wanted everyone to thrive. On her fiftieth birthday, she went and got a tattoo on her bum because she said no one would believe her, and she'd get the chance to legitimately flash people to prove them wrong.

When she was nearing the end, she had asked Lauren to take care of Cass, to keep her close even when she was difficult, even when she pushed away. She knew her daughter would struggle.

And Lauren had failed her. She hadn't gone to the funeral. Even though she'd known Cass would need someone, that she'd be hurting. It had all just happened, it was all still so raw. Barbara died, Cass betrayed her and she suddenly had to be the plucky best friend, the bigger person. If she had gone to that funeral, it would show that Cass could get away with anything and Lauren would still be there for her, like the pathetic little mouse she was. Like the shadow that couldn't escape.

But still, she had thought about going. She got dressed in black, but dithered, pacing back and forth in the hallway until Darren yelled that she was damaging the flooring, and then offered to take her out for lunch to take her mind off it.

He wasn't different at all after everything happened. That a week before the funeral he was calling Cass a liar, a troublemaker, someone broken who would drag Lauren down with her ... it amazed her now. The gall of the man. To be so certain, so above reproach that he still had a go at her about the floorboards whilst she betrayed her friend for a second time.

He'd wanted her not to go, she saw that now. He even insisted she change clothes, something that wasn't black, so she wouldn't be tempted to stop in. He knew Lauren was a stickler for blending in and following the rules. She wouldn't be so audacious as to turn up to a funeral in a red dress, so that's what he cajoled her into wearing. God, she'd been an idiot.

Barbara was a good woman, and Cass had needed someone. It wasn't the biggest regret out of all of this, but it was high on her list. She had been unyielding, and she had broken a promise.

'I'm sorry,' she whispered, half to the candle, half to Cass. 'I'm really sorry.'

Cass didn't move, the soft light from the flame making her hair angelic and her smile soft. She took her hand and squeezed.

'I know. Me too.'

At that point, Vee came running over, summoning stern looks from the staff.

'I want to go now, please,' she said, back straight, voice echoing as she frowned. 'Why is everyone whispering?'

'Because that's what everyone does when they think God is listening,' Cass said loudly, reaching out a hand for her daughter, and striding out towards the doors. Lauren was left to follow behind, trying to ignore the looks from the priests and other tourists, aghast but also slightly pleased for the distraction.

They ambled down the streets, looking in shop windows, tantalised by sweet treats and swayed by pointless souvenirs. They asked Vee if she wanted anything, pointing her to the small flamenco dresses in bright colours with polka dots, or little dancer dolls. She shook her head, giving Lauren a look.

Lauren tilted her head, trying to figure out what she was saying.

The little girl waited until she was sure her mother was looking at a shelf of shot glasses and pointed to a tray on another shelf. The look of irritation, that half-curved eyebrow and the thin lips, it was completely Cass. It almost made Lauren want to cry, that perfect impersonation that had happened naturally. It was like stepping back in time, an expression that moved through generations. She wondered if Barbara had done it too but she'd never seen her exasperated.

'Aunt Loll!' Vee hissed, jabbing her finger. Ah, she saw it now.

She nodded, picking up the padlock and taking it to the counter, grabbing a couple of bottles of water and a bar of chocolate to disguise her purchase. Vee, at last, looked relieved, nodding in approval.

Oh God, what if she thought the lock would stop Cass dying? Had she just completely derailed a child's development and grief processes? What if she was responsible for Vee's life going completely off track, all because of this moment where a grown-up lied to her about having control over death?

She could hear Cass's voice in her head: *Stop worrying, kids are kids. They do okay if you love them. Stop overthinking. You always get anxious when you overthink.* There had been so many panic attacks and anxious moments that Cass had weathered with her, holding her so tight that Lauren could relax into the tension. She had felt held, and safe, and loved, with Cass's voice tickling her ear and telling her she was going to be okay.

But after everything happened, it seemed unfair to conjure Cass's voice in her head, like summoning an imaginary friend who you didn't really believe in anymore.

Instead, she'd plodded on alone, no other voice to cancel out the ones telling her she was a failure, she was difficult, she was all alone. Life had been difficult without Cass, but even harder without her voice.

The panic attacks had been worse when Cass was gone. Debilitating, she supposed. She'd tried to hide them as best she could from Darren. He saw it as weakness, her choice to overthink, to worry, to make things complicated. Her mum had been the same too. She was just trying to be smart, and that made her break down. She just needed to think less, they said.

It was always wonderful to be told she was responsible for her own body turning on her. That it was her trying to be perfect, to get attention, to make everything a big deal. It was easier to disappear into bathrooms and say she had a bad stomach, or go up to bed and say she had the flu. They still called her weak, but at least it was her constitution, and not her mind, they were worried about.

Cass had always been the voice that calmed her. The one she kept with her, in her back pocket for times of trouble. She had missed that voice, almost as much as its flesh and blood counterpart. Maybe even more so.

'Hey, Loll, over here,' Cass waved her over to the shop window. 'Señorita Veronica has a task for you.'

Lauren turned to the little girl, smiling up with a cherubic grin.

'Oh dear.'

Cass nodded, her smile matching her daughter's. 'Yup.'

'Auntie Loll, I think you need to buy that dress,' Vee pointed up at the display window to the yellow strappy dress with little white and pink flowers. The skirt flowed out a little, and Lauren could already see how it would swish as she walked. She would put a pink flower in her dark hair, and she would walk with her back straight, head high, not shying away as people looked at her when she passed.

Lauren had a hundred pieces of clothing like that in her wardrobe – transformative ones, ones she bought when she was sure they would turn her into a different person. But whenever she put on that gorgeous dress, or that patterned skirt or that colourful top, no matter how good it looked, she got that sick, shaky feeling in her stomach that told her people would be looking at her. They'd notice her and judge her and dismiss her. It was easier to be invisible.

'Oh, sweetie, I don't think it's my style.'

Vee was unimpressed, and shook her head, hands on hips. 'Sorry, Auntie Loll, but that dress is for you and you have to have it. Storm says so.'

'Storm's in the hotel room,' she snorted.

'I can read his mind.' Vee was not to be argued with.

Cass cut in, 'Come on, Loll, just try it on for us, what's the harm? Maybe it's time to shine, right?'

'Is it?' she asked, searching Cass's eyes. The old Cass would know what this meant, how she hated being put on display. But maybe she didn't know how much worse it had gotten without anyone to push her boundaries or hush her fears with gentle words.

Cass reached out and squeezed her hand. 'Loll, it really, really is.'

The dress looked wonderful, as she was sure it would. It fit perfectly, but Lauren felt incredibly on show, even as she twirled for the two of them in the changing room.

'It's perfect!' Vee clapped her hands.

'The thing is, with a dress like that ...' Cass sighed, 'it's really your duty to go dancing.'

'Dancing?'

'Dancing!' Cass shimmied a little, laughing. 'Come on, Loll, you remember how, don't you? You're about to be thirty, not seventy.'

God, Lauren had loved to dance. She loved to move to the beat and ignore everyone else around her. She loved to look across the room when a certain song came on and find Cass's eyes. Then she'd disentangle herself from whichever boy she'd been with that night and make her way over to Lauren, and they'd laugh and sing along and twirl under the other's arms, clasping each other tightly.

'I've missed dancing.'

'We'll ask Nuria about somewhere with live music. And *you* will have your dress, Cinderella. My treat.'

'No. No treats. I'll buy it.'

Cass shook her head. 'If you buy it, you can justify not wearing it. I've only got a few deathbed cards, don't make me waste one if I can get away with guilt tripping instead. Much less bad juju for guilt trips.'

Lauren huffed and made snarky noises as she went back into the changing cubicle, handing the dress out from behind the curtain. Secretly, she was thrilled. Cass still knew her. Still knew what she would and wouldn't do in a situation.

When she walked out to the shop floor, Vee and Cass were already finished, holding out the bag to her.

'I'm going to wear my green and gold dress tonight,' Vee nodded, 'and Cassy is going to wear her pink one. Colours and pretty!'

Vee walked in between the two of them, holding a hand of each, so that they walked like a family, crossing through town looking at everything, stopping to take photos. Cass asked a stranger to take a photo of them all together on the bridge, smiling stiffly, their arms around each other. It was then that Vee remembered the lock.

'Me and Auntie Loll need to go over there,' she said, dragging her a few feet away from Cass and whispering, 'we need to do the lock!'

'You want me to ask your mum to go back to the hotel? Or do you want me to distract her a few minutes so you can lock it?'

Vee pressed her lips together, clearly thinking.

'She can stay.'

'I thought you didn't want her to know?' Vee shook her head, and Lauren sighed, kneeling down. 'Sweetheart, I don't know what you want from me. You need to tell me, and I'll do it.'

Vee looked up from beneath her lashes. 'You can be on it too. All of us.'

'No, Vee, it's for you and your mum, I wouldn't take that away.'

Vee simply shook her head. 'Can I have the pen, please?'

So she'd noticed the big marker Lauren had bought with the lock. She handed over both, then walked back to Cass.

'What's going on here?'

'Vee wanted to put a lock on the bridge,' Lauren's words sounded heavier than they needed to be. *Lighten up, Loll, not everything's so serious.* She could hear Cass's thoughts as clear as anything, and it was a relief when she looked at her face and saw that exact expression.

'Declaring her undying love for Storm the snow dog?'

'No, for you.'

'Oh,' Cass's lips twitched once, and then she pressed them together, her eyes blinking furiously. 'I'm not ready for this yet, Loll.'

'Just pretend it's for Storm, okay? Besides, apparently I've been added to the list. I wasn't allowed on before.'

'That's because she knows I'm going to haunt you until you come hang out with me,' Cass snorted, nudging Lauren as they walked over. 'But I'm gonna be a self-actualising ghost; instead of scaring you, I'm just going to make you do things that scare you.'

'Ooh, a ghost for a new age, so selfless, such a blessing.' Lauren rolled her eyes and tried not to think of growing old and being alone. Was that worse than dying young and beautiful? Probably not to Cass.

'Well, missy, what are we doing?' Cass knelt down and looked at the lock, grasped tightly in Veronica's hand. She was delicate in her penmanship; the simple *V* + *C* + *L* with a heart below it looked neat and precise. She had copied a nearby lock for inspiration with the heart.

'Shall I help you lock it, baby?' Cass took the lock gently, turning the key until it clicked, taking direction on placement from Vee. She held it as the little girl clicked it into place. Lauren stood back, watching the moment, wondering if she should take a photograph, if Vee would want this moment recorded. She decided against it, feeling too much like an interloper already. Cass held Vee up so she could throw the key into the water, kissing her cheek as she lowered her to the ground.

They peered over the edge, waiting for the sound of the key hitting the water. 'There we go, we're tied together forever.'

Vee nodded, clearly unsatisfied. Perhaps she had hoped for sparkles or fanfare, or some sort of sign that a magical document had been signed, an unbreakable promise had been made. Instead, other tourists walked by, traffic continued and the view of the sunset, beautiful as it was, could not be called magic.

There was nothing the adults could offer Veronica, except a hand from each of them as they walked back to the hotel, lost in their own thoughts.

*

'Dancing? You want to go dancing?' Nuria clapped her hands, 'I tell you where to go dancing. The best places for young pretty ladies.'

'Um ... young pretty ladies with a little one?' Lauren corrected.

Nuria was tidying the reception as she spoke, so Lauren tracked her movements, following her around the room. Cass had taken Vee for a nap, and she was desperate for one herself, but it was their last night in Seville, and she needed to make sure it was perfect.

'Family friendly. Good food, live music? Not a club or anything. We're ...' she struggled for the Spanish equivalent. 'We're old at heart.'

'Young people acting like old people,' Nuria huffed, 'a waste!'

Lauren's eyes slid to the floor and Nuria must have remembered what she knew about Cass.

'*Lo siento,* I'm sorry, I forgot. You want time with Veronica, of course. I have a place.'

Nuria's suggestion was only a few steps from the hotel, down winding back paths and out into a surprising courtyard. They followed her through, and were handed over to the waiter, who spoke in rapid Spanish with Nuria, before grinning at them.

'Please, this way.' He led them through as Nuria waved goodbye and shuffled back off to the hotel.

Lauren usually felt awkward and on show whenever she wore colour, but with Vee and Cass walking behind her, she felt like her brightness was a uniform. She got to be one of the beautiful ones this evening, and there wasn't that awful knot in her stomach telling her to go home and change into something dark. She had spent so long trying to be invisible, and yet it was just like it had been when they were younger – when she was with Cass, it felt okay to share a little of the light. Just enough to feel the warmth on her face.

They were seated in the courtyard, under a canopy of flowers and fairy lights, and as they were poured wine, Lauren sat back and allowed herself to feel completely at ease. Everything had been so tense, walking on eggshells around Vee and Cass, trying desperately to ignore how this whole thing would end. Ignoring the regret of all the years lost, and the anger at how everything had turned out. The shame of her own decisions and the part they had to play.

Instead, she sat in a beautiful restaurant with her friends, and listened as Vee chattered away about Isabel, Nuria's granddaughter, and the new words she'd learnt in Spanish.

The food was delicious, tapas followed by huge dishes of paella with crisp citrus bringing the seafood to life. They drank and laughed, and everything was easy. There was one moment where Cass looked over, flushed with the wine and the sun, and smiled at her. A smile that spoke of gratitude and relief. *Isn't this wonderful, aren't you glad we're here? Aren't we lucky?*

Lauren felt like she was taking a snapshot. That smile would sit like a carefully crafted Polaroid, in the vault of her memories, awakened every time she thought of Seville. The band started not long after Vee conceded defeat on her ice cream sundae. She was flagging a little, having barely napped that afternoon, but immediately perked up at the sight of the band, clapping along with the music.

Couples had already made their way to the space in front

of the band, dancing salsa to the rhythm, holding each other close. Lauren tapped her heels on the floor, fighting the urge to get up and dance. Cass had pulled Vee onto her lap and was nodding along gently. She looked completely relaxed. Lauren couldn't remember a version of Cass without tension. Sure, it was usually a chaotic, frenetic tension, one that could mean fun or fear or anything in between. But she was never completely satisfied, as she seemed now.

As Lauren looked across the courtyard to the band, she accidentally made eye contact with a man standing at the back. He smiled at her, and she looked away. Oh God, would he think she was flirting? That she wanted attention? She just wanted to dance and enjoy her time. She didn't want anything from anyone. She kept looking down at the table, rather than risk making eye contact again.

'*Hola*,' the voice came from above her. She turned to Cass, who grinned and pointed upwards.

He was barely twenty-two, if that. But tall and broad, with a lovely smile.

'English?'

'*Español* ...' she started, then smiled, wriggling her hand to suggest 'just a little'.

'*¿Bailamos?*' he pointed at the couples already moving back and forth.

Lauren looked to Cass in search of rescue, or an excuse. And yet, there was a thrill in the turnaround. All those years that Lauren sat on the sidelines whilst Cass was approached by hopeful men who looked at her like she was magic. Now, finally, someone saw her first. And Cass seemed pleased for her. No loss, no jealousy, no regret. Instead she cuddled her daughter and said, 'Go on then! It's just a dance!'

Lauren grinned awkwardly, taking the man's hand as he led her to the dance floor, twirling her into a start position. She hoped she could remember how to move. God, he was beautiful, all dark hair and intense eyes. They started rocking to the music, and Lauren suddenly felt like a teenager again. She moved to the rhythm, grinning as she twirled, as the man pulled her close, then pushed her away. It was invigorating, to dance, to be free completely.

They carried on, through a few different songs, Lauren turning to wave back at Cass, beckoning them up on the dance floor. Cass shook her head, soft smile on her face as she pointed at the sleeping child on her lap. How strange, to be the one looking back from the dance floor, the one to be sweaty and exhilarated, having the time of her life. It was addictive. Eventually, she pushed her dance partner away, thanking him and kissing him on both cheeks.

'That was wonderful,' she said, collapsing into the chair and downing a glass of water.

'Yes,' Cass smiled, stroking her daughter's hair as she slept, 'it really was. And you ticked it off the list. Dance with a stranger.'

'I'd even forgotten that was on the list!'

'Don't worry, babe, I'm planning it all out so we don't miss the good stuff,' Cass winked, reaching for her glass of wine.

'Tomorrow we're onto the next leg of the journey. How you feeling about seeing Uncle Jack?'

'Excited,' Cass said, 'nostalgic. I guess I wonder what life would have been like if I went with him all those years ago, when Mum died. If we'd be proper Aussies, barbecuing and snorkelling and surfing. Would have been a different life.'

'Do you regret it?'

Cass shook her head. 'I just wish Vee could have got to know them a bit more. The life he offered us was a good one. Maybe it was unfair for me to deny her that.'

'You raised her alone when you could have had help. Don't think it was easy for you either.'

Cass shook her head, looking down at her daughter with tenderness.

'It was penance. It was what had to be done,' she whispered, before shrugging it off and sipping at her wine. 'Besides, you know me, always been a little bit psychic. I've known how all this would end a long time ago.'

'You knew we'd be sitting in Spain together?'

Cass nodded slowly. 'I just thought it might have been a few years earlier. Cutting it a bit fine, babe. Making it the last hurrah.'

'Well, I always was a little slow. But the timing came right in the end.'

'Yeah, if Darren hadn't left, you might never have got a letter. You wouldn't have known about me or Veronica. Nothing would have changed. Guess we have one thing to thank the bastard for.'

'Two,' Lauren said, her eyes on Vee.

'Two,' Cass agreed.

PART FOUR

Australia

Chapter 17

Imagine the longest flight you can, with a usually angelic child who has fast become grouchy, tired and bored. Then imagine you've been seated separately from your travelling companions, and no one will swap with you. Then realise you've been seated next to a perfectly nice theologian professor called Frederick who keeps quoting bible passages and talking about how death is merely a state of being, and that the air stewards ran out of ice cream sandwiches just before they reached you. Imagine all of that, and you'd be somewhere in the realm of Lauren's pain.

The problem with Fred was that he wasn't even quoting the full verses and giving her context, he just kept saying, 'Matthew, 21: 45,' or things like that, even though she'd made it clear she wasn't religious. It was tempting to pretend to be asleep – which was one of the few options left because he kept talking through her choice of movie and tapping her on the shoulder to ask her things she couldn't possibly know about the flight.

Unfortunately, hovering on the edge of sleep left her half dreaming. Memories of Cass in the early days merged with the ones later on, when it was all drunkenness and tears, begging for forgiveness. It left Lauren unsettled, not sure which lifetime she was in whenever she woke. She dreamed of her mother, telling her she'd never do any better than Darren, and that she should try not to expect the world. She dreamed of a grown-up Veronica, her hair long like Cass's was, as she stood outside a club with a cigarette. She looked her square in the eye as she said, 'You're not my mother,' and Lauren awoke in tears. It was not a restful flight.

When they eventually touched down in Cairns, she could swear she'd been flying for a week. Time didn't seem to exist. She wasn't even sure what day it was.

Vee wobbled a little against her in the queue for customs. 'Auntie Loll?' she mumbled, clutching Storm to her chest.

'Yes, sweetness?'

'Do we have to do that again to go home?'

Lauren winced. 'Try not to think about it. That is a problem for future-us.'

Cass laughed. 'Let's live our lives that way. Much better idea. Future-Cass can worry about clean knickers.'

Vee frowned. 'That's rude.'

Cass raised an eyebrow at Lauren. 'Ah see, look, I have a parental teaching moment.' She knelt down in front of her daughter. 'Pumpkin, as long as you are not upsetting someone kind, or causing someone pain, I don't want you to ever worry about being rude. You tell the truth, you speak your mind, and you be heard, okay?'

Vee looked at her quizzically, then shrugged. 'Okay.'

'Also *knickers* is a funny word, so enjoy it ... oh, and also it's only rude because the patriarchy makes us feel like feminine things are embarrassing and have to be spoken in hushed tones ...' She shook her head, making a face. 'Don't worry about it, I'll write it all down. There's too much teaching to cram into an airport line.'

She struggled to get up again, reaching out to Lauren for support.

Lauren looked at her, exhausted. '*Now* was the time for "knickers are about the patriarchy"? Really? You didn't want to start with why people go to war, or how complicated the concept of truth is?'

'It's not that knickers are *about* the patriarchy, Loll. We're raising a girl here. We know how shitty it is to be a girl. I don't want her to be the quiet one who doesn't put her hand up even though she knows the answer. I want her to demand to be heard and not be ashamed of how smart she is. I want her to go for every opportunity open to her, and when she finds ones that aren't, I want her to bang on the door until they open up or cave in.'

Cass looked a bit winded, and Vee looked up at her in a sort of bemused wonder, shaking her head and offering her mother a one-armed hug.

As they stood waiting for the luggage, Lauren suddenly realised. Cass had said *they* were raising a girl. They were in it, the two of them together, and how she wished it would last. She had a role to play here, one that mattered. But they were in Australia, the last chunk of their journey, and time was running out.

*

Jack was just how he'd been all those years ago. A charmer, a gambler, a friendly drunk and someone who made eye contact just a *little* too frankly.

'Well, hey there, poppet!' He waved his board that read *Cassidy Jones and Co.* He wore a light T-shirt, khaki shorts and a baseball cap, rushing in to hug Cass. He held her tight, almost picking her up. 'Goodness, we need to feed you up, kid! And *this* must be Miss Veronica. I'm your Great Uncle Jack.'

Vee blinked, smiling tiredly. 'Hello. Do you have any dogs?'

Jack didn't even blink. 'Yes, I have three.'

'I like dogs.'

Cass snorted, holding Vee against her, stroking her hair. 'I think she's a little punch-drunk from the flight. Although she's right, she does love dogs.'

Jack turned his attention to Lauren, who wasn't expecting to be remembered.

'Hi, I'm—'

'Lauren, of course. I remember you, girl, it wasn't that long ago.' He gave her a hug, before reaching for their bags. 'I tried for ages to get Cass to move out here, and she said she had to be around for you, she couldn't leave just yet. And now you're here together!'

He started wheeling the cases to the exit, chattering away about the weather as he packed everything into the car. Lauren watched Cass, trying to imagine why she would have had to be around for her, back then. They weren't even in contact. She and Vee might have had a nice life out here. Surrounded by family and people who loved them.

We have a family, we are a family, she could hear Cass in her head again, being contrary. For her, the ragtag group of neighbours and the quiz team were family too. And considering how much they emailed and messaged, how Paul checked in and passed on their news, it seemed they felt that way too. Sandy had even softened towards her now she saw how happy Cass was. She'd said her aura looked blue instead of a muddy grey. A big compliment, apparently.

Cairns flew by as they exited the airport, Jack talking about all the things they could do, catching Cass up on what her cousins were doing, and who would be at the house. She sat in the front, seeming to genuinely enjoy being with her uncle, and Vee sat in the back with Lauren, resting her head on her leg, reaching for Lauren's hand and making her stroke her hair, guiding her to do what she wanted.

Lauren carried on absentmindedly, finding herself completely calm all of a sudden. The world had melted away to the sound of Cass's laughter and teasing, and Vee's soft snores on her leg as she stroked her hair.

'Lauren, what about you, poppet?' Jack called from the front.

'Sorry, what?'

'Jack said how did we feel about scuba diving tomorrow? He'll take us to the Great Barrier Reef.'

The thought of being encapsulated in a wet suit, her oxygen kept in a separate location from her lungs, made her chest feel like it was caving in. It was getting hard to breathe just thinking about it. Oh, but it would be beautiful. It would be an awful thing to miss, like going to Paris and never seeing the Eiffel Tower.

Don't be a scaredy-cat, she told herself firmly, willing herself to say yes. She didn't want to be left out. She didn't want to sit on the sidelines whilst everyone else had fun. That was how it had always been until this adventure. Now, there was this strange feeling that she could be the main character in her own life. That she had a responsibility to do so.

She felt the panic settling around her in the way it always had. The questions threatened to drown her. What if one of them died? What if they got caught on something and the oxygen ran out? What about Vee?

Cass's voice cut through the fog. 'Hey, Loll, how about snorkelling instead? We can paddle off the side of the boat, stick our heads in, still see lots of gorgeous stuff?'

Lauren's breath returned, and she looked up to see Cass smiling over her shoulder at her.

'You should dive though, if you want. I bet it's beautiful.'

'No, this is our trip together. Plus, there's lots to learn, and I'd worry about Vee and you. Let's just snorkel.'

How easily Cass could dismiss things with a casual shoulder shrug, as if being fearful wasn't something to be ashamed of. It was a relief, though, to be allowed to say no because Cass had. She was scared for a moment that Cass would push her into it, saying that she needed to learn and experience and grow.

As she watched Cass sit back in her seat, it was clear her energy was failing, and not just from the flight. She had a grey tinge and her brow was always half-furrowed. Things were getting worse, and Lauren wondered how long she was going to be able to keep jollying along. She knew how Cass got when she was hurting. Even a bout of the flu when they were studying led her to be a sharp-tongued, ungrateful nightmare. She was dreading the end, seeing how cruel she might become.

Lauren knew that Barbara had done her best but had twisted into bitterness and anger. She was relieved she'd never seen her after her 'going away party', as Babs had called it. One last hurrah, with expensive canapés and the best champagne, gorgeous young men hanging on her every word, everyone taking pictures and dancing and having the best time. Lauren remembered sitting on the bench in the back garden with Cass, sharing a cigarette and looking in at the party. Everyone was so beautiful, so effortlessly interesting.

'Do they know what this party is for?' she'd asked, unable to comprehend anyone being that happy to say goodbye to someone they loved. 'Do they think it's a normal going away party?'

Cass had stared into the house, her eyes hard as her mother threw back her head and laughed, gesturing for her glass to be topped up.

'Knowing Mum, probably. I had to pay two hundred quid to a professional make-up artist this afternoon, because she wouldn't stop crying about how she looked. Everything had to be *perfect*.'

After that one perfect night, Barbara Jones had locked herself away in that hospice like she was Rumpelstiltskin, protecting her memory like it was gold.

Cass was the only one to visit, and the more she visited, the more she cared for her mother, the more Babs resented her. The crueller she became. She would scream at her to let her die, to stop witnessing her disappearance. Cass would go out, get broken and drunk. Lauren would collect her from a club, or a stranger's house, and Cass would get up in the morning and return to Barbara's side.

The cycle continued for months. And when everything ended, when Babs was gone and Cass had betrayed her and Lauren was stubborn for the first time in her life ... it was too broken to fix. It was too much to expect that Cass would deal with this any better than Barbara. Lauren was waiting for Cass to turn on her, to make her the punching bag her mother had made her. That was the point of all this, wasn't it? That Lauren would be her witness at the end. *Too maudlin,* Cass's voice inside her head said, *so boring.* God, she needed to sleep.

Jack's home was large, one of those strange Australian creations up on stilts that made Lauren worry about exactly what kind of dangerous critter was waiting beneath. When they pulled up, he honked the horn twice and a miniature horde emerged from the front door, all loud and enthusiastic as they approached.

Cass turned back and laughed. 'Well, that's quite the welcome!'

Dolores, Jack's wife, was blonde and petite, but she looked like she could go out hunting in the bush and return with something to cook for dinner. She waved firmly, a big grin as she beckoned everyone down to the car. Their kids were mid-to-late twenties, and Lauren recognised the son, Jason, who'd come over to Barbara's party. He had shorter hair now, but still looked the same as he did then – oversized T-shirt and long shorts like a skateboarder. He held a toddler in his arms who wriggled to get free. The other two, Lissa and Annie, introduced themselves as they got out of the car. Annie held her baby girl in a sling across her front, and Lauren's stomach flipped a little with jealousy.

'This is Dot.' Annie lifted the baby's white sunhat, only managing to reveal her fair hair and the tip of her nose before placing it back again. 'Don't start Mum off on the name, she'll be here all day.'

Lissa's son Taylor was around Vee's age, and he immediately wanted to show her his treehouse. His mother tried to gently explain what jetlag was, but Vee seemed revived by being surrounded by so many people, all of whom were thrilled to meet her.

Lauren suddenly realised Vee had probably never seen so many family members before – in fact, she hadn't seen any. It was just her and Cass, the same way that, mostly, it had been Cass and Babs. They'd both carved families out of friends and co-workers and the people you met on the street by the boardwalk.

It was clear the little girl was overwhelmed by how many people wanted to know her. Taylor dragged her off to the treehouse, and Jason handed Lauren his child so he could get their bags out of the car. She froze, holding the little boy, who looked at her in surprise, before grinning at her.

Oh God, her chest hurt. She'd wasted all that time with

Darren, and now she was about to be a thirty-year-old divorcee. Dating had changed, it was all online now. All taps and swipes while you found someone who seemed perfect then sent you a picture of their penis at 8 a.m. on a Friday. Oh God, she was going to have to start all over again.

Lauren held the toddler close, rocking him back and forth as they went into the house for tea. She sneakily kissed his forehead as they sat down at the table, Jack introducing everyone and explaining their plans for the next few days.

Thankfully, dinner was served early, as the three of them were swaying in their seats by the evening. It had been warm, full of laughter and friendliness, sharing memories of Cass's mother and growing up.

Jack had stories about Cass too; how feisty and determined she was as a child, the time she broke her leg because she was 'learning to fly' like a superhero, or the detention she got for making the school bully cry. It was a balm to hear about these different sides of Cass, and Vee listened with an intense interest. Lauren knew she was looking for these traits in herself.

It wasn't clear if Jack knew why they were there, if he knew anything about Cass's current state beyond being a bit thin and pale. She must have told them, surely?

The dinner reminded Lauren of her own family, but without the tension. Food was passed around, gossip was shared, compliments given freely as if expected. It almost made her uncomfortable, how easy everything was.

It was when she saw Cass looking around though, suddenly surrounded by people who cared about her and her daughter, that Lauren put the pieces together. *Cass wanted Vee to live in Australia.*

Of course. They were her only family. They already loved her, there were other kids around, a huge support system. Vee could be happy here, exploring and wandering, letting her curiosity lead her to new places. There would be no worries about Darren, no disappointing British coastline. There was *colour* here, and Lauren was starting to see the importance of that.

Still, the realisation hurt, like picking off a scab only to find it hadn't fully healed. Blood pouring everywhere – she would lose Cass, and then she would lose Vee. Except it wasn't about her, she reminded herself, stabbing at her potato with her fork and distracting herself with chewing. If this was what was best for Vee, then she had to support them both. Cass was making a big decision. She'd only stayed in England that long for her anyway, apparently.

That night she couldn't shake it off, though. She lay in one of the guest bedrooms (available now that all the kids were grown up) and heard Vee and Cass's quiet voices in the room next door as she stared at the ceiling. It felt weird to be sleeping away from them; she had become so accustomed to their breathing, their sleepy snuffles, or the gentle nudges from Vee as she whispered that she needed a drink, please. The same was true when they were at uni, and Cass would come bounding into her bed after a night out, or if she'd had a bad dream, or if it was particularly cold and they refused to put the heating on. Cass became a regular presence in Lauren's room, her hair brushing against Lauren's face, or her pointy elbows digging into ribs. It had been automatic, unquestioned.

And now Lauren felt alone again.

She could hear Cass singing gently, the quiet plucking of the ukulele alongside. She longed to go in there, to sit with them and snuggle up, like the family she'd become a part of. A group. A pack.

But it didn't seem right, to intrude on those moments when Vee would have so few of them left with her mother.

Instead, Lauren got out her sketchbook, and continued drawing wolves. She'd found a strange calm in it – the pointy ears and soft furry stomachs, the strong legs and tails with a flick. She drew them hungry and dangerous, fangs bared. She drew them gentle, playful, more like dogs, with mothers guarding pups, or pulling sleds. She drew them in the snow, relaxed but watchful. A pack, she'd told Cass all those years ago. Possibly the only time she'd been the strong one, pulling Cass out of the darkness. *We're a pack, we're together, we're never alone.* When this was all over, she was going to be alone again. But this wasn't about her.

*

Lauren still wasn't quite herself by the time they went out on the boat the next day. She'd sat at the kitchen table and watched as this family came together to cook breakfast, to chat even more than they had the night before. They were all so colourful, so *vibrant*, and Vee was the star of the show, their most revered guest. Did she want blueberry pancakes? Did she want a chocolate milkshake? Had she tried this fruit, did she want seconds? They had to know, Lauren told herself, they had to see this as an audition. There was no way anyone was this hospitable.

She felt herself withdraw a little, blaming jetlag and tiredness. She could get away with that for a few days, at least. They were only staying for a week anyway, before moving on to the surf camp Cass had insisted on. She looked a little fragile, but she was hiding it well. Every time she looked at her, Lauren remembered another thing she wanted to say to Cass, another moment she wanted to recount. She wanted to fill her in on all the moments she hadn't been there for, read her all the text messages she hadn't sent. But there wasn't time, and the shadow of what had happened sat like a barrier. Eventually, they would have to talk about it. About Darren, about everything. Until they did, they couldn't be close again. But the fear of what would be unleashed, the possible cruelty and loss, how everything would be ruined ... it was almost too much to bear.

She tried, instead, to be inspired by the Jones girls, and carry on with the colour she'd embraced in Seville that night, unafraid of being seen. If anything, it was becoming easier. She wanted to scream, 'I'm here, don't forget me, I'm part of this too.'

Where this came from was unclear – Jack had been more than welcoming, she was never left out of a conversation. There was nothing there that she wasn't offered. But she wasn't family. Not anymore.

The boat ride was gorgeous. They sat on aquamarine waters

that twinkled in the sunlight, the boat bobbing up and down as they made their way to the spot Jack recommended. Vee was so *alive* here, so full of energy, as if something had been lifted. She was so distracted by all these people, all these new experiences and possibilities and colour, that she forgot to remember her mother might be gone soon.

'Okay, here we are,' Jack announced, coming round to hand out masks and snorkels. 'Now, we operate with respect for that world down there. No taking things, no trying to touch animals or coral or anything else you find. Just watch and be happy, right?'

'Right,' they nodded their agreement.

Cass gave her a look, raising an eyebrow and tilting her head. Lauren recognised that look – a quiet check that she was okay, that she didn't feel pushed into doing something she wasn't comfortable with. That look felt like a caress, a loving cuddle. She had seen it so many times when they were younger. She'd missed someone looking out for her.

Lauren held out a hand for the goggles. 'Excited to tick something off the list?'

'I even came prepared!' Cass held up an underwater camera.

The sea was warmed by the sun, and Lauren immediately felt calm as she trod water, trying not to think about how vast and deep the ocean was, and what might lie below. There was too much to worry about, it was best if she didn't think of anything at all.

Instead she stayed close to Cass and Vee as they floated along, bums floating but faces down in the water. The world beneath the surface was magical, there was no escaping it.

The colours seemed beyond bright, in a way she'd never imagined was possible. She never really swam when she went away with Darren. He always picked places that were by the sea, but with pools that were safer. The water always seemed like something to look at, rather than venture into.

The coral was unbelievable, and Lauren felt a distinct sadness that humans had destroyed something so wonderful. She watched as shoals of brightly coloured fish swam by, and poked Vee to get her attention, pointing after them. Cass waved back and forth, then pointed and they both swam after her, almost going into the back of her when she stopped. It was hard to tell what she was looking at, and it was only when Lauren lifted her head and saw other swimmers crowding around that she put her face back in the water in the right direction. The turtle swam right by her, nimble and carefree as humans took photographs and pointed at it. It knew it belonged there, it was accustomed to the visitors.

Lauren felt herself smiling, and then realised she was letting water into her mouthpiece. As she bobbed back up to the surface, she took the chance to wipe the steam away from her goggles, readjust and replace her mouthpiece, before descending again. She turned in a circle, not sure where Cass and Vee had gone. Just as Lauren was about to go back up to the surface, she saw a dark flash of fin out of the corner of her eye. She turned, thinking it was another shoal of fish.

When she saw it, she stilled, trying not to scream or move at all. The shark could only have been a baby, she didn't even know sharks could be that small, but that was definitely what it was. It flicked back and forth in the water, not quite agitated but like a bee uncertain how to escape through a glass window. When she unclenched her jaw, Lauren saw others around her, looking at it, taking pictures just like they had with the turtles. Surely, then, it couldn't be dangerous? Or were people just stupid?

As it swam off, its fin almost brushed past her. She felt the push of the water against her skin, before pushing herself up to the surface, her heart beating in her throat. She coughed, tearing the goggles off, almost crying.

She felt a hand on her shoulder. 'Loll, you okay? Did you see the turtle?' Cass pulled her mask up. 'Loll?'

Lauren turned. 'Did you see the shark?'

'Shark? We wouldn't be swimming here if there were sharks!' Cass laughed, nudging her, 'Such a worrywart. It was probably a really big trout or something! Things are huge here!'

Lauren shook her head, feeling her fingertips go numb. 'It was definitely a shark. My legs are tired, I'm gonna get back on the boat.'

She swam carefully, scouring the water around her for another sighting. When she reached the boat, Lauren quickly pulled herself up the side, then sat there, uncertain of what to do.

Jack arrived on the deck behind her. 'Too much for you?'

'I think I saw a shark.'

He shrugged, reapplying suntan lotion. 'Well probably, poppet, but they'd only be babies round these parts. Won't hurt you.'

Lauren nodded. 'Well, at least I'm not crazy. Cass tried to tell me it was a big trout!'

'Cassy is not the girl to ask about anything to do with critters, on land or sea! Girl once told me her mother had given her a hamster. I looked at the thing, it was a great dirty rat that had come up from the floorboards!' Jack had a loud laugh, which was kind of jarring when you felt light-headed. He stepped around Lauren and jumped straight into the water with a, '*Wahoo!*', ignoring the steps.

She couldn't help but laugh at that, a grown man still so excited to jump in the sea like a child. Vee would be happy here. She'd have a life most kids would dream of, surrounded by family, loved and treated well. She'd have adventures and learn new things, a whole new wilderness to explore. Still, the ache in Lauren's chest started to throb.

Cass swam over to the boat, shielding her eyes as she trod water. 'Ahoy there, captain! I'm coming up!'

Lauren scuttled back to give her room, but after a few moments, she still hadn't made it up the steps. Lauren peered over and saw Cass clinging to the bottom, her muscles clenched against the pressure of holding on. She kept trying to pull herself out, but immediately fell back again.

'Cass ...'

'I'm fine.' Cass gritted her teeth. 'Get me a towel, would you?'

Lauren did so, then paused at the top, before putting the towel down and reaching out a hand.

'Cass, come on, let me help.'

'I'm *fine*.'

Lauren huffed, 'If you don't take my bloody arm, I'm going to jump in and push you up from behind. Come on.'

Cass reached up for her hand, and Lauren pulled her up, surprised by how little effort it took. She was certainly thinner, which may have been why she wore that T-shirt over her swimsuit. She barely weighed a thing. It was disconcerting.

'You're still bloody stubborn.' Lauren threw the towel at her, and Cass laughed.

'Says you. Don't think I've ever met anyone more committed to a bad idea just because she'd already told people about it.'

'Which one was that?' Lauren tried to keep the tone light, but Cass hated accepting weakness. She knew where this could go, so easily.

'The one where you married a scumbag you were never that bothered about, because your mum convinced you that you couldn't do any better?'

Lauren took a breath, looking out at the water. 'Where's Vee?'

'Jack's with her. No response to that?'

'It *was* a shark earlier, you know, Jack said there are baby ones around here.'

Cass half screamed in frustration. 'I thought we were getting somewhere, Lauren. After you apologised about stuff, I thought everything with Darren—'

'Apologised?'

'In the church, in Spain.' Cass shivered a little, wrapping the towel around her shoulders, her hair falling in thin wet clumps around her pale face.

'I was apologising for not coming to your mum's funeral!'

Lauren yelped back. 'What do you think I should be apologising for?'

Cass shook her head, eyes to the sky. 'If you don't know that, things between us are more broken than I thought. And we don't have that much time left to fix them. Figure it out, Loll. You're a clever girl.'

'Stop being so patronising! You were the one who was such a fucking mess back then!'

'My mum was sick! I lost my best friend to a bloody moron who treated her like a prize shi-tzu rather than a person, and I had no fucking idea what I was doing with my life. Of course I was a fucking mess!'

Lauren stepped back, hands up. 'I can't do this now, in the middle of the bloody ocean with you. It was horrible back then, I was drowning. I was trying to look after you, and look after him and make everyone happy. I came home every night after smoking in the car and I cried in the shower so he couldn't hear me.'

'At least you had someone to notice you were in the shower, Loll. At least you had someone to answer your calls.' Cass's eyes were hard and cold, and she started shivering, gritting her teeth. She refused to back down, even if she was uncomfortable.

'You can't *blame* me for that! You can't! I was there for *years*. That last year of picking you up from random bars, or clubs, or passed out in takeaway shops ... protecting you from creepy guys, wondering if I needed to take you to the hospital. I even took you to get tested! I was *there*, for so long! It got too much for me. I needed to finish my post-grad course and take my exams and keep my job. I needed to stop my relationship from falling apart because of you. And you *hated* that. You hated that I chose me for once.'

Cass shook her head, reaching for another towel on the side, before padding off to the front of the boat, where there was sunlight. 'But you didn't choose you, Loll. You chose *him*.'

Chapter 18

There was an atmosphere, and there was nowhere to hide. They had another couple of days with Jack and Dolores, and it already felt like there was nowhere left to go. She should have apologised, she knew. She *did* pick Darren, and she was wrong. But if Cass hadn't pushed her, for so many years, to be her carer, to be her conscience, it wouldn't have happened. If Cass hadn't fallen apart so spectacularly, safe in the knowledge that Lauren would be there to pick up the pieces ... she wouldn't have had to make a decision in the first place. But then there would be no Vee, and that was pretty much impossible to comprehend.

Lauren tried to keep herself out of the way, letting the family bond. She sat out on the patio whilst they had tea, her own mug of fresh mint brought out so she could draw her wolves, watching the kids play in the garden. They seemed to have created an obstacle course where certain parts had to be jumped over, whilst others were crawled around or rolled through. Vee seemed relaxed here, and Lauren wondered if she would be the one to bring her here when this was all over, or if Jack would come to England.

Perhaps they would go home and Cass would be fine for another few months, and they'd just become polite acquaintances until she was gone. Lauren wondered if Cass would have enough people to invite to a 'going away' party, if she did the same as her mother. She doubted it, somehow. On the other hand, she could probably fill the room by wandering into a local pub and charming them into attending. It was a different sort of power to Barbara, but the root was the same – they were lovable. She heard soft footsteps come out onto the veranda, and pause behind her.

'Those are good, has Vee seen them?' Cass asked, placing her own mug of tea on the table.

Lauren shook her head. 'They're just doodles.'

'You always shrugged away your talents as if they weren't big and important.'

Lauren tried to laugh. 'Well, there you're wrong, because none of my talents are big or important.'

Cass plonked herself into a chair, delicate fingers tracing the lip of the mug. She seemed to be trying to find the words.

'You know I almost didn't have Vee?' She looked across the grass at her daughter, before meeting Lauren's eyes. 'Why would I, right? Single, alone, child of a man I despised. Proof forever of the one rule I'd broken. I was a fuck-up in every sense of the word, but when I loved someone, I stood by them, never betrayed them. That was the only good thing I knew about myself, and suddenly it was a lie.'

Lauren said nothing, but the pencil grasped between thumb and forefinger stilled.

'I dreamt about dying all the time. I'd dream I went to see Mum, but actually it was me, and I watched myself die. I saw your face as you told me to leave. Haunted me for months, that look of disgust.' Lauren took a breath, clasping the mug to her as she fidgeted. 'So I was going to get rid of the baby. I was going to sell Mum's house and move out here, where I could surf and swim and belong.'

'So what changed?' Lauren felt she needed to say something, even though Cass had already told her. Her desire to survive, to limit her chances of cancer. That's what made her grow and raise and care for another human being. A trade-off: one life to save another.

Cass pressed her lips together. 'I went to the nurse, and we talked about my plans. I told her I wasn't having that baby. No way, no how. I was a lone wolf, I was young, I didn't need a baby right now. And she turned to me, this little woman with all this red hair tied back in this ponytail, and she said, "Don't you know how lucky you are?" and I was so fucking pissed off, but I couldn't stop crying. I cried until I was sick. I don't think I've ever cried like that in front of someone else before. Well, except for you ...' Cass paused, wincing at the memory. 'She explained what she meant, that being pregnant could save my life, and I should consider it as an option, even if I had the baby adopted.'

Lauren felt her eyebrows peak, but tried to keep her facial expression neutral.

'I know, right?' Cass laughed, shaking her head. 'Not only would I be a liar and a cheater and a huge, crazy mess, but she wanted me to bring an unwanted kid into the world just to give myself more time. And I hated myself, because I considered it.'

Lauren wanted her to hurry up. *What changed your mind? What made you into Cass the mother?*

'You,' Cass answered the unasked question. 'I knew what I would do, I would give the baby to you. The perfect answer. The ultimate apology. I would carry this child, your child, keep her safe for you all these months, and then I'd bring her to you. Yes, you'd be upset at first, but when you saw her, you'd forgive me. You'd love me again.'

Lauren stared at her, horrified at how much she'd wished that life had been hers, only for a moment. Perhaps it all would have been different.

'So why didn't you do that?' she croaked out.

Cass's smile was sunshine. 'Because I fell in love with her. I couldn't let her go. No matter how much I loved you and wanted you to forgive me, I couldn't do it. It was suddenly impossible.'

Lauren nodded, feeling the loss in her fingertips. 'You made the right choice.'

'A rare occurrence.'

The silence stretched, and Lauren didn't even try to break it.

'I *am* sorry, you know,' Cass said, picking at the edge of the mug with her fingertips. 'For so many things, more than just Darren. I'm sorry I put so much on you back then. I didn't have anyone else. Everyone was fake.'

Lauren nodded, pencil still shading the wolf mother, holding a cub by the scruff of the neck.

'I only had you. And so ... I tested you, I guess.'

'That's what it was, with Darren?'

'No, my God, no! Lauren, honestly, I was just so drunk and hysterical and shocked, even though I knew Mum was going to die, I just hadn't prepared myself to be alone ... I don't even remember it.'

Lauren held up a hand, trying to push away the image of Cass, tears flowing, on her knees, begging to be forgiven, apologising, struggling to breathe because she was crying so hard. It had broken her heart then, to be cold.

It was hard to remember how cold she had become. She had been numb for so long by that point, barely inhabiting her body for fear of feeling anxious or afraid. Numb was easier. Quiet was easier. Letting Cass go, because Darren was right – she was a bad influence and a mess. She would always need Lauren to clean up her mess, but never call her to ask how she was.

'I should have apologised a long time ago, Cass. But when I think about it, the regret and the shame all bubble up, and it's easier to be angry than to miss you.'

The thought of how much time they'd wasted left a sour taste in her mouth.

'Hey, that's my kind of coping mechanism.' Cass laughed, raising her mug in a salute. 'So we're okay?'

Was that it? All those years and it came down to a couple of 'I'm sorry's and the fact that the fear of losing her again was worse than anything else? Lauren felt herself take her first truly deep breath in what felt like forever. Something had unlocked.

'Yes, we're okay,' she replied, her eyes looking out to the garden. 'Vee seems happy here.'

'It's a great place, loving family, wonderful home. I spent last night dreaming of our life here. Maybe I'd have met some surfer boy with beautiful hair, who'd carry Vee on his back, and make me bracelets from bits of shell and always smell like the sea. Maybe I would have settled, had a different life here. Been part of a family. Not had to do it alone.'

'You've built a family back home, though.'

Cass inclined her head. 'Sure, and I love them, and they love us, but ... it's different somehow. Like using a large piece of fabric to make a quilt, instead of patchworking the offcuts from other people's material. God, I might have had someone who'd take the four a.m. feed, or drive me to the hospital when she was sick, or look after me when we both had flu and I cried because it was hard to be alone.'

Lauren paused. 'I was thinking I shouldn't be here, you can spend the time with your family.'

'No, Loll, don't be stupid. It's about us. This whole thing, it's about us. We're tied together in a way that becomes unbreakable.' Cass sat back in the chair, feet up on the table, and produced the Big Book, suddenly scribbling in it.

'Adding more things or crossing them off?'

'A bit of both. You don't mind, do you? I want to write stuff down before I forget it.'

The silence was companionable, the same as it had been when they'd sat on the floor of a bedroom studying, or reading as they lay on the bed next to each other.

Vee was being chased by Taylor, shrieking as she ran past them. She took the time to wave before continuing her escape. This could be her life, surrounded by cousins who would play with her and family who would feed her up and keep her safe.

'How old is Jack, do you think?' Lauren asked, not lifting her eyes from the sketchbook.

'In his sixties? Dolores is a bit younger. Why?'

'No reason,' Lauren shrugged, 'they just have such a big family. I wonder if it's tiring for them, all the kids and grandkids?'

'I think they love it,' Cass said, before raising her head and sitting in her chair. 'Oh. *I* see.'

'See what?' Lauren's cheeks flushed.

'You're so transparent, Loll, always worrying about the future and what life will bring. Take a leaf out of my book, would you? Life isn't so terribly important.' Cass winked dramatically, laughing to herself.

Lauren didn't say anything, not really sure what she'd been accused of.

'I haven't decided if Vee will live here. I think it's a lot of change for her. I wanted to see how she liked it and get her opinion.'

Lauren nodded and said nothing.

'You want her, Loll? You want my daughter?' Cass's voice was small, and she looked up to the sky, her eyes becoming glassy.

Lauren stayed silent, not sure what the right answer was. Instead, she traced over that same drawing of the small wolf cub, scratches of pen and ink as it howled up at the moon.

Chapter 19

The days had passed quietly, being tourists, being guests. Jack went out of his way to teach and show them everything he could. He knew, Lauren realised now, how sick his niece was. It was in the way he held his head, the tilt of concern every time Cass was tired, or needed a break. He had seen his sister back then, he knew what this part of the journey entailed.

They were leaving to go to the surf camp when he approached her privately.

'Hey, Lauren, this arrived for you.' He handed her a large envelope, and she turned it over in her hands, inspecting the labels before snorting.

'My divorce papers. Excellent timing.'

'Am I congratulating you, or offering condolences?'

'Congratulations are fine. You know, ones that say it's better to realise you were an idiot than to keep on being one.'

Jack laughed, putting an arm around her. 'Good philosophy, kid. Look, I wanted to talk to you about those girls. You're the leader here, looking after them and everything ...'

'Am I?'

He frowned. 'You're the organiser, you made it all happen.

You brought my niece out here when she refused to come before. She said it was on your list together. She wouldn't come without you.'

Lauren's stomach clenched. *Oh God, everything has always been my fault. She would have been out here with her family. If I'd just got one letter, maybe all of this would have been different.* 'Oh.'

Jack waved away her concern. 'Look, she's not well, and she's stubborn as hell. So if you need me, you call me. And if she tells you not to call an ambulance or make a fuss, you make one anyway, okay?'

Lauren nodded.

'Promise, Lauren. Promise you'll call me when everything happens.'

How *ifs* changed to *whens* so quickly. Lauren took his hand, 'I promise. I'm tougher than I look.'

'Oh, I know, kid. Not many people can handle Cassidy. Fewer still bother!'

He gave her a brief squeeze before releasing her, walking over to the rental car where the bags were being rearranged to fit into the boot. 'Hey now, let's get this sorted, shall we?' she heard him say, clapping his hands together dramatically.

There were different types of love, and different types of bravery.

The drive down the coast was easy enough, being on the same side of the road. Cass had always been a fairly decent navigator, a fact which shocked most people. It was one of the things Lauren had liked best about their road trips in the past. They'd play music and laugh, and take turns driving, but she could always depend on Cass to get them where they needed to be.

The journey to the surf camp was a fair few hours down the coast, and when they arrived, it was almost empty. The little huts were set back from the main road, down a dirt path, and old surfboards held signs to guide their way.

'Heya, how's it going?' The guy behind the desk was reading the paper, his ginger dreadlocks scraped back in a loose bun. He grinned toothily. 'I'm Mac. Checking in?'

It was quiet, Mac explained as he took their bags through to the room, because the waves were good, and everyone had jumped on the bus to catch them. 'You've got your class tomorrow though, so until then, hang out, take it easy.'

Their room had three sets of bunk beds, and Lauren laughed as Vee tried out each of them to decide which was best. They wandered the grounds, sat in the beanbags and hammocks in the garden, nibbling on chocolate bars they bought from the tuck shop. There was an air of school trip about the whole place, which was comforting. It was quiet and relaxed, the hammocks swaying in a slight breeze. Lauren felt completely at peace, smiling as her fingertips trailed the ground.

She heard the click of the camera and opened one eye to find Vee standing over her with the phone.

'Cassy said to take a picture.' Vee pointed at her mother, not even attempting to take the blame.

Cass raised a hand without lifting the canvas hat that was placed over her eyes. 'I did. I said it was rare to see a relaxed Loll in the wild, up close like this. An endangered creature.'

'Ha,' Lauren snorted, adjusting herself as Vee decided to crawl into the hammock with her. 'Hello, what's this?'

Vee smiled up at her. 'Cassy said you were drawing more wolves. I want to see.'

'Please,' prompted Cass.

'*Please*,' Vee added, wide-eyed and over the top. 'Pleaaaaaaaase.'

Lauren reached into her bag with one hand, pulling the sketchbook free, and passed it over.

'Woah.' Vee thumbed the pages delicately, touching the tops of the fluffy ears, or tracing a sharp fang. 'Hey, it's me!'

It was, although Lauren was convinced it was a bad sketch, with Vee's face a little too round to be right. It was close enough to be her though, Storm the husky cuddled up against her neck, her eyes squeezed tight in joy.

'You're *very good*, Auntie Loll. Cassy, did you know Auntie Loll was good at drawing?'

Cass sat up, sharing a look of amusement with Lauren. 'Sounds just like my mum, right? "*Darling, you must meet Jemima – she's a fabulous ballet dancer, just fabulous.*"'

'"*Meet Dennis,*"' Lauren added, hooting with laughter, '"*he's terribly good at the* Sunday Times *crossword – always gets fifteen down, don't you, Dennis?*"'

'What? What's funny?' Vee was upset at being left out of the joke, and had a suspicion she was being laughed at.

'You sound a lot like your grandma,' Lauren gave her a squeeze, 'and it made us remember how funny and lovely she was, that's all.'

'You knew my grandma?'

'Sure did,' Lauren looked across at Cass, trying to figure

out how she was feeling. She had a strange smile on her face, the remnants of laughing about her mother, coupled with a realisation. She looked like she'd finally solved a maths problem she didn't really want the answer to.

'Let's see these wolfies then,' Cass said, gently tipping herself out of her hammock and ambling over. She leaned over to look, and a smile blossomed.

'You know, I think I know what we should do with these ...' She held up a finger, before retrieving the Big Book. She opened it on the second page and pointed to number seventeen.

Lauren sighed, 'Oh God, really?'

'Are you ever going to do it if you don't do it with me?'

'Probably not!' Lauren laughed, 'Is that a bad thing?'

'You tell me,' Cass shrugged, pretending not to care, her eyes to the sky, 'I mean, we *could* be driving into town right now to find somewhere ...'

'And probably ending up with a bunch of diseases and our arms falling off.'

'More of a long-term problem for you than for me there, babe.'

Vee frowned, crossing her arms and wriggling out of the hammock. The adults had been talking in riddles for too long. 'I want to know what's going on!'

Cass waited for Lauren to respond, one eyebrow raised in a challenge. 'It's up to you, Loll. How brave are you feeling?'

Lauren sighed, wondering why the little thrill of adventure still made her do stupid things when Cass was around.

'Veronica, me and your mum are off to get tattoos.'

*

'S'not fair,' Veronica huffed, sitting with the sketchbook in her lap as her mother was tattooed. 'I want one too. You get wolfs and I don't.'

'Wolves,' Cass said, wincing as the tattooist adjusted her grip on her wrist. 'And when you're eighteen, if you want one, you can have one. Just ... Loll, you'll keep her in line, right? No England flags, boys' names or things on her face, okay?'

'I just want a wolf too,' Vee said quietly, stroking the drawing of the cub on the page. 'That's my one.'

Lauren gave her a squeeze, keeping her taped-up wrist out of the way. Cass had made her go first, in case she chickened out, and she had to admit, it was nice to be nudged into something. For every anxious thought that popped into Lauren's head, Cass had a, 'So what?' to respond to it with. It was like a battleground. She vowed to say, 'So what?' more often.

'Well, when you're older, if you want that one, you can have it.'

She knew that didn't mean much to the little girl, who so desperately didn't want to be left out of anything.

'Hey, give me your arm,' Lauren said, getting her black biro out of her bag. She carefully started outlining the same image Vee clung to on the page, offering as much detail as she could on the girl's delicate wrist. By the time Cass was wrapped up, Vee's 'tattoo' was finished too, and she admired it, twisting her arm this way and that.

'I won't wash and it will stay there,' she said, nodding her head.

Lauren made a face. 'Umm ... how about you *do* wash, and I'll just draw it on every day again?'

'But if you're not with me?'

Lauren looked at that little face in distress, not sure how to answer. She was right. What if Vee lived in Australia after everything? What if she never saw her? What would she do when she had to go back to her life?

'Aunt Loll will be around, baby girl,' Cass calmed her, the same solid voice she'd used to calm Lauren multiple times over the years. 'And if she's not there at some point, she'll teach you how to draw your own one.'

Lauren nodded, saying nothing.

'Now, we can tick that off the list,' Cass said, taking her daughter's hand. 'I think we deserve some ice cream.'

That night, Lauren lay in the bottom bunk, listening to the snuffling noises from her travel companions. She kept looking at the outline of the wolf on her wrist, head back, howling, all strength and strong lines. Cass had chosen hers for her, opting for a more sedate one for herself – a wolf curled up softly into a ball, ready to sleep, but eyes still watching closely for change. Always ready to pounce.

It had seemed so easy – she had decided something, and had done it. There was no little voice whispering about whether it was tacky, or what people would think. That voice had always sounded like Darren. The one that asked her why she'd do something so stupid and asked if it would affect her job prospects sounded like her mother. The voice that quietly asked, full of exasperation, when she would finally stop worrying so much, sounded like her own. The imaginary version of Cass sat in the back of her mind, reclining with a glass of wine, and simply said, '*Don't worry. You'll figure it out. Way to go being brave, babe. And wasn't it fun?*'

Cass had been scribbling non-stop in the Big Book, and Lauren thought maybe she was keeping a diary of their adventures, listing all the things they were doing so Vee could have it later on. She hoped she'd crossed out some of the terrible ideas they'd written in their early twenties. But maybe there would be a time Vee would want to read that, to know that her mother wanted to skinny dip and take drugs and go dancing. Stupidity was appealing in nostalgia. *'Oh God,'* she could imagine Vee saying in the future, *'can you believe my mum?'*

It was still light outside, and the frosted windows at the top of the room did very little to keep anything out. Lauren slipped her hand into the front of her suitcase under her bunk and pulled out the paperwork Darren had sent her. The legal jargon didn't bother her – it was exactly how she'd expected, and it was a relief that everything was as he'd said. She didn't care, she just wanted what was hers, and to be done. There were so many endings, this one was the least of her issues.

Cass was right – she should have apologised. She had chosen Darren when she shouldn't have. She'd had a choice between a horrible truth and a palatable lie, and she'd been weak. She'd preferred to live in the dream, hoping everything would be okay if she just tried hard enough.

Lauren scribbled her signature, almost pushing the point of the pen through the page. It was time to wake up.

Chapter 20

Sometimes, there is such a thing as a perfect day. You can taste it in the air, a sweetness on the breeze that tells you everything is going to go your way. You might play the lottery, ask that special person out for a drink. You might simply do the same walk you do every day of the year, but notice a flower you've never seen before, or the smile of an old man waiting for the bus. You feel grateful to be alive. Lauren knew it was going to be a day like that the minute she saw Cass's smile that morning.

'Hello, sleepyhead,' she whispered, smiling. 'I see the fairies arrived in the night to end your time as a sad *Mrs*.'

'Just the beginning of a long process,' Lauren sat up, 'but I do feel better for it.'

'Of course, you do! You're going to be free to start again. So why don't you get up and come do some sunrise yoga with us?'

Lauren blinked. 'Sunrise? Is Vee up?'

She turned her head and saw the little girl waving from her bunk. 'I'm good at the sleeping one,' she said, splaying her arms wide and pretending to be asleep.

'Me too,' Lauren laughed, getting up. 'Okay, let's salute the sun as it's coming up. Insane.'

'You're way too easily pleased, Loll,' Cass said, padding out of the room barefoot and leading them to the garden they'd rested in the night before.

The air had a surprising crispness, and the camp felt quiet and sleepy. A few people in brightly coloured clothes assembled silently behind the woman dressed in purple, already stretching.

'Grab a mat and relax,' she intoned, not stopping her fluid movements.

They bumbled along, and Lauren felt herself looking around at other people, wondering if they were in their pyjamas too, looking for examples of imperfection, trying to ensure she wasn't the biggest mess there. And then she simply took a breath, and let it go.

She was here. She was in Australia with her dear friend, and her wonderful daughter. She was finally having adventures. Life was quiet and enormous, unexpected and yet, not at all overwhelming. She could be brave and still breathe. It was miraculous.

She stretched into her body, breathing deeply, entirely in the moment. For a while, she just spread her arms out in the child's pose and listened to the sound of her breath, feeling like time was endless. As she turned her head to the right, she saw Vee napping in *savasana* pose just as she'd promised, her little snores gentle in the breeze.

Cass seemed to be completely at peace, a look of relief on her face as she stretched and moved, her body looking stiffer than Lauren had realised. She'd been in pain, and had been silent. She hadn't punished others, or drawn attention. She'd been completely selfless in her discomfort, only making sure that Lauren and Vee were happy. She'd been looking after both of them, Lauren realised, letting them think it was the other way around. She felt this sudden rush of love for her friend, who had given her such a gift even as she was dealing with something so unbelievably terrifying.

When they finished yoga, they napped for a while in the shade of the trees, crawling into the hammocks and beanbags, or remaining on their mats. It was only the smell of pancakes that woke Lauren from her haze about an hour later, music playing on a rattling speaker in a hut in the garden.

That hut, it appeared, was the kitchen and dining area. People flooded out of their rooms, apparently starving as they queued up for pancakes, poured coffee from the urn and peeled fruit at their tables, sharing and passing things around.

Everyone had a story, it became clear at that breakfast table. Everyone was running to or from something, had fears and dreams and things they'd rather not talk about. For once, it was easy to be amongst these people, not to have to prove anything to anyone.

The pancakes were easily the best she'd ever eaten, and for the first time in a long time, Lauren felt ravenous, as though her body had awoken from a long sleep. She heaped fruit and maple syrup onto them and finished the entire plate, pausing every few chews to sigh in disbelief at how good they tasted. Did everyone taste this? Did everyone realise how extraordinary this was?

Cass ate half, then pushed her plate away, allowing Vee to pick at the fruit, identifying each piece before she ate it.

'Okay, guys, we've checked and the surf is up – great waves today. Let's get suited up and get down there. Leaving in ten!' Mac called out, scraping his hair up into a ponytail.

Everyone sprang into action, piling plates and scraping off leftovers, taking them over to the side of the kitchen, swilling out their coffee mugs. And then they were gone, to change and cover themselves in sun cream.

'Are you going to teach us to surf, Cassy?' Vee asked, pulling on the wet suit that was left in their room. She stood with her hands on her hips, superhero stance. 'I'm going to fight crime. I need a cape!'

Cass wiggled the zip on her own wet suit up, and sighed at how it flapped around her waist, but said nothing, plucking it away once and shaking her head.

Lauren took a deep breath in, zipping it up and resolving not to look at herself. It just had to be practical. She wasn't a fucking mermaid. Besides, this was for Cass. Cass had loved to surf. She'd come here as a teenager when she'd visited her uncle. She'd spoken for years about how surfing was the only sport she liked, that if she could become one with the water, she would.

Whenever they got near the sea, Cass seemed to come alive. Maybe that was why she'd ended up in Blackpool. The sea was changeable, unpredictable. Quiet and calm one moment and destructive the next. The sea could be vengeful, beautiful and overwhelming all at once, drowning you in desire for appreciation. Sounded about right.

The bus arrived at the abandoned beach, and they carried their boards to the sea. The seasoned surfers ran in, eager not to miss a moment. The rest hovered on the beach, waiting to be taught.

Mac, the receptionist, approached. 'All breezy, mates, so, let's get started.'

He was a good teacher, patient but direct. By the time they'd practised getting up on their boards on the sand for what felt like a hundred times, Vee was wiggling all over the place, desperate to get into the sea.

They watched from the beach as Cass went first, suddenly so confident in something she'd only done a handful of times over a decade ago. She was amazing, fluid as she swam, sensing the wave and jumping up on her board, a look of pure joy on her face. She pumped her arms in the air and shouted, 'Woohoo!' waving at Vee and Lauren before wobbling and falling off.

The moment she disappeared under the water, Lauren panicked. She counted, trying to keep Cass's voice in her head: *Don't worry, not everything's dangerous. I'll be fine.*

When she got to five seconds, Cass bobbed up again, laughing. 'That's what happens when you get cocky. Vee, ready to try?'

She was incredibly patient, Lauren noticed, explaining things, listening, waiting. Mac took over, helping Vee practise, perhaps noticing that Cass needed a breather. They stood a little way back, waves lapping their ankles as Vee tried to get up on her board and wobbled, before crouching down again.

'It's okay, baby, just try again. You're doing great!' Cass called out, waving and giving her a thumbs up.

She looked at Lauren. 'You need to stop worrying. She needs to live, and try things. Sometimes she'll get hurt. That's life.'

Lauren took a breath, 'I know, I just ...'

'You want everyone to be safe and okay, I know. There are endless dangers everywhere. But if there's no risk, there's no joy.'

Lauren nodded. 'I know.'

'And you'll worry anyway, I get it.' Cass stared ahead at her daughter as she swam back out to try again. 'Thing is, she'll need someone who encourages her to be adventurous. Not to wrap her in cotton wool. Someone who can be afraid for her without letting it stop her from doing things.'

Lauren said nothing. Vee would stay in Australia, that's what she was saying.

'Keep that little voice in check, Loll. It's your turn.' Cass grinned at her. 'Out you go.'

Lauren was surprised to realise she enjoyed it, letting the waves guide her, draw her back in to the shore. After about half an hour, Cass decided to take a break on the beach, and let the others carry on.

Lauren looked over from helping Vee balance and saw Cass scribbling in the Big Book again, looking up at them and waving. She looked older from a distance, small and thin with her short hair slicked back, hunched up as she scribbled.

Vee managed one more run, catching an excellent wave, and navigated her way to the sand, jumping and whooping as she did so. Cass dropped the book to stand up and run to her, throwing her arms around her in excitement. She kissed her cheeks and forehead, stroking back her hair.

'You were so good! You were great! You're amazing!'

Vee laughed as her mother spun her round, then placed a hand on her cheek, her little eyes intense.

'Cassy ... you okay?'

'Just a bit tired, sweets. Maybe a nap before dinner, I think. Want one too?'

'Babies take naps.'

'Babies, and politicians, and the Spanish, and people who want to be able to keep their eyes open to see the band tonight and have a dance.'

Vee rolled her eyes. 'Okay, but just a small nap.'

'Teeny-tiny,' Cass said, putting an arm around her, 'a nap-let, a nap-tini.'

Lauren snapped a photo of the moment from afar, revelling at how the afternoon sun bathed them both in a glorious gold colour. Today was a good day. It was so good that Lauren didn't want to ruin anything by worrying about their new tattoos, and how they should have kept them dry. Cass, of course, shrugged off the concern – it was a once-in-a-lifetime thing. A few hours falling in the ocean wasn't going to hurt, it wasn't like they spent half a day in the bath. Lauren struggled, peeking up the sleeve of her wetsuit to see if the cling film she'd applied that morning had stayed put. She didn't Google any *what-ifs* though, and that felt like progress to her. Why not believe everything would be fine? It was as likely as not, as Cass said. She didn't mention it again, and felt proud of herself.

By the time they returned to camp, showered and got into dry clothes, they were ravenous. Luckily, someone already had the barbecue going and they gorged themselves on what seemed to be the most delicious food they'd ever eaten – fresh, crisp salad and succulent pulled pork on toasted burger buns with grilled pineapple. Everything was full of flavour, like it had never seemed to be at home. It was as if all her senses were awakening after years of being muffled. The sounds of laughter, the smell of saltwater in her hair even after showering. The feel of grass beneath her bare feet. Lauren couldn't get over it. It was like being drunk. Everything seemed unbelievably beautiful.

After dinner, everyone seemed to laze around, dozing, completely relaxed. Some read books, one of the men in the beanbags strummed his guitar. It was like time was almost standing still. Cass and Vee curled up together on another beanbag, Cass flicking through the Big Book, and Vee retracing the wolf on her wrist in pen, where it had started to wash off.

Lauren's phone began to ring. Not wanting to disturb anyone (and aware that most people calling from the UK would not bring calming vibes to her life at this point) she walked around the back of the garden, following a path down to the herb garden. She didn't recognise the number, calling through an international app. Probably Darren's lawyer calling to confirm she'd received the papers.

'Hello?'

'Lauren?' a man's voice chirruped. 'It's Paul.'

'Oh! Hi.'

'Sorry about calling, I just thought it might be easier than video calling again.'

'It's fine,' she paused. 'Is everything okay? With Vee's homework and school and everything?'

'Oh yes, yes, absolutely, absolutely.' He coughed, then paused. 'It's almost half term.'

'Ah,' Lauren said, wondering where this would go, 'doing anything nice on your break?'

'Nothing very interesting. Just marking, organising stuff for next term ...' He trailed off and Lauren fought to find a way to cut to the chase.

'Um, Paul, I don't mean to be rude, but were you calling for a specific reason?' she said gently, hoping the delivery would mask the sharpness of her words.

'Oh! I guess I just wanted to see how you all were. If Vee was okay, if Cass was ... well, how her health was?'

'They're doing well, Vee's happy. She got to meet a lot of her Australian family. Cass is ... Cass is hiding how much pain she's in. She's tired and weary, but she surfed in the sea today and seemed so happy. It's been a good day.'

'Do you know what you're going to do when it's not a good day?' Paul asked. She could imagine him, tugging at his shirt collar, or running his hands through his hair. Sitting with a mug of tea in the cold weather, whilst she swished her long skirt around her bare feet and breathed in the warm smell of lemongrass from the garden.

'We'll be home soon, we just have to get home, and then ...'

'And then you'll disappear and it'll be someone else's problem?'

'Excuse me?'

'Look ... I'm ... I'm just worried for you, okay? I know Cassidy, I know she's full of adventure and she loves you so much, but she's not well, and she's pushed herself probably further than she should have already. How are you going to deal with her and Veronica?'

'What are you saying, Paul? That we need to come home now because I'm not capable of caring for my friend?'

'No ... what I'm saying is, being there when someone stops being themselves ... it's hard. It's heartbreaking. And Cass mentioned you're an anxious person ...'

'Then why did you help me arrange all this, if you didn't want it to happen? If you thought I couldn't handle it?'

Why was she arguing with this man she barely knew? Why was she trying to make a point, when really, he was making some pretty valid arguments?

'It's not ...' Paul sighed, then tried again. 'I was just trying to ask how *you* were, Lauren. I thought you might need a friend. I thought it might be a lot of pressure to be on this kind of holiday with someone like Cass.'

Lauren immediately deflated. 'Oh. God ... I'm sorry. I jumped down your throat a bit there, didn't I? I seem to keep doing that these days.'

'I'm sorry I didn't explain myself better. I think you're very capable.'

She took a breath, wondered how to move forward. 'It's been wonderful to have this time with both of them. To get to know Cass again. To see parts of her in Vee. I pushed her out of my life for the wrong reasons, and she was kind enough to let me back in.'

'She was excited about this trip. She said you needed it.'

'*I* needed it?' Lauren paused. 'Well, yeah, I suppose I did. And it felt good to keep a promise, to finally do the things we said we'd do.'

'Do you know what you'll do when you come home?'

'Start looking for jobs, I suppose. Or maybe look for places to start over. Do what Cass did – a clean slate.'

'Well ... if you're ever in Blackpool, it would be nice to talk.'

'About what?'

He paused. 'About ... anything.'

'*Ohhh!* Oh, okay. Sure. That would be nice.'

They said their goodbyes, and Lauren hovered in the herb garden a few moments longer. *What was that?* Could Paul actually be interested in *her*? Or would this be just one more man who loved Cass, and wanted a connection through her friend?

Back then it had been boys who wanted information – what did she like, what didn't she like? Did she have a boyfriend, how did they get her attention? For the first time, it didn't seem like that.

She went back to their room to nap, suddenly exhausted, and dreamt of Veronica. A grown-up Veronica, all long, crazy blonde hair like Cass's. She kept walking up to her and saying, '*But you promised I could meet my daddy – where is he?*' and shrugging her off when she tried to grasp her arm. She kept following this girl, and sometimes she was Cass, and sometimes she was Vee. Unbearably interchangeable, as though time didn't exist, and they couldn't be there at the same time.

When she reached for Cass the last time, she tripped and fell, hearing only Paul's voice as he said, 'It's a lot for anyone, Loll.'

She gasped awake before she hit the ground, and saw Cass and Vee staring at her in concern.

'Are you okay? You were mumbling.' Cass reached for her arm. 'Too much sun?'

'Something like that.' She sat up, narrowly avoiding hitting her head on the top bunk.

'Auntie Loll, there's going to be music! And dancing. You have to wear your pretty dress!' Vee's hands-on-hips stance had become something of a regular occurrence on this trip.

'Oi, bossy boots. Your aunt can wear what she wants.'

'No, she needs to wear bright colours and then she'll fall in love and won't be sad about her silly husband.' Vee met Lauren's gaze head on, as if the phrase had been plucked from her thoughts.

'Huh, interesting philosophy there, kid,' Lauren laughed. 'I'm not sad, and I certainly don't need to fall in love. But colours, yes, I think you're right.'

'They make you happy!'

'I agree,' she said, surprised to find the clenched-stomach feeling was gone when she slipped the dress over her head and her wrists were adorned with different bangles and bracelets from the Jones girls' armoury.

'Let's take a picture together,' Cass said, reaching out her arm with the camera as they cuddled in. 'It's rare you get a photo of a perfect day.'

Lauren shook off the remnants of that dream, any thoughts of the future, of the past, or anything but that day. Cass had said it was a perfect day, and it was. She wasn't going to let her brain ruin it.

The perfect day slid into a sweet evening. Everything brought them joy, from the band in the back garden playing bluegrass, to the collection of guitarists in the lounge singing sweeter songs. She and Vee danced, swinging their arms back and forth, laughing as they moved. She felt *fun*, she felt like she was actually herself, that Loll who came to life years before when a strange girl in a club toilet asked for her help. The drinks flowed freely, ridiculously cheap and served in a random array of mugs and glasses, and even Cass got up to dance. She moved more gently, swaying rather than jumping, but she joined in, happy because they were happy.

The evening ended when the sun started to come up. They sat in one of the oversized beanbags, savouring their mugs of wine, Vee asleep on a selection of cushions and blankets in front of them.

Cass watched the couples slow dancing to a softer melody, the guitarist playing on his own as they waltzed.

'I regret never falling in love,' Cass said, twitching her nose. 'I think I would have been good at it, eventually.'

'You were good at being fallen in love *with*, does that count?' Lauren smiled.

Cass shook her head. 'No, to be in love you've got to be vulnerable. The only person I was ever vulnerable with was you.'

Lauren didn't really know what to say about that, so she said nothing.

'Did you keep your dress? The one to wear next time?'

It took Lauren a moment to figure out what Cass was talking about. The second-time dress.

She had been terrified to tell Cass she was getting married. It was during that bad time, when Lauren was desperately trying to hold down working and studying for her post-grad, and Cass was spiralling into party-mad destruction, jumping between jobs and ways to block out Barbara's decline.

There hadn't been much to tell, either.

Darren had been reading the paper, munching noisily on a bacon sandwich, when he had suddenly stopped and looked at her. 'I think we should get married.'

He was tired of wasting time, all the people at work were getting married, and *their* wedding would be much better. They had more taste. They'd throw a wedding people would be talking about for years.

He went on about the food, and the champagne, and how pleased her mother would be. How they could honeymoon anywhere she wanted, somewhere fancy with those little huts on the beach. Aruba, would she like Aruba? He'd been talking so long she hadn't even realised she hadn't said yes. But really, he hadn't asked a question. She'd imagined telling her mother and receiving that final perfect pat on the head, the excitement of planning a wedding together and bonding over dresses and tablecloths. And yet a stone sat resolutely in her stomach. That little voice that told her Darren was only ever meant to be temporary. She dismissed it as anxiety. She was always worrying, always thinking too much. She couldn't trust her brain – it lied a lot.

When it came to telling Cass, she knew it was going to be

painful. There would be arguments and sharp words and who knew if Cass would even be sober when she told her? Things had been falling apart for a while now, and it seemed like Darren was right: Cass wasn't really someone she had anything in common with anymore. And then, just like Cass, she surprised her.

'Well, everyone needs a trial run,' she had breezed over her mimosa, raising her glass. 'Personally, I think you'll get bored of the knobhead before you ever make it up the aisle, but here's to making mistakes and learning from them.'

'Well that's not patronising at all!'

'You forget I know you better than you know yourself sometimes.' Cass had stuck out her tongue.

'Still patronising!'

'Nope, just true. Still, I bet you'll get some decent presents from the knobhead's posh friends. And then when you get married the *second* time, it could be a really chill, quiet affair where no one's looking at you and we get to dance all night to your favourite hits.'

'Well I'm glad you've planned my second wedding. Why wouldn't this be a quiet affair?'

Cass hadn't even responded, just raised an eyebrow and downed the remainder of her drink. Of course, she was right. Lauren had rattled with discomfort. She *was* making a mistake, this wasn't her future. It was so clear to see when she was with Cass, and yet, when she wasn't ...

Cass had simply patted her hand and gestured for the bill, and just like that they were walking down the street, arm in arm, like they had a couple of years before. She led her to a bridal shop, something unusual and kooky. The silver swirly writing above the door read *Missy's* and the bell rang as they walked through. They didn't have an appointment, but Cass had sweet-talked the owner, spun her an earnest yarn about how they were such good friends, and they rarely got to see each other. How it would mean *so much* to be able to share this experience with her friend. How the fiancé was loaded and would drop some serious cash on the dress.

She got her way, and watched as Lauren had delicately fingered the dresses on the hangers, too scared to make a choice. Cass stood by her side, nodding as her hand hovered over one. 'Try it!'

When Lauren came back out, she shone. The dress was simple, sixties in style, short with three-quarter-length sleeves and a boat neck with beading. Lauren remembered how wearing that dress felt like the lights being turned on. Cass had clapped and whooped and made her twirl, pinning a veil in her hair whilst they sipped flat prosecco the owner had in the fridge.

'You know I won't end up wearing something like this though,' Lauren said, meeting Cass's eyes in the mirror as she adjusted the veil. 'It won't be enough for them. It's not grand, or attention seeking. It's little mousy Lauren, trying to hide away again.'

'But it's the opposite, when you really look at it. When you notice the detail of the pattern in the fabric, the pearls that are sewn in. The strength and structure of the skirt. It's completely extraordinary. It's you, Loll.'

She shone in that moment, in the light of Cass's flattery. It was easy to mock the effect on others until she turned it your way. Lauren splayed the skirt, looking at herself in the mirror and twirling as it moved with her.

'Wedding number two,' Cass had nudged her, smile unwavering. 'That one will be simple, relaxed. Registry office and a dance in a cute barn. You'll wear this and the guy will wear jeans and a waistcoat and we'll all dance to a live salsa band and your mother will be miserable but no one will care.'

Lauren felt herself tearing up, and pressed her lips together, Cass raising an eyebrow as she stroked the sleeves of the dress.

'Thank you for this. For being happy for me.'

'I'm not happy for you, Loll. I think if you marry that man it'll be one of your biggest regrets. But, we all need regrets, right? We all need stories.'

'Will you pretend on the day?' Lauren asked.

'As best I can, if you want me to. Though I'm also gonna have an escape car ready. Maybe the Batmobile? Something cool. I'll have a case packed for you, and if you decide you want to do a total dramatic run from the church slow-mo style, I'll be waiting.'

She'd left the shop that day with Cass, feeling more than ever that Darren was wrong. Cass was still her friend, still the person who knew her best in the world. She was hurting, and her mother was sick, and there were a hundred other things, but she still loved Lauren better than anyone else ever had.

Cass had gone back and bought the dress for her. She'd sent it to the house with the tag, *For the second time around*. But it arrived only days after everything else happened, after Babs died. After they fell apart. The dress had felt like an obstinate apology, a defiant admission of guilt. A reminder that she was making a mistake.

She had put it away, bought an over-the-top dress that her mother had loved, and tried to ignore the clenched feeling in her stomach as everyone looked at her on her wedding day.

Lauren wanted to look at the dress again, suddenly. To run her fingertips over the fabric and notice how detailed it was, how special. That her friend had seen the most beautiful thing in that shop and decided it was for her. That was a gift.

She looked at Cass, lit by the light of the fire, short hair and protruding collarbones, and still no less magic than she always had been.

'I'd forgotten about the dress,' she said, trying to find the words. 'I kept it. I thought ... when it arrived, it was after everything ... I thought it was one of your apologies, but the lady said it had been ordered months before.'

'God, apologising by buying you a wedding dress?' Cass winced. 'I'm not insane.'

Lauren couldn't help but laugh, 'I loved it though, maybe I'll try it on when I get home.'

'It can be your something old for when you get married again.'

'I can't even imagine the possibility of that right now.'

Starting over, starting again? Finding someone you chose, over and over again each day, who complemented you instead of drowning you out. The idea of finding someone she was sure about, without the doubt or gnawing worry ... how would she make that choice without Cass there to tell her she'd picked a winner or a loser?

'I know, but you will, one day,' Cass said, then paused. 'I regret you never falling in love either.'

'You have to stop thinking for more than five minutes to fall in love.' Lauren laughed again.

'So do it. Take a chance. Who knows?'

Lauren said nothing. As if it was that easy.

It was nice to dream though. To imagine a world where she started over, becoming that person she'd always thought she might be. She tried to imagine herself in a little flat with a balcony, looking out on a beautiful view, or living on a boat. She could do anything, go anywhere. There were too many possibilities, so many that none seemed appealing. The world was suddenly too big.

'I want her to stay with you,' Cass said, staring out at the dancers, a lilt of drunkenness in her voice. 'Vee, I mean. After.'

'I thought ...' Lauren paused. 'What about Jack?'

'They've had their kids, they don't need to be raising one again. Although it'd be nice if you brought her out here to see them every now and then.'

'Has this whole trip been one of your tests, Cass?'

She held up her hands. 'That makes it sound like I've been scheming, and I have, but not in the way you think. I was just giving you time. Not everyone wants to raise their dead friend's kid whilst going through a divorce and having to find a new job. I wouldn't blame you.'

'I want to be there for her,' Lauren said immediately.

'I know.'

'I'd look after her.'

'I know.'

'You think I'd worry too much?'

'I know you would, but that's okay. You learn to let them breathe. And didn't you once say I was the voice in your head? I'll stop you from suffocating her, make sure you give her the freedom she needs.'

They sipped at their wine in silence.

'I'm not sure what to say. It feels weird to say thank you,' Lauren said.

'Then don't,' Cass shrugged.

'Do you feel you've got what you wanted from our trip? Are you happy?'

Cass nuzzled back into the beanbag, nestling in as she considered it. 'Well, I guess in some ways it's worse, because now I really don't wanna go. But I'm feeling it now. I've been trying to hide it but I know you've noticed. It's starting to feel ... hard to be alive, I guess.'

'Cass—'

'But everything I wanted has happened. I got to see you and Vee have these experiences I wanted for you, this growth and strength.'

'You wanted for *us*?'

Cass's smile was like a light bulb. 'Of course. This was for you too, Loll. So you could grow and live, and do all the stuff you'd never do without me there. I mean, I bet you didn't do one thing on that list in the time we were apart, even though it was *your* book, *your* list?'

'God, you're right. That's pathetic. *I'm* pathetic.'

Cass shook her head. 'You just have to remember that it's important for you to do a lot of living. I'm not going to be here to push you. But you'll have Vee. She's good at teaching you how to be in the moment, how to feel alive. Kids have that *thing*. Like the excitement at a rainbow or a fifty-pence bottle of bubbles.'

'What if I do a bad job, with her? What if I fuck up?'

'Impossible,' Cass said. 'I am asking you, dear Loll, to love my absolutely perfect daughter for the rest of your life. To give her everything you have. That's all.' She grinned. 'She has only the best parts of me. And she has the best parts of herself which is even better. She'll look after you, and you'll look after her. That was the plan.' She wriggled her fingertips as if presenting a final number on stage. 'I even named her Veronica, just for you.'

'Cass, what does that even mean?'

'It means that I knew. I knew it would come to this. You were always meant to be part of our lives, Loll. You were meant to be her fairy godmother. I named her Veronica for your grandmother, the woman who believed in you, who knew you were strong in your own way, that you could do anything. Now you get to be that for Vee, and she gets to be that for you. Strong, amazing women looking after each other.'

Lauren shook her head, struggling to keep it together.

'We missed out on that time together, but you still get it with her, and that's what matters.' Cass looked up to hide the shine in her eyes. 'At the beginning I felt guilty for keeping her, because of how she came to be. Like it was another betrayal. But ... I finally loved someone more than anything else in the world. She helped me survive, gave me a purpose.'

Cass pressed her lips together, tried to take a breath as she looked at her daughter sleeping in front of them.

'You know how everyone tells you to live every day like it's your last? I did. I do. I knew no matter how much I did or how many pills I took or therapies I tried or however many parts of me they cut away, I was gonna leave this world early, just like my mum.

'I knew when I had this little girl that one day she would be raised by someone else. I'd hoped it would be you. It was always meant to be you. And if one day you go from "Auntie Loll" to "Mum", I won't be annoyed, I promise. I'll be pleased.'

'That's mad,' Lauren protested. 'She's your daughter, she's you all over again. You just have to look at her to see it.'

'Exactly, you'll have me back again, but a better version. And she'll keep you doing silly things, pushing you and having adventures. And you'll give her what she needs – structure, stability, all that family stuff. The stuff you gave me.'

'Is this your final selfless fucking act or something? Your apology gift for everything, *giving* me your daughter? It's mad, it's too much,' Lauren shook her head, not really sure what to say or do. She had wanted this, hadn't she? She had wanted Vee for herself, to love her and care for her and remind her every day about Cass and how magical she was. Now it seemed like she'd been tricked into it. She felt guilty again, somehow.

Cass smiled. 'When you put it like that, I guess it is a gift, isn't it? The best gift I can think of, for each of you. You get my Vee, and she gets my Loll. Not selfless at all, it's just right. A perfect circle. You remember how your dad always said I was the sun and you were the moon?'

'Because you were bright and interesting and I was dull and moody,' Lauren huffed and Cass laughed, nudging her.

'No ... although yes about the moody. We needed each other because we were different. I needed that calm soothing thing you have, and you needed that frazzle of nutty energy. I'm the sun and you're the moon and we're both needed. And now we're taking turns looking after the world.'

Cass pointed at Vee, pleased with herself at the analogy. Lauren swallowed a sob.

'And you'll look after each other,' Cass continued, 'the only two remaining people to ever really know and love Cassidy Jones.'

She had to hand it to her, Cass had always managed to manipulate a situation so she got exactly what she wanted from people. She said it, and watched as Cass laughed.

'Remember you asked if I was testing you? I wasn't. I was training you, for her. You've completed your training. The only thing left to do is stop being so afraid to live. Because I promise you, dying is scarier.'

Lauren did nothing but reach out a hand, tears streaming down her face, interlocking her fingers with Cass's. Their hands clasped, tattooed wrists tying them together as they looked at the young girl between them, a legacy for them both.

Sometimes joy and loss both taste like saltwater.

Chapter 21

Cass's scribbles in the Big Book had become more frantic. She picked it up every second moment, either worried she'd leave it somewhere, or afraid she'd forget what she'd started writing. She sat in the back seat of the car, hunched over the book whilst Vee fiddled with the radio and Lauren concentrated on the road.

Lauren had posted her divorce papers that morning, and even though she knew it was only the start of the long process ahead, it felt good to get that part out of the way. She had no idea what she'd be doing with her career, but she had been tasked with caring for the one thing Cassidy Jones loved more than anything else. The sun and moon, like Cass said. She had a starring role. The full moon to Cass's setting sun. She had a purpose.

It was just the pain of what would happen in the lead-up to the end that scared her. The days in the car contemplating on the open road didn't help, her mind searching for answers that simply didn't exist yet. Vee seemed to agree.

'Where now, Auntie Loll?'

'We are going to a rainforest. It's this big park called the Blue Mountains.'

'I liked the surfing. And the dancing.'

'You'll like the rainforest too. There's apparently also ... *drum roll* ... a chocolate shop. We can go walk around then taste a bunch of chocolate.'

'Okay.' Vee turned in her seat. 'Cassy, what do you think?'

'I think ...' Cass finished her current scribble with a flourish. 'That the beauty of the rainforest will definitely inspire me to eat some chocolate. And maybe you will learn some stuff to do a project for Mr T. Lots of interesting plant-type stuff!'

'More school,' Vee pouted, crossing her arms.

'Don't be like that, you get to tell a story about your big adventure! Everyone will be so jealous,' Lauren said, her eyes meeting Cass's in the mirror, asking if this lie was acceptable. Cass nodded with the wisdom of motherhood.

There was so much to ask her, to check with her. How would she do everything right, how could she raise her the way Cass would? And how would she explain to her parents that she was caring for Cass's daughter? Would she tell them Vee was Darren's? That would unravel everything. Sometimes, it was easier to say nothing. Yet, hadn't just "going along with everything" all these years been part of the issue? Perhaps she should be honest and open, and if they didn't like it, that was fine.

Lauren was learning to live with the idea that she could do what she wanted without permission or acceptance. She had been given a chance, in this trip, in finding Cassidy again, in Veronica. Whilst there would be hard times ahead, the air tasted a little sweeter now that she was allowed to breathe it. She got to choose her life, and she chose this one. They would go back home to Blackpool and make as much of the time as they could.

They seemed to be driving forever, the road stretching on and on. They stopped frequently, for snacks and petrol and lunch, just to break the time up. No one spoke much, enjoying the peace and quiet of the journey, or perhaps dealing with their own thoughts of home and what would happen next. Vee did her homework and played around on a tablet, showing an intense concentration in the furrow of her brow. And still, Cass scribbled on and on in the Big Book.

By the time they reached the mountains, it was early afternoon the next day, and Lauren felt like she could sleep for a lifetime. They checked into a bed and breakfast with a view of the sun setting, the haze of colour surrounding the mountains in the distance.

'See, that's why they're called blue,' Cass pointed out, her hand on Vee's shoulder.

'But *why* are they blue though?'

Cass shrugged. 'The atmosphere? I don't know. We'll find out tomorrow.'

She wrote furiously through dinner, until even Veronica lost her patience. 'It's rude to do things at dinner.'

Cass looked up, like a child caught being naughty, then held her pen up, closing the book. 'You're right, baby, I'm sorry. Tell me about your favourite part of the trip.'

Vee blinked. 'The surfing.'

'Yes, but that was the most recent. What about the

beautiful dancing in Seville? What about the huskies, or meeting Santa?'

The child wracked her brains. 'I liked the hammocks. And the burgers.'

Cass laughed. 'Good thing we took photos if your memory is that bad!' Under her breath she added, 'Doesn't look good for me, does it?'

Lauren heard and squeezed her hand, shaking her head.

'I want to take a photo,' Vee said suddenly, scrambling for Cass's phone.

'Um—'

'Please and thank you!' Vee added in a hurry, fearful the phone would be taken away.

Cass handed the phone over. 'What are you taking a photo of?'

Vee turned the phone towards the two adults, indicating they should put their heads together. They smiled sweetly, leaning against each other as Vee counted down from three. The minute she reached one they pulled faces, sticking tongues out and flaring nostrils. It was a grotesque and hilarious photograph, and Lauren was weirdly pleased to be in it. She wasn't always worrying, she wasn't always wondering what people thought of her. Sometimes she was just a girl sitting in a hotel dining room, pushing her nose up so it looked like a snout. *Fucking ridiculous, and wonderful.* Vee was grouchy about having her photograph ruined, but Cass tickled her into submission, coaxing a begrudging smile.

That night, they fell asleep on the huge bed together, lying on top of the covers. Vee was between them with Storm nestled in the crook of her arm. They had been reading a story together, laughing along as Cass did the impressions of each animal.

'You know, this is what I imagined when I thought about having a family,' Lauren whispered, 'this kind of moment.'

'This is what I imagined when I thought I might have someone to share it with,' Cass replied, smiling even as her eyes were closed. 'You realise why this is the way it is?'

'What is the way it is?'

'Timing, moments, righting wrongs, everything. It's because you're my fucking soulmate, Loll. That's what it is. The universe knows. It won't let me screw us up again.'

'Oh well, that's really comforting, that hard, factual evidence. Thanks for that.' Lauren laughed quietly, curling up on her side to look at Cass. She paused, unsure if she should ruin this moment. 'Do we need to talk about stuff? About everything back then?'

Cass shook her head sleepily. 'Oh, you know, let's just not. You know I'm sorry, right? Let's just put it down to life being hard, and us being different types of fuck-ups in our early twenties. And let's be grateful that dickhead's gone, and we're together. We won! Let's just be grateful. Is that okay? Is that enough?'

Lauren nodded, grasping her hand. She wondered if she really did have anything more to say, anything more she needed to know. Her friend had betrayed her what felt like a lifetime ago, slipping away into grief and self-destruction. Her fiancé had lied and she'd believed the wrong person. She had married him anyway. Did they need to talk about it more than that? Two confused twenty-somethings and some terrible choices.

Cass had done something awful, and had spent her life punishing herself. The kind of punishing that only Lauren would be able to understand. A life alone, because that was what she deserved.

It was time to end that now. She found relief in getting it out of the way. It was done, it didn't matter anymore. Only this mattered. The three of them, together.

That was how it would stay when they got home. She would be here on this ride until the end, that much was clear.

'Come on, get some sleep. We have an early start tomorrow with a big, exciting day,' Lauren said.

'See, you're a natural at this mum thing already, you always were. You were excellent at looking after me.'

Yeah, until I wasn't, Lauren replied in her head, trying to keep hold of that calm she'd found. *If* only she'd been there for Cass, *if* only she'd not prioritised Darren, *if* only they'd travelled sooner. But then Veronica wouldn't exist, and Cass might already be gone by now. An unbroken friendship couldn't change biology. Cass was sure everything was happening the way it was meant to. If she could believe that, nearing the end, Lauren had no right to feel otherwise. No more mooning over lost time or bad decisions. In the end, it all came down to the same thing.

'Love you, Cass,' she said quietly, hoping she was already asleep.

'Love you, Loll,' Cass mumbled back as she curled up. 'Always.'

*

The hike through the Blue Mountains was beautiful, a plethora of colour and sound. It was so much more than simply a forest, or a jungle. Even the mess of trees, fighting for life as the sunlight skipped through holes in the canopy felt unearthly.

They'd started their day early, planning out their route through the park, and Cass had been insistent that they had to do it. She'd missed out when she was in Australia as a teen, and she wasn't missing out again. So they'd slathered themselves in sun cream, packed their backpacks with water bottles and snacks, and jumped on the bus to the starting point.

Lauren had started to relax finally. She could see how everything would work now. The shadows of the past were lifted, all had been forgiven and she was no longer shackled to the person she always had been. She could be something else. The smallest shift, and the resentment had started to crumble away. Colour had returned. Cass had done that for her.

That didn't make the hike any easier, but Lauren was determined not to grumble, or moan or worry too much. They were coming to the end of their adventure, the weeks and months ahead would be hard enough. It was important to be present.

The heat was intense, and it was hard to breathe because of the moisture in the air. Lauren wiped the sweat from her forehead with the bottom of her T-shirt, and offered a bottle of water to Vee. The little girl was struggling, weary arms flailing as she tried to propel herself up the steps carved out of rock.

It had been an hour since they had commented on how beautiful it all was, that had drained away into exhaustion as they simply tried to find a vantage point. Yes, there were signs and other people scattered here and there, but Lauren knew they would have to make it out of the rainforest itself, climbing up to the road to get the bus, or to stop in one of the restaurants or cafés to truly appreciate the view.

Cass was the only one who seemed to be in love with the rainforest, eyes taking it all in like she couldn't believe the colour. Trying to match up this version of Cassidy with the one who was all heeled boots and sparkly leggings on the dance floor at university was almost impossible. These memories would sit side by side, a before and after, a sign that people could grow and change and wear green khaki shorts without the judgement of their past selves.

'I'm tired!' Vee sighed, a permanent pout marring her features.

'Oh look. kiddo, we're almost at the top, okay? And then we'll catch our breath before we go to the chocolate shop!' Cass told her daughter, reaching out to pat her arm. Lauren didn't mention that the chocolate shop may be on the other side of the canyon. Whatever it took to get to the top. All she wanted was to know they'd be standing at the top soon, breathing air that didn't fight her lungs when she inhaled.

Cass gave Vee a teasing smile, nudging her as she adjusted her hat. 'Look, if I can do it, you can do it.'

She hurried ahead, taking two steps at a time so she could reach the next landing. The lush greenery framed her perfectly, the bright blue sky peeking through the canopy. They looked up at her, standing there all triumphant, struggling for breath, grinning at them with her skinny arms waving about, her floppy hat shielding her from the sun. Lauren almost reached for her phone to take a picture, there was so much joy and cheekiness in the movement. And then, almost in slow motion, Cass fell.

In that moment, time seemed infinite, like her body wouldn't move quickly enough. All she could register was Veronica's painful scream of 'Mummy!' before she went hurtling up the steps to the landing, throwing herself on top of Cass. 'Mummy, Mummy!'

Lauren could feel her brain shutting down in panic. It was becoming hard to even see, the beating in her chest a painful gallop that made her dizzy.

Hey there, Loll, it's fine, Cass's voice inside her head said, calm and soothing. *You just have to be calm for Vee, okay? You have to take control and not be scared.*

Lauren nodded to herself, running up the steps and trying not to look at Vee's face, streaming with tears as she pawed at her mother.

'Vee, sweetheart, this is very important, okay? You need to go up ahead, up those steps and anyone you find, you ask them for help and to call an ambulance.'

Vee looked frozen in panic. 'I can't!'

'You absolutely can – I'm going to lift your mum and we'll be right behind you, okay? But the sooner we get help, the better.'

She felt like she was on autopilot, calling after her, 'Keep yelling back so I know where you are, okay?'

'Okay!' Vee looked back one more time before scampering up the trail.

Lauren looked at Cass, unconscious but breathing. She briefly checked for any cuts, and prayed that any moment, Cass would wake up, laughing about what a fright she'd given them. Dehydration, exhaustion, that had to be all it was. She fanned her, tried pouring some water on her face. Should she even be moving her? There was no phone signal this low down, and even if there was, how would she tell them where they were? No, she was making the right decision. They had to get to the road.

Just make a decision, Loll, and go with it. Trust yourself, you're smart. You can do this.

She crouched down, putting an arm under Cass and standing up with her. It was so strangely reminiscent of that year when she'd had to keep barging into bars, pubs and clubs to rescue her, unable to stand up on her own. She'd turned up in her pyjamas most nights, nodding at the bouncers who had started to recognise her, knowing she was there to make their lives easier. She'd find Cass passed out in the toilets or curled around a stranger in the smoking area, and lift her up, take her home, tuck her into bed. She was capable of looking after her, she always had been strong enough.

Lauren took the full weight of her onto her own body, realising just how weightless and frail Cass had become. It was hard because of the heat and the pressure, and she had to keep that fearful little voice in her head at bay, the one that told her everything was about to go terribly wrong. The one that kept replaying Cass's fall and Veronica's scream. But she could do it, she could absolutely carry her.

'Don't do this now,' she whispered as she held Cass round the waist, trying not to drag her feet as she climbed the steps. 'I didn't even properly apologise for my part in all this. You want to hear that, don't you? You want to hear me grovel and beg and tell you I was wrong?'

She heaved up another few steps, then stopped. 'I'm meant to look after Vee, Cass, and I don't know what to do. You still need to give me directions! We've still got to go home and have a big fancy party like Babs did.'

Another two steps, teetering as she pushed forward, almost dizzy with exertion.

'Come on, we haven't finished the book yet, you can't go. We haven't gone to bingo and pissed off all the old ladies, or been to one of those fancy spas and eaten the cucumber out of all the water jugs. I need you for that, we need to do it together. Please?'

'Loll!' Vee's voice came from above. 'A lady called an ambulance. They said stay there.'

The little girl started her descent, leaping back down to get to them, and Lauren watched with a detached sort of fear, hoping she didn't fall, hoping this wasn't the end, hoping that everything would be all right. She allowed her legs to buckle, collapsing in relief as she guided Cass back down to the ground.

Vee launched herself at them both, stroking back hair from Cass's face as she spoke gently.

'It'll be okay, Mummy, it'll be okay. Storm says you're strong.'

The sight of the little girl, tears streaming down her face as she tried to comfort her mother, was too much. She had called her *Mummy*. She knew what was happening.

Lauren put an arm around Veronica, holding her close but saying nothing. In her head, she ran through every single thing she meant to say. Every missed text message, life moment, joke about her mother. She wanted to scream that she'd only just got her friend back, life had only just started to sparkle again. *Please don't leave, everything's always broken without you. I don't know how to be me without you.*

As the sound of the air ambulance became more distinct, blocking out the light above them, Lauren held them both close to her. She knew what she needed to tell Cass. Everything burned down to the two things that were always true:

I'm sorry, and I love you.

Chapter 22

Then

'Loll! Loooollllll!' Cass yelled, hollering on the front door. Her tongue felt fuzzy and fluffy, and it was hard to focus. She was sure that was Loll's front door. It had that stupid doormat with some joke on it. She hammered on the door again.

Why wasn't Loll answering? She'd been avoiding her for weeks, replying late to her text messages, never around to meet up. She had to work, she had to study, she had to plan the fucking wedding of the year. Didn't matter that Cass was alone, that her mum was dying. That her mum had died.

She'd called Lauren thirty-two times since it happened that afternoon, and her best friend hadn't answered once. She hadn't even sent a text. It had to be Darren. Darren had gotten to her, convinced her that Cass was a bad influence. Speak of the bastard.

'Cass, you're drunk.' Darren sighed, rubbing his hand across his eyes. He was still dressed in his shirt and grey trousers from work. It couldn't be that late then. Loll would be home soon.

'And you're a dickhead.' She strode into the house, pushing past him. 'Where's Loll? She s'no' answering.'

She rested her hand on the wall, feeling the world start to spin. At least she'd made it to Loll's before passing out. That was something.

'Maybe she didn't want to talk to you,' Darren answered. 'Come in, by the way. Make yourself at home, as always.'

She tried to glare, but struggled to focus. 'I need to see her.'

'Surprised you can see anything, the state you're in,' Darren snorted, walking over to the kitchen, brushing past her in retaliation.

Cass took a deep breath. 'Darren, just … just can we not? Not now?'

'What, you want to call a truce? Is it the end of the world?'

Cass forced herself to meet his eyes. 'Yes. My mum just died.'

'Oh.' The shock was clear on his face, he suddenly didn't know how to be mean to someone when they were in pain. Even when it was Cass. 'I'm sorry.'

'Thanks. I just want Loll. I want Loll and then I'll go home.'

Her voice broke on the word home. It had been empty for a while, but still, what was home without your mum, your only family?

She heard the clink of glasses, and when she looked, Darren was holding out a tumbler of whisky and gesturing to the sofa. He listened to her, as if he were a stranger, not that narcissistic arsehole her friend had tied herself to. He nodded and made eye contact, sympathetic noises and sad eyes. He touched her hand, patting it gently, whilst he topped up the tumbler. Finally, she thought through her drunken haze, maybe this is the nice guy he's been hiding, the one only Loll sees. Maybe we'll be all right with each other from now on. He knows I'm human, I'm not trying to hurt anyone. He knows we both love Loll.

Darren spoke softly, about how much he missed Loll, how late she worked, how hard she was trying to be the best. He knew it wasn't fair to miss her, but he did. He couldn't complain, but she understood, didn't she? She understood what it was like to miss Loll, how horrible it was to be alone?

She nodded, feeling the tears well up as she struggled to balance. She'd be alone now, always. Except for Loll. She'd always have Loll. Where was she, why wasn't she here? She'd see them getting along and she'd be pleased, she'd know it was a new chapter. Maybe everything would be better from now on. Even without her mum around.

She could sleep, she knew. She could feel the abyss of unconsciousness in her near future, and she revelled in it. Tomorrow would be horrible, but at least she'd be asleep. She hadn't slept properly for weeks, she always needed to be blacked out from the booze. It was the only way to get rest.

Darren's hand rubbed her back, and she felt like a child, like someone cared. She couldn't remember the last time someone had hugged her. Her mum had stopped, in the end. She'd been cruel to try and stop her coming to the hospice, tried to push her away. She didn't want to be seen as weak. And still, Cass went, to the spiteful words and outraged eyes, because where else could she go, who else did she have? She wanted a hug from her Loll, that would make it better. Someone to put their arms around her and tell her she was loved.

When lips touched hers, she wasn't really sure what was happening. They were soft but fuzzy, tasted of whisky and pizza sauce, and these hands seemed to come from nowhere, touching her back and tugging at her clothes, rough fingertips reaching for her skin.

'Nngh,' she mumbled, not really sure if it was easier to kiss back in the hopes that whoever this body was, it would let her sleep soon. Unconsciousness felt strange, like walking through the corridors of your own mind, feeling your body through a pane of glass, not quite yours, but not quite other. She was Cass, wearing a body as a suit. Something far away and ill-fitting.

She reached for him, she remembered that much. She had pulled him to her. It had happened so many times before, the easiest way to oblivion with a man she didn't know. Except this time it wasn't a man she didn't know. It was a man she despised.

When she jolted awake, he was sitting across from her on the sofa, fully dressed, drinking a cup of coffee like nothing had happened. The whisky was back in the cupboard, the glasses washed up and put away. There was even a plate of fucking biscuits on the coffee table.

'She's never going to forgive you for this, you know,' Darren said, dipping a biscuit in his coffee, his expression thoughtful.

Cass felt terror clutch at her heart as she looked down at herself. She couldn't have, really? Why? Why would she have done that? The impending hangover rang about her throat. She was going to be sick. Why would he do that? He hated her. He loved Loll.

'It's the one thing she loves most about me, how much I hate you,' Darren snorted. 'Fucked up, really, for a best friend, don't you think? She's so obsessed with being in your shadow, being

more boring than you, more quiet. Being invisible. And now you've gone and slept with her fiancé.'

'But—' Cass blinked, trying to understand, 'but she'll be angry at you too! You betrayed her too! Why would you do that?'

Darren shrugged, a smug smile on his face. It was how relaxed he was that made Cass panic. He just lounged on the sofa, drinking his coffee, no guilt, no worries at all.

'Opportunity, I guess.'

'So you're just another lad who'll take a shag whenever he can get it?'

'And you're just another slag who doesn't care who she fucks as long as someone wants her.'

Cass felt her chest crumble. This was too much. How was this happening?

'How can you possibly hate me this much?' She tried to stop her voice from trembling.

'It's easy. You think the world should love you. You think you deserve things just because you're pretty and charming. You make Lauren run around after you, getting up at three a.m. to find you in some club, or listen to you whenever you need to moan.'

'She's my friend, I love her.'

'You don't love her, she's like a pet to you. She's anxious and doesn't want to let people down, and that's worse when you're around. She's never going to be the person she could be if you're here, dragging her down with your … drama.'

Cass blinked. 'But … but I love her. You don't understand us. We're … we're us. She knows.' The room started to spin and Cass gripped the edge of the sofa. 'Why would you do it? I don't understand.'

It wasn't true. She'd known men who'd screwed her as if they hated her, who wanted to dominate and control her. Men she'd teased and embarrassed who wanted to destroy her. She knew how men could be. She knew they always said the same thing – it was her fault, it was who she was, what she'd said, how she'd treated them. And yet, she'd reached for him. She'd reached out in the dark for a moment, just to be in someone's arms. This was her fault. Darren smiled as he saw the realisation on her face.

'Who do you think she'll choose, Cass? The person she's been in the shadow of for all these years, always causing trouble and drama? Or the dependable fiancé who was tricked by a drunk, vindictive girl who couldn't stand her friend having something she couldn't?'

'You can't have planned this, you're not smart.' She stood up, wobbling slightly, the desire to vomit suddenly visceral.

He raised his hands, so sure of himself, the way he was when he chose wine at a restaurant, or started talking about his salary. 'If you'd pushed me away, Cass, I would have stopped. You're always testing people, aren't you? I saw an opportunity to test you. And now you'll have to live with the consequences.'

'She's my best friend. She knows me. She's never even been particularly bothered about you!' Cass felt like a child, fists clenched, shouting at the adult who wouldn't be baited.

'She's marrying me.'

'After this comes out? We'll see,' Cass spat, grabbing her bag and heading towards the door.

Darren's voice rang out behind her.

'You could solve the problem by going away. You have no reason to stay anymore now, right? Your mum's gone. You've betrayed Lauren. Why not save her feelings and just go?'

Cass rounded with so much speed she thought she might trip over, rage emanating from her fingertips. 'Because like fuck am I going and leaving her with you! I'm going to tell her the truth, and then we'll both be gone and you can enjoy your pathetic little life.'

Cass rushed straight out to find Lauren, who had been in exams all day. She called and called, desperate to get to her first.

When she finally got a call back, a couple of hours later, Cass wasn't sure what news to start with – her loss or her betrayal. She tried to explain, she tried to make it okay. If you told the truth, everything would be fine. That's what her mum had said. That people couldn't help but love her, that they'd always forgive her as long as she was honest and said sorry. She knew she was a fucking mess, she knew she'd done a bad thing. But surely he was worse? And surely Loll would still love her anyway? She always had before.

She had thought the playing field would be fair, though, that was the problem. That for Lauren, it was a choice between the two people who had betrayed her – the best friend and the boyfriend. The oldest story in time. She hadn't accounted for a different turn of events.

'Darren said it didn't happen.' Loll's cold voice was clipped as she called her in the morning to 'sort this whole thing out'.

'What?'

'He says it didn't happen. You came over drunk and he made you coffee, and you were talking about your mum and suddenly

you tried to climb into his lap and kiss him. He said you were really drunk.'

'That's not what happened!'

Lauren groaned, exasperated. 'Why would he shag you, Cass? He thinks you're a mess. He hates you, he's always hated you.'

'And I've always hated him!'

'That's never stopped you from fucking someone before,' Lauren said, and Cass could hear those words as clearly as if they'd come from Darren's mouth.

'This is what he wants!' Cass said desperately. 'He wants me gone, he wants you to hate me.'

'Then he's got what he wanted,' Lauren said. 'I put up with a lot from you, being your little sidekick, always being your shoulder to cry on. Being invisible because people can't see past the magic of Cassidy Jones. And I didn't mind, because I thought you loved me. But you're a liar. You tried to take what's mine, and finally, you found someone who didn't want you.'

'That's not … Loll, please—'

'I'm sorry, Cass,' Lauren said, her voice clipped and tight so that Cass couldn't even imagine any tears. 'I can't even think about you without wanting you to drop dead. This is too much. You're too much. I never thought … I knew you were a mess but … we're done. Okay? We're done.'

'Loll, please don't—'

The line was dead, and Cass curled up in her childhood room, surrounded by objects she'd treasured and posters she'd adored, wondering why her mother had lied to her.

*

Lauren's falling apart was of a different sort. She didn't rant or rave or scream. She just reverted to type. She sat at her kitchen table and watched her fiancé as he straightened his tie and pressed buttons on their fancy coffee machine. She went to work, and went to study, and hid from the world. The anxiety that had been building up got worse, and there was no Cass to hold her hand, to remind her to breathe. She stood in the toilet cubicle at work, clutching her own hand, pressing her thumb into her palm with such force that she left a red imprint.

She was alone in the world again. Pretending to be strong, when the ground felt like it was shaking, her chest in a vice as she thought to herself that she must be dying. On the outside, the world was still, and inside she was trembling.

Her GP gave her medication without even questioning it – she had a nervous disposition, she was under pressure, she was anxious. It softened the hard edges, but made her feel untethered. The memories felt further away, the times she spent with Cass, the holidays, the laughter, they faded into something she hoped might be a nostalgia.

It was just growing up, Darren said. She was becoming a new type of person. He never apologised, or tried to make anything up to her, because he had nothing to feel guilty about. Instead, Cass was suddenly out of their lives, a hole, a cauterised bullet wound, tissue growing in and around but never quite covering it over. A loss that throbbed daily.

Lauren thought there'd be more from Cass – more apologies, more drunken voicemails, turning up at the front door to demand to be heard, to fight for their friendship. When she didn't, it was a relief, but confirmed that she'd never really cared that much anyway. She was just Cassidy Jones's sidekick. It would have hurt, if she could feel anything at all.

Other people fell apart outwardly. They drank or cried or wanted to destroy the world. Lauren's destruction was like a slow rotting from the inside, like the cliffs that crumble into the sea. She became the exact opposite of what Darren expected – she was more nervous, more timid and scared and tired. She wanted to buck herself up, go for her dreams, reach out and be the best.

But there was no voice in her head anymore, telling her that she could do it, that she was brilliant and wonderful and loved. That she was capable of excellent things. That voice had died the moment Cass did what she did. And who could trust the voice of a liar, anyway?

Now

They kept talking about how clean the hospital was, how friendly and efficient the nurses were. How everyone was so impressive. Almost a week passed and Cass didn't wake up, not really. There had been a brief flurry of activity, her lips mouthing words, eyes fluttering, but she slipped back into the coma. Seeing that hope snatched from Veronica, the howl of grief as her mother disappeared again ... Lauren knew she would never forget that sight as long as she lived. The same with Cass falling, it played on repeat like a showreel behind her eyelids each night, daring her to try and sleep.

Jack and Dolores had driven down immediately, and even just to have someone to try to distract Veronica whilst she dealt with insurance and paperwork and the throbbing grief in her stomach was a blessing. Jack kept telling Cass stories, talking to her in gentle tones as he held her hand and spoke about her childhood, her mother, her memories. Vee sat on the bed, listening attentively, watching her mother's face for any signs that she understood.

She wouldn't give up hope. She and Storm had whispered conversations where she worked out magical ways to bring Cass back. Every morning she sat on Cass's bed, gripping her hand, her own wrist extended in demand of her matching tattoo. Every morning, Lauren drew it on without question.

Vee's latest quest was to fill the room with colour. Cass loved colour, she needed it to stay alive. So her brightest red polka-dot scarf was wrapped over her pale hospital gown, and the room was filled with hand-drawn pictures of their adventures – huskies in Finland, the dancers in Seville, stick figures surfing with big smiles. Cass's pashminas and skirts were draped over the backs of chairs and hanging from the doors, as if a fashion show would lure her back from sleep.

'Cassy, see how colourful it is! We have all your favourite things!' Veronica's voice was trying to lure her mother back, like a child promised sweets and treats. 'And if you wake up, Auntie Loll says she'll even go on a roller-coaster!'

'Hey!' Lauren tried to play along, keep upbeat and cheerful. 'Well, *okay,* if that's really what needs to be done, I'll do it.'

They sat for a few moments, Veronica scanning Cass's face for activity, looking for the twitch of a lip or the flutter of an eyelash. She had already tried kissing her, to wake up her sleeping beauty. That had been the first plan.

Her little shoulders slumped and she looked up to Lauren. 'Cassy's not coming back, is she?'

Lauren paused. Here was the moment, her first moment as a parent. Should she give a comforting lie? Could she take away all hope? Cass's voice was wry in her mind, laughing at her panic.

Poor Loll, you never get an easy question, do you? Be honest. She'll love you for telling the truth.

Lauren took a deep breath and took Veronica's hand. 'Sweetheart, I want her to come back more than anything in the world, but no ... I don't think it's going to happen.'

Vee pressed her lips together, trying hard to be brave, a look that was so purely her mother's that Lauren burst into tears, holding her arms open so that Vee could join her. They cried together.

Cass slipped away that night, with Vee curled up on her chest, and Lauren asleep on the chair, grasping her hand, resting her head on the bed.

When she woke and realised, she tensed her jaw, shocked that there were any tears left at all. She had to do the paperwork, she had to figure out how to get her home, she had to tell Jack and Dolores.

You have to be sad, Cass's voice was clear, *and you have to look after her. That's it, Loll. Don't get lost in lists. There'll be time for that.*

It was so tempting to run away from everything, bury herself in practical adult things, the things that needed to be done. Just like she had before. Instead, she waited, letting Vee sleep a little longer, holding off the moment when reality would peek in like unwanted sun behind the curtains, and this new day, this new life, would start. A life without Cass. Let her sleep a little longer.

Chapter 23

The plane ride back to England was sombre and exhausting. Lauren kept going to ask the air hostess for a gin and tonic, and then remembering she was a guardian now. She had to hold her feelings to care for Vee's.

The little girl sat numbly, staring at the screen, watching some animated movie, Storm the husky at her side. She kept stroking her own wrist, the remnants of the most recent wolf drawing now faded, only the odd biro line showing.

It was Lauren's job to care for her now. To make decisions and make the ones that Cass would have made. She had to figure out how to get Cass home to England, and that had been a headache.

Sorry I couldn't make it easier for you, babe, not really my style.

It was easy to imagine what Cass would say, it always had been. And having this time together, this last journey, had just enlivened that little voice in her head. The kindness she was capable of, the forgiveness. How she had always believed in fairness, a trade-off – a coffee for a hurtful word, a beautiful book for a misunderstanding, a child for a betrayal.

Lauren had been sure she would have a panic attack, she could hear the words swirling in the back of her mind, each worry competing for attention, eager to tell her how awful everything would be. How everyone would judge her, how she'd do a bad job, how Vee would come to hate her. Whenever these thoughts threatened, she stroked Vee's hair, or touched the Big Book. It seemed to keep the thoughts at bay.

She kept thinking of how she called Paul to tell him, and he was so terribly quiet, a sad little, 'Oh,' that made her question whether he'd heard her properly. In the background she'd heard Sandy say, 'She's left us, hasn't she?' and the honking nose blowing into a hanky that could only be Barry.

'How are you?' he'd asked in those tender tones. 'How's Veronica?'

What words are there to reply when someone asks that? Sometimes there are only lies that you hope will become truths: 'We'll be okay.'

The plane journey was broken up by fitful bouts of sleep, nonsensical dreams of the past where Cass in her smeared green eyeshadow and huge curly blonde hair had grabbed her hand, led her through the club. She'd taken her to the bar and said, 'Meet my friend Loll.' Cass winked and she always woke up, this ache in her chest for those days, and how much simpler it would have been if everything went to plan. She eventually caved and ordered a glass of wine whilst Vee was sleeping, her face pushed against Storm, using the toy as a pillow.

It was tempting to use this flight as preparation – she had to have everything worked out by the time they landed. Death left this void that seemed to be filled with paperwork and decisions, and yet, it seemed, as always Cass had prepared for that. This had been her story, and she decided how it ended and what happened after she was gone.

Cass hadn't just been ticking off their adventures in the Big Book, or writing in memories as she had scribbled away. She'd started an entirely new book. Their list had only ever taken up the first ten or eleven pages, ideas and dreams cramped in on the paper as if there would never be enough room. Halfway through the book, a new story began, in Cass's swirly, slanted writing.

The title was written in capitals and underlined:

LOOKING AFTER YOU

So this had been what she'd been working on, frantically scribbling as she felt the end grow closer.

She'd tried to cover as much as she'd learnt of motherhood as she could, all the ways she knew to make her child happy, keep their life ticking over. A journal, a memory box, an advice column, all with Cass's voice singing out in laughter from behind smudged ink.

Really, it was a Vee manual, and Lauren had never been so grateful in all her life. All the things she saw now that Cass was trying to teach her when she'd talk about Vee – how she'd only drink hot chocolate if it was stirred a certain way, and she only liked the red jelly babies, or green apples. She had been trying to prepare her for the role she'd picked out for Lauren long ago.

Each of these facts about Veronica was written down, everything she could remember, from allergies and fears to the lyrics to the special toothbrush song. Cass told her that when she'd been through treatment last time, Vee's imaginary friend Matilda had arrived. *She might come back, after I'm gone. Be nice to Matilda. She likes banana cake and ponies. Don't try and hurry her along, she'll go when Vee's ready. Don't panic about it.*

A mother who even knew the dietary requirements of her daughter's imaginary friend. Something like guilt sat in Lauren's chest. She had doubted her. She had known an angry, sad, confused, brilliant girl when they were nineteen and she'd assumed she was just doing okay as a mum. She should have known she was excellent. If you loved Cass, she would give you the world. She would give you everything she could.

Here were all the conversations she had meant to have with her friend, the unsent text messages and unshared stories – Cass had shared them here. So Lauren wouldn't panic, and wouldn't feel alone.

There were pages and pages of instructions for being Veronica's mother. Her memories, her lessons, her naughty moments. *I'm not trying to make you a copy of me, Loll, just use this when you need someone who knows. And don't let me be forgotten. So someone can tell her about how much she cried when she was born, and how when I tried to change her nappy for the first time, I threw up on her. Keep my memories safe, Loll. Use them when you need to.*

Halfway through, there was a set of bullet points titled, *Looking after Loll*. The first one made her snort.

- *Don't be afraid to have a glass of wine – you don't have to be a guard dog, she'll be fine.*

'God, you still know me better than I know myself,' she mumbled under her breath, taking a sip of the wine from her plastic cup, and looking down at Vee's sleeping face, bottom lip jutting.

The book was like a lifeline, a physical thing that remained of the woman who had existed only in her mind and memories for years. This trip could have been a dream, except she was coming home with a daughter to a completely new life.

- *Don't coop her up and make her afraid of the things you're afraid of. But don't feel like you have to be Wonder Woman either – you're always trying to be perfect.*
- *Share the things you love, like skiing and writing huge lists and eating oven-grilled cheese sandwiches in bed on Friday nights. But maybe try and do a few of the things I love too? Just so she remembers (and you do too).*
- *You've probably learnt this one already, but don't choose the easier thing over the hard truth.*
- *Always know you are worth more than what someone deigns to give you. You're the moon. You are a glorious moon, Loll. People might be blinded by the sun, but the moon has magic all her own.*
- *Do things that scare you, like falling in love, or trying*

a job that could go wrong, or going on that rickety old roller-coaster. That's the only way she'll see how to live.

- *Value your happiness – it matters. It always mattered. Don't just settle for life.*

Lauren felt that was a rather poignant place to end, and wondered if Cass had known that it would be the last entry. It was only when she turned the page that she saw, *Wear some fucking colours!* that she laughed, hysterically, trying to quieten herself as they turned into tears. She checked to make sure Vee was undisturbed, briefly stroking her hair back from her face, before allowing herself to cry properly. She was returning home to a new life, but this time, she got to keep Cassidy with her.

Chapter 24

A Few Months Later

'Hey, Vee, you ready?' Loll called up the stairs, grasping the bannister. 'Do you want breakfast here or shall we get something on the pier?'

Vee poked her head over from the landing. 'Doughnuts for breakfast?'

Loll paused, thinking of what her mother would say about setting up bad habits for life. Then she thought about what Cass would say. 'It's a Saturday, let's live a little.'

'Is Mr T coming to the pier today?'

Loll shook her head. 'Nope, you're stuck with just me, that okay?'

Vee grinned, nodding, before thundering down the stairs.

Paul had been around. They all had, that ragtag family who had joined together to help a young woman who was all alone raise her child. They were doing it again. The same, but different. The sun and the moon.

It had been weird to live in the little house that was once Cass's, but they'd agreed it didn't seem right to move, not just yet. When Vee felt like it was time, they would. There was no hurry. Matilda had turned up briefly to necessitate cooking banana bread every few days (Cass had included a recipe in the book) but there'd been less talk of her the last couple of weeks. She seemed to have other places to be.

Living in Cass's house with so many of her things around, it felt like sitting in a hug. Well, there were the odd moments where there was something dull stuck in her chest that she'd never manage to extract, so it'd just sit there, aching. But even that felt right, somehow. She'd get up in Cass's bedroom and wonder if there was a time she should change it, just to claim it as hers, but it had already been decorated in her style. It was exactly what she would have chosen, and when Barry revealed that Cass had asked him to repaint it whilst they were away, Lauren wasn't surprised. Touched, and tearful, but not surprised. Her heart just swelled with gratitude. She had it when she sat in bed with Vee, reading to her, and saw that mobile hanging by the window, an uneven moon and sun circling each other, never meeting.

Vee liked to say every morning to her, 'You are a glorious moon, Auntie Loll.'

'And you are the beautiful Earth, baby girl,' she always replied, as if she were channelling Cass.

She was a stand-in, always second best, like Nuria said. And yet, she was the best person for the job. She had the family that Cass had created for them – the people in the community who wanted to help, the strangers who wanted to become friends. The endless food people brought. Paul had been there, never asking for anything, but asking her how she was, whether her divorce had come through. Making her laugh. Making Vee laugh. Making it feel okay to be happy every now and then.

The phone rang as Vee ran down the stairs, and Loll took a breath before answering it.

'Hey, Mum, we're just heading out, can I give you a call later?' She rested the phone in the crook of her hand as she expertly plaited Vee's hair into two pigtails.

'Well, that's a bit rude, Lauren,' her mother huffed. 'I was just calling to see how you were. You and little Veronica.'

'I know, Mum, and I appreciate it. But we've got our Saturday-morning routine, you know that.'

'I hope you're wrapping that child up warmly, she'll get a cold going down to that beach without enough layers on.'

Loll took a deep breath, closed her eyes, and then opened one to look at Veronica, sticking her tongue out.

'I am, I don't need you to tell me that.'

'I've been a mother, Lauren, I know things you don't.'

'And I know Vee. And Cass,' she turned around to check the back door, gesturing for Vee to sit down at the table. She softened her voice, 'I will need you, Mum, I will ask you for advice and help. But you've got to let me come to you. Right now, honestly, I've got this. I was meant to do this.'

She waited for her mother to huff, make a sharp comment or even hang up on her. Instead, Martha laughed.

'Good for you,' she said, 'such confidence! But don't forget her coat. I'll call you later.'

Loll smiled to herself, shaking her head. Her mother was changing. Or rather, she had changed, and her mother was responding. It seemed easier, somehow, since she decided not to let her mother make her feel small. She had been given an important task, and she was going to do it.

Martha had even been quietly supportive of her working. She was using her law degree, at least. Cass's colleagues at the charity had given Loll a little work, looking over contracts for tenants they felt had been illegally evicted by landlords. It was sad, but good work. She felt like she was helping. Even in her tiny way, she was doing something useful. That had always been the goal. To be good for something more than herself. She was starting to put together cases. Starting to care again. There was potential everywhere.

Vee sat at the kitchen table and reached into the special box they had placed there. She held her wrist out, a demanding look on her face.

'A new one already?'

'Well if you didn't make me scrub so hard when I clean ...' Vee said and Loll stuck her tongue out.

'We'll have to find somewhere else to put them when the hot weather comes and the school notices,' she said, peeling the sticky label back and placing it face down on Vee's wrist, daubing the back with water.

'No, they have to be nice to me because I miss Cassy,' Vee said with such certainty that Loll laughed. She was definitely her mother's daughter.

The temporary tattoos had arrived a week after they got home. Cass had ordered them, stealthy as always. They were Loll's wolf drawings, different cubs and grown wolves, some together, some alone. She had ordered three hundred and sixty-five different temporary tattoos for Vee, so she'd never have to feel like she wasn't one of the pack. It was just creative and crazy enough to be the thing that helped Vee heal.

She smiled for the first time that day, and every day after, the moment of applying that tattoo, or even just looking at it. Laying her wrist next to Loll's at night seemed to make her happier.

'Okay, all done, let's go!'

Loll helped Vee into her little yellow rain jacket, her pink gloves in the pocket. She slipped Cass's long bottle-green coat over her own clothes, a red jumper and black trousers, and picked up the polka-dot umbrella, just in case.

They walked to the pier in quiet companionship, and as she so often did on a Saturday, Loll wondered whether Vee was okay, how badly she missed her mother, and whether she was happy. This was her routine. Her time to worry. She kept it in shifts. Saturday walk was worry time, and during that time she chatted with the little version of Cass she kept in her head.

You're doing fine, Loll, you're a natural.

But what if she's unhappy?

Well I should fucking hope so, she just lost her mother. I'm not forgettable, am I?

Never.

Then calm down. You're doing such a good job. And when you're ready, you can build on this life instead of just living in it.

I'm just borrowing it for a while, Loll thought to herself.

Good, that's what I designed it for.

It was chilly, but dry, and they stood looking over the edge of the pier into the waves, choppy and insistent under a sky that promised spring. This was where they'd sprinkled Cass's ashes, and came to talk to her. Vee said Cass had always wanted to be a mermaid.

Loll laughed to herself about plumbing hidden depths, and missed Cass fiercely, the only other person who would have understood and laughed along. Then, she realised, today had to be the day.

They stood before the roller-coaster, and Loll held out her hand, palm up. 'Come on.'

'Really?' Vee squealed, taking her hand and dragging her to the ticket desk, where they gave the young kid more than the ticket price, because that's what Cass would have done.

As the rickety cart climbed the rail, Loll felt herself start to shake.

'You're okay,' Vee said, smiling at her, 'it's good to be scared sometimes. Lift up your hands and scream.'

It was there, at that moment, she felt it. Hovering at the top of the track, about to fall, the girl in the green coat being seen from the shore. She clasped hands with Vee as they started to slide forward.

Here we go …

Acknowledgements

Some books take a little more time and love to get out into the world, and there are some people to thank for their dedication in making it so.

Firstly, big love and thanks to my super agent Hayley Steed, who believed in this book from the beginning and was steadfast in her determination to find it a good home. To my editor at One More Chapter, Hannah Todd, whose joyful (and sometimes emotional!) notes made Loll and Cass more authentic and loveable – thank you for loving this book and showering it with your skill and enthusiasm.

A huge, stonking, great big thank you is due to Lynsey James, the other half of Team Cheerleader, who, true to the name, has always had my back. During the tearful, hair-pulling submission phase, to the worries about edits, storyline, promotion and questions of what the hell I was doing, Lynsey, you're a superstar. This book wouldn't exist without you.

As always, thank you to Shaun. For reminding me to take a break, feeding me jellybeans, pouring me a glass of wine and listening to me work out plot points when you have no idea what the hell I'm on about. For always asking how the book's going. And just for being you.

And finally, to you, dear reader. Thank you. For reading this book. If you don't know me, or if you knew me when I wrote slightly different novels, you took a chance and I hope it paid off.